Dolores Park

a novel

**Volume three of a series:
"My Years of Apprenticeship at Love"**

by
Michael Lyons

Library of Congress Cataloging in publication Data

Lyons, Michael
        Dolores Park
I. Title

ISBN: 0-9655842-3-2

Published by HiT MoteL Press

Designed by Michael Lyons

a novel by

Michael Lyons

Dolores
Park

"Careful consideration of the realities of the organism, both psychological and physiological, would lead a dispassionate observer to the conclusion that the ideal human mode of life is routine punctuated by orgies."
— Aldous Huxley

To the House

Dolores Park

Table of Contents

Individual Romance

Group Mind

Group Marriage

Individual Romance

1

Dahlia

A woman sat down beside a man in the only aisle seat left just seconds before the house lights dimmed and theater began. As the play slowly came up, the man —Walker — noticed that the woman had long dark hair finely falling over her shoulders down the middle of her back, straight and free. Walker was not so forward-thinking as to leave the aisle seat open in hopes of possibly engaging a woman, although he certainly wanted to; he was with his friend Bob, the director of the play who wanted to be more in the center to better observe, and Walker was sitting beside him.

Using the spy technique of sweeping the eyes left in a sidelong glance without moving the head, Walker casually looked at her face. He was struck by how good-looking she was. He wondered if she might be latina. She looked to be in her early 30s, and lanky. Big shoulders and big hands. Her face was noble. She had freckles on her cheeks. She was movie-star beautiful, except that her eyes had a child's shining wildness which enlivened this beauty and lifted it out of being something unapproachable to being real.

He turned to take in more of this lovely brunette. She must have sensed his gaze; suddenly she turned and their eyes met! He managed a quick smile of chagrin; she just looked at him, with her doe eyes unblinking.

She saw his large masculine face. He was fair skinned, had long, curly, light-brown hair. His face had all the masculine attributes of good looks, in spite of an adolescence ravaged by acne. His eyes were as blue as the sky. A girlfriend had once said he had Mick Jagger lips. His face was so masculine looking that early in college he had been teased about having a "camp" jaw.

They smiled at each other.

As Walker settled into his plush chair he became more and more aware of her presence. Even though he was intently interested in the performance as it progressed on stage, he found himself being more and more aware of the woman next to him. The play was *An American Yoga*. He noticed how easy her breathing was.

At a certain point in the piece, the actor — who was playing a North Beach barker with greasy slicked back hair and a skinny tie — began making outrageous remarks about muff divers and fur pie. Some people got up and left the theater as he cat-called to them out of his monologue. Walker was delighted that the woman beside him enjoyed the sexual humor. A closer look told her age: she has some lovely laugh lines at the corner of her eyes. And yet her laughter was a girl's peal of delight, which just seemed to bubble up and escape in spite of the indecorousness of the material. Several times they shared a laugh.

At the intermission, Walker, relieved that she was by herself, decided to chance a friendly comment: "It's good, isn't it?"

"Yeah," she agreed. "I don't get out to a lot of theater, but I wanted to see this one."

When she stood up and laid her long-sleeve girls-school sweater into her seat, Walker noticed her trim shape fitting snugly into cords and the hint of bust hidden in a logger's flannel shirt. She leaned over toward him and said, "Will you keep an eye on my sweater for a minute?"

"Yeah, sure," he said. He sat there, feeling a little ridiculous being the custodian of her stuff. I ought to go out into the lobby and talk to her, he kept telling himself. When he finally got up the nerve to go out there, he didn't see her anywhere among the crowd. He got back to his seat before she returned.

The climax of the play was stunning. The actor moved and writhed in front of a screen upon which was projected a film that had been recorded in a camera that had been thrown off the Golden Gate Bridge on an elastic bungie cord. The audience gasped in amazement. The actor dancing against the moving background of the fall made the audience feel like they were sliding off the edge of the continent. It gave one a sense of being part of a great fall into oblivion as if one were participating in some modern rushy high-speed art sacrifice. The woman sitting next to Walker seemed moved too. They looked at each other with recognition and confirmation. He wanted to strike up a spontaneous conversation with her. However, he hesitated because of his extreme shyness, and not wanting to invade her space. But when Bob said, "Walker, there's going to be a cast party after the show," a light bulb went on in Walker's mind. This would be a good thing to invite this woman to. He smiled at her, and began, in a kind of big brotherly way, to include her into the after-theater glow whose circle was quickly edging toward them. The actor on the stage was holding a bouquet of flowers and was introducing the director. The spot light coursed through the audience and encompassed Walker and the woman as Bob stood and nodded to the crowd. Somewhere in the timeless movement of thoughts, while Walker was processing the fear he always got before that initial encounter with a woman, the fear that some look in his face would put her off, the fear that once again he would be creamed by rejection, he noticed the woman had slipped out of her seat and left! He leaped up, strode quickly to the lobby of the theatre and spotted her drinking a glass of wine. He swallowed his fear with a big gulp and said, "Why don't you stay for the cast party. Drink some more wine."

She tossed her hair with an inviting shake of her head and a small portion of it fell in front of her ears. She had an earnest, almost Madonna-like calm to her face which became considerably more girlish as she wiggled her shoulders and then sticking her tongue between her teeth, smiled and said, "Okay."

Beer and Calistoga water had been sent for, fruit and cheese were laid out.

"What's your name?" he asked.

"Dahlia."

Walker worried that his southern accent would give him away.

"Are you new in town?" she asked.

Walker hitched himself up trying to make himself look like an old blues hound and sang in a gravely voice, the lyrics from a song: "I just got in from Texas, babe."

She laughed and told him that she had just moved from Hawaii. You could see that both Walker and Dahlia and felt edgy and uncomfortable amid the gush and swirl of the actor crowd, the way they so easily and with florid aplomb hailed each other and kissed each other on the cheeks and carried on with great exaggerated emotional physical encounters. Walker envied and felt intimidated by their ease with community. Dahlia wondered about the authenticity of the thespian salutation. The man and the woman were alone together in this crowd.

Walker generally told her about the theater, the warehouse scene in Berkeley, keeping the conversation on Ernst and the theater ensemble, The Blake St. Hawkeyes. Occasionally Bob would wander in and out of their conversation, interjecting various asides about the theater piece, being charming. Walker's partying style (if you could call it that) was to hang back around the keg, swapping lies with the good ole boys. Walker was grateful to watch how Bob put Dahlia at ease. Ernst had practically invented solo performance, a new art form in the Bay area, by incorporating liberal borrowing from Grotowski, Artaud, tribal ritual, jazz and tai chi. Dahlia seemed particularly interested in the theater collective.

Walker asked her: "Can I call you sometime?"

"Well I guess so."

She gave him her phone number and he wrote it on a match book.

After a particularly long lull in the conversation when his out of the blue, off in the blue eyes just seemed to drift off into space Dahlia picked up on it and asked Walker, "Where did you go? Where did you go just then?"

"Sorry," he said, drawing himself back, "I was just worrying about my dog. She's in the car, down in the parking lot."

"Want to check on her?" asked Dahlia.

They let Sunshine the dog, out of the van, and walked down the jetty at Fort Mason. Whole Oriental families were fishing at night, listening to disco music, chatting easily. Off in the distance was a clear view of Alcatraz. Dahlia, wearing her long-sleeved school-girl sweater draped over her shoulders rubbed her forearms, hugging herself. Though Walker sensed she wanted to be touched, he did not touch her.

Back in the theater, they helped strike the set. Dahlia carried three heavy lights at once! It was then that he became aware of her beautiful, straight, broad, brave shoulders.

Although she seemed to want to continue partying at a jazz club called Bajones on Valencia, Walker was driver to Ernst this night and they had to get back to Berkeley.

Walker opened the door and let her into the back of the van. He felt relieved that Dahlia was perceptive enough and that he and Bob were trustworthy enough for her to feel OK about going with them.

"Well this is a traveling 'poor man's salon'," Walker said, indicating the back of the van. "It's like a nest." The sleeping compartment was dense with tapestries covering the windows. Big inviting pillows were neatly arranged on a big mattress. "It's a little like Freud's study, don't you think? Or Sara Bernhardt's studio packed with stuff." While he worried about what she would think of him if she knew he lived in his van, she thought about all the books she had read on Freud and pictures she had seen of his study. She wondered what it would be like to make love on that couch.

Walker reached back onto the bed / bench and pushed aside his beloved regulation-Army down-filled mummy sleeping bag. "In this bag, I have spent many an hour zipped up like like King Tut in a sarcophagus, snoozing into a transcendental dream."

Dahlia sat on the edge of the bed platform where she could lean forward and drape her arms on the front seat. She pointed between the seats in front to a radio mounted beneath the dash. "Is that a short wave?"

"No, it's a CB," Walker said. "Are you into CBs? What's yer handle?"

"Oh, I don't have a handle," she said. "But we have a short wave at the house where I live. What's your handle?"

Walker thought back to the mid 70s when, during a previous attempt to live in Berkeley, he worked as a cab driver in Berkeley and Oakland. He shuddered thinking about all the pimps in flamboyant clothes and prostitutes in hot pants he used to pick up on MacArthur or Telegraph Ave. motels and ferry about in the night. Whenever he could he used to go up to the top of the Berkeley hills and watch the bay. Listening to Terrible Thing and The Rug Man. Walker's handle back then had been Krishna Glass. Boy that was weird. He had come under the influence of JD Salinger, and thought of himself, in a literary sense, as a brother in the

Glass family.

"Oh, I don't have one either," Walker said. "I just like to have it in case I get stuck in some place like New Mexico."

Dahlia gave them directions to her place. Walker revved the VW bus up to climb the long Divisadero incline from Fort Mason and as the road climbed and climbed they began to see beyond the huge plush mansions to the neighborhoods of lighted houses following the contour of the hillsides, stretching off and circulating around the pristine skyscrapers of the brightly lighted city. It was so steep Walker remarked: "Woah! We might go tumbling backward down the hill end over end like a football! . . . Has that ever happened?"

"Nope. It's never happened," Bob said.

Dahlia said, slightly defensively, "I only know the way the buses go."

Walker steered the oblong van down impossibly steep hills. "Man this little van is climbing halfway to the stars."

She lived in a huge building that the was nearly the whole block long in the Mission. It had once been a Sears department store. He pulled into the parking lot off Valencia and drove up to where he could be in sight of its industrial glass door. Walker went around and slid the van door open to let her out.

He walked with her a little ways toward the door, to be out of sight of Ernie so he could make his move. Walker took her arm gently and she turned to face him.

"I'm glad to meet you," he said. "I hope we can become friends."

She smiled at him, and looked hopeful. "Me, too."

He let his arm slide further up around her shoulder and pulled her to him. She yielded to his pressure gracefully, allowed herself to be pressed close to him, and indeed, grasping him in turn hugged him back. Walker felt glorious.

"I'll call you soon," he promised.

2

Home

Dahlia unlocked the glass door to her building, made sure it closed securely behind her, with a loud ka-thank and climbed a wide flight of stairs to the first landing. She zigzagged up two more flights of wide, flood-lit, carpeted stairs until she came to a big metal door leading to their penthouse. She opened it and continued past towering wood racks of camping equipment, up another long flight of stairs. She felt herself feeling at home, relaxing in the familiar smell of garlic and bracing herself for the rising burble of sounds going on up the stairs.

The sounds quickly rose to an ululating wail from the great holy humming hive of her tribe as she came up the stairs into the huge penthouse room. It was the size of a small warehouse. Spread out across the floor are about a dozen futons; there are no other furnishings in the room. Dahlia lives in a commune. On each futon is a couple making sound. Some couples are sitting in lotus position facing each other, holding hands and chanting. Some couples are talking together low. Other couples are supine, hugging and OMing. It was dark, but Dahlia knew many couples were engaging in sexual intercourse and channeling the heavy breathing, sighs, moans and gasps of their passion into OMing. Dahlia smiled and felt a focusing of her attention as mindfulness oriented her being. She thought, another typical midnight in the Loft.

She wondered where Mario was. He was usually one of the loudest. She smiled and thought about how excited he became when they used to have sex. He was so pleased with their lovemaking. "That was one of the most intense feelings in my cock; it went on forever. It was the best ever!!" he'd say. She smiled with satisfaction. It felt good to help make him surrender to Her like that.

Katie walked by. She too was still wearing her street clothes, a dowdy dress. Katie had straight long hair in a glamorous 40s do —parted and swept to one side. She was very petite, in her late 30s, older than most of the other

House women. She was as American as apple pie. Many of
the commune women who worked downtown as secretaries
prided themselves in being Mayor Dianne Feinstein clones,
wearing the dowdy dress, with big bow scarves and Nikes —
it was disguise. Though Katie perpetually had a kind of
hangdog demeanor, she could be quite animated and joyful
at home. "Hi," she said. "Did you enjoy your night out?"

"Yeah, it was good. I went to dinner and the theater."

Katie teased: "Well, that sounds like a *cultured* way to
spend the evening." She did a fake take as if she were a
supercilious person looking down her nose at the hoi poloi.

"Yeah, it was cool. I enjoyed it a lot," Dahlia answered.
"Do you have a session tonight."

"Yep." Katie grinned. "I'm getting together with Aaron."
Katie actually beamed, smiled and blushed thinking about
the great oral sex she had given Aaron during their last
session. He was so cute when he apologized for cuming.
"Aaron and I were just finishing going over the
spreadsheet."

Dahlia knew that Katie was very sweet on Aaron. Those
two went back just about the longest of any couples in the
commune — 12 years. "Well, I better turn in. Six o'clock
comes awful early," Dahlia said, taking leave.

"Yea," said Katie, "and we have that big finance meeting
tomorrow."

Dahlia continued up one more flight of stairs to the loft
above the main floor of the penthouse. It too was awash in
another dozen futons and moaning couples in an even more
dense arrangement. It was darker and hard to tell how many
couples were getting into sex under the covers. Dahlia had to
walk around the lovely Wyoming and Ursu fucking in the
upright sitting position. Ursu was sitting with his legs
outstretched and Wyoming was sitting on top of him. She
had her long legs stretched out and clasped around his back
and was ooching herself back and forth on his lap. She was
riding him pretty hard letting her hair fall back as she looked
at the ceiling, moaning loudly in orgasm. Go for it girl!
thought Dahlia. Feel the body of enjoyment awareness.

The big penthouse had tall windows and the loft floor
cut across the windows in the middle, thus letting light in
above as below. Guided by a distant street light, maybe a

klieg light from St. Luke's hospital down the street, Dahlia went into the communal closet area at one side of the loft. It had a small light in the back of it too. Each member of the commune was assigned a closet area no more than two feet wide. There were four long aisles with the closets back to back. Some people managed to get shelves, and even a narrow chest of drawers in their space. It was like living in a space station, living as close to other people as you possibly could. Dahlia hung up her jacket. She stripped off her pants, and folded them into a drawer.

In her panties and camisole she walked back across the loft, trying to avoid looking to see who was sleeping with whom and where, just trying to be in her own thoughts. She hoisted up one end of her futon. It was one of the last left still rolled up from the great pile at the other end of the loft. She wrestled it across the floor, meandering among other supine couples, careful not to disturb anyone. Let's see, I don't want to plunk down my futon right next to Mario, that's for sure. She couldn't make out where he was in the gloom. I thought I heard him downstairs. It would be best to avoid sleeping near Malcolm too, she thought, because she was having a beef with him, and it wouldn't be good to have to listen to him getting into all kinds of good sex with Pia.

Dahlia lived in a sangha. The Sangha of the Dorje Chang — The Church of the Divine Couple. Maybe not church, maybe residential therapeutic community was more like it. Or group marriage. The House, as they called themselves, had consciously designed their family/church/ marriage to be more or less like the traditional Tibetan Tantric Buddhists sangha. Dahlia sleeps with a different person almost every night. They are the same different people of her small group marriage in sequential rotation. In her immediate small group was herself, Lucia and Jesse, (who were away at the land), Morey, Malcolm, Pia and Dianne. Dahlia's group marriage to 3 men and 3 women is part of the commune of 42 people. A few people had left during the recent shake-up when they had to sell the farm and move from Hawaii to San Francisco.

The small group marriage contracts to stay together for a year or so, then dissolves and reforms with another small group. Dahlia has been in this therapeutic community for more than 10 years. She is used to very passionate sex in the tantric tradition of sex as a kind of co-centering meditation in which you were supposed to be able to ask for and receive devotion from another as well as give devotion. The practice of mindfulness in sex, asked that you be aware of the going together with someone to a timeless, spaceless, flowing state of consciousness and dwell there as long as possible as part of your training to reach this place in meditation. Sex was a medium to find grace or a vehicle to take the lovers "out of body," to take them out of this enjoyment- or fruit-body back up the tree to the place whence it grew, into the life force or "form body' or dharmakaya, a place no longer limited by time and space. It is a state of enlightenment resulting from the accumulated merit of good action; and its powers sustain the communion of Buddhist saints. Here the Buddhas are in paradise as embodied truth, the ecstasy of enlightenment. The practice had started with Chase — their nickname for Charles Lang — the group therapist out of whose clinical practice the House had evolved over the years into a full time graduate school of Tantric Buddhist psychology. He was the charismatic leader. For them sex was a medium they could enter into and have with them always as general and diffused feelings. Grace.

The pattern of sleeping together in the small group, turn and turn about, is established by a purely mathematical rotation through all possible combinations of all the members of the small group so that there was no favoritism. The men found sleeping with other men frightening and difficult at first but grew to find it liberating when they confronted together their deep-seated fears of being homosexual. There was very little homosexual activity among the men; the women were a lot less inhibited about getting into sex with each other. There were also "round robins" in which you chose someone else from the house that you hadn't slept with in a while or they chose you. And then, there were nights off, in which you could sleep with anyone you wanted. You could even sleep alone on those nights, though it was frowned upon. The only solitary activities were that of: "sitting" in meditation, contemplation of a tankha or being locked in a deep visual feedback kind of meditation of one's self in the mirror. And reading. If you slept with anyone outside the House, it was with group knowledge at least, if not prior group approval. Each night, 20 couples slept together on futons on the main floor, or on the floor of the loft upstairs. Each child had a room of their own. People had sex under covers or sometimes sitting upright out in the open, in full view and in full knowledge of everyone. To be sure, this kind of intensive group therapy got to psychological material in real time. It felt incredible to own your own sexuality to such an extent that you felt like it was safe to be having sex with one of the ones you loved in full sight of your friends. It made the couple feel like a god and goddess consorting in concert with the hopes and good wishes of the community. At least that was how it was supposed to work. However, it brought up a lot of jealousy, fear, shame, anger and competition for everyone. You might find yourself sleeping with someone one night right next to someone else with whom you had outrageously satisfying sex with the night before. You can only do this if you have a lot of communication, if you can bring the jealousy, fear, shame, anger and competitiveness to small group and big group therapy for examination every day and if you have individual psychotherapy at least once a week. The therapist of the house was Chase, the teacher, the father-confessor who as the big bad Freudian daddy had to absorb projections which were more amplified by this confrontational style of therapy. He was Father-Mother to all of them.

Dahlia wondered if Chase was up. He was the man who had created this monster, who had to take on the transferences of his whole practice: an empathic man.

She felt him looking at her! I wonder what Chase is doing. I wonder if Chase is up. In the dark she scanned across the loft toward the corner above the kitchen where each of the kids had their own room, and where Chase, had his office, looking for him.

As if her eyes might be drawn by heat, she began to make out the shape of someone in lotus posture in the dark. She caught her breath. It was Chase! Was he looking at her? Or perhaps he was just meditating.

Though she couldn't make out detail, his image was forever imprinted on her mind. No one had ever looked into her soul the way he had. He always looked like he was both angry and falling in love. He was 52, older than almost everyone in the House, his thick shock of hair prematurely white. Everyone was mesmerized by his dark eyes. Chase had a high widow's peak. It made him look almost devilish at times yet he was cherubic and portly and that made him cuddly. He had the most animated eyebrows, close down to his eyes. And his eyes . . . they were like black holes shining in the light of your psyche, drawing you in. They made him look absolutely fierce, almost cruel. He was unflinching. He had seen everything in human behavior during his work with schizophrenics in the wards of Bellevue where he had done his internship. He was a medical doctor. Chase often looked angry and frightening, and you didn't want to disappoint him.

In fact, he was an indefatigable lover —the best Dahlia had ever had. He had taught them all how to pursue sexual pleasure assiduously.

Sex was seen as part of a regular devotion, and thus no one was pressured to perform. This did indeed lead to the expanded relationships with many people. It was very exciting to try and grow. He had at one time or another helped all the women with getting more out of sex. Many of the women could, with Chase's help and instruction, experience multiple orgasm that went on for 1/2 hour or more. Easily. This was slowly built up like the way you confront any hysterical illness. For example a person with fear of heights should be slowly walked over a high bridge in the company of trusted friends. Another who fears to drive on the expressway, can gradually be led into it. A person who has a lot of disgust with their own nudity, might have to sit naked in group.

Chase knew that no matter how much pain he put them through, they would look back on their experience going through it and love each other more. He was creating a kind of brotherhood and sisterhood, a family they would never forget. An anti-family to make up for the dysfunctional ones they came from. That was his trip, to get them into as much sex as they could possibly handle. With as many partners as they could possibly handle. That is what the ancient gurus had done and it had worked.

Dahlia thought about the sleeping arrangements in

Hawaii, they had been able to have these cabanas with one wall open to the sea on their private plantation. That had been wonderful, if terrifying with the challenging group gropes carried out on the wall to wall mattresses, against the ameliorating surge and crash of the pounding ocean shore.

Dahlia felt her asshole twitch. God the things Chase had done to her, when they were last in session. She felt his presence in her mind. He really was a guru, trying to help everybody be reborn into a good life. She felt a kind of sad resignation because this birthing process was both painful and joyful.

Dahlia lay back and listened to the raucous moaning and OMing and heavy breathing of the House. God if my parents had any idea what we are up to. It is a hell of an experiment we are in. She peered into the darkness of the loft to see if she could get some kind of idea who was sleeping with whom.

Where was Mario? Dahlia felt a twinge of anger and sadness about not being able to have any sessions with Mario any more. She had been "in love" with Mario and her ego was still smarting over the House finding it necessary for the group to separate them. "You'll be much better friends for it in the future," they had said.

She smiled and recalled how she used to be "in love" with Mario. It had been so obvious. In Hawaii, whenever they went to the beach as a House, Mario and she would always end up together. She thought about how she could really abandon herself with Mario, how much fun it was for them to get off. He could go on and on. As always this "dependency" quickly drew the suspicion of the House. They finally separated us. Dependency — thy name is evil, she thought. There it was in all its hideousness, and I wanted it. We just can't have this kind of dependency in the house. People who get along outside in the world are people whose projections mesh. Ignorance, lust malice jealousy. These were their demons to fight and they were all fighting them together. Ignorance, lust malice jealousy, will I ever be free?

Ah. There was Morey. Dahlia smiled at the sight of him lying on top of who? Ah, it was Rachel, his major throb. The two of them were going at it like a pair of snakes in heat, and OMing at each other in that deep passionate way he had.

Morey was on top of Rachel, his legs spread wide and her legs intertwined around his legs as he was very slowly, infinitesimally fucking —hardly moving at all. Thank heaven for cool guys thought Dahlia, guys you can love and not get too hung up on. He was a real pal. She dragged her futon, over to a spot not too far from where Morey and Rachel were carrying on.

As she unrolled her futon, Dahlia thought: Why must I always be in this endless strife. She heard the loud rising and falling glissandos and sighs and roars of OMing initiates and passionate couples channeling their pleasure into prayer. It sounded like some strange discordant symphony for a new world. She fluffed out the bedclothes from last night. There. That was settled. There wouldn't be any more shadows from her past to bother her this night.

In her thin strap T-shirt and panties she went back down to the bathrooms on the main floor below the loft, next to the kitchen. In the kitchen she saw old Theo puttering with the sprouts system. She chose a bathroom that was unoccupied and was careful not to turn on the light until she closed the door so she wouldn't disturb the sleepers outside bedded down on the floor. In the large industrial, multi-sink, multi-throne, group-shower facility, Dahlia looked at herself in the mirror. Her long hair was luxurious and lustrous — that new herbal rinse she bought for herself was doing the job. She liked how her hair felt on her bare shoulders in the thin cotton camisole. She wore no makeup. She smiled at her fresh face in the mirror. She had soft brown sensitive eyes which showed that she was an empathic, sensitive woman. Her skin was too fair to indicate her mother was Mexican, but there was a definite Latin fire in the way she held herself. She lathered up and washed her face with the big white bar of ivory soap the House buys. Then she chose her tooth brush out of a long rack — a red one with her name embossed in tape on it. When she was finished washing, she sat on the open throne and urinated. As she left, the flash of harsh florescent light falling momentary from the opened door onto the landscape of wrinkled bedclothes and supine couples made it look for an instant like a writhing bed of snakes out of a Doré print.

Scott was coming out of the other bathroom. Except for

padding along in a pair of blue flip-flops, he was completely naked. He looked like a homyunkle man, his posture bent over like a clerk or a banker. He was prematurely bald. Yet his body was lithe and muscular from much physical activity —a kind of muscular Barney Fife. He asked Dahlia, "Who's your session person tonight?"

"O, nobody," Dahlia answered. "I went out to a play tonight."

"Oh," he said, with a look of resigned sympathy on his face. "No session?"

"Well," he continued, "Christine, Wendy, Harve, Brad and I had dinner together and Christine and I had a good talk." Scott smiled thinking about getting into sex with Christine last night. He remembered how much fun it was to pause his stroke. It made the whole experience more intense. He made a mental note: if the notion of taking a break or pausing came to mind then I should do it.

Dahlia brushed nimbly past him in her bare feet and skivies, heading up the stairway to the loft. Back upstairs she crept across the creaky loft floor, and slipped under the bedclothes snug in her heavenly futon. Dahlia looked at the cheapo plastic battery operated wrist watch she kept attached to her futon. She pressed the button so that the little light came on and she read the time: 1:03. Dahlia put the watch beside her pillow. She had the alarm set for 5:30.

She lay there alone, thinking of the night's meeting of a new man. She wondered how it would go. She'd have to be careful if it turned out to be something worth pursuing at all. Because the House would get involved.

As Dahlia was drifting off to sleep, safe in the company of her family, Walker pulled the van into the warehouse parking lot in Berkeley. He had dropped Bob off at his apartment a few blocks away. Walker carried his sleeping bag in from the van. He opened the door, let himself into the cavernous warehouse making sure the door locked behind him. The building was in a rough neighborhood near the Oakland border in auto row. It was dark and no one else was there. On the stage of the theater he plunked himself down on his orange therma-rest. He lay on his back with his hands under his head, staring up through the skylight thinking of the lovely Dahlia. He drifted off to sleep smiling.

3

Group Wedding Portrait

Walker called Dahlia from a pay phone at the laundromat on the corner of Blake and Shattuck close to the warehouse theater. As he was living out of the van, on his way to Canada, Walker didn't have a telephone. His heart was beating wildly with a mixture of fear and vague hope. His palms got a little sweaty holding onto the receiver as it rang, for through the magic of hope and electronics he might conjure up the ideal of his mind and Dahlia was his ideal type. Walker loved tall, dark, long-haired Latin women.

A man answered.

"Hello."

Walker thought it must be a roommate. "Hello, this is Walker. I'm a friend of Dahlia's. Is she there?"

"Well, she's busy right now. Can she call you back?"

" Uh, I'm not at my own phone. I'll have to call her back."

"Can you leave a message?"

"Just tell her Walker called."

It would take many phone calls like this from the sad laundromat at the corner before he talked to the girl of his dreams.

Around that time there was a "group marriage portrait" of the whole House taken at the Noe Valley Church. Mandatory presence had everyone in the House standing on the wooden steps in front of the quaint New England church. Chase even had Jesse and Lucia called in from the Land. Since most of the people in the House were transplanted Easterners, they liked the no frills Quaker shire-town look of the church complete with a wooden spire and cross on top transplanted to San Francisco. They also secretly enjoyed the symbolism of it. In the group portrait of the marriage, you see attractive average people mostly in their 30s, many in their 20s, not so many in their 40s, and not even a handful in their 50s. They fill four rows of steps. The five kids in front —Luke, Dhyana, Maggie, Mark and Jason. Chase (the father of Luke and Mark) is in the center; Serena (his wife, their mother) by his side. Aaron and Katie and Morey and Lucia and Dahlia in the front row.

Anyone with an eye for physical beauty might be drawn to Rachel, for her good looks, or Jade, she also has a kind of cruel sexual wildness about here, or Lucia who has a stunning European model face and shy knowing smile, or Wyoming looking like a thinking man's Ava Gardner with a mane of wild Jewish hair. It might strike you that all the women have a kind of wild beauty. You might notice only Denise is overweight, and indeed everyone looked tanned and fit —the men positively rugged as they were mostly carpenters and landscapers fresh off the farm in Hawaii. You would notice a sense of relaxed comfortable closeness in the ease with which the group hung together. Almost all the women had glorious long hair. In the utility and modesty of their clothes you see an American portrait of middle class people who have become stalwart, upright, pioneering hippie folk. The men all had trim short haircuts. (There are a few bad haircuts worn by the younger members identifying with the punk aesthetic —Lissa, Mario, Jade.) There was an unduly large concentration of therapists in the group; a fact which might present itself through the tentative assiduousness of their regard.

Across the back row are some of the swarthy male landscapers. Bradley, fearless high climbing tree trimmer; Scott (former diminutive accountant, now almost buff with cuts and definition; stalwart Morey, head landscaper; Big Tom; Robert, who was actually a graduate student in psychology currently on a heavy physical work yoga. (Robert should be with the therapists standing closer to Chase: Wyoming, Adrienne, Malcolm, Denise, Serena, David and Jessica.

In the second to the last row from the back, in the same row with Jesse, a mechanical engineer and Harve, an architect were the Phelan brothers — Malcolm, a programmer and at the other end of the row Kevin, an electrical engineer.

Kevin, 25

I was born and spent my first 17 years in Edinburg on the island of Great Britain, Europe.

I came to the House through my brother, and though he is much older than me and we are almost in different generations we have gotten closer from being here. My parents were very old when I was born. We had moved to better council housing by then but were by no means well off. It had been pretty tough for the older siblings.

I hated sports and was obese. At age 8 I was able to beat anyone in my family at chess and started playing tournaments around Edinburg. I was obsessive in primary school. High school was a breeze; I took up the guitar and was in a rock band but my social skills with girls were poor due to extreme reticence. I was a good student because I realized education was the only way to get out of the slums of Edinburg. I managed to get a scholarship to a top notch engineering college, the London Polytech Institute. I got an electrical engineer degree. My brother invited me over to visit this community he was in Hawaii. Shy, I was a virgin when I came to the House on the Big Island. The wild House women, in particular Wyoming and Frieda soon put an end to that situation and I've been in love with one or another of them ever since.

Malcolm, 34

I'm Kevin's older brother. I too have the Phelan wanderlust. I had lived all over the world working on programming contracts, a free lance programmer of IBM's premier language PL-5. I met the House in Hawaii, brought in by Wyoming who I had the hots for at the time. Wyoming and I are married. I was born in Singapore. My father was a sergeant in the British military, a lifer and had taken us to live all over the world: Hong Kong, Malaysia, India. He believed in the Raj. He was one of the lucky soldiers saved at Dunkirk.

I'm also a graduate student in psychotherapy at the Integral Institute in San Francisco at the moment. I'm in a group marriage with Dahlia, Pia, Jesse, Lucia, and Dianne and Morey. My current favorite is Frieda.

Frieda, 35

I've been in the house 12 years. I work in the landscaping crew preferring the physical work, though at times I have worked as a secretary. I've got a Masters in Sociology. I was working as a social worker in New York when I met Chase.

I was married before I got married to the House. I met my husband in 1963, we wanted the 'American Dream': a large home in the suburbs with children and many cars. I got pregnant in 1964, though the situation was resolved by a trip to Sweden for a legal abortion after I found out about my husbands affairs. I felt the loss deeply. We got divorced.

I was born just down the coast from here, San Mateo. I grew up in Marin, my father was a broker. I was crazy about horses when I was a girl. We owned several. I used to be quite an accomplished horsewoman, riding in shows. I stopped after I entered university at Radcliff.

I started in individual therapy with Chase at his practice on 12th Avenue, then moved to group therapy and was part of the beginning of the House. I've been in several group marriages within the House, Tom and I were really tight for a while, now I've been getting closer to his brother Eric. I've also gotten into wild crazy deep romantic sexual attractions with Ursu and Morey and Aaron all of which taught me a lot about dependencies and how I always pull for that.

Rachel, 30

My name is Rachel and I have lived several distinctly different lives in my 30 years. Life at this time is the best ever.

My childhood was horrible until the age of nine when it got worse. I found myself the object of my fathers sexual activities. I had to suffer my father's sexual advances until I ran away from home at the age of 14. I watched him deteriorate into violent alcoholism and pigishness. Though it wasn't always bad. I got to love hiking and the woods. That's where I'd go and camp out when things got really bad. When I was 14 years old, I packed my favorite possessions, took the $500 I saved from my job at the Dairy Queen in Yreka, took my tent and sleeping bag and took the bus to San Francisco. There I was lucky to hook up with a feminist co-op in the Haight. I got my GED in night school, started doing secretarial work, started work as a secretary in a law firm, went to school to become a legal assistant. I've been more or less on my own until I met Rob. Even though I'm considered beautiful and men hit on me a lot, they soon come to see me as a bitch. Robert helped me out a lot. He was the first man I ever loved. When we went to Hawaii, on my first ever vacation we got involved with the House. Rob wanted to do it, and I wanted to be with him. I never had an orgasm until Chase showed me how. Chase said I was compulsively workaholic in order not to be overwhelmed by the feeling of abandonment and rage that was always present. He said I had lost the ability to feel or express feelings having had to stuff these way down deep inside from my traumatic childhood. He worked with me a lot. Finding out about my orgasm, women's orgasm and being in the House for four years now has let me pursue a pleasurable life, and this and my best friends who share the same goals are my priorities. THANK YOU, Chase!

Morey, 34

I was born Syracuse, New York, of an overbearing Jewish mother. And I was a good little Jewish boy going to Sabbath services etc.

I loved sports and was a good student.

At age 14 my face broke out with acne, and it got worse and worse over the years all through school and high school, covering my back. Acne Vulgaris. No amount of bacterial and lamp treatments could stop it. My social skills with girls were poor.

I subsequently put more attention on music and hiking and sports. Hangin' with the guys. I went to college in New York and majored in Business.

I met my first wife in my junior year, the first girl I had fallen in love with. She was a fantastic musician and it was the late 60s and she urged me to play and I took up the harmonica to play back up and we really got into the blues. We decided to record her music. Neither the music nor our marriage worked out.

I started going to therapy with Chase in New York, and got involved with the start of the House. He has shown me a lot and been one of the best friends I ever had.

Since 1979 I have been researching pleasure. We have
been living together and learning sensuality from each other
for many years. I love women and I don't stay away from
them anymore. I am hooked.

I still play blues harmonica. I've got over two dozen
harps in my brief case now. I enjoy playing with the other
musicians, Kevin and Bradley around the house. We've
even set up on the street and been buskers downtown in
front of the BART station.

Jade, 24

This August will be my 25th birthday. I had been going
to school all my life. Started college when I was 16. Got a
masters degree when I was 21, and started working on my
Ph.D. in literature. I liked the French romantics. Stendahl.
Tuisant de L'Ouverture. I like the way they looked at the
Nouveau Mond.

I met Harve at a party some graduate students in
architecture invited me to. We started getting together, and
then he brought me into the House.

Chase said that I do well in the structured rigid reward
systems of school because it makes up for the neglect and
lack of love I had in my early life.

And now I'm here in the house, working in
landscaping. As far as I'm concerned the pursuit of a
pleasurable life, and best friends who shared the same goals
were priorities that were head and shoulders above anything
else.

Serena, 49

I'm a 49 year old former wife and mother —still a
mother — perhaps now more than ever since we live with a
bunch of my best friends, family style. Like the great big
spread out Italian family I always wanted to be part of.

My husband Chase and I were married and already had
Mark when he started shifting his practice into group
therapy and Aaron, Katie, Janette, Lucia, Dave all moved
into the house my grandmother left to us in 1970 in New
York city and started to experiment with open marriage and
LSD.

I feel like I have the richest life in the world as a result of it. I've got to admit it was really a stretch for me, though, with my "good girl" upbringing. In my mind I was to marry a doctor (I did), have a big house (I did—but no white picket fence), 2 kids and we even have a dog.

When I met Chase 15 years ago now that middle class fantasy evaporated and we were inspired to pioneer our own unique life-style and relationship. All of us took years of group therapy and spiritual Buddhism and communication courses to enrich our lives. Gradually we opened it up to more people who had the courage to pursue their own souls on this earth and the Sangha of Dorje Chang was born.

I feel so fortunate to be a partner with my best friends in this journey. Last fall, I attended, upon Chase's urging —I wasn't goin' to go, my 20 year high school reunion and was amazed at how different I was from those old people there. What a kick! All aspects of my life are amazing: my sex life is great, I'm home everyday with my family, constantly meet new people and am surrounded with positive, responsible friends in love with their lives.

Tom, 25

Hello: I'm Tom, 25. I'm here in the House. My brother Eric is here too. And I feel so alive. We're part of the most fun household in the world. For the last two and a half years, I lived on a coffee plantation on the Big Island of Hawaii with my family of friends. We grew some of the best Blue Mountain Kona coffee you've ever tasted.

I came to the house through Brad and Jennifer, after I was going to get married but the house talked me out of it. I came into the house with Apalonia this beautiful Italian girl but she got freaked out and had to go home.

I remember being freaked out when everybody talked to us about dependency, and I was so bummed out when she left, but getting into sex with Wyoming and Jennifer, and Bridget and Katie took my mind off all that. Coming into this group was a giant step towards a fun and pleasurable life. However, I really had no idea of what a wonderful, exciting adventure I was beginning. I especially love playing with Wyoming's pussy. I'm learning a trade too, becoming a landscaper and a gardener.

Pia, 34

I am a short Jewish woman from Manhattan and I speak
with a slight Brooklyn accent. My parents were born in this
country, and did well in the garment district. My father
owned his own buildings. They used to take me and my
brother on trips to the Bahamas and Cuba. I became a fabric
designer and managed a boutique in Chelsea. I enjoyed
dressing up the tall thin models, which I am not. I met Chase
when Lucia, one of my models, who was in therapy,
suggested I get into it. I had been in therapy before when I
was a kid growing up. My parents believed in it and were
into psychoanalysis for years. It was a glamorous life there
for a while, the fashion circuit but I retired from that to
dedicate my life to living with this extended family now. I
still have a passion for clothes and recently bought a blue
suede coat from North Beach Leather. I've been designing
and sewing some clothes for the girls in the House.

Chase, 52

Well I'm Chase and I could say I'm the chief, cook and
bottle washer around here. We are sort of a loose tribe. A
family. An intentional community. A group. A sangha. We
are training some very fine therapists here, and we are all
getting much further along in exploring the real potentialities
of being human. It has not been easy. But things have turned
out really well for us. We are a going concern.

About myself. Well. I am unusual in that I was raised
among Indians. I was born Charles Lang on a farm in the
Badlands. Back in South Dakota where I was a kid there
were Indians and I spent a lot of time with them out in the
woods fishing and camping. It really made me see how
different us white folks are from them. We are always
angling for something, always got some agenda. It wasn't
until much later that I understood how pervasive this
Narcissus complex is in our culture. From a very early age, I
was drawn to indigenous cultures and their spiritual
practices. I was particularly fascinated by the . . . paranormal
which I like to call super-sensory — beyond ordinary senses.
It struck me that native people live with a foot in two worlds.
They seemed to be in touch with the Source upon which they
relied for assistance through supernatural forces to assist

them in their everyday lives. Perhaps super-sensory is a better word than supernatural. It is beyond the ordinary senses; I think it has to be a spiritually cultivated Sense.

My clinical practice has emerged out of my private practice and has evolved over the past 15 years. It started out after NYU Med school in Queens, did my internship at New York Flushing Hospital Medical Center then going to the psyche wards of the VA hospital during Vietnam. I was a conscientious objector and my advisor got me into a learning analysis with the psychiatrist Julius Goldstein and they found a place for me in the VA hospital. I became a conscientious objector when I got exposed to Buddhism on a trip to India and Asia when I was an undergraduate helping an archeologist take temple measurements. In Nepal I was amazed at the similarities between American Indian and Tibetan tribal rituals. And too, their circular mandala paintings: they were both about the self finding a place to stand and from which to move out of lower levels to higher ones. When I got back I attended a series of lectures by Joseph Campbell at NYU Stonybrook and even talked to him. I got involved with the Vedanta society where I first learned to meditate and I took initiation into Buddhism in New York on the Lower East Side with Lama Drayan Ling, a Buddhist of the Tibetan Marpa tradition whose root guru is Kalu Rimpoche. From there I got a job working with the psych wards of Bellevue Hospital and finally clinical practice out of an office with a group of psychiatrists in Manhattan. Over the years I've done analysis with several therapists and always found it to be the best money I ever spent. I've made several retreats to Southeast Asia and Nepal even shortly after the war in 1973 and 74. I met my wife Serena — she was a nurse — and we have two children. Our life style has evolved considerably over the years as has my therapy practice.

My therapy is a hodgepodge of psychoanalytic theory. From group therapy I took the importance of expressing problems to a significant other. From Reich and others I took the idea of defense as a motor event and the role of body armor in character formation. From traditional analysis I took the free association. From Primal Scream therapy I took the re-enactment of the engramatic process of traumatic episodes. From Zen and Buddhism I realized the tremendous importance of meditation, the no-nonsense straight-forwardness, minimizing intellectualization and "sitting." Sitting means just that, having to sit with and free associate, analyze, repeat, and work through the material that comes up in therapy.

Group therapy brings up psychological material in real time, and around here we are doing intense non-standard group therapy and have managed to quite increase the "group velocity" which is the frequency and intensity with which issues present themselves for analysis. We are learning the Buddhist practice of mindfulness, which feels like a super-sensory process. It involves a different metaphor for the self and methodologies for knowing the self. This came about through the use of LSD and the 2500 year old metaphysical psychology of Tantric Buddhism that really took me deep with one great insight after another. With LSD we had first begun to see the inner lights. We had set about to correlate these inner light phenomena with the latest developments made in the natural science description of neurophysiology. But it wasn't until we began to read the accounts of the yogis and Tibetan monks who had developed a system of explaining the lights, a system of chakras and Kundalini that systematized the mastery over the mind and body that I began to realize a way to bring these insights into clinical practice. Soon the individuals in my group therapy clinic were taking a lot of LSD in sessions and working through the freakouts, and we began to live together in the big house we bought along the East River. We began to experience at first hand the profound effect upon character of communal life. These marathon group therapy sessions with LSD evolved into a kind of western puja.

The values, methods and goals in the large canon of esoteric Tantric Buddhist literature were adapted, made modern and amended by group activity. To the Buddhist, meditation and mindfulness is not only a scientific method it is also a field of study. For some 3000 years Buddhist have been researching its rich history, and have formed a huge science and technology and body of writing around it.

Gradually the therapy has become what Buddha said to do so long ago: practice the 8-fold way — Right View, Right

Understanding, Right Thought, Right Speech, Right Action, Right Livelihood, Right Concentration, Right Mindfulness. One comes to have great respect for the complexities of Buddhist methodologies for living a richer, deeper, more satisfying emotional life.

We found that the limited cortical experience of western man—the "normal" genital character structure of consciousness described by Freud, along with what he believed were its necessary superego-imposed restrictions—can be expanded.

Liberation of the nervous system from these restrictions was found to establish pre-genital polymorphous sensateness. When this liberation happens, consciousness deepens to encompass subcortical events described in Eastern yogic psychology — the interoceptive sensations of lights and sounds, described in yogic literature as the raising of the Kundalini and the frequent experiencing of beatific visions.

Most of the people in the house do not come from such terrible backgrounds, suffer psychotic breaks, suicide or other psychotic states, brought on by severe mental and physical abuse. Only a few, like Rachel and Theo and Dianneand Bradley and Lissa do have the potential for severe psychotic breakdown but they are responding well and hanging in. Although at times we all dip into the Hell Realm, and other realms and learn to deal with it. Most of the people of theHouse, the sangha, like most Americans, come from a background of neglect and live in the Hungry Ghost realm. They don't get stuck in the Hell Realm of schizophrenia or psychotics but more in the realm of narcissism, they are just completely out of touch with what it is like to feel real. They seek to fill their lives with grasping and consumerism, — this is the Hungry Ghost Realm; the antidote is real spiritual nourishment. We manage to go in and out of the other realms, the God Realm, the Animal Realm, on this great mandala Wheel of Life hopefully getting off more and more at the Human Realm. We've managed to keep ourselves out of the Animal realm by developing a detached and spiritual sexuality. We have a great group process to monitor that we don't drift into the false God realm. Living together, we have pulled ourselves as close as possible to each other. We can do this by turning trials into opportunities and forcing ourselves to confront the Hungry Ghost narcissism and egoism that pervades so much of modern life. Our methods keep everybody on their toes to achieve a perpetual deconstruction of consciousness.

What we have here is a spiritual marriage. This is simply where two people can ask for and give and receive devotion. You need to be present with each other, WITH your fear and your anger. You need to own the anger instead of flipping it off onto others through projective identification.

It is very important that men understand the anima and women understand the animus. That is what a spiritual marriage is about. Forcing each to come to terms with the other in a supportive environment. So, I am like cupid and I really want to see these young people get together and really love each other and I keep all their problems in mind and I think about them. That's my job. I think about yogas and ways for them to overcome their problems. I am training therapists here and sexual surrogates.

Shame, guilt, and anxiety are seen as illusions, not pure experiences of reality but the outcome of attitudes developed in an environment of social injustice - the nuclear family. In the Freudian account of consciousness the superego intercedes between the self and reality, standing against it, denying or resisting it, fearing to perceive it. These illusions of the genital character personality due to the super-imposition of inhibition by the superego are treated exactly as a chronic psychosomatic symptoms of the culture's purposive repression of extra-genital feeling —their origins and manifestations are examined in the group atmosphere of support, and confronted with various actions called "yogas." I and others in the group conduct specific sex education. I do at times cross the boundaries of traditional analysis and give specific hands on sexual instructions to the group and to individuals.

Meditation is the most valuable method of all. Meditation brings you beneath the occurrences of every day into your own central nervous system and beneath that to a Universal Mind, which really does permeate the universe and is knowable by some of the more highly evolved species with consciousness in the universe. Though we have not met any others besides what is on this planet. We may one day meet them through meditation. Freud's description of mystical experiences as "oceanic" were, I think, dismissive and perhaps indicative of the experience of the God Realm; they are not the mystical experiences that Buddha described as essential to his psychology of analytic meditation.

We have evolved a life style that includes sophisticated group-therapeutic and bioenergetic technologies. I am very interested in the Tibetan sangha and its future for the exploration of liberation through meditation and mindfulness. I have created a commune, a sangha, a spiritual community. I am the unofficial mentor to several students doing graduate work in psychology though I am a no longer a member of the AMA, due to an unfortunate incident involving a clash of methodologies. We've evolved quite a democratic group here. They disagree with me often and come to each other's aid.

My style of therapy, though like Reich using strong counter action to punch through the character armor, has been tempered with what I saw in the Tibetan Buddhist paradigm: its ability to bless these defenses. For I learned to look at the two sided nature of these guardians. We ask what are they guarding, and what they are guarding is nothing less then exposing the individual to the raw transcendental energies of the life force.

The main payoff from studying meditation, is being able to shift the metaphor of the self from being a spatial metaphor of disparate parts cut off from each other to being a temporal one that allows ambiguity and flow. This empowers you to move into the ambiguity, feeling both excited and anxious. Feeling the ambiguity lets you be in the temporal dimension.

Theo, 55

I have the dubious distinction of being the oldest man in the house, 55. Oldest person I think. I'm the tallest too. Man I really appreciate getting loving from these young healthy smart liberated women in the House. I have gone through a lot of changes.

I was an itinerant professor of Asian History moving

around some swell places in academe. Traveled all over the orient, Malaysia, Nepal, Japan, Thailand. India. Studied everything about Buddhism from art to Zen. Studied Japanese, Tibetan, Sanskrit, German. Even did a stint as a Professor of Oriental History at the University of Hawaii.

I met Chase when we were both initiates with Lama Rgpo in Nepal and in the US. We were OK Buddhists. Brothers of the Habit.

4

The Van man's hope as electron in a circuit

Walker was jobbing out of his van, doing a little
carpentry, painting, landscaping. In between jobs, he wrote
resumes, cover letters, qualifications briefs. In order to try
and get a little of the trickle down Reganomics he waged
war with the outside world through the mails, dropping letter
bombs, where his high hopes exploded. He would rent time
on the electrical typewriters in the basement of the Berkeley
library. They each had a little chrome meter, in which you
inserted your quarter and it turned on the juice to the electric
typewriter. If you were really broke there were a couple of
antiquated beat-up mechanical typewriters you could use for
free. All sorts of amazingly eccentric street people —
scholars, poets, economists, crackpots espousing every
philosophy and obsession under the sun, worked out their
theories there. The Berkeley public library was a poor man's
bedlam, and if you were really lucky you could research
children's books up on the fourth floor looking out a glorious
window at the Golden Gate spanning the bay. One of
Walker's cover letters for his resumé went like this:

```
Walker Underwood
2019 Blake St.
Berkeley Ca, 94704

Dear Sirs;
    I recently left my college teaching position
where I taught physics and electronics and came out
here to the Bay Area, wanting to write computer
programs that teach  physics, electronics, math.
Ideas have been accruing about this in my mind for a
long time. Recently in the August '82 issue of Byte,
there was an interesting article about creating
"neat" computer microworlds, and how these engage
very fundamental learning and metaphor (to carry
meaning) properties in the adolescent mind, as
discussed in the pedagogical theories of Piaget.
    I understand your company is writing teaching
software for the micro-computers now. You must of
course, realize, with the expanded capability of the
new 16 and 32 bit machines, that all those
```

incredible programs that could only be done on
university mainframe machines can now be done on
little home computers. As well, great new user
oriented languages are engaging more and more young
people into the world of computers. Those programs,
like the biological simulation of life from bonding
rules for amino acids called autopoesis, or Conway's
Game of Life, or the larger programs of Quantum
Mechanics, the manipulation of matrices, and related
matric processes like curved geometries, and Markov
chains, Feynman diagrams, scattering, can now be
done at home with the desk top computer. How I
longed for one of these labor saving machines with
interactive language when I was going to college
pondering the weighty mathematical tomes,
manipulating tensors bristling with indices! The
language of group theory and operators streamlined
things somewhat, but that is so abstract, nothing
like experiencing the simulation of seeing these
phenomena unfold before your eyes in high resolution
color! Think of it! Programs relating to entropy and
information theory, game simulation of human
interaction, Maxwell's daemon, anything that can be
thought of in terms of vector spaces or state
variables. What terrific antennae this gives the
race! I wonder if you might possibly suggest some
people who are interested in making these kinds of
teaching microworlds into task domains or problem
spaces designed for virtual streamlined experience.
        Sincerely
        Walker Underwood

But the jobs weren't coming during that bottoming out
of the recessionary period of beginning Reaganomics. As the
recession deepened the resumes became more baroque, the
lies got sweeter, but his own voice became more and more
lost.

However, since meeting Dahlia there might be some
hope. After a few more trips to the phone in the laundromat
Walker was getting exasperated. Finally he got The Dahlia.
She said: "My girlfriend's mother is coming into town this
Friday and I've got to spend the day with her."

There was a long pause.

"But we can get together on Saturday."

"Alllrigght!" Walker's heart leapt for joy.

"Do you know La Boheme?" she asked. "Meet me at La
Boheme. It's at Mission and 24th, across from the BART
station."

"Got it."

On the trip over the Bay Bridge to meet his date that Saturday the world took on a hyper-real luminescent contrast. There is nothing so sharp as the visionary imagination of a young man filled with the possibilities of love. It is a windy trip over the Bay Bridge and Walker has to grip the steering wheel hard with both hands. His knuckles are as white as the whitecaps broiling in the bay. You don't exactly drive a VW van, it is more like sailing it. But Walker doesn't notice. He's got the warm tingling glow of anticipated love inside of him. As he came off the Bay Bridge on a warm bright October night he felt as if he had entered the City of Dreams.

How lucky he was, how filled with hope he was, to have bought the van, quit his college teaching job in Austin and spent the whole summer traveling and camping out of his van, then to end up back in Berkeley, among friends at the warehouse, but to top it all off to possibly get something going with a chick! For dates he'd leave Sunshine behind with his friend the poet Darrell Gray who had a house with a fenced back yard in Oakland.

The thought of getting into sex with her crossed his mind in a vague sort of way.

He looked into the back of his van and thought, Siegfried! The van had a large queen size mattress dominating the entire back part of the van. Walker sang in an operatic baritone: "My ship of love is ready to attack." He just had to have the sumptuous mattress because it was the only one he had found that could accommodate his lank, six-foot-three frame. He had multicolored curtains over the windows and the passageway between the bucket seats. Beneath the mattress platform was his whole kitchen in boxes: a little Bluet butane stove, lots of whole grains, back-packer food, desert caravan food. He had an f.m. radio as well as an unlicensed C.B.

But this was a first date, and his own sexual history did not leave a great deal of real hope for anything, certainly not this first date!?

Besides, Walker had just about sworn off women.

Walker's sexual libido which had been down to just about absolute 0 in Texas was rising ever since he hit the sunny dessert of California. It's not that he didn't like women. Oh yes, he liked women, once had really loved them, had almost been married a couple or three times. At the university in Austin, Walker had lived with several women, MaryJo on Enfield and then later after she bought a house off Lamar. She really wanted to be married, but she could never have orgasm, unless an inordinate amount of hand frigging was used.

Then later after a short period of sadness he had shared an apartment with Terry while she was in graduate school. He should have married that one. But things had gradually drifted apart when he got more and more into hanging out with bohemian poets and musicians down on 6th St.

Then he drifted around for a while, and there was no one in particular.

There was a lovely young woman / girl 18 —actually 17 — when they met on a bus, and she turned out to be good friends with the daughter of one of the people on the faculty of the trade school where Walker had worked as a teacher. Walker and the young high school girl were kind of suited to each other. They started meeting down near the river by the foot bridge near the high school and going for walks. It was good to be broke together, ride bikes, walk dogs, camp out, make candles for a living. But they had drifted apart when a friend introduced him to a woman his own age - 30 - and she lived on a farm, the very farm where "The Texas Chain Saw Massacre" movie was made. Walker should have known.

Even though he had been introduced by a friend, the friend nor the woman had told him that she had herpes and silly and naive he had ended up getting it. It came on after they had already gone their separate ways.

It was his first intimation of mortality, and after that Walker had no more love affairs. By the time he managed to get enough money to get the van together and get out of Texas he had entered a state of near quarantine, where his anger had taken up residence in the old guilt. The herpes was like a fever, like a cold, but what his mind did with it was way out of proportion. He often thought about getting a gun, going to her door and when she opened it shooting her in the face. Then he'd shudder in fear of his own evil impulses and turn his anger into guilt. His ego beat up on him with guilt.

His body was polluted with some little crystalline entities alien invaders from the world of matter seeking to take over. He had spent so many nights in fear, —my eyes, my eyes! What if it got in my eyes and I went blind! He developed an obsession for washing his hands. But gradually through books he learned about it.

It resided in the spine and when agitated by stress reared up its hexahedronal head and exploded — sending shards of RNA to take over the cellular machinery and reproduce itself. He had been a vegetarian for a long time but now he had to develop a life that was more stress free. That is why he had left Texas to come out here to the west coast —to find some understanding.

He had to do some serious management of spoiled identity. Especially where romantic encounters with women were concerned. And now here he was on his way to a date with the lovely Dahlia, all these thoughts and other doubts running through his mind.

And anyway, he tells himself, the whole issue wouldn't even come up on the first date and besides if it did, he was not under attack at the moment, *and* he had a condom. Anyway it was a total non-issue on the first date. Relax and feel the hope he told himself.

From the descent off the Bay Bridge, he is on the freeway. They call it a freeway here, he tells himself, I've got to remember that. A freeway, not an expressway, not a thruway, not the interstate, but the freeway that snakes over the labyrinthine streets of the city. At the twilight hour when the lights are coming on, the city is fluid. It rises up and down, spangled, burnished, looks Byzantine, a mosaic of space-time tesserae within frames within frames within frames. There is the smell of coffee in the air. Hills Brothers. Think drink for an intellectual city.

There is an absolute sharpness to his vision as he looks from the still bluish heavens beyond the hills ringing the city silhouetted against the golden west. The great wall of Daly City boxes snake up and down the hills like boxcars on a long train. All the little houses, parallel the grid of the downtown skyscrapers.

Man, this is not Austin any more. Not Berkeley either.

This is a city with three telephone books! He was moving quiet as an electron, through the aether. He was just one of the many red tail-lighted electrons in the current of the freeways. He is traveling in one of the many traces of an integrated circuit and he is wired with radio and neon lights. The city is a microprocessor. Each house or apartment in the city is a transistor in the integrated circuit. They convert the utilities into information. The utilities provide electrical power and communication analogous to providing the voltages that bias the registers and logic and arithmetic units. Who designed this huge integrated circuit? Who were the architects of this space in time. He would get to know this city: its roads, its businesses, its libraries, its history, its organization of memory. Maybe even help organize its memory, its meaning, its logic, its truth. Getting ready to change lanes he thought about how in a traffic flow the spaces between cars are Poisson distributed. There ought to be a way to sample data and exploit this mathematical phenomenology in real time. That coupled with radar sensing of other cars, and circuitry embedded in the roads or the side of the roads ought to lead to smart roads where people could move at high speeds all watched over by benevolent time series of bump car field hubris. That would be cool, wouldn't it?

He changes lanes, goes off an exit ramp which brings him into neighborhood. Driving down Potrero, 'neath the shadow of a large round friendly green hill, he notices puffy dark clouds to the north. He drives on until he comes to the corner of Mission and 24th. There on the red brick plaza surrounding the subway station a crowd of Jesus people are being harangued by a swarthy Latino with a bull horn.

Walker parks the van and walks back a few blocks down Mission. The glorious tingling surges through him, straightens his walk, assures his gate. This is a good place. Wake up! You are in the city. Notice. Watch out. See what is going on. Hunker down to the hum. The hissssss. Hot breath of cityspeak blowing old newspapers by teeth grates in convection canyons. On Mission St. low-rider sedans are growling, pacing on the pavement like panthers. Loud disco and heavy-on-the-emotion Mexican music picks up the solidarity out of the air and blasts it out of the cockpits. You can get a citation in the Mission for having a broken speaker.

Sidewalk still crowded with merchants moving racks of clothes fluttering in the breeze, racks of electronic goodies, banks and robot tellers, hookers and throngs of dark faces going home from work.

In La Boheme Dahlia was sitting in a way-off corner alone. Walker dodged and picked his way across the crowded room toward the vacant chair at her table. She was sitting up tall in a peasant shirt tucked into long skirts made of heavy blue jean denim that fit her snugly around her slim waist. She had a real inviting way of scrunching up her shoulders and turning around to look at him with a smile when she saw him.

She looked different from the other women in the room, more self-assured, strong, though modest, non-provocative. No one would bother this woman, yet he found her so approachable. Her eyes were large, wondrous and dark. Her untroubled forehead suggested the calm gentleness of her ways. He was so glad to see her, like a man looking at the jailer who was to release him from the prison his own mind kept him in. She lifted a cup of chamomile tea to her lips and carefully sipped the hot liquid. Easy and self-assured were her moves and her smile was as innocent as a child's, as was the curious non-judgmental penetration of her gaze.

"What have you been doing?" she asked.

"Oh, I've been looking into some teaching jobs," he said. Walker's mind added, Oh, God. Now I've done it. She thinks I'm unemployed. "In the meantime I've been doing some construction work," he added quickly, moving his long torso back and forth in a John Wayne swagger.

He got up and followed a tall straight African woman, sauntering among the tables up to the counter. The harried humorous and hirsute young counterman seemed to have four arms serving lattés, lemonades, teas and tarts with great aplomb.

"What magnificent creatures! here in San Francisco," he said to Dahlia indicating some of the bohemians. They watched dykes in leather Amelia Erhart jackets swaggering to and fro. Next to them, a table of tall stern ancient men, with long gray locks or an obvious toupee pontificated over the scene like elder walruses basking in some past glories.

Later, he told Dahlia of his desire to be a writer. He usually hesitated telling people this, but since he was a stranger in a strange land, he decided he may as well be himself. "Sometimes," he said, "I use the resume as a literary form. After all it is a kind of creative fiction."

She laughed at this lack of proper respect. It was all a bit awkward, as first meetings usually are, but there was much good will.

"I studied poli-sci in college," Dahlia said.

"Oh, boy, he said shaking his head in dismay at his own political apathy —this was partly because he wasn't a citizen and had never voted in America — "I'm afraid I'll have to get you to underline the names in the paper for me. I don't follow politics too much."

"Well, I use it more for office work right now," she said.

They watched as a very calm woman bought a bag of garlic from one of the little oriental street urchins who just could barely reach up to her table.

"I write too, mostly journals and stuff," she said. "I've written my own autobiography." She thought about how Chase was always encouraging everybody to write to pay attention to their feelings, and to speak well. That was a big part of the Buddhist practice. Chase was constantly admonishing them to pay attention to the feelings, to the sensations. Learn how to describe them, to anticipate them, to protect them, to cherish them.

"I have too," he said, "but it was weird. It was like a Biographia Literia, just about stuff that I learned. I'm afraid I don't know myself any better."

Dahlia smiled at the alternative diary she was keeping and the title she had recently given to this literary effort: Diary of a Commune Nympho. Of course that was her secret. She said, "Yeah, it's hard to tell yourself who you really are, let alone someone else." She smiled in a feeling way. "Well. . . you have to do a little every day. When I come home I make like I am writing a letter to a very trusted friend. Maybe only to say, 'Hi,' or sometimes to tell her how the day went, sometimes to ask for help dealing with things." She didn't tell him it was about honoring the deity within, or how it serves the purpose of fiercely pursuing pleasure. Chase wanted them to use writing as a kind of self-seduction, an ally in the pursuit of pleasure.

"Wow, yeah," said Walker, that's the great way to do writing. To think of it as a letter to a friend, to be communicating with somebody you love and trust."

Dahlia's diary entry from earlier this day read:

Sept 24, 1982 Had another argument with Malcolm. I think it's because we are so much alike. He's up against telling the truth and I'm up against the same and being nice about it. I know he's out there spinning his wheels but I know he'll be back. I was really nervous when it came time for our session but we made a lot of sound and broke through. It all seemed kind of surreal —where I was in my head before. We actually had a great time. When I held his cock in my hand it was actually throbbing. Those horny Scots. As I stroked his cock up and down it was actually twitching in my hand. He's a good guy even when he gets on my nerves.

Just then some bearded drunk was coming out of his own private drunken ecstasy/hell and was staggering around and grinning stupidly in the middle of the room. He was wobbling about, and as he turned, he made his hands like holding a machine gun, shooting at some virtual enemy ahead. He shouted, "STAY DOWN! Don't do that, stay down." Walker and Dahlia paused their conversation to see whether there was any active danger. The whole coffee shop was stealing glances at him. After a while he left.

"My, it's like bedlam in here isn't it?" she said. "Anyway," she continued, by way of finishing her thought, "I write mostly for self-analysis."

They perused the Bay Guardian trying to decide where to go on the first date. "How about the Great American Music Hall?" she suggested. "Have you ever been there?"

"No I haven't," he said, sliding his chair around to be beside her. As he looked over her shoulder at the paper, he inhaled her soft scent.

"Pharo Sanders is playing the sax," she said.

"Wow, I like him a lot," he said. "Remember that stuff he did with Leon Thomas. It was awesome. He had this wonderful jazz yodel, sounded like a soulful camel in heat. Didn't he? "

Dahlia laughed.

He looked a little nervous, "What does it cost?"

"Cover charge is 20 dollars."

"Oohh, man, that's a little too steep for me," Walker said. "I'm kind of between paychecks at the moment."

They decided to go to a bar called Major Ponds. It was ladies' night free, so Walker only had to pay for himself. He and Dahlia squeezed into a standing place at the bar, each being careful not to touch the other.

"Since you had to pay for your cover, I'll buy the first round," she said.

They drank sevral glasses of wine, and she danced with somebody on the tiny dance floor after he demurred. The band, KICK, had the audience sing along on one song: "Coming down from love and I wonder why it takes so long. Coming down from love and I wonder why it takes so long."

She matched him glass for glass of wine. He spent the last of his money on a last round at closing time.

She was a vision of loveliness leaning back with her arms against the bar. She was just inviting him to put her hands on her and he did. He slowly pulled her to him, held her and kissed her.

It was a warm fall evening, even at 2 am. A storm was in the air. Dark clouds of fear hovered at the periphery of his sexual history which he tried not to notice but which kept seeping up. Subconsciously he began to rapidly go over all the bad sexual experiences he had had in his life, starting with the first encounter at age 14. His first experience if your could call it that was with a whore. He recalled going down to Mexico to a whorehouse with Jose Mendez. These were plump, stupid whores. Who only lay back on the bed and spread their legs. No caress, no help, no nothing. Of course I couldn't get it up. And there on the bed next to me, Jose was laughing. So I was embarrassed. My manhood was not yet ready to demonstrate itself. And in those days, pre-pill, good girls didn't have sex. I met some good women after that, had some good relationships. Then went for a long time where I was just going from one person to another. I had gotten the clap several times, while a teenager going down to Mexico. And there was no one to tell. You couldn't go to the doctor, couldn't tell your parents. It was very frightening. No damn wonder I'm afraid of sex.

He felt Fear reaching out for him then and trying to get

ahold of his mind for a while, wanting to talk to him from the shadows, offering to play back old movies in his head. Then I started getting much later a kind of psychosomatic NSU. Because I wasn't having any feelings in my relationships. Then finally a couple of years ago I developed herpes. That really devastated and devitalized me. It was such a blow to my sexual self image. It is really guilt and fear about sex that keeps getting reinforced by VD. That is why I'm afraid of sex.

But the yearning for love was coursing through his drunken veins and it was stronger than the barricades of fear and he pushed through and squeezed into her bucket seat in the van and started to hug her. He asked her to lie down on the big mattress in the back of the van, just to hug for a while, nothing more, as the terrifying crash-BANG! of thunder shook animals from their sleep. He drew the curtains, and they took off some clothes, for the windows were steaming up, and they wanted to rub more skin on skin. And then taking refuge from the storm he put on a condom and entered her and they made love.

What great release!

He knew he would have to tell her, about his social disease but not yet. He'd worn a condom. Here just a few days ago he was never going to get together with a woman again, and now. . . "Well," he thought, "a man is entitled to a little pleasure in this life."

Snug in a sleeping bag, they drifted off to sleep under the patter of rain on the van roof. Walker was delighted once during the night to wake up in a sea of cozy quilts and bedclothes when all was still and the moon broke through the skies into the van and he spent a few moments watching over her lovingly, cherishing the memory of her face innocent in sleep.

5

The Love Poem

Dahlia looked good in her long skirts as she high stepped from the van dashing quickly back up into the Loft. She would slip through the cracks of the morning hustle and bustle and not have to account for the night's activity.

It was a strange thing for Walker to sleep with somebody. For several hours after she left, Walker felt the impression of Dahlia's lovely nude body plastered into his own. He decided to write a poem in order to keep that presence for at least a few hours more. When he got back to Berkeley, he grabbed his pack with his notebook and headed for the Med. It would be cool if I could blow her away with a beautiful love poem, he thought. I'll send it to her.

Walker kind of pictured himself as a member of the old-school literati, like Pound sending notes all over the place, it was like he hadn't got used to the telephone yet. He did know that nobody sent notes by mail much any more. (She'll see I'm from the old school, he thought, — hope she doesn't think the old Catholic school.)

Walker laid his blue spiral notebook on a marble table in the Med on Telegraph Avenue. He took his favorite good-flow Parker pen out of his shirt pocket and laid it on the table too. He sipped a machiato and recalled the lines of Sir John Suckling: *Out upon it: I have loved thee three whole days all together, and am like to love thee three more, if fair prove the weather.* Wonder who he really was. That was back when women had bodices you could unlace from the front. He was probably a breast man.

But that won't do. It's too flip. It's not sufficiently serious and respectful of the auspiciousness of the situation. Hmmm. If I could just write her a simple love poem. Something from the heart. Something to make sense of the way things are for me. Something about the way I feel the world, so bottled up, about to explode. Walker took pen and wrote the first line of the poem:

Like a volcano on Venus

Volcano is right, he thought, the way I exploded last night when I came. God I needed that. Like the i. I need to get the symbolic letter i, in there. Make it stand for my dick. Somehow. I'll make it the little i. And he wrote:

and i, a little Venusian man

That's cool, my dick as a little Venusian man. And the dot on the i is like the sun, setting over water. He drew a big i on his note book page.

Let's see, maybe I could say something about what it felt like to watch her sleep in the van, in the wee hours of the morn. I felt like caring for her like I'm her mother. Walker wrote:

quiet / baby's sleeping, / and i a little Venusian man / recently arrived from that very hot planet / (a place that is good for men and dogs / but not very good for women and horses)

Oh, oh, women and dogs. Better not do that. It's OK for Texas, but won't do for here. He copied what he had again:

quiet / baby's sleeping, / and i a little Venusian man / recently invited to stay for a while in your hot wet cave,

O God no, that won't do, go back. He wrote again differently:

quiet / baby's sleeping, / and i a little Venusian man / stirring upon this hot new land, / peeked out the venetian blinds.

That's pretty funny, a little Venusian man looking out some venetian blinds. I want to give the feeling that this really is some kind of new land. Like that H.G. Wells book about traveling to the moon with a spherical ship where they just opened and closed blinds. Cool. I watched her turn over in bed and admired her lovely behind. *She* is this new found land, she is the planet? A planet with two moons! He wrote:

And now the planet turns and I must confess i peaked.
As the moon rose moving along the sloping curve of the
latent volcano between your legs.

O god, between your legs, she'll never accept that.

It's like the lover becomes the moon rising over the
terrain of his love. A land of archetypes coming together; or
maybe just looking at her rump under the bedclothes. Want
to be sexy but not offensive.

What. I . . . think about soaring over your lovely white
moon-like curves. Walker added:

The moon was big moving along the sloping curve
of the latent volcano across the bay.

Ha, ha. Now the little Venusian man is looking out some
venetian blinds at a volcano. Maybe get something going
about how love blinds, too. Nooo. It's got to be light and fun,
don't want to tick her off with something heavy. Maybe
something about the planets, something archetypal, Men
from Mars and Women from Venus. I've got to stop all this
damn word play. That's not poetry!

Walker took a sip of his coffee and noticed no fewer than
three other tables occupied by men younger than he, writing
in notebooks.

Walker thought: maybe I should try for something
immortal like the troubadours. But those guys were really
addressing the feminine sides of themselves, and writing
about God and death and spiritual love. Those were intrepid
cocksmen of yore before they had a cure for syphilis. Walker
shuddered. He wrote:

In the starry night i felt Venus
smooth and bridal white
was watching over us two
new lovers accepted into her Way.

Well that's fairly timeless. But conventional. God it's
like this poem has three characters now! i and I and Venus
are talking. We are definitely into some kind of archetypal
thing here. It is as if she were the one doling out love, from

outside. We are of two minds, (hope Dahlia doesn't think I am schizophrenic.) Venus and I are like mom and pop, and i is me. "Venus" is like the female side of my psyche, and "I" is like the superego — the one watching out and always looking and making sure things are going right. And "i" is the wild and crazy cockeyed id. Is this getting heavy or what? God, I'm glad I don't have to stimulate the libido of a 17 year old girl. *I want to hold your hand, yhan yhan. When I . . feel like . . . something.* Got to get something that would excite the libido of this 30-plus Latin beauty. Something like the brute, Stanley Kowolski, crying for Stella in the rain. He wrote:

As i watched you sleeping, / having trusted yourself / with intimate horniness / to my adult care,

Yess. Intimate horniness. That's fairly mature. Isn't it?

Well, what have we got so far. He turned to a new page of his notebook. As he started to recopy onto the new page, he thought of a title and started with that. He wrote:

> *for you (from Venus and I and i)*
> *quiet*
> *baby's sleeping,*
> *and i a little Venusian man*
> *stirring by your side in this hot new land,*
> *peeked out the venetian blinds.*
> *The moon was big moving along the sloping curve*
> *of the latent volcano across the bay.*
> *In the starry night i felt Venus*
> *smooth and bridal white*
> *was watching over us two*
> *new lovers accepted into her way.*
> *As i watched you sleeping,*
> *having trusted yourself*
> *with intimate horniness*
> *to my adult care,*
> *I heard Venus say:*

But, but. Why would Venus be doing the talking? It is fake and away from the real feelings. Well, you can't express your real feelings. Ascribe them to some external source then, a god. But that went out thousands of years ago didn't it?

"Oh, God. I don't know," sighed Walker. Maybe I should try to get some nice clean cut rock thing going in it. I need to get something that sounds like it came from rock. *Teen angel can you hear me.* Oh no. Dying in a car wreck, that won't do. Venus. Yes. Goddess of love. Madonna. *(Get into the groove boy (you've got to prove your love to me)).* The lines in songs are so simple and obvious. That is what I want, obvious — but not sentimental, emotional directness, it refers to nothing outside itself, it is lived. It is compelling. I am looking for something tough, something you can be extremely proud to say to a group of people, something with so much feeling in the words that you can't help but act them out a little bit. That is the beatnik — the poor guy pounded down and hounded by modern life trying to come up with something true, unique, his own. Why is this so difficult?!

Maybe something like: *There is a rose in Spanish Harlem / a red rose, up in Spanish Harlem / it is a special one; it's never seen the sun, it only comes out when the moon in on the run* ...

Uumnhm yeah, something like that would be cool. Lets see, *There is a Dahlia in the Mission and with her I've achieved fission She is the one, with whom I'll have some fun, da dad da da da da*

No! That's ridiculous! She'll think I'm trying to parody love. Walker wrote:

> but no not love of that i am respectful
> from that I do not turn lightly.

Yes turning like the planets. I've got a Venusian man or is a Venusian woman and a lunar man or is it a lunar woman. What am I trying to say?!

That I see a lot of hope for us. That I think you are going to be a big change in my life. That even though I'm horny for your person; you can trust me. I've got my I and my i, and sometimes my i leads my I around. And I'm confused by this, so I'll ascribe it to some external forces, the force of love — Venus. Yeah, that sounds pretty good. OK basically what I am trying to tell her is, that I'm not a lout; I'm more a

sensitive brute. Tempus Fugit baby. You'll be sorry if we
don't get it on while we have the time. So how can I say that
in a cool new and fresh way. Say it in a way that is not
cloying or demanding, or needy, even though I am. You will
be sorry when I'm gone, you will mourn my passing when
I'm gone. There ain't but one way out and it's straight up.
Think! Beatnik! *Like wow baby, me and you could really
exist together.* Or maybe I should just somehow blurt it out: I
want to rub up against your booty!

Walker looked into the staid old Med. A few more
beatniks and street people had wandered in. He tried to
imagine Madonna doing a disco number around the tables
singing: I want to rub up against your booty!

Walker sighed. I'm no good at this. I said I was a writer.
I didn't say I was a poet. Not a poet who writes lines that are
so meaningful and obvious that they just settle into your
unconscious, and become a part of a your life, infectious
lines.

I'm really more of a journalist writer, aren't I? Trying to
write this poem has cleaved me into two minds. Most of
what passes for poetry is word play, or the maudlin
ruminations of the depressed. What I want is something to
come in as natural as a dream and infect this woman with
love for me. I need incantations, spells. Where have I ever
really been touched by poetry like that. When you get hit by
some real poetry you are struck by lightning, galvanized and
evangelized: you walk around dazed, stunned, a wolf
howling at the moon-faced cow people.

Walker recalled a roommate, Roger. Man that guy was
always getting laid. He had the most magical things to say to
women. Sometimes we collaborated on poems. How did that
one go? Mourn my way, I think it was. Something like:

*It is neither here — nor there — that I mourn my way —
a chipped pearl in the drawer — or a python behind glass —
I ask — clear questions as a good citizen will — about truth
and justice and politics and pain. — But I question not love*

We had taken turns, writing it. The Exquisite Corpse.
Man that was really good. I can't believe I can remember so
much of it. It must have really affected me. Now that's what

poems should do. Maybe I should just roll a bunch of our poem into mine. It had the *carp diem* theme — *mourn my way*.

It has politics. Yes. Politics. Dahlia said she was a poly-sci major. She likes politics, and civic responsibility. I've got to show her that I am an upstanding citizen. I'll use his straight simple declarative sentence for that. Walker wrote:

> *I ask clear questions as a good citizen will*
> *about truth and justice and politics and pain.*

The poem also had that direct statement about being poor. Yeah, that's something I need to do. I need to make things right about appearing to be kind of broke too. I've got to confront that perception straight on with something short and clear. Walker wrote:

> *and though poor / I manage elegance*

I've got to make her think I've got some prospects, or at least that not having money, doesn't mean I'm not rich. Yeah that's a good spin on it. That I have seen money, that I once had some trinkets. Walker copied down more of the words of the roommates' poem from memory:

> *My jewels are junk / are gems of cheap and laughable lamentations, / they are / and though poor / I manage elegance*

Wow, I could never write anything as good as that. Maybe I'll just incorporate some of his poem in mine. We used to collaborate. It will be like the Red Badge of Courage, tell a lie to get to a deeper truth. All's fair in love and war.

But what ending will it have. Walker wrote:

> *but I question not love / Love helps us lift the tools to repair*
> *And I hope that we can be a pair.*

Ugh, another pun. Deliver us!

Parts of the roommates' poem began to merge together
with Walker's as he recopied the lines from here and there.

He took it immediately to the electric typewriter at the
library. He typed:

```
for you (from Venus and I and i)

quiet
baby's sleeping,
and i a little Venusian man,
stirring by your side in this hot new land,
peeked out the venetian blinds.
The moon was big moving along the sloping curve
of the latent volcano across the bay.
In the starry night i felt Venus
smooth and bridal white
was watching over us two
new lovers accepted into Her way.
As i watched you sleeping,
having trusted yourself
with intimate horniness
to my adult care,
i wanted to say
it is neither here nor there
that I
mourn my way.
For "I" is only a temporary construct,
a chipped pearl in the drawer,
or a python behind glass. . .
I ask
clear questions as a good citizen will
about truth and justice and politics and pain!
But I question not love.
My jewels are junk,
are gems of cheap and laughable lamentations.
They are.
And though poor,
I manage elegance.
But no not love,
from that i do not stir easily.
Love makes me
lift up the tools.
Let us repair.
```

6

Porpoises at the Drip-Dry Lounge

Dahlia was very pissed off by the poem. On the phone when he called her she said, "I don't know if we ought to see each other."

"Why?" he asked.

"Because of that foolish letter you wrote me. And it didn't even sound like you."

Walker was sure his impetuous ardor had spoiled the fruit of his passion for all time. He scrambled: "Writing doesn't always sound like the way you talk, because it's a one-way communication," he said, "and you don't get the immediate feedback of talking to somebody face to face."

"Well, I don't know . . ."

He could feel her through the phone line —balking like a skittish coltish cutie. "Well, why don't we meet at some neutral cafe and try to figure it out. I just merely wanted to indicate that I took it more seriously than a game of handball."

Dahlia brought along her friend, Pia, because she was in her group and though it would ordinarily be required to discuss Walker in the group, Dahlia had decided to just bring Pia in on it because it wasn't that far along and might not go further. Dahlia was the House Manger and one of the most powerful people in the house, except for perhaps Serena who was still legally married to Chase and mother of his two kids. Serena and Dahlia were the alpha females and had a great deal of influence on the women.

Pia was curious and teased Dahlia: "I'd like to meet your new *suitor*."

"What!? Hoo-hoo." Dahlia replied with a hoot of derision. That word was calculated to raise the scorn response, because romantic behavior was considered duplicitous in the House.

At La Boheme Walker saw the girls engrossed in each other at a table in the corner. Walker felt like he was interrupting something when he came up. Pia managed a weak smile at Walker as though she was a little miffed at having this *guy* interrupt her *tete-a-tete* with Dahlia. They began to size each other up. Pia had thick reddish hair. She was over-dressed for La Boheme: silk sharkskin big-shouldered open jacket of subtle purple shot though with yellows. Dahlia was wearing white jeans and had on a dark sleeveless muscle T-shirt under a school-girl sweater. Walker shook Pia's hand across the table and smiled. Pia was shorter than Dahlia, in her 30s too. As far as Walker knew Pia was just Dahlia's friend.

As Pia spoke, Walker knew she was from New York. "I grew up in Chelsea," she said, "and it should have prepared me for living in San Francisco." Pia raised and lowered her eyebrows to indicate the gay climate. This was lost on Walker who tried to act like he understood. She continued: "I had a textile business there." Now, Pia worked as a plant person traveling around San Francisco in a van and taking care of plants in offices. She was a nice Jewish girl from New York.

Walker, Pia, and Dahlia set off for The Saloon in North Beach on public transportation. Walker had left Sunshine with his poet friend in Oakland; he lived in a house with a back yard. Walker was totally like a peasant his first time on BART. He had to be shown everything to do. He didn't even have the right change, Dahlia had to give him some money. He couldn't figure out which slot in the ticket machine to submit his coin of the realm to. Once he finally got the ticket he couldn't figure out where it goes in the turnstiles. All the while the ladies were patient. Smiling.

"Wow! Going under the city in a subway," he shouted with enthusiasm. "I have always wanted to live in a city with a subway." The two women looked at him as if he were a bit of a hick. "BART virgin," Pia teased, shaking her head in mock condescension. She sneered pointing derisively, "He's a BART virgin! Never been on before." She gave him the horse laugh. "Hya hyna ha."

After emerging at street level downtown they ran for a bus, going down Market Street. Walker observed the powerful action of Pia's haunches, while running, and after they got into the bus, all out of breath and exhilarated, to the stares of rows of lonely males, Walker cheered, "Primates on the prowl." The girls laughed.

For naive Walker, having Pia along on their date relieved the awesome sexual tension between himself and Dahlia. He treated Pia like a sister. Or maybe a little Jewish matchmaker? Perhaps even an ally in his campaign to win Dahlia's heart.

Walker didn't know it but the two women slept together. He thought that the building where they lived was like an apartment house of lofts and that Dahlia and Pia were maybe neighbors or roommates.

But Pia was kind of in love with Dahlia. She admired Dahlia's long languid leggy leanness. The last time in their session, they were under the covers on Pia's futon, completely naked and they were holding each other close and OMing.

This is how Pia wrote about the session in her diary:
October 7, 1982

My pussy was on fire, it was making me weak. I had not let Morey bring me to orgasm in our previous session. I just really had the hots for Dahlia but didn't want to freak her out. So I would casually, ever so often, languidly let my pussy touch against Dahlia's leg. At first Dahlia withdrew but then the last time she didn't withdraw and I started riding and hunching Dahlia's leg while in a close OMing embrace. Then when Dahlia reached down and put her warm hand over my pussy, I just about came out of her skin! I squeezed her to me and started bucking and bucking. And moaning into her ear, I came.

Then of course in the next group session it was necessary for the two women to tell the rest of the group marriage about becoming closer in their relationship. This might be as simple as saying they "had gotten into physical stuff." It was required to tell the group about new sexual activity so that it could be closely monitored. In group, one sexual partner looks into the other partners eyes, and holding each other's gaze in the contact of real intimacy — this is called "hooking up"— tries to respectfully own the powerful feelings of sexual pleasure they had gotten into with that person. Pia said, "I really liked it when you put your hand on my vagina last night. When you did that it made me feel a part of all womanhood."

Dahlia acknowledge it with a nodding of the head, a little blush. Getting into sex with women really is powerful because you have to let go of the competition. They didn't have a *great* passion for each other but it was definitely the sisterhood.

At this point other members of the group marriage could elicit details, if it was felt necessary, to keep a watch on the intention behind the sexual activity. This was to ensure there was not dominance and submissiveness or anything but the most spiritual and pleasurable of motivations.

Pia wanted to say, "I love Dahlia." But didn't. She had to swallow her sense of being the suitor in a one-sided relationship. But it bugged her; she'd think derisively: I'm a visitor to the wonderland of Oz, populated mainly by 'Friends of Dahlia'. I don't like always being the tag along woman, the invisible girl. She is so fine. It is hard to stand next to her light.

Walker felt really at ease with Pia, teased her and played with her verbally. Since the white, college-educated Walker had made a few bucks mowing lawns for black folks in Oakland, he could go out to dinner with them at a little Italian restaurant. He sounded so California sophisticated to be going out for 'pasta' instead of spaghetti.

Across the dinner table Walker noticed Pia looking at Dahlia with much love. The thought did occur to him: Maybe they are lovers.

As they were walking across Broadway, to the catcalls of the barkers, Dahlia put her arm around Walker, and he in turn put his arm around Pia and the man with two women walked past North Beach flesh pots amid barkers' shouts promising wall- to-wall flesh. The Saloon turns out to be a classic rhythm & blues dive that you entered through a swinging door. The band was in high form laying out a soaring high energy sound playing loud wild blues of thunderous psychedelic feeling. Walker and Dahlia danced a lot. It was so funky and hot in there he stripped down to his T-shirt and felt really happy to be rockin' and swingin' and groovin' to this funky rhythm & blues.

"They call this the Drip-Dry lounge," Dahlia shouted over the smoke filled din.

At intermissions they went outside and standing in the alley in front of god and everybody smoked a little of the famous killer California smoke. When they went back in for the next round of dancing this pushed the scene into almost psychedelic jazz with colors moving in the mix. Later, back in the alley at the second break, drunk *and* stoned, Walker stood grinning in the alley just above Carol Doda's topless place on the corner of Broadway and Columbus, looking at the city beyond, and a slow glow come across his face slipping into ecstasy and Dahlia was close to him and the girls were looking up at him and him thinking about their fine smooth curves and surfaces of their women's body 'neath those tight jeans and he doubled over in a big laugh and when he stood back up he said, "Not even the porpoises in the ocean can percolate drugs through the system by dancing."

Several different women-friends of Dahlia and Pia kept coming up, being introduced and checking him over. It turned out a total of five women from the "House" were there. Walker met Leslie, Beverly and Wyoming. Walker was stunned by Wyoming, a beautiful swinging brunette, extroverted, feisty and flirtatious. He found out that she was called that because, though she was a nice Jewish girl from New York, she had spent several years teaching in a rural school in Wyoming and was always talking about wanting to move back to the Big Sky country and be free. Currently she was a graduate student in psychology and worked as a maid to make ends meet. Leslie worked around town as a domestic also and had wild frizzy hair and a kind of harried rawboned almost undernourished waif look of someone who had come from Appalachia. Beverly was a secretary who worked downtown, and had a big toothy grin and smiling flashing eyes.

Walker and the four women squeezed into a cab back to the loft in the Mission. It was November and they were wearing lots of clothes. Walker had never *seen* so much dark-haired beauty at once. None wore make-up and the skin on their faces was taut and unblemished and had a fire and a glowing to it.

Beverly and Wyoming were on a session. Beverly loved how they were supposed, when outside of the House, to still maintain the passion and feeling they had for each other inside of the session.

Beverly had been obsessing about Wyoming all day. Ever since Wyoming and Chase had given a demonstration of the long orgasm two nights ago. She could see her, lying on a futon in the middle of the loft, the whole House siting close up around them in lotus position. This is how Beverly described it in her diary entry:

Oct. 7, 1982.

Wyoming is naked with her legs spread, her legs pulled way back and her pussy open and her asshole exposed. She looked really wild. We were all feeling for her. Chase was demonstrating how to massage her vagina. There was Wyoming on a futon with her feet up and her pussy spread and Chase with two fingers inside her vagina and his thumb on her clitoris pointing out, "This is the introitus, a most sensitive spot under the hood here behind the lips."

It was all a very supportive environment with members of the House gently touching her and / or each other in a network of connectivity, and chanting OM and sighing and letting big noise make them unafraid.

Chase took my hand and pulled me closer to Wyoming He said to gently place my two fingers on her introitus and feel it. There was Wyoming on the table smiling up at me warmly and the heat coming out of her pink swollen vagina as I slid my two fingers gently inside was radiant. It felt incredible. It gave me and everyone a soft glowing feeling.

Others were invited to touch Wyoming. There were a dozen hands gently touching her legs, stomach, shoulders head. Then when we were all concentrated on the giant group grope, and working with Chase we propelled Wyoming into a screeching, wailing, moaning, god-awful orgasm that must have lasted easily 15 minutes. She kept coming and coming in my hand. I have been so turned on by it that I haven't been able to think of much else since. I feel a special connection with Wyoming. And I'm glad Chase let me be the one to help take her to this higher place.

In fact the next day in the law office downtown where I worked my pussy became wet and dripping just thinking about it and I had had to stop and go to the bathroom and take my panties off because they got wet. I just sat on the

toilet seat in the stall, and slid my finger in and out of my
pussy slowly feeling it get all wet and hot and I came right
there in the bathroom, shooting juice on the seat and into the
toilet. Got it was hot. I am just so turned on. Then I went
back and draped my panties over a divider in the bottom
drawer of my filing cabinet so they could drip-dry. I didn't
want to get them wet. I then took my bare ass personage
outside into the cold to see if that would take my mind off
sex.

In the car Beverly looked at Wyoming with thanks and breathed a silent sigh of gratitude for helping them all feel, the aliveness of their skin.

After the taxi dropped them off at the loft and Wyoming had conducted the collection of shares to pay for the cab fare, Walker and Dahlia crawled into the back of his van and stretched out on the large mattress, under a big down coverlet.

It was late and they were loaded. Of course that still couldn't ameliorate Walker's fear and guilt. She told him, "I'm having my period and don't want to get into intercourse." Yet she went on and touched and teased him, and pulled his aching swollen cock with her expert gentle hands. He fingered her trigger; suddenly his gun shot off into the sheets just for fun. They got a few hours sleep.

Later as the early Sunday morning light was filtering through the hung-over van windows, he put on a condom and plunged his cock into her cunt. Her period started to flow. That made him her blood husband. She looked at him and held him with her eyes. She said, "I see a lot of pain in your face."

After dozing off again Dahlia drifted into a wild late morning dream: In it she saw Walker as a member of the House. She was back in Hawaii, and the whole House is sleeping in a big pile in their cabana with one wall open to the sea. It was really weird and wet and she awoke sweating. She kissed him, got a few clothes on, gathered up the rest and he slid the door open to let her go. She was smiling at this hot dream and ran into her building. She wanted to get it down in her diary asap.

Oct. 8 1982
Dream in which Walker was a member of the house. In

my dream we were sleeping in the cabana by the sea and the mats all dissolved into the sea and we just sank under and were a pod of porpoises! I could see them from the sky —a shadowy shape moving beneath the warm sea. I guess it was cause I really had to pee.

My eyes could see under water I remember being able to breath from my back! Below me I saw Walker, I think it was Walker, but come to think of it he had a big satisfied smile which was like Mario's smile. I signaled to him with my fin to perform a docking procedure. Mario/Walker rolled, swimming under me with his belly facing up. I remember being able to sort of feel his long thin penis extending out and into my vagina hole. Then as we two are mating, he holds me real tight and directs a sonic pulse into my mind that travels down my spine to meet up with the fire coming up from his penis and it made my whole body quiver and start and I was trying to wake up on the mattress in the van.

But then I drifted back into the dream bardo with more control it was like a lucid dream and I was given a most powerful sensation: I remember thinking that my mind has expanded to fill the extra large brain they have! I had to urinate yet I felt my whole vagina was full of sensation, my clitoris felt bigger and longer than ever before. Walker is carrying me, driving me up to the surface.

In the dream he lets out a high speed click-stream of laughter then launches us both up out of the water into the air and we separate doing back flips away from each other, and we slapped the water with a flick of the tail. As we re-enter the water I remember seeing it close like an iris behind us. Just as I was about to awaken I saw him swim quickly back to the surface, blow water out of his hole as sperm ejaculated out of his long thin extended penis! Whew, was that wet or what?

7

Zapped

The following Sunday, Pia, Walker and Dahlia and Walker's dog Sunshine went to Muir Beach. The women almost looked like they were little girls playing dress up. They had on long warm dark dresses with vests, starched white blouses and some lace here and there. Pia was wearing a black velvet choker necklace with a cameo and Dahlia some elegant beads in her long dark hair. Bless their hearts, thought Walker.

Walker spread out an old sleeping bag, and they lounged on it. When Walker came back from a stroll on the beach with the wild and gentle Sunshine, the two women were snuggled up in a spoon with each other against the cold. The taller Dahlia had her front to the back of the shorter Pia.

"Mmmmmmm, warm bodies!" purred Walker as he snuggled up behind Dahlia, making a 3rd spoon. The girls giggled at his lasciviousness.

"Let's make a Dahlia sandwich," he suggested, and reached his long reach around both of them. Pia turned to face Dahlia, and he squeezed both of them tight. The girls were delighted and giddy, Walker felt wondrously brave. Easy hugging and touching, two women!

As they hugged each other, thoughts of a *manage a trois* slipped in and out of his mind but he pushed them away. In unison they became aware of nothing but the sound of waves: Concussioning shore pound, sheath slack slide. It was forward rush, momentary silence, backward sucking roll over small stones. Their breathing gradually fell into the long rhythm of the ocean, which had a period of about 9 seconds. In unison they began to AUM on the exhale, long relaxing sighs riding out on the waves of white noise.

Others people may have looked their way on the beach, but really they were the only ones there. Walker began to notice some curious dogs coming around Sunshine. "Uh, oh," he remarked. "Sunshine is coming into heat and attracting curious males. I better get her into the van."

They drove to an old maritime inn — whitewashed and Tudor — called the Pelican, close by. They were like children having tea, playing like adults. It was all very polite. While Dahlia was just being sociable, Pia and Walker seemed to be about establishing themselves to each other as artists, he a writer, and she a worker in textiles and fine papers. After a while, Dahlia seemed to tire of feeling excluded from the obvious attention by inattention or superficial attention she was getting from Walker. She looked kind of lost, kept trying to crack Walker's veneer of being the charming, brotherly male. Pia said she was going to go over to her gym and have a workout. Walker further asserted his big brother stance by saying, "What you need, is to do about 3 sets of 10 reps each of deep squats with heavy weight." This got her laughing. Outside, Walker grabbed the surprised Dahlia and hoisted her way up into the air, just in case she had the feeling of being left out.

On the way back to the City, winding over hairpin turns through a eucalyptus forest the two women were sitting delightfully close to each other occupying the same front seat, Dahlia being held by Pia from behind.

"Have you ever been married?" Walker asked.

"No," said Pia.

"Yes," said Dahlia. "I was married once before but got divorced. I'm married now."

Walker is shocked and quiet for a while. As they were about to go across the Golden Gate bridge the women insisted, against his protest, that they pay the toll. Back in town, Pia asked to be dropped off near her gym at Divisadero and Haight. "What are you going to do?" she asked Dahlia.

"I'm going to hang out with Walker," she said, looking at him.

Yes!! thought Walker. At last I get her to myself. Dahlia and Walker went into the El Rondel restaurant on Valencia St. Although Walker liked being out with the two women, he was glad to get Dahlia alone.

While they were looking at menus Walker said, "You know, the first thing I noticed about you was how easily you breathe."

"That's funny, because I used to have asthma as a kid."

"Really! My mother has asthma," Walker said. "I have a good friend back in Texas who has it, too. It can be quite terrifying, can't it."

"Yes, it sure can. In therapy I learned that it is related to troubles and repression from my mother," said Dahlia. "It is really terrifying not to be able to breathe. At the time you just feel so constrained, that you are not going to breathe!" With that Dahlia slipped into a pensive, quiet mood.

It was at that moment, right there in the restaurant, surrounded by little Mexican families eating their Sunday dinner out, that Walker was zapped by Dahlia. It happened when she held him with her eyes. She was very used to this from years of therapy. She knew that it was one thing to be introspective and analytical, but it was quite another to stand vulnerable before another in mutual recognition of vulnerability that really broke through. Many people go through their whole lives without it happening. And it happened to Walker right there. For him it was like getting hold of high voltage that you can't let go, that doesn't burn, or shock, but stuns you with a good magnetic feeling. It was a dawning of sympatico, a recognition of flare or mutuality of style when the other emerges out of privacy in intimacy and the facade of sociability between them was let down and they started to appear to each other as they really are.

We look but we are constantly searching for the object, penetrating. But to relax and gaze, to see the space in between, the space of relationship. . . For a moment he is arrested in the moment and he knows somehow that this moment is for always, and if he could he would hold it and hold her until the end of the world, and he was transported — his body flew across space and time through those two worlds of the Self and the Other to be captured by the curved spacetime of her brow and pulled into her orbit through the orbs in the troughs of her eye sockets. And in that tiny reflection of ourselves beheld in the eye of the beloved we see our infinity not as something lost but instead as that which contains our destiny.

And to think these eyes were opening wide for him was almost too much to imagine, and he got scared down to his shoes at being seen, and he did not know how to be in it or to return it, for he knew he must become the person who has the right to occupy the view of and become central in the world of this creature he wanted more than anything in the universe.

Walker was zapped by Dahlia's approachable look. Her sensitive vulnerable ways aroused in him a feeling of wanting to protect her. It is not lust, or a sexual thing; it is something....in the language of two bodies, the mute language of the eyes, of their regard. Dahlia started to look especially beautiful to him after that. There was an alert sensitivity to her intelligence, a feline smoothness to her movements, a great sureness about her, that he had not seen before.

There was something about her fragility and how she had overcome her illness, that gave her a great strength. Or it was the way the other emerged out of great privacy in the humility with which she had shared with him her home life with her parents. But mostly it was those big, sad, dark eyes, being so serious. And too, she is a big-hearted girl, a country woman, who likes to let people have what they have longings for. And Walker had longings for Dahlia. He liked that about her.

Outside in the middle of the crosswalk going across Valencia he grabbed her and kissed her and shouted over the traffic, "In San Francisco they kiss in the middle of the street!"

She was a little shocked at this. "O, you have such big sad dark eyes," he said, spoofing her off to lighten up the situation and take her mind off a sad mood she had fallen into over her thinking about "parental programming" as she called it. He didn't know it at the time, but he had fallen captive to those big sad dark eyes, and the vulnerable dark side of her Latin beauty. With his light hair, blue eyes and winsome smile, Walker went very well indeed with Dahlia's intense and lunar darkness.

The passion of love was upon him. He walked with his arm around her up Valencia St. Then all of a sudden he pushed her into a dark alcove! "You've got to watch out for these dark alcoves," he said as he swirled her up into it, expertly cupping one hand behind her head, protecting her, and another arm around her waist, and with great grace swept her into a wall, protecting her with his hands, mashing up against her and kissing her gently on the cheeks and the forehead, as one does to change the mind of a petulant child. Joy kisses on alternate cheeks to confuse, soothing kisses on the forehead to smooth a wrinkled brow, and then one on the lips, like feeding a small bird. Then gently he cupped a breast in his hand, but by then he had an erection pressing against her through his trousers, and he started to feel embarrassed to be doing that to her, as though he were molesting a girl, and he grew shy and withdrew.

"Don't stop," she said, looking into his eyes quizzically. But he had withdrawn.

"Does that happen to you very often?" he asked, trying to cover up his chagrin with conversation, trying to rearrange and compose himself, trying to think of something else, — beat up old trash cans festooned with rank dripping garbage often worked — so he could walk down the street without drawing attention to the protuberance in his pants.

She smiled and her face went all delightful and blushing she said, "Not in a long time."

8

The Strawboss of Skillful Means

Dahlia asked Walker: "Why don't you come to my house some time."

"Yeah, that would be nice. I'd love to." Walker thought: All right! She's going to introduce me to her roommates. To see if I get the stamp of approval.

"Come up to dinner on Monday night," she said. "You can meet some of my friends. We get started around 5:30."

He arrived at 6:30. She came downstairs to meet him, after he announced his presence into a speaker at the front door and she buzzed him through. She found him wandering around on a lower floor, not knowing how to get up to the penthouse. They got into an open heartfelt hug, then they went up.

Up the wide stairs, Walker found himself in a large open room. And all these people!—5 small groups of from 5 to 9 people each, all sitting on the carpet, cross-legged, engaged in intense conversations.

O my god, thought Walker. I've fallen into a gaggle of moonies, or a bunch of Rajaneeshian divideps. Or worse! Maybe this is one of those weird cults that sacrifices outsiders. Better watch my step.

"Are you hungry, do you want anything to eat?" Dahlia asked him.

The inside is bare and spotlessly clean, the carpet shampooed. There is a smell of good strong garlic and vegetarian cooking going on. Noticing that they had already finished eating dinner he said, "No, thanks."

"Well, why don't you take off your shoes," she said, "and sit in with us for a while."

He sat down on the carpeted floor with her in her group.

The House got together after dinner every day, for small groups, either on the first floor or upstairs in the loft. Most people sat cross-legged in meditation pose on circular meditation cushions or had pulled up a sleeping pillow. If you did not sit in good attention meditation pose, someone would ask why.

Walker recognized Pia and nodded at her as he took his place in the circle in a space made by some people moving aside to make room for him. People looked at him blankly. Pia looked distracted and distressed. The others in Dahlia's group hardly acknowledged Walker's presence. They continued to focus intently on Pia. She seemed to be in some intense argument with a slender chap with a crisp British demeanor; indeed he was Scottish. Malcolm, a really good looking Scottish guy, was in a face to face verbal grapple with Pia. He was sweating under the hairline and looked at Walker with an almost hostile imperiousness. Malcolm and Pia were in the middle of some kind of argument. The other people in the group were a man, Morey, shorter, more powerfully built and a woman, Frieda, a fay and slender older woman, maybe early 40s who looked like a hippie who had led a hard life. Jane another tall, extremely quiet, hippie-looking woman.

Pia glanced at the faces of the other people to judge the impact of her emotional outburst.

Malcolm shook his head, as if to dispel collusion. He looked hot around the edges from taking some verbal abuse. He replied with a smile, "I mean this Jewish mother thing you get into really is blocking our relationship. I'm finding it very castrating."

"What? !"

"I'd really like to have a relationship with you but somehow before I do that I've got to let you castrate me first?! No way!"

Pia looked shocked. Then scowled. She was about to explode but she didn't answer. She slumped down. She slumped over like a famine victim, her mouth was twisted into a whine.

"Like I'm getting a lot of non-verbal communications from you."

Morey, a stocky rosy-cheeked open man, reached over and touched Pia's knee with care and commanded, "Sit up!"

"Why are you acting so pissed at Malcolm?" Frieda said. Silence.

Malcolm had his defenses up too, and was scrambling for some kind of superiority in the verbal struggle. "Like I see you as this little girl who is outraged at her father for not paying attention to her and you are projecting that on me. That I'm your father!"

Pia took umbrage, "Oh, you're *SUCH* an intellectual, aren't you. You think you know it all." Pia looked down. She started to cry.

Dahlia defended her: "Yes, Malcolm. Can't you see she's *trying* to hook up." The other women seemed to show support to Pia. It looked like it was, once again, the men against the women.

Dahlia admonished her: "Come on Pia, hook up."

Pia didn't answer.

The others were intently scrutinizing her.

Having no experience with therapy, Walker was shocked by Pia's crying. Pia was crying! Now a cowboy sees a girl crying, he is moved, he can't stand to see the little girls cry. He leaned over to Dahlia next to him and whispered, "Why is she crying?"

Dahlia, noticing Walker's discomfort, leaned back over toward him and said, "It's an anxiety attack."

Walker was extremely reticent to speak, had the horrendous but common fear and shyness of groups. But he liked people. He listened politely to them "getting heavy" but not knowing to what they were referring, his attention wandered. He felt like he should give these people some civil indifference room to talk. He didn't think he should be in the middle of what looked like a couple — Pia and Malcolm — fighting.

He noticed real hand-painted tantric tankhas — many of them, some with gold, hanging on the plain red brick walls around the room. Through the windows and the sliding glass door he could see that the penthouse was surrounded by a thick garden of shrubs and flowers. Beyond, was the vast vista of the city. And noticing others wandering in and out, Walker asked if he could go outside. There, on the deck of the penthouse, overlooking the city he wandered in a huge garden. A vast area of the roof had been decked. Plants grew out of various sized buckets and urns. There were even some arbors, upon which climbed jasmine and trumpet vines. Climbing trellises were beans and loofa, their gourds tenderly supported in little slings.

What *AM* I doing here he thought. Then Walker noticed what a terrific view of the city. He walked over to the edge of the roof, leaned against the parapet and scanned the city sky line. He began to ponder what lay ahead for him here. It was late afternoon in the fall sun. There, beyond, was the city. Downtown was a far-off clamoring of intricately cut many-faceted jewels of glass and stone and steel climbing into the clear sky. Beyond, --the blue bay and the hills around, burnished golden by summer. And the ringed diadem of the city was crowned by the jewel of the pyramid building. And this here was the tough Mexican Mission district, below Bernal heights. He liked it because it was family and reminded him of Texas.

Walker's thoughts turned from the promise this town held for him, to being accepted among these gentle people. Walker knew they were gentle, because they cared for plants. Perhaps they love each other too. He focused on the beautiful plants, from flats of sprouts, from little peonies to mature trees and admired the hand of the horticulturists who knew plants. He knew not plants, yet he liked them very much. He liked these people too, who like the plants, were natural. They seemed open, vulnerable somehow. It was obvious they were some kind of a commune. He had always been interested in communes. He thought of Steven Gaskin and the Farm. This season's plants for this season's people. There were new beginnings in the air. It felt good to be alive in a new adventure, meeting people. They didn't know where he was from, nor he they. But he felt like he wanted to trust them.

What Walker didn't know was that the community in which Dahlia lived was a sangha. He knew it was some kind of Buddhist or religious community. He certainly didn't know that they all lived in the one open space, he thought they lived in various apartments throughout the building and convened in the loft for meetings. Walker didn't know Dahlia was in a *group* marriage.

They thought of themselves first as a group. They knew they had some aspects of a cult, that is their devotion and dependency on a charismatic figure, Chase, (though they would be hard pressed to admit that). They preferred to think of themselves as being devoted to the Group Mind, that the

Group Mind was the functioning head. In the House life had been an ongoing graduate school of group therapy for years and many of the members had become quite accomplished at this kind of therapy. Several had or were getting doctorates in clinical psychology and counseling from prestigious institutions. The House was an intentional Tibetan Tantric Buddhist community called a sangha which incorporated and extend modern group therapy. They were a tantric group. They called themselves the Sangha of Dorje Chang, the Church of the Divine Couple. Chase and others of the House had spent time in the Buddhist community; several including Chase had been initiated and performed sadhanas.

They identified with the concept of the sangha; the imagery in their cult was predominantly Tibetan Buddhist art and philosophy. This was reflected in conversational preoccupations and attitudes. Discussions revolved around LSD experiences, sexual experiences, experiences of getting in touch with the core self and feeling it related to a universal Source. Many had begun to experience nature as a personal deity —a god, the source off all. The commune had purchased and built a camp with an orchard and garden on land near Mount Shasta. They made long trecks every weekend onto the Land and it kept this consciousness fresh. Their former life on the coffee plantation they owned in the paradise of Hawaii had been in many ways unforgettably idyllic. They had created a small paradise on earth. In addition to the religious group the unspoken group experience could easily change into the fight or flight group, like an army or a mob defending some cherished belief.

Most of the members had tried out other beliefs, disciplines and psychologies. Those few who had been involved with Rajaneesh now had little sympathy with the bright orange uniforms. They rejected Rajaneeshe's size, overly stated presence, antagonistic political stance — arguing that the sangha by contrast was a residential therapeutic group and an unofficial family. They believed that the world should return to that loose confederation of more or less heterogeneous tribal units before the Roman empire.

The whole House was the sangha community and the small groups were marriages. Some 35 persons and 5 kids were residents in the Loft. Most had been there for a dozen years, all through the 70s. The newest had been there for 3 years. Most were white, some were Latin.

The House purchased all needs: food, flatware, cooking utensils, toiletries — soap, tampons, toothpaste. They did their own carpentry, and wiring. The idea was to develop mindfulness in all actions and they wanted to create the best possible environment for doing this. The setting was safe.

Some worked for the House. Morey, Aaron, Tom, Greg, Bridget, Dahlia, Katie, Rachel, David, Mario, Leslie, Pia and others. The rest of the women did secretarial work, or were maids taking the bus out to rich people's houses. Most of the men did landscaping and gardening, some were engineers and programmers. A lot of the women worked in landscaping too. The people of the House see work as the yoga of action, an opportunity to maintain a self-awareness in a service, something to grow in, something to make them confront their own personalities. All had tripped extensively, some every weekend for several years.

Group Activities. There were two kinds of groups: a committee and small group.

The committee is problem centered, task oriented often led by a chairperson. The committee memberships vary with occasion over longer and shorter periods of time.

The small group is an arranged marriage which contracts to stay together for a certain fixed time — a year or two. The group marriage is for exploring interpersonal communication of great interest to the participants. It gave one an opportunity to check his tolerance for psychic stress arising from ambiguity, intrapsychic conflict, interpersonal conflict, uncertainty and risk. Also maximum joy.

The two kinds of groups take place on many occasions. What is learned by relating in small group will transfer to the more anonymous committee.

People arose early and were off to work by seven. Futons were rolled up and placed in a neat pile upstairs in the loft. The floor was cleared and vacuumed by 8. Some of the women swam every morning before they got down to their jobs.

Sundays: mornings were spent cleaning the loft. Cleaning, vacuuming, scrubbing, hitting every corner. Lunch was served at noon, the rest of the day was spent in marathon Big Group which is where the whole House sat in lotus posture with good attention around in a large circle and talked to each other, about all kinds of major issues facing the House, as well as focused on a particular small group's problems. There were various tantric meditation rituals that took place in the big circle that tapped into awesome energies of consciousness.

Mondays was small group meetings followed by 'sessions.' In a session you talked to and breathed with and got into hugs with and otherwise became physically close with people in your small group. You had a session at least once a week with each person in your small group, rotating through the group and starting over in succession.

Tuesdays were free.

Wednesday, Thursday, Friday were devoted to group meetings and sessions.

Saturday was a free day.

The prominent and central interest was in having feelings. Most of the time was spent discussing feelings, confronting those who were having difficulty in having feelings, and in implementing insights gained from these confrontations along with developing verbal ability and integrating. The main focus of the House was the negation of the individual ego and with that the hold that karma has on the individual was loosened. This was greatly facilitated by the complete lack of privacy. The lack of privacy was one of the most difficult things the members of the commune had to undergo. The men found sleeping with other men difficult at first, but with the confrontation of the fear of homosexuality this became a liberating thing. There was little homosexual activity.

There was very little solitary activity, except listening to stereos through headphones and reading. Boredom and monotony were confronted as disruptive ego defenses. There was no television watching or purely diversionary activities although the teenagers were allowed the normal video games and skate boarding adventures with their peers.

One of the most important functions of the Sangha is the raising of children. Many people in the House took an active interest in raising the children. Each child had a room of his own. Each child had a committee of from 6 to 9 people, plus support people. Each person on the committee pursued his relationship with the child giving and getting what they could. Raising children confronted bachelor selfishness and brought up a lot for people by forcing them to relive their own childhoods of neglect. Also it allowed the parents time to grow. And the kids were always surrounded with fresh adults to tire out.

There was a core staff. Dahlia was the House Manager, and generally one of the most important people there, although on the surface people were supposed to be equal, some were more equal than others. Real ability to facilitate action in a wise and compassionate way, called in Buddhism, "skillful means", is the goal of sangha life and is highly prized.

The week's activities were scheduled by the "Strawboss," a paid position that each communard held for a week. The Strawboss generally saw to it that things were interconnected all week long — basically it was playing Mother to 40 intense people. This week Dahlia was also the Strawboss and it made it easier for her to bring Walker in. This was lucky for Walker because she could just bring him over, without much prior discussion in her group.

There was a general feeling of strong physical activity and awareness and the members took a lot of pleasure out of just being there close with each other. The women especially seemed to enjoy it. The House women had a very comfortable kind of body integration, they walked from their hips, like the way native girls did, from hard work and a comfortable supportive sexuality. People often said they don't get enough time to be with each other.

Attention and conduct. Socializing and lightness were generally frowned upon as being a kind of ego defense, a politeness role, Mr. Nice Guy around your mother's house. Considerable time was spent in contemplation, reviewing material and emotions, pondering the inter personal relations of the group's interactions and the group dynamics.

After a while, a long while, Dahlia came outside onto the rooftop and started talking to Walker. "Why don't you come back inside and hang out? And just be there with the group?"

"I came here to see *you*, really," he said, "and this might be an unfortunate word to use, but I came here in some sort of preliminary *courtship* procedures that I don't understand and now I feel like I have to *court* all your friends. I don't really mean it like that but..."

But suddenly he realized from the look on her face that this was not appropriate at all, and this drove him further into inappropriateness —he kept trying to get her into a hug, for in truth, he felt like doing ballet, a *tour jeté* on the rooftop he felt so good, and she was extremely shy about doing that around her House, and Walker at last saw that and backed off.

As they got ready to go back inside, his courage failed him again, at the thought of being the outsider about to re-enter their group for a second time, and he covered it with nervous laughter saying, "But I find them so *serious*," he said. "I'll just have to wipe this smile off my face." He covered his face with his hand, drawing it down over his smile, but this made him laugh even more and he had to use the drastic technique of biting the inside of his cheeks. They jumped back over the sliding glass threshold into the room.

"Could you make me a tea," he said," so I'll at least have something in my hand while I'm socializing." He whispered this as though in conspiracy.

Back in the small group, Pia was still red-faced sweaty and teary-eyed. And they carried on further. Then Malcolm said, "I feel a little weird in this. Here is this person, Walker, and we haven't even acknowledged his presence yet."

Then all eyes turned to him. Walker managed to talk about various *safe* subjects, job hunting and the economy. He mentioned his studies in meditation to show at least some affinity with this group, who, it seemed obvious, had something to do with Buddhism. The group seemed barely able to tolerate this relative banality as passions were simmering below the surface. He felt they were impatient and preoccupied and he tried to be brief. Finally it was time for the groups to break up.

Walker was brought into the kitchen where he ate some fruit and helped with clean up. This was a microworld, with its own structure. Dahlia walked around with a clip board, people kept coming up to her looking for direction. Walker was told, Dahlia was "strawboss" for the week.

The intent of the Strawboss job was to give everyone the opportunity to take on the responsibility for conducting the orchestration of the House affairs for a week. Each week a new person would transition into strawboss, take up the thread of events from the previous week and remain until the next week. This meant getting up early to see that every one was awakened. Checking out and coordinating all the various committees.

There was the kitchen to coordinate. The strawboss had to make sure who the dinner cooks were, who the breakfast cooks were. Who did the kids lunches. Who preps. Someone had to draw up menus, going into exacting analysis of the protein content of each meal insuring no salt, butter, meat — of course, sweetener, coffee etc, the list was endless, — passed the sangha lips.

There were shopping runs that had to be made to Farmers market for vast amounts of produce, to the health food store, Rainbow. The co-op bought in bulk; delicious organic tofu and nut butters came in big 5-gallon containers. The sundry inventories had to be kept up.

In the kitchen Walker met a tall skinny man named Theo, much older than the rest. He was in charge of sprouts. He had developed an elaborate sprouting system with microprocessor controls that he had adapted from his gardening irrigation experience, that involved a stack of large round bamboo steaming trays. There was a bean person. A person to wash and sort produce. The person who made yogurt, sauerkraut, mayonnaise (no eggs) and salsa etc. The Deep Cleaner. This week the Deep Cleaner was Scott. He came into the kitchen wearing only a pair of striped boxer shorts and a carpenter's utility belt full of cleansers and brushes.

Theo teased him: "Goin' in, Scott?"

Scott did a take like Barney Fife, "Yep, gonna fight the slime oozing through the bricks on the North Wall."

Theo put on an air of awe and mock reverence, got into a kind of catechism questioning mode: "What does the Deep Cleaner work for, Scott?"

Scott stood at attention and like the little tin soldier said, "The Deep Cleaner works for Love. For cleanliness is next to godliness and godliness is next to love." Theo and Scott winked at each other in delight.

There was the refrigerator, the floors, counters and dishes, both AM and PM that needed cleaning. Garbage from kitchen and bathrooms taken out. The plants and vehicles needed to be maintained. Kitchen books had to be maintained. The kids areas and all areas maintained. Rug shampooed.

There was a safety/disaster person who was watchful for preparedness. Everything from malfunctioning air cleaners to conducting earthquake drills.

There was a Medical coordinator who kept track of the sick people and did surveys, education and got people interested in self help. Because they all lived together in such close quarters, flus and colds seemed to rage through the people like wildfire in a forest. In some ways sickness was one of the few ways you could get time to yourself. Other small group members held groups with the sick person supine and admonished them to use the time well.

Then there were the ongoing projects of the commune. There was a huge land committee which administered their farm in the Siskyou forest. These people were involved in maintaining the eco- co-op: shelter, water, and road preservation; agriculture, alternative energy education,—and investigating the possibility of earning a livelihood there.

There was the clean up and storage committee. There was the committee of the library/common area who updated the strawboss logs, forms, posted notes etc. There was a committee for writing and publishing Chase's books.

There was a good sized library dealing with transcendental and humanistic psychology and enlightenment, all the books were there: Alloport, Bion, Campbell, Freud, Huxley, Jung, Kline, Laing, Lowen, Maslow, Pearls, Rogers, Watts, . . .

A community involvement committee brought in guest speakers, arranged anti-nuke activity and did community service. A real estate committee was researching land purchases in Marin, Mexico and New Zealand (the best place to be in case they dropped the big one.)

There was a lot of seriousness and power attached to the strawboss position. It put you much more out in the open with people. It confronts the tendency in a person to be self isolating, 'hiding out' is the term the people used for it. It defeated the walls and guards people put up. It got you real involved. During the week of early rising and late to bed and all the contact and responsibility a person could really feel his image.

Walker stayed for a while, waiting for Big Group, —the whole House —to convene. While he waited he got his Rubic's cube out of his back pack and entertained a couple of the teenage boys, Jason and John who were passing by. Though no adults in the house were up on the cube, the teenagers were involved with it at school. Walker was quite an expert, had developed a finite group algebra (non-Abelian) which used the commutator operator from quantum mechanics all expressed in his own original visual pattern notation. He could return the cube to its initial state of original symmetry in at most 2 minutes from any random state. A number of the people in the House enjoyed this from afar and he noticed the women looking at him. Dahlia seemed especially pleased.

Walker was a cube lover. The cube was actually a vector space he could hold in his hands. A little world, a crystal ball. He could apply the operators { $F, R, U, B, L, D, I, -$ } which formed a group of transformations operating on this vector space. He developed a group algebra adapted to the symmetry of the cube, that is using independent subgroups of corner and edge operators.

His group algebra was also adapted for a person to hold the cube in his left hand and do the operations with the right hand. Pursuant of this he tried to use only the R, U and F operators. The algebra is useful for comparing to find operators with the fewest number of moves for speed in handling and ease of memorization. Though it was easy to memorize, he was a little embarrassed that he took this abstract approach to the cube, and envied native seers who could just visualize where they were moving things, like those speed demon teenagers. But his algebraic approach gave him an opportunity to experience abstraction on a level you just couldn't get anyplace but quantum mechanics.

Though the group of cube symmetry operators had, of

course, the properties of closure, identity and inverses it was non-associative —that is Right face twist followed by a Front face twist was not the same as a Front face twist followed by a Right face twist. He was able to adapt the famous Heisenberg commutator from quantum mechanics to express this non-commutativity. He used this paradigm-shifting statement of uncertainty which bespoke with such poignancy man's coming of age in the universe naturally in his algebra. And lo and behold! It turned out the commutator was a generator of the corner subgroup.

The cube was a wonderful thing to play with. This little vector space of position and orientation, of moving through, of spins and flips was the stuff of Quantum Mechanics not seen so much in the everyday macroscopic world of large matter. He coined the name 'cubon' for the little individual cubes that together make up the whole cube in honor of the electron, neutron, proton, pion, photon, graviton etc. that were the individual parts of some configuration. By developing conjugations of the commutator it got even simpler. And he was very proud of the pattern notation language he had developed. It associated a kind of ideogramic symbol for what one needed to do with the cube, with the string of operations that would do it. The symbols of notation and its associated string of operators all fit together like neat little Japanese designs in boxes. By writing small with a number 5 pencil he got the whole algebra to fit on the front and back of a business card

For Big Group the whole house got into a large circle that filled the floor. They did some beautiful chanting which Walker enjoyed. Then they talked and interacted with each other with the same kind of familiar intimacy of small groups. Walker was amazed at how some of the people talked across the space to others and said loving things about their relationship and their encounters during the day.

No therapy was being conducted by Chase at this meeting and Walker did not even notice him as standing out from the rest of the people. The give and take in Big Group was almost spontaneous. It was shining at times. They mostly discussed money business and logistics. Walker couldn't wait to get out of there and was glad to say thanks and good-by to Dahlia as soon as it was possible to move without drawing attention to himself. Walker had no clue of the sleeping arrangements or the night's activities. He thought they lived in the building in separate rooms and this penthouse was like their community center.

In the nighttime people began sessions with individuals in their small group. If session partners were fairly new to each other, they might spend time looking at scrapbooks or pictures and getting to know each other. Then chanting and making sound together while sitting in meditation pose opposite each other or supine in a hug. Eventually people started showering and bringing out futons and getting ready to sleep together with their session person.

Sex was seen as part of a regular devotion, and thus no one was pressured to perform. Instead of the genitally focused feelings in the " genital character" the House was able to expand those intense feelings into a general and diffused brotherly and sisterly love. Instead of sex being a male dominated orgasms obsessed affair, it was a mutually engaging, pleasuring that occurred. The situation of being in a fantasy was openly explored and shown to be isolating and impersonal. The object was to become more involved and intimate and holistic with the people in your group and with the rest of the House. For the most part the men and women of the tribe enjoyed this sexual generosity and it made them very happy. The idea was to pursue a more pleasurable life while being in authentic feelings.

Chase required that each member of the House write a journal. It was a kind of homework, part psychology and part erotic foreplay. Chase encouraged the writers to use potent, true, feeling language as anticipatory preparation for better sex with their partners and toward savoring the afterglow of intimacy and self-understanding.

Here for example are some randomly selected diary entries for this day November 12, 1982.

Jesse Nov 12, 1982

Thoughts about Rachel: Feels like she is really falling in love with me. She has been putting more attention on me than before and it feels like love. I get goose bumps all over when she has her attention on me. I mean, like all the other women in the House love me too, but she seems to have this special feeling for me and I can feel it. She looks at me differently than she has before.

Thoughts about Dahlia: She seems to be falling in love with me, too. When she has her attention on me, I can not only feel it physically but mentally, too. I love when she asks me to do things for her in the house. She really is so beautiful!

Thoughts about Jane: Loved to be out with her in a session. Seems like she does better out doors. I do to. She's had a hard life but it has made her so strong. Love to smile at her as I pass her on the hill. Feel so much compassion for her.

Thoughts about Chase: Love Chase. He's really a good friend. Always wants me to do more. He's helping me a lot through a transition period in my relationship with Wyoming and Rob.

Mario November 12, 1982
We talked in group about Dahlia and I being able to have a session. We still haven't had one, and after going several months without that activity I haven't given it too much thought. Yesterday I saw Dahlia and Pia were napping on a futon. Dahlia rolled over and I got turned on. I have to admit Dahlia is still the one I think of getting into feelings with the most. I miss how we laughed and hugged and kissed.

Wyoming November 12, 1982 Chase and I had an amazing physical session together. I told him about some of my sexual activities in the Group, with Ursu and Brad. Then he had me get undressed in front of him, then he got undressed and we breathed and AUMed for a while and got into sex. I was really turned on. He was using this rhythmic one, two, three pause stroke. He just told me to lie back and relax. Then he started asking me questions about the imagery of my orgasm. I noticed that when he would pause me at the top of the high peaks I used to get blasted. My vision would tunnel or cloud over with color and tears it felt so good. My eyes would water. It would be a struggle to keep my attention focused on sex or where I was, I was falling, dissolving into something. I told him this. We were both really high from the experience and I felt much clearer. I'll have to get Tom and Ursu to explore this with me.

Pia 1982.11.12
Got into sexual intercourse with Chase during our session. He was inside me and he helped me to relax my body. He kept telling me to tell myself that I want to relax my body, break the habit of tensing up my legs, my stomach. He was great working with me. I felt totally accepted by him, no matter how I look. I was able to relax and feel like I don't have to do anything but lay relaxed and feel every stroke. He will produce the orgasm in my body. He told me we weren't going to go for orgasm, just for relaxation and we did. When I relax my mind is on enjoying pleasure.

Rachel 11/12/1982
I feel myself getting so close to him, Jesse is so really nice. I feel I love him. Each time we get together it is getting better and better. I felt more aware of my orgasms coming. This morning when we got into sex I felt my orgasm widen and concentrate than widen again when he stroked me then paused. We had a great ride together. Afterwards I let him look at my pussy in the morning light — I didn't care if other people were around — so he could see how full and rosy red my lips were. He said they looked beautiful. I had my legs wrapped around his hips and we leaned against some futons. He was up inside me and I was stroking his back while he felt my back muscles, and my ass and my stretched out legs with his right hand. I thought what a fun position. I gave him one final soft slow stroke and I could feel him really hard up inside me. It made me flush all over my upper body. It was hard to disengage and slide off of him and leave him standing high, happy and wanting more.

People in the House felt very accomplished in their ability to give and get sexual pleasure. The way sexual love was portrayed in the culture and the media —people being overcome by forces beyond their control and swept away into spontaneous sexual activities leaving a trail of clothes to the bedroom seemed quite laughable. It was a matter of honor to keep the focus on sex with the partners to whom you had committed yourself to within the group marriage. This made the House feel like the most completely secure and safe environment in the world.

There were not any elaborate seductions and other games that needed to be played. In fact if you did not take chances and "go for the feelings" then you had to give an account in group the next day. Clothing was optional most of the time especially in the evening. Sex was seen as a way of knowing, they used the phrase "feeling you with my mouth," instead of eating pussy or sucking cock when they spoke about oral sex. The emphasis was on carrying the sexual energy generated in sex over to the next session with an other lover rather than dissipating it in orgasm.

Chase had started out a disciple of Reich using strong counter action to punch through the character armor, but then he saw in the Tibetan Buddhist paradigm the ability to bless even these defenses for he learned to look at the two sided nature of these guardians. He asks what are they guarding, and what they are guarding is nothing less then exposing the individual to the raw transcendental energies of the life force. "It is through them we must go."

He wanted the people to be like surrogates for each other. "Don't forget, you are like surrogates with each other," he'd say. "You are standing in at that moment you are a channel for the life force you are conducting and being conducted. Give yourself over to it."

Dahlia didn't have a session that night. The strawboss sleeps alone. This is what she wrote in the Strawboss Log:
Tues. November 12, 1982 Strawboss: Dahlia

Day #2 on the strawboss job—I've been having quite a lot of trouble with anger and competition. I've been acting like Aaron is my father And taking myself out of the picture with the working on the budget.

Some trouble with leaving herself out of business opened up for Katie, seems she puts herself down like she is too crazy. It also felt that it was angry in the way she expects others to be telling her what to do. And acting like there is nothing to feel good about the project of getting tax exempt status for the Institute.

We had a group at lunch today—the way Chase sounded got me concerned that we are stringing it out on this project.

I talked in the Lunch group with Aaron, for myself it felt less anxious and more prepared, I also had some feelings about keeping the books that seemed to please Aaron. He felt kind of tired or overburdened. My feeling is that he will feel something about where he comes from soon.

I sat in the mirror and realized I wasn't angry at either Katie or Aaron & I would much rather be having my feelings with them. I feel like acting out the anger is very self destructive. Sitting with it is going to be a big yoga for me.

Rachel seems to have more energy now, with some symptoms still lingering on. It feels good to see some improvement. Some stuff opened up for Rachel with her illness. Mostly that she is getting isolated—she talked about some fears of what will happen because she is missing a lot of class work and some trouble that has left her feeling out of it a lot and opened up some trouble with cynicism about getting closer, we'll try to help her more in group tonight.

Lucia and I got a lot of work done on the Co-op and & Katie balanced some books this afternoon, felt better after hooking up at lunch.

Marcia & Brad are still going slow and stayed home from work today, still not healthy enough to do go to work. They spend a lot of time together, it would probably be good for them to talk in group also. Marcia is still sick & staying in bed most of the day—we talked about her seeing the doctor last night & decided to wait until Thursday. How does Marcia feel about that? Maybe I'll ask her later.

I enjoyed the group last night. I brought a new friend — Walker to the house. I feel Walker projecting his mother on me, thinking he has to prove something to me. I enjoy being with him and would like to talk with him in group.

It felt like everyone was more present than it has felt for awhile.

It has been six months since I was last strawboss.—The job in itself seems almost effortless—everyone here seems very aware of what needs to be done & how to go about it— the attitude is very positive also. All of that helped me to see the kind of pressure the job brings up for me, thinking it is all up to me. In my family I never wanted any responsibility because it always meant I would find out how inadequate, stupid, selfish, etc. I was—both my mother and father laid that on me. It feels like a painful space to be in my head.

Dahlia was sleeping near her small group and could if she wanted to, hear bits of conversation between Malcolm and Frieda or between Pia and Morey.

The session of Malcolm and Frieda, an experienced couple who had the proper detachment, was going exceptionally well. Malcolm was feeling honored and trusted by Frieda in the way she spread her legs for him. For her, sessions with Malcolm always made her feel very sexy. Malcolm is always attentive. He let his hand just rest on her vagina, and felt it opening like a flower. He actually felt an electrical charge run over his finger tip and he gently touched her little tiny clit sticking up like the little jack in the pulpit.

Frieda had been thinking about him stroking her clit more slowly and using shorter strokes with his electric hands. She showed him just how tiny the stroke can be. Then she lay back and let him take over gently teasing her clitoris. It was a marvel of communication the way he continued the motion of feeling her. He got this image of going real slow, my god he thought, it felt like it was kissing my finger, sipping the touch off my finger. She leaned back and relaxed and thrust her hips up to him, so his finger slipped deeper. They both experienced the most sensational tingly electricity jumping across the gap between his finger tips and the wet lips of her cunt. Malcolm almost expected blue sparks to leap from his hands and fry this very excited woman who had lovingly given herself to him so completely.

It felt so incredible, it was like a tingly numbness passed up from her quim into his arm and up to his shoulder.

Malcolm thought: God, I must explore the energy of this. I wonder if I could get this blue tingly energy to run up my penis. He decided to see if he could just substitute his penis in place of his finger. Placing a hand on each of her legs He spread them and just rested his penis on her clitoris where his finger had been. It was incredible, he just followed the heat down in. And the two of them hooked up in sex. After he moved it in and out for a while he just sunk to her lower depths and pinned and held her there. It made Frieda feel like she was pinned and writhing, impaled on his stake. She enjoyed giving herself over to this power. And they relaxed into it.

He got this vision of the two of them like two bodies floating through the universe together. Malcolm leaned over and told her, "I felt an electrical jolt up my penis and into my spine! Wow. It was the most I've ever felt through you."

Frieda felt it too. She said: "Yes! Success! It is just what I wanted."

Then he got a long slow easy motion going. He stayed with the short, slow stroke most of the time.

Malcolm whispered in her ear, "Wow, I feel like we are flying through the night."

Frieda said, "Oh man it's sensational."

But, of course, this did not happen as often as one might like. Just as often a couple would have to stop and talk and deal with the defenses. Pia and Morey had a breakthrough night too. But it started off difficult. It went like this. After they get under the covers they were holding each other and OMing and enjoying the spirituality of that experience, and Morey smiling softly, looks deeply into her eyes, trying to hook up in empathy, gently kisses her. She suddenly feels rocked to the core. She swoons. Her entire body spasms in waves of pleasure that ripple through every part of her. But this frightens her terribly. However, she is mindful enough to realize that instead of surrendering and letting herself be swept away, she feels a jolt of fear. She knows the main thing is to be in the feelings. In the moment. Even if they are unpleasant.

Pia suddenly sits up and gasps for breath. Morey is sensitive to this. He and Chase and the other men are working together with Pia.

Here the couple just retreat back into the earlier stages of breathing and OMing together and see if the sound work will push through the fear. Soon they stop all together and Morey asks her, "What is coming up for you? Where did she go just then?" Neither he nor she would feign heat of passion and to cover up fear with a giggle and a kiss and push through into the sex act. That's not where it's at here at the House. You have to honor that resistance too. In their session Pia said, "I find myself having difficulty letting go. I'm not yet as free as I thought."

And Morey said, "Yea I could feel you tensing up and holding your breath."

Pia: "And I kept my butt and thighs tight. I felt my mind wandering and losing connection."

And they slept on that.

Morey knows Pia's history, and this has happened before. They are working on it. The last time they were in group and talking about it he had told her, "It made me feel like you were saying I'm not trustworthy. That you couldn't trust me enough to let yourself go with me."

Now Pia had been working on sexual issues with her therapist and the men and women in her group marriage. Her work was cut out for her. The history of Pia's liberation from these episodes of panic and frigidity began when she started working intensely with Chase.

Over time Chase taught her how to pay attention to her mannerisms, and examine the rigidity of these boundaries especially during sex. Then in session Chase has her take off her panties and sit on the edge of the chair. Without getting undressed himself, and keeping intimate, empathic eye contact —that only a therapist and patient can get — and speaking in a low assured tone he says, "Spread your vagina for me a little bit. I want to feel the lips."

Chase put one finger gently inside her pussy. He told her to relax and pay attention to what she was feeling. He slowly and gently moved his finger in and out of her cunt and got Pia to feel the tension in her stomach if it was keeping her from relaxing and feeling more pleasure. She admitted that she also tended to hold in her stomach because she felt a bit heavier than she'd like to be. Chase assigned her the yoga of sitting in small group sangha, naked.

Chase said that she was afraid of letting go, and that

holding her belly tight was part of a whole pattern of muscle control that they were working on and that was keeping her from getting fully aroused sexually.

"While I am touching you here, I want you to think about sucking cock. My cock, Morey's cock, anybody's cock.

For the next few sessions Chase massaged Pia's vagina with his hand until she was able to have orgasm. She found that she was more relaxed in the shower and able to use the bathroom in the presence of men. She started to enjoy sex.

With the help of Chase and Morey and the other men in her sangha, Pia paid attention to her mannerisms, especially during sex. She saw how her self-conscious body language projected a tacit message that proclaimed: 'I don't trust you enough to relax and enjoy myself with you. Looking good is more important to me than feeling good.'

In a later session Chase had Pia feel his cock with her mouth. As she did it, he told her, "I want you to really feel Morey's cock with your mouth. Come to know it, let yourself go, abandon yourself to the power you will have over him, and let him surrender himself to you." Chase told her, "It will help you confront your prejudices about Morey's body type and personality." It had come out in therapy that Pia felt some prejudice against Morey's body type. Morey was a landscaper and though he was a short and squat man, he was an older man. And he was so incredibly hairy. Chase told her, "Sex is a kind of meditation. It's not about who is dominating and who is being dominated. You need to figure that out."

Finally for that Tuesday night's session with Morey she had been assigned by Chase to suck Morey's cock. Chase said, "You have to become generous not only with the other person but with yourself. You have to know you have a lot to offer and you have to come to know your own generosity. That is the reward."

She had gone into the session knowing she must surrender to her own desires. Chase told me to give Morey the best cock suck of his life. She told herself then I will let go of my prejudices about Morey's body type and personality, I know it will happen. But she fought it that night.

Pia and Morey slept through the night. Toward morning she got this mixed feeling of joy, sadness, excitement and peace as she stopped fighting. In the morning Morey like all men had a huge monstrous boner. With a mischievous grin on her face Pia slid down under the covers and held the monster in her hand, strangled it a little bit. Morey moaned. Pia strangled it a little bit more and jerked it from side to side. I'll show you who's boss she thinks and then she slowly took the monster's head into her mouth. His cock is the hardest I have ever seen. As I slide my lips over the head of his cock I feel a rush through my body. I fall in love with his cock. It is like a little baby.

Morey sat up and twisted around on his side so he could gently stroke the outside of her pussy with his hand as he was feeling her hot wet mouth slide down over his cock. Pia breaths out a long auming sigh and relaxes her spine. He is stroking my clit lightly, she thinks. I am pushing out, the sensation is spreading throughout my body. I am falling in love with Morey's cock. The tingling increases in my body. My pussy feels so warm and soft. He pushes me off him over to the right side, spreads my legs with his hands and lets his hairy knuckles graze over the outside of my pussy. My pussy contracts. I am holding his cock in my hand. I love to feel it engorge in my hand, I want it in my pussy. I am thinking about him fucking me furiously.

In group that following night, speaking about the physical stuff they had gotten into that morning, Pia wanted Morey to go first, to talk about it first. He does. "What a great way to wake up! With you feeling my cock in your mouth. I felt like a new man, rejuvenated and I sprung out of bed. I worked on building a rock wall all day. Then I came home and did the shopping run to Rainbow. I was happy all day.

In the days to come Pia let herself have more and more experiences with men. As Pia examined her programmed feelings toward men, she decided to risk being her 'own true self with them— whatever that is.' When she did, she discovered that without all that body stiffness she was indeed the authentically sexy woman she always knew she could be.

9

A Night to Remember

Walker got a little job crawling around on his hands and knees under a house with this 70-year old man jacking up the house with hydraulic car jacks, cutting out rotten joists and replacing them. He was glad to have the work.

By Friday, he was so out of it tired after working all day that he wasn't good for anything. He ended up in the poet Daryll Gray's basement flat. The poet was in the low ceiling kitchen preparing an excellent stone soup. Walker loved the long high-speed intellectual conversations they got into about Korzybski, Jung, the Vedas, atomic particles of meaning, Heizenburg and uncertainty and synchronicity. Jiving to jazz, hanging with the 'boys,' Walker instigated: "Let's go to the Starlight Ball room and waltz some of the babes around."

No response to that one.

Later Walker was practicing his lateral side-snap dragon-kick. "Well, let's go downtown to the LUX and see three Kung-fu movies for $1.50."

"Ah, I don't know man."

The in-and-out conversation of a bunch of really broke guys went like that. Such was the lonely life of the bachelor.

He decided to call it a night but not before making one last late night attempt —lonely horny loser that he was — at getting another woman, some woman he had met somewhere —Betty Anne— to go get one of the last cable car rides (they were shutting down the cable cars for a good part of a year to work on them) or maybe walk the Golden Gate bridge in the full moon. He got turned down because it was "ladies night."

Walker was beginning to think that much as he might like Dahlia it was hopeless. He said to himself, this is going to be *way* too hard to get involved with her. She is already married, to the commune. He thought he ought to try and meet some other women. For it certainly didn't look too good with Dahlia. Isn't dating fun?

But he really missed her and he ended up trying to call

her up at the aundromat. He called up Dahlia, that Friday night, and left a message with Mario that he would call her Saturday morning. And sure enough Saturday morning he was able to catch her in —it was early when he called —and she came to the phone all lovely and sleepy voiced over the phone, before breakfast, and they discussed meeting later in the day.

When he got to the Loft she made it a point of taking him aside, sitting him down on a sleeping bag spread out on the floor and opening a big photo album. She began showing him pictures of her life.

"I want to show you my pictures because it will help you get to know me," she said.

Walker rarely got to know very much about the women in his life. He was always too polite to pry. People let you know what they want to let you know. It was delightful and disarming the way that Dahlia was taking the time and telling him about her life.

For Dahlia the horse ran threaded through the memories of her childhood. She had grown up alone on a farm in the mountains of Colorado with her brother and parents. In one of the pictures she looked like a little Shirley Temple doll. "My mother gave me a permanent which was in fashion at the time."

"Oh, yeah, my sisters had those too."

There weren't any other girls her age around, and life was pretty lonely. At last she came to know a beautiful horse, Winsome. The horse was kept in an old farm down the road by a kindly old cowboy whose ways were ways of gentleness, who befriended her, and taught her the true and gentle way to be with the horses. When she was a teenager they sold the farm and moved to Hawaii, where she rode horses by the sea. Walker pictured her like in a TV commercial: the long-haired Dahlia on the back of a stallion her hair flowing in the breeze, like the horses mane, galloping through the surf.

But soon enough she gave up those wild seaside rides for college and boys. She took a degree in Poli-sci. She married in the Officer's Club, and settled into the life, as a lobbyist. Her husband and she would take groups of friends sailing from Kona where they had a coffee plantation, to Honolulu.

"Being with this large a group of people at sea got pretty strange," she said: "It makes you very childlike to be out on the ocean for a day or more. You have to get into this very basic physical rhythm or get sick."

"Ever been to Hawaii?" she asked.

"Nope."

Walker innocently enough had thought to enlist Dahlia's aid and suggestions in trying to find some decent clothes. He needed some to wear to an interview (should one occur). He, Dahlia and Pia decided to hit the various Goodwill stores and haberdasheries in the Mission. Dahlia immediately saw it as Walker going into some kind of male courtship ritual to turn the women of their lives into their mother. It was not a good idea to engage her in a motherly role, she had no desire to see that he got properly clothed. So she and Pia dismissed him to his quest, pulled out of formation and shopped for some fabric to make children's clothes.

Down the street the First Annual Indian Street Fair was happening on Valencia Street, behind the old stone Armory. Dahlia and Walker connected up again there. Sharing a Heinekens from a paper sack, they dug on a bunch of the braves whooping it up, beneath enormous speaker towers, flashing electric guitars in loin cloths in the open air.

Then they headed off toward Fort Mason with the object of getting one of the last cable-car rides, and a drink, while digging the sunset down on the Bay. There was a tiredness to her. She was subdued, non-verbal. People in the House took things very seriously and were supposed to be mindful of the deeper reality of relationship at all times. Being in analysis full-time required having to face unpleasant and un-comfortable things about yourself, for analysis is considered successful if it makes unconscious fears and anxieties overt. There were a lot of time consuming rituals and activities; becoming an adept is very tiring work. But Walker read it as a sign of resistivity and lack of interest. He feared it and wanted to blast it away; because he was afraid it meant the beginning of the end of a fine romance for him. If he had been trained in the ways of group psychotherapy, he might have seen that he himself was providing distraction from the anxiety Dahlia had of the group.

He saw the giant Mark DiSuvero sculpture — a large swing, standing in a massive wood and I-beam frame on the bluff above Fort Mason. It was made out of a gigantic tractor tire split along its circumference and splayed out hanging by chains from a huge steel girder superstructure, three stories tall.

He took her hand like children on a school yard and led her over to his huge manta ray looking swing. Got it going with pushes, after she stretched out her sweet anatomy, galumping along on the back of this huge black manta ray thing floating out and in against the sky, looking across at the frieze of whitewashed surfaces climbing Pacific Heights.

He wanted to push this strange manta ray so high that it would just take right on off outa there and float away into the sky. Swing slow and gentle and sure enough her mood changed. Yes, Dahlia began to sashay on this fine sunlit autumn day. As they walked out onto the spiral jetty at the Aquatic Park below Ghiradelli Square, Walker casually inquired for information about her past.

The jetty is a short spiral and at the end, Walker leaned on the top rail looking out at the sun reflected off the undulating Bay, breathed deep the fresh salt air on this glorious and beautiful day, felt incredibly high and alive. A bunch of *cholos* adroitly scrambled up an obelisk and perched there like preening lords.

A little girl in a red riding suit screamed for her father, who was standing just a few feet away, fishing. For some reason of vibrational affinity, the little girl ran up to Dahlia. Dahlia asked her, "Where is your Daddy?"

And the child pointed with a mischievous grin, "Over there."

As they walked on Dahlia spoke of the children in the commune. "At the loft, none of the children know who their fathers are. And the youngest one, doesn't know who her mother is."

"Wow."

"Yea, we didn't have it so together when the older kids were born, but we're getting it more together. The youngest kid, she makes fun of kids like that. She will sometimes act like they do, mimicking them crying for their Daddies the way they do at school, where she sees that kind of behavior.

You see we have this co-parenting situation at the loft, where everyone takes responsibility for the children."

"Like a Kibbutz?" Walker asked.

"Somewhat. We're interested in breaking the cycle of parents passing on neuroses to their kids. You see, this way they don't grow up being obsessed by one person, like in the nuclear family. For example if a kid falls and hurts himself, he or she has lots of parents to run to. They don't end up getting fixated and becoming dependent on one person. Co-parenting taught about how obsessive love is, — always trying to be finding the surrogate mother."

"You mean that for you," Walker hesitated in romantic despair, "one person is interchangeable with any other?"

"No, not for me, I'm the old way," she said with an encouraging grin.

They walked on, to the large concrete bleachers at the Marina below Ghiradelli Square where a bunch of drummers were into a rocking rhythm on their congas, timbales, bottles and horns. The band played real good for free. A trumpeter was holding the last lingering variations of Summertime, (and the Living is Easy) like he was trying to slow time down, as if this was the last sundown of the last summer day, and he really loved the summer and feared the winter, and he could somehow impress his metabolism through the shinny brass horn into time, and intercede for us somehow like the way the horn pressed its yellow sound through an affinity of round shape like the sun does into to the eyes as the blue bay stretched away to the wan sky.

They sat down on the bleachers. "Mmmmm still warm from the sun."

Dahlia said, "I really like to come here, it is my favorite spot in the whole city to come and watch the sun set."

Walker pulled her to him, he sitting with his back to the wall on the large ledge and she sitting between his legs relaxing with her back into him. He held her close, inhaling the warmth of her.

The sun got redder and redder, then oranger and oranger and warm and fiery from soaking up the heat and passion of the world's day. It puffed up and seemed to burst: and splash everyone with yellow light. Yellow light streamed down across the breasts of joggers, across the backs of strollers pushing perambulators with babies, glimmering off the undulating waters, leading off on a bright path into itself like the dot of an i. The horn player felt it too, for he began to linger and softly held long Miles Davis tones, and the other musicians were slowed down to say Ya! man, and ooh YAhhh.

Houses rose and fell on the tip topsy turvey hills of this stone city of eleven mystical peaks while tall buildings piled up vertical crystals like geodes of feldspar and over it all dominating it like a triumphant tuning fork, or some unearthly alien invader, the micro-wave Sutro tower.

This was an old city. It felt like they were in some great sun washed painting from the old world, a landscape, a cityscape, a seascape, — with pillars —huge columns like gates becoming portals to the unknown world. Many life times had passed in this spot, looking at the sun set in golden west. Sitting at the edge of the bay, watching the ships passing, sunlight streaming down, Walker was filled with the presence of place. This was her place. A power spot. It was natural, anyone could recognize it.

Walker became overwhelmed and uncomfortable with the intimacy of the silent communing moments they shared. Hoping not to disturb the moment, but somewhere inside realizing he was making a wrong dumb move, he said, "Thank you for bringing me here." He just knew she would think him a pedestrian schlep for being trapped in bourgeois politeness, trying to make this inoffensive prattle pass for intimacy. Or, he thought she could think even worse of him for appearing as he felt right now, thinking of her as a small boy would, thanking a whore for giving away — candy bars. But he had to goof on it, even if it got her goat, because it *is* special when somebody takes you to their power spot.

"You're always being so polite," she chided, grabbing his upper arms and giving him three shoulder shakes and looking into his eyes.

"Never hurts to be polite," he blushed.

And she settled in and was not going to take it away from him, but help it go longer, and he held her there watching the sun set and listening to the horn player for longer than he had held anyone and it was just the horn going off and his soul drifting out with it on the long warm shining rifts. Walker had a melt down of feeling. He just dissolved into himself. He thought so much of her, felt the pulls of strong feelings —it was a confused admiration and gratitude mixed with lust and love. He knew he must work out some way to be both lover and casual friend to this radiant being. And it is in those moments when, whatever you want to call it, — the source of life — communicates to us through a language of images soaring along on feelings. And the image of a flare came to him. It was like Wake up! Woa! His mind began racing as he thought about his feelings for Dahlia. He saw his own life prior to meeting her as a car wreck on the side of the road that he was driving past. There's a flair burning beside the wreckage of your life. He was lost, a discrete being wandering around the chaos of the dark void; she was like a flare burning by the wayside, telling him of dangerous turns, warning of dangers, but showing the safe passage. He felt that she could make him confront questions that had been bothering him so long that they had been buried, or hidden behind walls, so that he couldn't even see them anymore. He had to get back to the truth. I've got to tell her about the herpes! I've got to give her the option of rejecting me.

I am both trying to get closer and stay apart from Dahlia. Sex and guile had gotten us introduced, and I had moved into some kind of preliminary courtship procedures. We have a flair for each other's style! Which was a cool, classy style. There was a mutual recognition of this fantasy, him the tall, fair haired, blue-eyed *outremonter*, she tall, Latin, long dark hair, serious dark eyes. He looked for humor, intelligence but most of all a sense of mystic ecstasy, that's the style of will he had most affinity for. The mystic personality is kinetic with feelings, and it feels through a kinetic sense. He had felt this affinity flair at the moment of being zapped by one of her feelers. When you have been zapped you are nude— defenseless, to the current they seem to be throwing your way, and when the one you have been zapped by approaches, there are networks of connotation in their smile, fields of electricity in their walk, in who they are, and you need to surround yourself with a well grounded cage, if you are even to approach them and live, you need to let yourself be enlivened by this electricity.

His mind is racing along as he struggles think of something to say, to blurt out some kind of truth to her. But he couldn't say anything to her. He longed to say:

The sky attains the degree of obscurity as the night reigns, supreme on the earth, —because the earth never attains the density of matter —because matter is always in fusion, and the air is in diffusion and if ever it was possible to feel the union of our body with the sky it is through feelings. We are able to become detached from our feelings, because we become detached from the sky, we get into little rooms, with fluorescent lighting, and if we are not able to be in touch with our FEELINGS which are on fire, we become separated from ourselves, and we begin to slip away from ourselves without end, and we are no longer able to get in touch with ourselves and with the divinity that is under our skin under which we cannot get, which will not lift off. The feelings are the untouchable parts of our exterior image, because they represent the extensibility of our entire being and if the feelings don't fly like the wind and penetrate the impenetrable, and if the feelings move you and can only move you to be worn in movement.

It was like a flare up, not of anger, due to a strong disaffinity, but of a surrender to being able to send off and pick up feelings from someone, to be more than just another other for someone, to have them be more than just other to you. To let someone else in, to let them influence you, and you them, to be a marker on their pathway. It is not love, not devotion, but a being for, and recognition of being. There is the kind of inevitable relief for the discrete being going around in the chaos of the dark void to be involved with flare of mutual flair, an agitated relief, like traveler on the dark curve, the flare bracing his attention for what was coming up, showing him that somebody cares, somebody is there, there is safe passage.

But didn't.

"I meet a lot of people," Dahlia began, interrupting what was turning into a long solipsistic silence, "and I try to find out where they are coming from. Try to find out what their upbringing was like, what their parents were like and how they were programmed. That way when people reject you, or do something weird, you know it's not necessarily them, but their programming that is what they are really reacting to."

"That's a good idea," Walker said, "disassociating the personality from the being." Walker was startled by this insight. What an amazingly sharp chick, he thought.

"I've heard of this before but never been able to make it work much, in an interactive way, with people. Oh well, sometimes in meditation I have had this — been able to have this disassociation of my personality from my being."

Dahlia thought about the watcher equivalent in Buddhism. What was his name? She screwed up her forehead trying to remember. "Yeah, there's an avatar of this in Buddhism, can't think of his name right now."

Walker said, "I think it is one of the ancient techniques, whereby a person who could disassociate himself from his body would feel no pain and therefore no fear. Not even of death." This was very important to him. He recalled how he had learned self-hypnosis to try to do something about the level of stress in his life which seemed to help with the herpes. "I learned the art of self-hypnosis from" —and he thought he might tell her but his defenses took over and he turned it — "believe it or not, the Texas bureau of MHMR," he thought for a moment " —Mental Health and Mental Retardation." He made his eyes go humorously wide, but he longed to add that self-hypnosis had been what got him through the early stages of herpes. But didn't. He had, to a certain extent, learned how to control his autonomic nervous system with it and the level of stress. "I had learned to take long trips of inner visualization. I actually started to believe or imagine that I could somehow cross the brain/blood barrier." He longed to tell her more about this stuff but this was not the time.

Dahlia was thinking about how to tell him about the group marriage and wondered what *he* might think. After a slight pause she continued "At the loft we all live together — so many people — and we really grind and file away on each other."

She was quiet too for a while, and then she brought up something out of the blue: "I felt like I didn't want to come over to your place on Tuesday, yet I felt that you wanted me to."

She sighed and said, as if anticipating what he was

thinking, "Romanticism is for dopes."

"I'm very romantic, myself. I believe in romanticism," Walker returned.

"You tend to think these feelings are focused in the other person in romantic love," she said, "rather than in yourself. Those feelings of being so high are focused in YOU. You're the one who generates love."

They stayed staring out at the sea, past several attempts of Walker's agitation to move. Lights came on in Tiburon and Larkspur; Angel Island faded into darkness.

Realizing the talking had come to an impasse, he hugged her from behind for a long time, and then they started humming together. At first Walker felt weird doing this in a public place, but after all, this was California, and it seemed all right. This made him relax and forget the chill. He kept putting his hands under her armpits to keep them warm, feeling her shoulders, and her stomach and breasts, squeezing her to him. Like some strange Kundalini his penis kept getting erect and creeping up her backbone. She enjoyed leaning and ooching herself into him.

Later they went to a place called Maxwell's Plum, a really up-town tourist place at Ghiradelli Square. The ceiling of the place has a stunning design of embedded cut-stone and colored glass powerfully back-lit which made it a palace of light. The architect had designed a pavilion honoring light and it made you feel like you were afloat on the crystal planes in a huge lattice. Walker stood transfixed at the cut glass mandalas on the walls, while seeing the whole ceiling over the fashionable dining room was a magic carpet of lighted gem stones. He was astounded to see great mandalas, made of concentric rings of blue green yellow red colored stones, with a bright white light behind them. The light shone through the concentric rings of stones blue green yellow red. Some patterns so large they might cover the ceiling of an entire room red red; blue blue; green green.

The two lovers came under the influence of the blue blue stones intermixed with the red red interspersed with the green. Mandalas! Like a light show at some kind of subliminal rock opera. The eye moved outward and inward following the concentric nodes of radiant back lit gems tones blue blue, green green, yellow yellow yellow, red red red.

"It reminds me of orifices," she said, "like many mouths."

Walker thought she seemed a little coy in saying this, and seemed to shape her mouth around the vowels of her speech.

"Like the lowest chakra, the anus," she continued. She blushed a little and said, "There is so much apprehension associated with each orifice."

Dahlia flashed on that particularly scary House yoga called Asshole Feelings. OOOhhh the very word. Basically the idea of the house was to have people get into as much sex with other people as they possibly could in a tightly-confined open community marriage in order to bring about a rapid destruction of the ego. And one of the ways to do this was a "circle meditation" in which the members of the small group, all clean and flushed out, got around in a very tight circle touching, and the one in back gently inserted his longest finger into the anus of the one in front. It was SO strong, feeling someone's finger like a hot jet shooting all the way up inside your body flushing the cheeks. By god that will definitely break down your sense of distance from the others. They had also done it in big group.

It made a woman or anyone for that matter feel really vulnerable to present their ass to another, to have their anal orifice pierced by another. It was terribly strange —and then later in the moments of passion to allow your lover to do that to you too. It was awesome, powerful.

———

Thinking about being open, being able to merge, to drop away the boundaries of personal narcissism that kept us apart Dahlia suddenly had a quick flashback: *she was back in the cabana on the beach in Hawaii. All of them doing LSD. It was a beautiful bamboo cabana with wooden floors at the ocean's edge. The men had built it for complete privacy and inaccessibility except by swimming or boat. They felt safe. They were a colony, a tribe at the edge of the universe. Anywhere in time. Civilization seemed a million miles away beyond the darkness.*

You looked out and could see they were on a long stretch of beach, alone for miles. The atmosphere was hot and did not move in the cabana as if its own saturated weight were dragging it down. And feeling warmed by it she opened her legs to it, not a shred of clothing on her beautiful body.

Waves. She could hear them crashing close by, but she couldn't see them. Then she realized it was because it was dark; pinpoints of sparkling light dotted the night sky out the open wall over the sea.

They were floating among the stars. She remembered lying against the freshly laundered and wind dried cotton sheets on the futon. The only sensations she can feel — Cleanliness against her naked skin, the heat of the men and women as they reached out for embrace. FOR THE GROUP, she thinks as the excitement tingles down her breasts to between her legs. In the candle light flicker. She could see skin all shades from white to tan, mostly tanned as if it were one big entity that she was part of yet that moved through her while she was part and looked on.

Lust, life force moves slowly through the group. It moves, snaking its way along the canvas of the cotton futons seeping up into naked bodies, a conflagration of feeling, painting her fragrant coconut-oiled skin with lust, desire, trust, and patience.

She remembered her face being inches from her Daily Person —who had it been then? Mario? And she leaned in, putting her hand on his cheek as he kissed her. She immersed herself in his presence completely, letting the feel of him wash over her like the waves on the beach outside the open wall. Her breath coming quicker, as she strains and surrenders to the life force warming her body and turning her on. It really had been a time when each individual could melt into the universal ocean pouring his fluid back in to merge with the universal mind.

Head back, mouth open, eyes closed. Sharp breaths. The life force just presents itself. Along her stomach now. He leaves kisses, sweetly stinging nips and bites, to melt into the skin below her navel while she breathes her mantra of Aums. Auming and moaning relinquishing control, being subsumed into a world where she could transcend herself and feel the Source, the anima giving it all away. If for only a few moments to touch that which is eternal generosity. She reaches out and touches the life force in his erect penis, simply and existentially there.

Sound. Ahhhhs out of open mouths. Aums resonate from all cavities, moans rise up. Mixing with others intoning anthems in a tongue unknown. From underneath him she lifts her cunt up to him. Hips search for hips until his cock slides smoothly into her, her eyes open, her cunt open like a flower, for him taking all he has in sacred sacral union.

He gingerly pushed his penis into her hot wet cunt, the water eddying around it as he slid easily into her and moved gently with the tide's rhythm. It was incredibly slow. As she moved her hips against his ridged cock, water coursed in and around them as she slid him into and out of her, their motion synched to the far distant crashing of waves on the shore. Buddha time, unconscious time took over; seconds stretched into minutes, minutes into hours. The tide rose with them. They made sound together to keep from coming. Sound flowed out and influenced other lovers of her group marriage. Admonished not to cum, the idea was to prove they were all equal instruments of the life force.

She was possessed by this life force and she did not want it to let go. She had gotten close with everyone in her group marriage those nights. Chase had set up a big brass gong that was struck at odd intervals, thus signaling when it was time to change partners. . . Gong.

After, Mario took his penis out of my vagina and moved on. Next was Tom. I saw Bridget give Tom one last kiss before he came over and we got into a hug. I rolled over and got on top of him. I saw Jesse lie down between Bridget's spread thighs. I was kissing with Tom and started to moan when I impaled myself on his hard penis. . . Gong

Next felt Wyoming's tongue make contact with my clitoris. I shuddered and reached down to run my hand through Wyoming's hair. . . Gong

Jesse had been next. He got up to kneel beside my head. Jesse was fully erect and I reached out to grab his phallus. I turned my head and took the tip in my mouth to begin sucking him with a slow and steady rhythm. I then took more and more of his erection into my hungry mouth. Jesse simply knelt there with his hands on my head, I'm his "wife" I remember thinking, as he was moaning and groaning in erotic bliss. But he must not cum. I paused and saw Wyoming splayed out like a dog on her hands and knees reaching back with her hand touching Tom on his balls as he slowly put his penis into her vagina. . . . Gong.

Then Ursu had his tongue buried deeply in my hot pussy.

Men were putting their penises in her mouth and pussy where other men had put their penises. Men were putting their mouths where other men had put their penises. Women were putting their mouths where men had put their penises, and where other women had put their mouths. As she had.

Mario's brown eyes were open staring at her from above. The pleading in his eyes feeds her smile. Tom's steely blues were staring up at her from beneath her as she rode him like her horse. Wyoming's dark eyes, gazed upon her with loving compassion as they held each other close. Bridget's green eyes were happy to feast on her. Jesse's bright blue eyes were open wide with lust for her. Her dark eyes were filled with compassion for her brothers and sisters. And closed as she comes squeezing against Morey her last partner for the night. I, me, you, we, they, he, she, these distinctions dissolved in the little cabana by the sea.

Man that was hot, she thought, awakening herself from the flashback to the restaurant scene. Walker wondered what she was driving at with her reference to the anal chakra. He knew intelligence was the best aphrodisiac and let it work on him as well as for him. He found intellectual flirting erotic. The thought also crossed his mind that she might be interested in anal sex. Maybe we'll get an opportunity later, to investigate buggery. He became shocked and freaked out at the thought of it, and quickly changed the subject: "When I look at the mandala," he said, 'I see it as radiating energy nodes, like the pattern you see when they scatter light off the head of a pin, and this creates wave interferences with the atoms in their lattice, and like, gives a projection of what the lattice looks like. I think of it as a representation of the radiant energy source emanating from all things — emanating from, by and through all things."

Dahlia smiled and looked thoughtful.

Walker shifted into his teacher mode, "That's quite a different take we each had on the mandala. Mine wouldn't have been nearly so personal," he said, goofing on his own pedantry.

She just smiled at his critique.

Walker broached the subject of anality then, just to show he wasn't a prude. "I think about the anal chakra," he said as he looked around, at the tres chic and elegant ladies, and the waiters carrying trays of plates of food to the elegant tables. A few sidelong glances assured them they were out of hearing range of any tender ears. Dahlia smiled in amusement at his conspiratorial demeanor.

She decided to have some fun with him. Boldly she crossed her arms looked studious like a schoolmarm and asked, "What DO you think of the anal chakra?"

"I think about the anus chakra in the Freudian terms, being anal compulsive, being orderly, or leaving a mess around, that others have to clean up. 'Get your shit together,' you know."

Dahlia laughed. She had heard that association before.

"But it is like that," he continued. "You have to start taking care of yourself. That is what the first chakra is telling us. That you have to get your food trip, and your money trip, and your work trip together. You have to become self-sufficient. That is the first step on the road to enlightenment."

"Yes, you have to be able to take care of yourself," she agreed. "But you know what?" She looked at him in a challenging way. "You have a nice ass."

Walker blushed.

"Then the next chakra," he continued, regaining his pedantic composure "above that is the genital chakra, right?"

"Yeah", said Dahlia, "then she raised her eyebrows like Groucho Marx, Yeahhhhaa!"

Walker had to smile as he was being teased by a master. She thinks she is so smart.

"That is saying that you have to get your sex trip together," he said. "Get your love life together. Don't go about being obsessed."

He thought about that a minute and though it did sound a little like the old monk that he usually thought of himself as. Avoid sex. Avoid commitment. Walker felt himself on a roll. He was trying to telegraph something to Dahlia about their own situation. He was often doing that. Presenting some idea in a presentational mode, but realizing that it was the most direct statement about how he felt, at that moment, that he could possibly make. For him the world was digital, run by rules, axioms, abstract.

"Then the next chakra is the solar plexus, right?" he continued. "That is saying that you have to study your breathing, get into stamina, get into the control and understanding of your own autonomic nervous system." Walker looked around, and was kind of amazed at this conversation being carried on in the most uptown tourist watering hole in San Francisco.

"These are still mostly on the physical plane," he continued, "and it is all the farther that I have come. The next chakra, the heart, I haven't really been able to get my hands on. I might be wrong, but I don't think it is so physical as the others. That is the one I am working on now. The heart chakra and love."

She smiled at him, admiring the run-down.

But basically she was getting a little tired of this tourist lecturing her. She was thinking, I want this relationship with Walker, I like this romantic ass, I'm not done with strange ass in the House, and if we have to think of it as, god forbid —boyfriend and girlfriend — then so be it. I'm going to take this boy home with me tonight.

"Then, let's see," he continued, "there are seven right?"

"Yep, right," she said.

"There is the crown chakra," he continued, "the intellect, which I have developed a lot, we are very top heavy in the west. I think I understand that one pretty good. . . And what are the other two?

"Well there's the third eye," she said, "the intuition."

"Right. . . And one that relates to the thymus gland. . . But it's also the voice. . . Isn't it?" he asked. "Finding one's own voice. . ." The throat chakra was somehow in his mind, convolved with the thymus, the throat and that with immunity, or that part of the body which differentiates between self and others. He knew it related somehow, to the correct processing of information. Perhaps somehow, it rather than the heart chakra was the one that connected the planes, the physical and the spiritual planes. Maybe the heart really was on the physical plane.

"But it's like a path that unfolds, isn't it? Have you ever read the Diamond Sutra?" Dahlia asked.

"Yes, I have. What was it about? I don't recall it that good," he tested. He really hadn't read that classical sutra.

"It was mainly about various techniques of meditation as I recall," she said.

"Yes," he said interjecting his own interpretation, "It was based on the central metaphor — it is an old metaphor — that the mind is a diamond, and that we are polishing it, if I recall." He looked at her side ways so she couldn't tell he was looking to see if he was more or less on base.

"Well in a way, yes," she said

"I use that idea when I meditate," he said, "like when you get in the lotus position," and here Walker touched various parts of his body —chest, throat, forehead, made the mudra of touching his forefingers to his thumbs, looking furtively around to make sure the dowagers weren't watching his overly animated conversation.

"That's what is really beautiful about those books," he continued, "they get you swinging with a central metaphor, and take you for a long wonderful ride with that. Like when I meditate, I sometimes visualize that I am a candle, and can see the various colored flames around me, or sometimes I can visualize the chakras, but another great one is the one out of the Diamond Sutra, that in the lotus position," and here Walker stood up on one leg and crossed the other over it, and made the finger mudra, touching himself in various points, saying, "you feel like you get yourself inside a diamond, and that you can bounce light around on the inside of all these facets or planes of your being, that is what I see, the outline of the human form with all these lights bouncing around inside."

For a few moments there Walker was blissed out — so many things were going on, here they were two lovers in this crystalline room, talking about the Diamond Sutra.

"Well, I've got to make a bathroom run," Dahlia said.

"Me, too."

After they met up with each other on the way out the door, Dahlia observed cynically, "Looks like they put all their energy into the upstairs." Walker smiled. Sometimes he kind of liked bitchiness in women.

They walked over to the Good Food restaurant on Bay Street. Here they ordered one ultimate four cheese lasagna to split. While waiting for the order another long lacunae in the conversation occurred, in which the topic of lassitude was crossed over into the topic of one's self. Walker said, "I am trying to write this piece on mental imagery and visualization for the holistic newspaper *Common Ground*, to see if I can get them to send me to this big imagery convention that they are holding in San Francisco next month. I'd like to go on a press pass.

"See I am interested in exploring the relationship between chakras and glands. 'Bout all I've been able to come up with is this piece about gland trouble. Goes: people are apes with gland trouble / apes are primates with gland trouble / primates are mammals with gland trouble / mammals are lizards with gland trouble / lizards are frogs with gland trouble / frogs are fish with gland trouble / fish are worms with gland trouble / worms are amoebae with gland trouble / amoebae are algae with gland trouble."

Dahlia started laughing. She was surprised.

"It's kind of a goof on evolution," he smiled.

Later while drinking coffee after the meal, Walker mused, "It would be nice if I could sleep with you in the loft sometime. . ." She smiled and opened her eyes with delight. She sighed with relief: he asked.

Walker continued, "Couldn't I just be like some kind of. . . protuberance in your sleeping bag? Like when you sneak boys into a girl's dorm?"

She laughed. This is what she wanted. She said: "You might trip over a naked body!"

"We could just hold hands all night or something."

"Hold hands!" She hooted in derision. "We do a lot more than that!"

"You mean," said Walker,— (with a sharp inhalation, excited, acting shocked, hand on palpitating heart, his voice rising, feigning shocked jealousy) "you get into SEX! Together?"

"Yes! We all sleep together one night a week. It really brings up a lot of feelings at the group meetings. Then one night a week, we pick someone not in our small group, and spend the night being close to them.

"We have many interactions," she continued. "That is why we throw ourselves together, so we can agitate and grate on the programming that controls us."

Dahlia didn't want to go dancing so she said, "Why don't we go over to the loft and see what's happening."

When they got up to the Loft, there were already one or two people who had put out their futons and were getting ready for bed. Walker felt weird, watched over, remarked upon and duly noted by these indefatigable spiritual hedonists — her very dear friends. He was such an outsider; but Dahlia was doing her best, with a bemused grin, to keep him calm. They went into the kitchen, and drew out the act of making coffee, some de-caffeinated Kona coffee that Dahlia had come up with. He tried to be helpful with some woman obviously having difficulty pulling a stuffed hefty trash bag out, but she managed quite well without him — thank you.

They made nervous small talk on the edge of the carpet of the main room. Then they walked around looking at the wonderful collection of hand-painted on-fabric tankhas. Walker was drawn to one depicting the Wheel of Life, or the Wheel of Becoming. They stepped over one Loftist and looked as it clearly depicted the animal world, and a supernatural world; it depicted the hungry ghosts with huge distended bellies, and long skinny necks. Another tankha showed a horrible huge monster — the Mahakala — in connubial conjugation with a powerful consort, and she was all contorted around in a beautiful lay. She had a most powerful back. Walker thought: man, let a woman with a back like that get ahold of me, it could be my undoing. "Notice how the center of the painting is centered right on her asshole," Dahlia smiled.

She brought out her futon and they sat on it for a while. They smoked part of a joint. Walker kept his back to the others, in order to afford them more privacy. Then she went upstairs for a long time.

Walker lay back on her futon.

He noticed that some of the women were walking around in the nude, so he put his glasses back on. Wow. It was like being back stage at some sexual ballet. These were strong lean vegetarian women. Not *Playboy* beautiful, but not an ounce of flab on them anywhere. These were all American girls (rather women). He was very nervous. They have a level of sexual relaxedness, a sophistication he lacked and his inhibition made him nervous. He noticed that men and women used the same bathroom.

When Dahlia returned, she stood at the foot of the futon and with a sexy grin pulled her shirt over her head, baring her sweet little white breasts. She said, "Well, it's time for bed." Then she stripped off her slacks, showing her smooth, tall, lithe body, as she folded them. Stepping high out of her panties, she lay down beside him.

Walker felt that all eyes were upon him. House members were doubtless saying to themselves, "Now who is this tall stranger, Dahlia has brought into our midst". . . And another might think, "Stranger in the house, Oh well, guess I'll just relax in my nudity." And another might conclud, "Dahlia really is into having a lot of feelings with different men, and no wonder, she's a beautiful person." And all these smiling and knowing looks seemed so many warm embraces in a group mind. The effect was Pentecostal, all sleeping in one big meltdown for each other.

"I notice the bathrooms are unisex," he said.

"Of course," she snorted, "you don't think we'd have separate bathrooms!"

Walker knew he'd have to strip, so that she would save face. He did so, sitting down, modestly, and quickly ooching out of his clothes. He left his underwear on, and quickly slid beneath covers. It felt so good to rub up and hug on her warm bare body. But he was determined that he was not going to let himself get carried away, and make love to her in front of all these people.

Upstairs in the loft, he could hear others AUMing and moaning. He thought of calling the humane society, thinking there were ailing animals in the house. Because sometimes their AUMs would be elongated into long sighs of pleasure, and glissandos of delight, would at times reached primal scream levels. And there were chuckles and laughter chuffy gusty expelations of air as the communards were lovingly hugged tightly. Walker, the awkward swain, and Dahlia the experienced Tantric Sex Surrogate Therapist, got into hugging and AUMing together. Dahlia let out with loud

AUMs, and sighs, really let herself go, much more so than she had previously in the van.

They hugged and squeezed and AUMed together for hours. Walker felt their bodies resonate, and the space between them dissolve, somehow. They were one.

—At last, he thought. This is it. The relaxed, brotherly, real full-on hug. This is tantra. Not the kind he had read about in books, but the real thing.

For the first time, he felt somewhat relaxed, rather than all purposive and driving toward some kind of orgasm. This made a strong impression on Walker. He felt like a babe reborn, or like a shy 16 year old virgin, her first time out.

He was totally new to this kind of loving. At one point he became amazed that they were two persons at all. In the auming and breathing and hugging, he would press his head against hers, and could hear the bones, and cavities inside their bodies, resonate at their natural frequencies and he saw sequence successions of color tones. Fading into a rich blackness. Or maybe this was the void, in which all fission and fusion was virtually there anyway.

Gradually his anxiety about love making in a room full of people began to recede, to be replaced with the revelation that he was safe and watched over by all these loving people.

He chanted softly, flatly at first, hiding from any would be spectators. But there was no hiding from Dahlia, he was in bone resonance with her. This resonance came slowly, dimly, and stealthily, in spite of his inhibitions — gained greater impetus, growing and increasing, finally to achieve a mighty breathtaking diapason as he became one of the many, people hugging, having the air squeezed out of their guts with huge bear hugs, and finally the auming slid into sighs, into moans, into great howling cat-screeches of orgasm around him. The depth of this lovely Dahlia person, this divine other he was with, sank into him.

The full-on hug. She got really hot as he hugged and petted her, and kissed her but whenever they'd start to really wind up into a randy screw someone would come in through the sliding glass door! There would be knowing guffaws or slightly embarrassed titters.

At one point, while working up to an extremely passionate embrace, she looked up at people coming through the door and said, "Hi, Mario."

All this caused Walker to feel silly, and he began to just want to laugh and hug and carry on. He felt protected, relaxed.

Love was in the air. He felt closer than he had ever felt to any human being, he felt that he had just been re-mothered by her at this his rebirth. And as only a baby coming into adolescence he felt too inhibited to penetrate her with his penis, so he brought her off a time or two with his elegant and gentle hands, and although she kept after, ducking like a sleek water otter under his arms when he would withdraw them in silly laughter from some interruption, he didn't want to go 'all the way.'

"For that, you've got to come over to my place," he said— a lover instituting discipline.

She pouted. "It's very frustrating, I want to feel you inside of me."

But he was far off, into the tantric aesthetic of caretza. He felt an incredible lightness when he was lying on her or she laying on him. It bordered on the miraculous, this lightness. Like it was some kind of field between them, a field or great strength, and for the first time he knew that it was possible to make a sexual partner stronger, through sex, rather than to make them weak. For the first time he could have the feelings first. It was the beginning of unmechanical sex.

And while she couldn't let him sleep, kept prodding him, reaching for his cock, trying to get his underpants off, he was feeling light, giddy, like a young girl. Silly, elated, inhibited, self-conscious. Like he had just been initiated for the first time into real love.

He awoke the next morning, got dressed and left quickly with a really good feeling all day. He vowed to put more time in with these people, and maybe one day join them.

10

Love Torqued on His Thoughts

Lightness stayed with Walker all the next day, until the group meeting Monday night, the next chance to see her. These nights were open to visits from outsiders. There, in small group, Dahlia was crying. It so upset Walker that he couldn't swallow.

In the small circle of five people forming the small group, Morey, who was sitting next to Dahlia, gently reached out and touched her knee and looked her in the eyes with sympathy. "Hook up," he said, trying to help her stay in focus when Dahlia's attention would wander from exploring the deeper memory or association of her current distress. He'd say. "Come on, hook up."

"I just feel like this hungry maw of unfulfilled love," she sobbed. "I had a dream last night, in which I went around with my sleeping bag, asking others if I could sleep with them."

Walker was immediately shocked. He thought: She must be talking about how she felt being with me the last time we were together.

"I could feel a lot of pain," she continued, "and awkwardness. I'm not even sure what the pain was about. Probably a lot of it was the pain I've been creating when I fight my feelings."

It made Walker feel sad, very sad that she was sad. Because if you are hung up on someone, and they are sad, then you are sad. But what could he do about it. He realized the House wanted him to see this, that crying is just an anxiety attack or that crying is feeling the return of ancient pain. And yet, Walker chose to interpret her crying as representing an underlying flaw or lack of resolve or belief in the lifestyle of the Loft. He immediately began having fantasies of being the hero to come and rescue this damsel from the commune. It might be that she could use his help.

Walker saw himself in a fantasy where he was throwing

a three- pronged grappling hook up over the parapet of their building and pulling himself up several stories like a human spidcrmun, the rope swaying on the side of the building. Then he saw himself carrying off this lovely Lady, swinging off with her under his arm like some barbaric Tarzan on a vine. He'd take her back to his cave and they'd live happily ever after.

Realistically he knew that if he was going to have any hope of pulling off something like this plan of busting her out of the brain-washing commune, it was going to take a while. He'd have to stay in town, he'd have to get an apartment and a job. He'd probably have to infiltrate the commune by joining.

And that's how his life changing decision to get off the road and settle for a while in the Bay Area was made. Toward that rescue, Walker wanted to present a more professional, acceptable persona to the people at the House. He wasn't ready to join them.

Shortly after that he landed an apartment in Berkeley. And a new job teaching at a private college in Concord, a satellite city east of the Berkeley hills through the Caldecott tunnel. Teaching a class the first semester is quite a scramble, but one Walker was used to, for this is the function of the Bachelor — to stay at least one or two lectures ahead of the students.

Dahlia asked Walker up to their land in the Siskyou forest on Mount Shasta. They wanted him to go up North. 'Up North' was a state of mind for them: it was participating in wildness; it was escaping the city which felt totally insane to these very sane people. For Walker this invitation to be part of this feeling community was frightening. It was like they were inviting him to start participating in what . . . What ? . . . He didn't know. The universal orgasm?

Walker knew he would have a problem with the authoritarian aspect of their leader Chase. The thought that Chase might call him a tight-ass really bothered him. The thought of spending all that time in close quarters in a couple of large tents in the winter up on some remote land that you wouldn't be able to up and leave if you wanted to with the commune was terrifying to him.

He told her he'd think about it. Meanwhile he was in that

first semester turmoil. Suddenly he found himself having a lot of lessons and labs to prepare. The more things change. . . As he told his new found friends at the Loft, "I left a college town where I was teaching college and moved to a college town, where I got a job teaching college."

He looked upon his new job as an opportunity to fulfill his purpose on this earth which was to inspire the overly-practical minds of technicians with the wonders of physics. He couldn't come out and say it to the students of the trade school but for Walker mathematics was the language god blew into maternal matter to energize form. For him physics was somehow like feelings. Magnetism was the colorless color, the color before color, the quiet force bringing things together, but also pulling them apart.

He really had it bad for this girl. And that was good! Sexual fantasies were saturating his mind to the core as he sat under the steady hum in a fluorescent-lit classroom trying to pull together a lesson. He'd imagine Dahlia, as a fresh-faced ingenue student in his class, wearing nylons from the early 60s (before panty hose), legs crossed and looking at him lovingly with her big playful dark eyes. And he'd shake his head trying to dispel the pleasant takeover, thinking: man, I'm fucking high. I'm starting to know all these women. Keep it casual, let it gel, was his mantra. Gonna keep it casual, gonna let it gel.

For his first week Walker prepared a lab on resonant circuits, essentially a radio tuner. He had set up an antenna conducting myriad radio station frequencies into a tuning circuit: which was a coil, (essentially a ferrite-core electromagnet) in parallel with a variable capacitor. Changing the capacitor changed the resonance frequency to admit the chosen signal. They would be looking at the output with an oscilloscope.

All set up and ready to go, Walker was about to flip the switch to power up the circuit when he paused in thought. He admired all the hidden uses of magnetism in his circuit: the antenna has a coil wound around an iron-core magnet making it an electromagnet when touched by the radio waves; there were magnetic cores in the transformers, in the power supplies and those used for coupling and isolating the signal in the scope. The scope's electron beam sweep for driving the display was a pulsed coil causing its magnetic field to focus and position the beam on the screen. The resonance with which his circuit tunes into radio waves, the step up transformers in the ballast of the overhead lights with which to see the experiment. . .

What else in magnetism did Walker, electrodynamic being, obsessively attracted lover, knight-with-whom-the-Force-was-strong, further admire?

Its universality as one of the four forces of the universe: its mysterious invisibility, working at a distance without touch and through walls: its contrariness, repelling like, attracting unlike: its restlessness in the form of electromagnetic waves spanning the spectrum of radio, power line frequencies, microwaves, infrared, visible light, ultraviolet, x-rays and gamma rays carrying information into all niches and realms of existence — (Maxwell's rainbow, surely evolution would have exploited this dual nature of the electromagnetic field, look at how it had the human eye evolve right in the center of yellow of the visible light part of the EM spectrum): its serpentine compressibility to coil up as a potential in a solenoid: its perpetual convolution endlessly exerting force on current and having current exerting force on it: its potency in motors, turbines, dynamos, step-up transformers in electric sub-stations delivering power to industry and our homes in the great dynamo of alternating current grid: its capacity due to the bi-stable coercivity of its hysteresis to hold in memory, —tape, disk, array, brain? — the mega-terabytes of information and images contained in words, pictures, movies and sounds, that influence our daily lives: its playfulness in speakers, radio tuners and transmitters, VCR tape heads and motors, CD-ROMs, and magnetic tape: its indispensability in credit card generators and readers: its vehicular ramifications in high speed magnetically levitated trains: its mass moving abilities from little charges in particle accelerators to bullets in recoilless coil rifles to orbiting payloads in mass drivers: its omniscient perspicacity in radar: its modernity generating heat in microwave ovens: its phenomenological sensitivity in converting motion, torque, force, rotation through sensors, detectors and transducers into electrical displays used in gauges — (for a moment Walker found himself looking at all the gauges on all the old cars and trucks and busses he had ever driven and thinking about magnetism giving him information as he was looking out the window at a countryside passing by, as if he was in a world of a thousand eyes all looking back at him.): its agile acumen in its ability to covert signals to motion working in feedback servo motor control: its navigational constancy in aligning all compass points north due to the circulating electric currents resulting from the earth's great molten metallic core 2000 miles beneath our feet sloshing around like wine in a glass converting the earth's rotational motion to moving current which induces magnetism out the poles: its recording in cooling magnetized magma of the expansion of plate tectonics in the spreading in the ocean floor: its gradation of colors in the aurora borealis, which is caused by gas being ionized by a wind of charged solar particles captured at the North Pole by the earths densely packed magnetic field there after they have been ejected from the sun in huge solar quakes belching great looping promontories arching millions of miles out into space : its astronomical currency in spinning electrons, magnetic star quakes, pulsars, neutron stars and black holes and the quantum analogies of this in spinning protons and electrons: its permeability, coercivity, saturation effect on materials: its variability of states in matter, diamagnetic unattractiveness in silver, paramagnetic weakness in soft matter, ferromagnetic strength in iron, —an easily malleable and universally available metal (the 'water' of magnetism): its great strength in extremely low-temperature super-conducting magnets: its penetrability creating images of the inner structure of our bodies in magnetic resonance imaging and magnetoencephalography and images of the inner structure of matter with the cyclotron and cloud chamber: its central role in inspiring Einstein to work out the special theory of relativity to explain the reciprocal electrodynamic action of a magnet when seen in different frames of reference — (Walker recalled struggling with using relativity in the derivation of magnetism from electrostatics in the Berkeley Physics Book Vol. 2, trying to make the jump in the frame of reference from statics to electrodynamics of moving bodies, wondering if there wasn't just some easy space if you could find the right coordinate system, in units of velocity maybe, or acceleration so that all the equations just looked like simple algebra, like Euclid's and Archimedes' plane Geometry.): its weirdness being a compact effluvial field of virtual photons, the " messenger particles" of electromagnetic field, that are within and without all things: its righteousness in electronic article surveillance strips embedded in books and objects to set of alarms when stolen to fight the perennial war against book theft: its domesticity in the attraction between refrigerators and little ceramic vegetables . . .

"Uh, Mr. Underwood?" A student was calling back his attention to the present.

Walker blinked his eyes and said to himself: Trade school students say Mister out here in the burbs, I like that. These people want to work with their hands.

Time came for Walker to let Dahlia know whether he was going on the trip, and he was too paranoid about groups and distracted about keeping up with the new job, so he told her he couldn't go. She seemed hurt on the phone and argued. He said, "I just don't feel comfortable making the trip and I have too much to do at work." And the situation snowballed into emotional distance.

But at work he found that his mind would just lock onto her and he couldn't stop day-dreaming about her. For example, a couple of days later his discussion on hysteresis was on the verge of becoming hysterical. He was instructing his students in the use of the load line across the hysteresis curve and right in the middle of it he paused and imagined her sweeping her elegant hands across the desk to lick a finger and turn a page and suddenly { No Time }. Forget Time. How he longed to have her work on him with those hands.

During an illustration of the knee of the Demagnetization Curve: he'd see her in his imagination sitting in one of the empty desks. She'd open her knees in her little one piece wooden desk and he could see frilly panties at the top of those legs beyond even the tops of the nylons. He'd be putting up equations about the Flux of

Magnetism through a core. Letters from the Greek alphabet: mu — permeability, and epsilon — coercivity began to march across the field of discussion like fluxions creeping of their own accord, like drunken characters in an Alice in Wonderland movie.

Quickly he'd turn back to the board and fire off a few more axioms and come down like thunder onto the black board, making his equations bristle with indices. But it would come out: The magnetic susceptibility gives the ratio between the angle of the dangle and the heat of the meat which increases the angle of repose. Or: When a cowboy is placed in a magnetic field, its atoms respond to the magnetic flux by either getting aligned and adding their own magnetic fields to that of the applied field — going along with the flow, — or by opposing the field and subtracting from it. There is an overall increase in magnetism in the loved being.

As the days wore on, he dove into the lectures like a madman, trying to forget but also looking forward to her appearances in his imagination there in front of him every day. He almost freaked-out the trade-school students by showing them a film of the Crab Nebula to illustrate digital pulse technique. The pulsar at its core is the biggest pulsar of them all. He couldn't keep his mind off her. The attraction he had for her was due to his high permeability; she was saturating him with her presence.

Instead of acting out the heroic deeds of rescuing her by kidnapping from the commune, he had to settle for words.

```
Dear Dahlia,

    It is half-past midnight, beginning a new Monday
and I am thinking of you as I seem to be doing more
and more since we have gotten to know each other
over the last month. You are away, up at the Land,
to which you kindly invited me, and I chickened-out,
as I started a new job and felt pressed to get my
image together.
    There is much I want to say to you, especially
since we parted without saying good-bye at the end
of Monday night in the loft.
    Seeing you cry that night made me sad, and I
couldn't eat for I didn't understand that these were
tears of compassion for the world and the way it has
```

made us. I see in you a most compassionate being, one who is truly far evolved, one who sleeps comfortable at night and has a clear open face because you live in the truth, one who breathes easy. You have devastated me with your big sad dark eyes, got me wondering what made them look so gentle and deep and so filled with compassion for your good brothers and sisters there at the loft. I don't understand the forces of personality, but you are so beautiful and I thank the forces that have drawn us together.

Hearing the sense that you make in what you have said to me and seeing you cry, those tears have fallen like gentle rain from those big dark eyes into my world, and you have made me grow for you have shown me how there is great strength in the fragility of your compassion. I am starting, just beginning to get in touch with the being in me, the self that is beyond the programming, the shadows I flee and fear, and the masques I present to the world.

What I want to say is that I desire for us to always remain friends for there is long life ahead, and all the time in the world, and maybe someday when we are old, maybe we can go away and take a vacation amongst the stars, where your name is surely written as one of the great compassion artist for you create compassion in people and send them back with keener sensitivity and the ability to know their own feelings.

I felt an incredible lightness with you, the night in the loft, and a bone resonance in the auming that I never even imagined before. This lightness and strength I must pursue.

Go lightly on my fragile being as I open to you. I trust you beyond all others, and worry about you, for taking on all these feelings but know it is good for us. I open and close at your touch like flowers to the sun and rain in their seasons.

Let us have this season, and many more of the turn of the earth ball around the sun ball.

Please excuse this mushy letter, I have always put my faith in writing, I'll try to be cool in the future but as you go through the days know that I love you and watch over you as you have done for me. See you.

Love,
   — Walker

He imagines the lovely Dahlia as his TA, (the world's second oldest profession.) She is in a little plaid miniskirt with pleats, when she is standing you can see her lovely long legs all the way up to where the miniskirt hits her leg way above the knee. She's got a white slip top with thin straps. She is sitting on the edge of a desk. Lolling her lovely legs back and forth.

She leans back on the desk and brings one knee up, cupping it in her outstretched hands. She leans back a little further and he sees all the way up to her cute little panties. She smiles.

Her legs look shapely, and her feet are in clunky superfly pumps that say fuck-me-with-these-shoes-on.

Her hair drapes back and she shakes it and it shivers loosely down past her bare shoulders. Her straight-across strong shoulders, and . . .and that cute way she had of scrunching her shoulders into him sometimes.

In his thoughts she was present there with him and she enjoyed teasing him, opening and closing her legs.

She swings down off the desk and says, "Here, I'll clean the board for you."

She stood with her legs apart in front of the black board. She leaned forward so that her miniskirt just draped over her lovely round ass, and she moved the eraser slowly over the marks, her haunches moved independently of each other, and the thin strap on her T-shirt fell down off her shoulder. She had taken her shoes off and her legs were bare, and she stood on her tiptoes showing her insoles and higher up in the shadows, her asshole up under the little miniskirt. (Wow she's taken off her panties too.) With these wonders of the universe she made him stand erect in the dark shadow at the center of her being.

As she reaches up to the top of the board, she is looking over her shoulder at Walker, and slowly licks the ball of her thumb, then puts it between her lips and gives it a big wet kiss. Sucking her thumb ever so seductively she looks at him with her big dark eyes.

She stared at him from the blackboard with eyes that knew the secret knowledge he didn't have, something that the base animal in him was clawing to get at. She didn't just know magnetism she *was* it. Where she walked, her animal magnetism made all cocks stand erect like compass arrows and point to her true north.

She scrunched her shoulder and tossed her long hair

which moved back and forth on the bare skin of her shoulders and back. In her eyes was an abandoned and fiercely burning look.

She is scrubbing the board with big movements rotating her lovely white thigh and bum. Then flopping her wet rag into a bucket of water and ringing it out — really shredding it, she gazes up at him inquisitively.

Walker's cock got so hard it was about to bust out of his fly. His core being is being aligned by the field effect of her presence. If he wasn't at school he'd have to whip it out and whack off. As it is, he made sure he was sitting down behind a desk when this fantasy came upon him.

She comes over sits on a desk chair with her legs spread apart, opens his fly and his cock flings itself out bouncing to a statuesque standstill. She reaches up and hangs the bucket of water on his erect penis. His boner is so hard and full to bursting, that it doesn't even dip down with the weight.

"My," she says touching him at the base of the monstrous thing, running her hot hands over his hairy balls, then definitively letting the palm of her hand pick up the aura radiating from its hot head.

"You are truly the woman of my dreams," he moans.

She takes the pail off and sets it down on the desk. She turns back to his member and bending over near it she lets her hair down to fall over it and shaking her head so her hair dances on it, and she reaches out to pull down the stiff cantilever member, ever erect and pointing, but can't. She stands, and putting her hand on top of it pushes down hard like you might push down the spring loaded toaster slot. And the cock is so ridged that when she bends it down, instead of going down it lifts Walker's legs off the floor!

"My that's torque!" They both laugh.

He loved to feel that girl, snuggling into his big hug. He could spend an age slowly drawing his hands over her belly and slim hips and thighs. He sometimes grabbed her hips when they were dancing. They were really the most powerful part of a girl. But you had to like her little white breasts and he liked how he could see them down the slit of her blouse sometimes. They had the most supple nipples, no matter how hard he knocked them down with his tongue they would spring back up erect again. But it was looking into her big sad dark eyes that got him. He became lost in their compassion.

She really does have that rare quality among women: true compassion for man. But what would that mean. It might mean that she was able to have only a fleeting interest in any one individual man? Or it might really mean that she was a front angel used to lure men into religious cults and make slaves of their mind?

What he wouldn't give to have his lips close to her face now. He liked to kiss and rub up against her smooth cheeks and then move the trail of kisses above —to her forehead. He could banish cares, unfurl angry crinkled brows, kissing them smooth, and the mind behind it. It was heavenly to nuzzle into her long black hair hanging down, to uncover the nape of her neck into which to nestle and nibble.

Yes, he definitely had it bad for this girl.

.

11

Nuclear Dread Oroborous
Transcending the Night Club Blear

In order to try and get some kind of perspective on the
House (or maybe it was to put off until further research
could be conducted), Walker had begun a study of
Buddhism, especially its art. He thought studying the
energies and forms expressed in the spiritual tankha
paintings might be an easier way into the House for him. He
had even started a class in tankha painting at the Jung
institute. The Bay Area was awesome, you could take just
about any kind of class in any subject you wanted.

The House was very active in the Nuclear Freeze
movement. Their outreach effort was a think-tank called The
Center for Culture-Independent Awareness which sponsored
a series of lectures. By pooling their money, the people of
the House were able to pay the going rate for famous lecture
circuit speakers and to hire halls where these people could
address the community during the Nuclear Freeze campaign.
The House was trying to be more active in helping the
world. They were moving through the Hinayana yoga to the
Mahayana yoga, trying to uplift the whole community. Some
of these speakers were famous ecologists and peace activists.
Chase enjoyed this generosity and commitment immensely
and moved proudly in the background, a big red
paterfamilias Indian-chief of a guy. In the interest of debate
they also engaged one speaker who was a hawk from the
Pentagon and another who was an ex- CIA. Chase relished
the irony of having an ex-CIA working for him and availed
himself to the opportunity to psychoanalyze these guys. The
CIA spook had however been very persuasive when he
pointed out that the psychoanalyst and the strategic analyst
were both concerned with the problem of evil in the world.

Walker went along to one of the talks which was held in
the basement of the Noe Valley Ministry, a large white New
England gabled church. The House had rented the facility for
the evening. The young men of the House, most of whom

worked in carpentry and landscaping had built a raised stage. There was a podium with water and behind that a comfortable seat. The women of the House had arranged tall lilies and sprays of roses. It was beautiful. Any thinker would have been proud to appear in that setting; the maharishi would have loved it. The speaker was a petite radiant woman and her subject was Psychic Numbing in the Nuclear Age.

On the wall behind the speaker's platform, above the sprays of flowers, the House had hung seven of the best paintings from their tankha collection. These were real tankhas, —5 feet long by 4 feet wide with elaborate brocade borders. Each tankha had a veiled curtain which was rolled up to expose the image. These paintings were at least equal to those in the Asian Collection at the San Francisco museum and it was rare and generous to see them outside the House.

Walker was drawn to the Tankhas. The tankhas worked their magic by creating a field of arcing loops of rich energy reaching out and gathering in all who let themselves be gathered in.

As Walker helped with setting up the folding chairs, he felt himself being drawn to the energy focused in the tankhas at the head of the hall. When he stood up from his work or even looked over at them, he kept noticing them, they seemed to impress themselves on the retina of his eye even when he looked away. After the chairs were set up, he took the opportunity to stand in front of these ancient doorways to a magical world and inspect them more closely. He rolled down the sleeves of his white shirt and eyed the tankhas from across the room. Something about their imagery was drawing him to them. He put his Goodwill tweed sport coat back on (with elbow patches, please). Walker liked to look like a journalist or a Berkeley grad. In a state of contemplation he walked in review past the row of tankhas hanging behind the stage. He stopped in front of one showing a god whose skin was an alien blue with many arms standing behind his foxy consort. She was wearing only a short apron —made of a few beads around her waist, and jewelry: necklace, anklets, bracelets and earrings. Her face was turned up to the heavens, her eyes were moons of consternation and joy, her upper lip was curled in a rictus of passion. She was being ravished by her big blue stud clasping her from behind with at least 6 strong arms. He was three faced: a white face looking east, a black one facing straight ahead, and red one facing to the right. Between the couple's legs could be seen the tiger's skin, legs and tails dangling off of him. He seemed to be really giving it to her from behind. There was a rainbow ring of fire around the couple. Damn, thought Walker, those deities in that old-time religion really knew how to tear off a piece of ass, didn't they?

In the lower right corner of the picture, beneath the couple was a huge monstrous black Mahakala swinging a sword. Fierce Tibetan hell hounds were leaping out of his back into the flames around him. In the opposite corner a philosopher king was floating in cool clouds. There were also various sages and deities surrounded by halos and rainbows in the upper part of the image. Did those old artists know how to create drama in their painting or what. Some tankha paintings drew you in with so much bilateral symmetry they were like an abstract *trop d'oile* into which you could fall.

All the tankhas seemed to have at least one huge bug-eyed wrathful *mahakala*. They are about destroying illusion. Then he notices the Bramastra. There was a Rorschach animism in it. And a most disturbing gestalt of a skull.

Pia had sidled up to him and was enjoying his obvious infatuation with the magic paintings.

"Someone has thoughtfully chosen the Bramastra," he said, pointing to a huge fearful monster made of smoke and night, fulminating in the gloom.

Pia gave him a knowing smile.

"Was that you?"

"No it was Chase's idea."

"Wow, it reminds me of what Robert Oppenheimer said when they first exploded the atomic bomb at Trinity. He invoked Shiva, Lord of Death and Destroyer of Worlds, and he quoted something from the Bagavad Gita: 'And now, I am become Death'."

"Yes, it is apropos don't you think?" Pia then glided off and left him to his thoughts.

There was a much more formal arrangement in the Mandala of Sang-due. The mandala is like a web, and Walker let himself be drawn into the web. It appeared to Walker's fantastical sci-fi imagination to be a stargate or worm hole portal into spacetime. It showed the space/time realms all surrounded by a ring of fire as a great citadel seen from above. His studying it closer revealed diagonal lines joining the four corners, dividing the square into four quarters of the compass: east — white, south — yellow, west — red, north — green. Glancing around the periphery outside the central image, Walker took in a large black deity at the top flanked by an emaciated priest about to drink what appeared to be a broth of brains from a human skull! At the bottom of the painting were huge wrathful Mahakalas dancing in flames. Each had three bulging eyes and a necklace of skulls.

Walker's eyes moved over the tankha painting, so rich, so dense, so psychedelic. A stream of energy fanned out from the circle and formed maybe an idea floating in the air, and next to it a forest and next to it a stream and next to it a mountain.

The painting, with its plethora of interconnected life forms doing a rhythmic mitosis raga was alive with semantic connections leaping and arcing across its quadrants. There's life out there in the universe on other planets, and it is trying to communicate with us; only we just didn't have a clue how to pick it up. He thought: These paintings are maybe bait or antennae to capture it.

Walker started thinking about his own design for a tankha. He had been reading a lot about tankha painting lately. This great spiritual art appealed to him — the surrealism of it and the formalism of it. Best of all it spoke to an ideal of an anonymous art, an egoless art, an art uncorrupted by commercialism.

Walker knew that even though he didn't have any great drawing talent, tankhas were in some ways a paint by number thing, in which the subjects and the look were well prescribed, down to fitting on a grid. The creativity was in the use of colors. His teacher was a petit Tibetan monk, with a pencil mustache, deep quiet eyes and small slow-moving elegant hands. The teacher started the students off by showing them how to make a ruler, which would be used over and over to keep the proportions and relationships among the shapes, symbols, and icons in the painting exact. Walker had only stayed for the one class. His lack of drawing talent made him too embarrassed to continue.

The tankha paintings always had at least three layers of communication: the verbal, in the sense they illustrate a story or sutra; the physical in which they were rhythmic; and the mental in that they were hallucinatory, surreal. The tankha paintings really spoke to him. They appealed to his sense of the abstract. They were like abstract diagrams of mental processes, of Jungian journeys.

Standing before the wall of tankhas Walker fell into a reverie, designing his own tankha. It started with him wishing and whispering to himself: 'make it new. Make it new.' Almost like a mantra. What would it be like to make it new, to make a tankha for our time. Well I'd like to get something pulsating out of the center, like the probability waves holding electrons in their orbital shells. Yeah, that'd be cool. And we'd have to have the circle in the square of course. Only what about making my circle the oroborous, have it chasing its tail. Yeah, have to have the oroborous. Walker thought about an explanation he had seen once which used the oroborous, that ancient symbol for the universe, to present the ongoing search for the basic force of the universe. It assigned the various domains of the force to the spatial distances over which it held dominion. A Jungian pie chart!

Starting from the eye of the snake and traveling along its body for about 1/3 of it's length, represents from the size of the known universe down to cosmic distances down to planetary down to the size of a mountain, down to the height of man. Over this domain gravity reigns. The next third, around the bottom of the turn and back up the snake's body, represents distances going from human size down to atomic dimensions. Here electromagnetism dominates. For the next 1/6th of the way, smaller and smaller distances inside the nucleus are represented. Here the Weak force dominates. The final 1/6th of the way, represents the smallest distances, between quanta in a field, where the Strong interactions dominate. As the distances decrease the energies increase.

The Weak force and electromagnetism were unified just a few years ago, as onward the quest for the great unified field theory goes. The strong force becomes equivalent to the others, and then as further and further the distance decreases, Gravity itself is included in the super-unification, represented by the snake swallowing its own tail, or the Klein bottle pouring back in upon itself.

Wow, it was a tankha taking shape. Yes, that's what I'll call it: Klein Bottle Oroborous Tankha. He began invoking the avatars of this new world tankha. Inside the large outer circle of the snake, would be inscribed a big square. Diagonals of the square would make four sections, each a different color, red, green, white and yellowish orange for the 4 forces. Instead of the old bearded sages from Buddhist lore, he'd have bearded physicists and scientists from the history of science, and beneath each scientist some signifying apparatus and/or his symbol.

Walker began to recall their faces from textbooks. There was Isaac Newton: gravity and motion with his most famous sign, F=ma; Dalton juggling atoms; Mendaleov, standing on a tile floor each tile an element of his periodic table; there was Maxwell. Walker thought of the beloved Maxwell equations, now being worn on T-shirts, with the tag line: "And God said, 'Let there be light'." The tragic Boltzman with his great entropy equation connecting the macrocosm with the microcosm. Einstein and $E=mc^2$; Planck and his constant of action. There would be the befuddled Mr. Thompson, in his bowler hat wandering around in the wonderland of the atom; Bohr in a chalk talk with an uncertain Heizenburg; and Dirac against a background of vacuum and antimatter. These were the sages in the canonical mandala.

Yet instead of a great citadel, they were prisoners in a Klein bottle. Walker liked the Klein bottle as the symbol of a new world order instead of the Christian cross with its almost cynical association that the world would hang a feeling seer out to dry. The cross just cleaved space and time into an abstract grid, and was the rubric under which reason enslaved the transcendent. On the other hand, the Klein bottle was a much more natural and a new paradigm of the synchronic and the diachronic because it flowed back in upon itself each part effecting the other part. Walker smiled: when you stood back and looked at his tankha you would see the scientists were each tiling their patch into a quilt of paradigm patches that flowed out of the Klein bottle and curved back in on itself encompassing the whole world. All the motions of heavenly bodies, and the way we communicate at a distance and the chemistry we have used to make out lives better and live longer, to increase the possibility that people would know more, was spilling out and flowing down and some coating the surface of the bottle, which was the universe.

Then the fleshed out image grew abstract, it became a Klein bottle, a model of a 4-dimensional spacetime manifold, a topological wonder that lifts itself out of the three dimension of space into the 4th dimension of time where it makes a twist and comes back on itself. It was the current model of our universe, what the physicists were uncovering. The lovely undulating transparent Klein bottle model looking like some kind of amoeba or jellyfish god hanging there in space suddenly flattened itself out to the simple circle of the oroborous, the snake eating its tail. It is an image of the universe trying to know itself and they were all embroidering a paradigm that shot out of the Klein bottle and curved back in on itself encompassing the whole world.

Walker began to feel like he better make some effort to mingle with the other people from House. They had finished building a cozy room out of the basement meeting hall. He went upstairs and out the huge church door that opened onto a large concrete area leading to the sidewalk and the street. A big 4-wheel drive white Toyota truck from the House pulled up. It was a warm November evening. Quite a few people were milling around outside. Dahlia was busy being the master of ceremonies and Walker was hanging outside watching the crowd. There were lots of people, many of them hugging each other, some hugging and sighing together and auming at the same time. Obviously these were House people. Walker also noticed Chase the great chief of the commune moving about on the periphery. He had a big blustery exterior and looked powerful and vaguely frightening to Walker.

A couple from the House got out of the 4x4 and joined the milling crowd. Dahlia sidled up next to Walker, took his arm, brought him over to them and introduced them to him. "This is Lucia and Jesse. They have been up at our land for almost 6 months."

Lucia's eyes were bright and full of feeling. Her well-tanned peachy complexion had a soft warm rosy glow. Her face radiated joy from every freckle. Several members of the House were milling around her, as if they were trying to bask in the glow of nature she had brought back from the land with her. Something warm and real rippled through Lucia's hippie, Jewish, Brooklyn-girl face when she smiled.

Walker stuck out his hand for a shake, though hugging was the accustomed means of encounter. Dahlia leaned closer into him and said, "Isn't Lucia just beautiful."

It was time for the speaker to give her talk. Everyone filed in and took their chairs in the meeting hall. Dahlia mounted the stage and spoke briefly about the Center for Culture-Independent Awareness and the series of talks it was sponsoring. Then she introduced the speaker who approached the podium as Dahlia left the stage. The speaker was a petite woman, just slightly over five feet. She had soft long blonde hair and an intelligent, innocent face. Here eyes were soft and secure. She looked like a little *Alice in Wonderland* in slacks, surrounded by the tasteful riot of flowers. But when she made eye contact with the audience; you knew she was fierce. Her soft brown eyes which were bright and intelligent and empathic touched everyone. She began her talk.

"We are the first generation to come of age since the first nuclear bombing in 1945, 37 years ago."

She remained silent. After a moment or two she raised her gaze and said: "The image of the mushroom cloud, through the schools and the media, has been driven deep into our minds. We became the first generation to grow up with the idea that our whole world could go up in smoke at any moment. We became the first generation to grow up with the idea that there might not be a future." She paused a long time to let the undeniable truth in that statement sink in.

She turned as if pacing and thinking aloud. "Think about

the nuclear warhead." The speaker paused for a moment, as if she were imagining the shape of the missile in her mind. "Think about how much power each one carried. One megaton of explosives! Each warhead carries a third of the entire devastation power of World War II! How did things ever get like this!"

"The U.S. and Russia have amassed an arsenal," she continued, "with 36,000 times the destructive power of World War II. One Trident sub carries multiple entry warheads, each with enough energy to destroy 200 cities."

Walker shivered in his Nikes: Yes, by god. That was the unit now. They are measuring the destructive powers of atomic bombs in units of World War II! Units of World War II. What would the units be called. WW's? Three A-bombs make a ww. Grrreaaat! God, there's something terribly cynical and terribly human about that!

As the talk continued, the movie screen of Walker's mind began to run old newsreel clips of World War II reportage; movies and TV shows came up. He tried to see them all at once —all the war film explosions he had ever seen in his life go off at once —trying to imagine the new unit: the World War II, the new improved giant economy size unit for devastation and heartbreak. He tried to hold in his mind the sight of World War IIs falling out of the sky. He tried to visualize the ashes and the mushroom clouds, and the firestorms and the spew of bricks and buildings and bodies when one Intercontinental Ballistic Missile fell unleashing the firepower of WW II in a few seconds, and another ICBM with it's WW II and four and six and ten and seventeen ICBMs and thirty and fifty ICBMs fell and each concentrating a World War II in a neighborhood the size of the Mission and if they got past the anti-missile missiles — through the window of vulnerability with which we looked at the world of foreign affairs, and they would —Death would be raining all over the world. It was falling on the cornfields of Iowa, into the deserts of Arizona, sizzling into the seas off the Atlantic and making them boil. And they came down, one came down and 5 came down and 70 came down, came down like giants feet stomping out everything on the earth, the cities, the forests, ooooooh it hurt so bad, like some ... he imagined some angry child throwing a tantrum, and pounding and pounding on his mothers breast and screaming and screaming. Kicking his mother, something he really loved and needed. And slowly the earth ball, the great earth mother this crawling, balling, brawling, sprawling soup of creation.... he sees it traumatized, beginning to crack up and chunks of her and her beings falling off like solar flares into the cryogenic coldness of the black pall of space.

Walker slumped down in his chair cringing before the horror in his mind as he imagined those ICBMs coursing through the blackness of space over the oceans headed for the cities, he felt fearful and beat down, humbled, stuck, staked out, as he imagined the heavy rain of ICBMs falling on the lights of the cities of the world at night, slowly making them wink out.

He shivered and shook himself to draw back out of himself to the lecture. The young woman orator exhorting the audience into understanding, who had at first appeared as a young girl, now had suddenly become more like a feisty old schoolmarm lecturing them. "A growing mind can not deal with an etiology of no-future. It has to numb itself out. It has to numb itself out and not ever look at this possibility of its future going up in smoke."

"This psychic numbing as a defense mechanism due to nuclear dread spread to other areas of the mind. So that as it became possible to no longer feel certain things, it became easier to no longer feel other things." Walker began seeing the image that he had often seen of his own mind: it was that of a compartmentalized maze. He had often felt the walls of the compartments breaking down and giving way when pushed over by analogy and punched through by metaphor.

At that moment she began to speak about Jung and the Image. "The Image and the Symbol are like a more primitive intimate language of the self. And they have been lost."

Walker was very touched to see this little Alice in Wonderland figure lamenting, "We can't image any more," she continued, "in the sense that we can't communicate with certain areas of our own minds. More and more parts of our minds became inaccessible, turned off. Instead of the ability to image, which is a more primitive unification of feeling and knowing and being-present and responsible, we allow public image makers to do it for us on TV. We live on status and hero worship instead of really relating to each other."

Walker was stunned. Maybe this was why he often felt the life he was living was a movie he was watching. Maybe this was why he always felt this kind of standoffish distance. Being around the House people, who were so involved with having and sharing feelings, made him notice his ghostlike distance all the more. It was quite painful. Walker was practically panting with agitation. He was sweating. He writhed around in his metal chair becoming more and more agitated. He tried to be still for fear the chair would squeak, disturbing the audience. This was really speaking to him. Here was an explanation of why his mind had always felt so compartmentalized. Psychic Numbing from Nuclear Dread had deep-sixed his head, ever since those duck and kiss your ass good-bye drills back in grade school. Psychic Numbing from Nuclear Dread. Psychic Numbing from Nuclear Dread.

Walker began to feel sad about all the lost feelings he might have been able to have. He saw himself wandering all the classrooms and cubicles of school and jobs of his life, among the neat rows of desks in school leading to cubicles in work. Yes, it was all very compartmentalized. He saw himself as strangely trapped in this labyrinth which was at once flat and three dimensional which he could look at as if looking at a flat map and as a world he was inside of. He looked up at the tankhas behind the speaker. One showed a great sage holding court in a temple on an island. This tankha showed a huge circular rainbow around the temple on the island and undulating in and out of the arching rainbow were rainbow-colored streamers, spinning off, unraveling into different realms creating as it went floating worlds, worlds flowing down rivers, worlds in clouds. The streamers fanned out from the central circle into the void becoming clouds and streams and animals and people and trees — filling the void. Walker suddenly felt overcome with sadness and a sense of loss. He shook his head to hold back tears.

The speaker began to trace the effect of this psychic numbing through current history. Then she went on to trace the current economic woes in the world, the sexual revolution and the generation gap to psychic numbing from nuclear dread. "To be sure," she continued, "Nuclear Dread of the idea that there might not be a tomorrow, fanned the flames of the sexual revolution but that too was a way of not really feeling for another person." Walker looked at Dahlia across the room. He noticed several members of the House nodding in rapt agreement.

"The general all purpose pandemic nuclear dread," she continued, "caused by the sense of there being the possibility, nay the probability of no future and the resultant psychic numbing and isolation that leads to an inability to relate to other people spread into increased violence. The Psychic Numbing from Nuclear Dread gave us the economic principles of waste. For why bother to steward a space ship bound to a collision course with oblivion? Why not rape the ecology. Why recycle for tomorrow if there is to be no tomorrow."

Walker felt his anger rising, there was a keen edge to his senses brought on by the penetrating cogency of the analysis.

"Our whole generation grew up with the idea that there might not be a future," she said. "This was the split, the big schism, the generation gap of why we don't trust our elders any more, because they got us into such a mess."

She ended the talk by sharing with the audience, what it felt like to break through this Psychic Numbing from Nuclear Dread.

"It was in the spring," she began. "And I used to go up to this high field in Marin overlooking the sea. I'd spread my quilt and sit down in the tall grasses blowing in the wind. And I could watch the ocean and lie back and look at the sky. And really feel the earth beneath me."

She paused for a moment and sighed.

"I really felt that the earth loved me and cared for me and asked me to care for it." She made a gesture like a little child trying to hug the huge earth ball. "And I would start to cry softly and think of what a mess we have made of things." She paused and sighed.

"I don't have any answers, but I know we must start by confronting this psychic numbing."

Tears were welling up behind Walker's eyes, and threatened to break through. He had never felt that way about the earth before. Walker felt chills running up and down his spine.

There was warm applause. After a while Dahlia took the stage, thanked the audience and opened the meeting to discussion. In the sharing that followed, Dahlia talked about how she could identify with this as an aspect of primal pain. Other people from the House took up this theme and built an elaborate and incredible analogy around the word "nuclear" and related the psychic numbing to the pain of the nuclear family.

Walker longed to stand up and talk. His stance raced through his mind. What about High Tech. High Tech will bring it off. High Tech will save our bacon. Walker felt the sweats in his forehead, a fever in the blood bringing chills running down his arms. He didn't know what it was, if it was the fear that he always felt when he even thought about addressing someone even if they were somebody he knew — especially if they were somebody he knew. Or if it was a deeper fear. He wanted to get on top of his fear by talking about the Accelerated Particle Beam weapon, Star Wars — Reagan's ray-gun. High tech would save the race, wouldn't it?

Now the House cannot rest leaving things that need to be analyzed and they began to interrogate the speaker.

"Do you have anyone?" asked Dahlia. "I mean do you have a support group, do you live with anyone?"

The lady orator blushed a bit and smiled. "Yes, I live with my boyfriend." She put her hand over her eyes to block out the lights, scanned the room then pointed to a man in the back of the room, sitting among their friends. "Timothy. That's him there." Timothy stood up, for all to scrutinize. Meanwhile several attendees were leaving. The lady smiled at her boyfriend, a kind of sympathetic smile for having to draw him in to what was becoming a session.

Someone, from the House asked, "How have you managed to cope with not having a numbed out psyche?"

"Well, not very well. I keep busy. I write."

The speaker was seated on stage in what was rapidly becoming the hot seat. She grew defensive and stiffened. "I think of myself as being in service of the world. I've worked on my career, trying to get these lecture tours going."

"But isn't that working on your image?" asked Rachel.

The lady orator was taken aback by this and looked aghast.

Walker thought, this is beginning to feel a little weird. The people from the House, who were the majority of the audience, kept on wanting to get the woman who had put together this thoughtful, liberating, and feeling presentation to talk about her struggle on a more personal level. They kept asking her questions about her family. Meanwhile other people, who had come to the free lecture and discussion, were driven to distraction by this line of pursuit. Some furrowed their brows, glared at the House people and left.

Walker felt like coming to her aid. He felt that the House was way out of line. This whole beautiful discussion was being personalized into *us versus them*, the hawks versus the doves. And it's much deeper than that. Walker felt that he needed to defend science, against these Luddites. They seemed to be polarizing the situation into the good anti-nuclear people against the bad Pentagon people.

He knew it was not the scientist's fault. He thought about what a heady rush it is to do quantum mechanics. It was an honor to understand this incredible paradigm of nature. The problem is this intelligence sits on top of the slower, more primitive aggressive mind that had survived evolution by using the brain as a weapon. He wanted to cry out, the nuclear bomb is something we don't understand yet! It is something like a virus or a disease, that either will challenge our ingenuity, or destroy it.

Still there was a warm openness to the lady, and the discussion heated up. But Walker was practically writhing in his chair, as something penetrated through the fog of psychic numbing!

By now the House members were reveling in the play on the word "nuclear" — the nucleus of the atom, the nucleus of the cell, the nuclear bomb, the nuclear family. It began to take over Walker's mind. He got into one of those poetic states where everything is all rolled together in one huge semantic knot. It was like when he first heard Ginsburg read the "Plutonium Ode" back in Austin. Walker flashed on the incredible poignancy of *that* moment. The poem was an embodiment of that vast penetrating power of the intellect, that has allowed man to penetrate into matter. Ginsburg whips the audience into a state of fever as we participate in a kind of sacrifice as the poet tries to penetrate matter with his own mind, tries to surround this evil plutonium — one thimble-full enough to give cancer to all humanity — offers to sacrifice himself, to assuage the hurt, with his bard yarp, his fat lovely body, like the ancient times when the tribes sacrificed their members to change the seasons, to change the astronomical force to put something in the way of what is coming down.

Then Walker allowed himself to imagine that he was up there on that bluff in Marin described in the lady's story. He imagines the child throwing the tantrum in his thoughts before, had turned into the lovely young woman who had given the talke as she lay in the grass of a high field in Marin crying for the earth and the trees and all the young living things coming up. But there is the snake crawling through the grass toward her blanket.

He wants to protect her. With his mind he makes the snake rise up out of the grass into the air. The snake circles back upon itself. The oroborous, of course. The ancient symbol of the universe, a snake coming back around on itself eating its own tail. It is the symbol of the generation of the child devouring the parents, or is it the image of the parents devouring the children. The transcendent that which is of itself by itself.

Walker watched as his mind worked at putting the speaker into the painting. He got the image of Wyeth's famous archetypal painting "Christina's World." It was as if he were detached, a docent giving a tour speaking of a paintings hanging somewhere, in the museum of his mind? "Now here you can see, in the great citadel of science, Walker has put the figure of this little girl lying in the grass crying. But you can see where he has raised the whole citadel up, on a cliff, and the girl is outside the citadel. The citadel is not central, but has been moved, just a little juxtaposed fringe off to the side."

"And moving toward the center of the mandala, as we move into present time, when you start to get more and more European physicists living in America, Walker has put in the figures of Oppenheimer and von Neuman. He has put in the faces of the many scientists who fled War and began working on the Manhattan project. It was von Neuman who invented the trigger." And then the docent Walker began a side lecture on Von Neuman: "He went on to invent the Theory of Games and Economic behavior. This allowed von Neuman to sit in on the biggest poker game of all: the Atomic Energy Commission. He saw his ideas on gaming become integral to the making of foreign policy into a poker game.

"On the outer edges of Walker's Klein Bottle Oroborous Tankha, the artist has painted nebulas. In the center is the archetypal image of the mushroom cloud, anti-matter and void. The vacuum.

"Now the scientists are penetrating deeper and deeper into the heart of matter, releasing higher and higher energies. Yukawa. The hyphenated names like Neimann and Gell-Man and the 8-fold way. The divine mysteries of group theory. Walker loved group theory, the story of symmetry. Surely that has to be the crowning intellectual jewel in the center of mankind's forehead."

Walker's focus shifted from the tankha he was painting in his mind with the bright young woman in it to the tankhas that surrounded her, and then to one in particular, the Bramastra Mahakala. The "docent" continued. "The bomb is a group totem. It is the scariest image of all. It is the one thing we fear most. It has the power to alter the history of life on this planet. The Bramastra, the all-knowledge of the stars. This was the ancient icon in Buddhism, an energy force that could be controlled by a mantra. It could be focused to kill the fetus in the womb and thus used as a contraceptive. It could radiate out in spherical potential and destroy everything like the atomic bomb. It fills all our lives. And yet, in a way it could bring us closer together, just from the fear of all dying together. It could make us worship life, starting from the nucleus of the cells and the fact that radiation can mutate them. For we are all cells in some great evolving corporate body. Evolving toward some kind of light, some kind of total illumination. The bomb represents that instantaneous illumination, in which we are vaporized by the energy of the sun. The bomb is a material object invented by pure mathematics. It is some kind of idealized intelligence with ungodly godly power forcing itself into our world from another dimension. And they are treating the whole situation like a poker game! That is what is really obscene. That is the idea behind the arms race. They want to keep upping the ante in order to bankrupt the Soviet economy. That is what the so called window of vulnerability is, it is this time in which we gamble on waiting for the accelerated particle beam weapon. This is the ace of spades in the hole. They know that if they get this fifth generation of computers, the new hardware of very large scale integration, then that will give them the digital guidance circuitry for the laser weapon. They know we already have the accelerators and know a lot about what's at the heart of matter. It seems like these boys who brought us out of the depression are going to get their way all the way on down the line. I don't know. They must be smarter than us."

By now Walker was about to explode. He couldn't be silent any more and he blurted out. "I'd like to ask you: What do you think about the Star Wars initiative? There's supposed to be a lot of spin off about that. What America is doing, I think, is playing a very dangerous game of bluff with the Star Wars. They want to up the ante of the weapons race so high that they will bankrupt Russia. They are trying to get this orbiting laser out there that supposedly will knock down any incoming missiles, and what's more, the spin off from doing that, in terms of laser technology, they'll use the laser to zap nuclear waste. So THAT will make nuclear power OK! And also the computers that will evolve out of that will be very powerful. Do you think there is any hope in that?"

The people in the audience and the house were kind of shocked into silence.

"And," Walker continued, "they know that with this machine, they can zap nuclear waste with the accelerated particle beam and transmute it into stuff with a much shorter half life. So that will alleviate the main drawback that the American public sees to nuclear power —the disposal of nuclear waste. Thus the American public will buy it ALL.

From the stage, the speaker looked relieved to be getting the subject back on track. She said, "I mean it's not all the scientist's fault. Sure it is inspiring to think about man opening this mysterious secret at the heart of matter, the secrets of the universe have always and always will cause humans to ponder, but we have let our analytical brain get too far ahead, of our right holistic brain."

Then Walker started talking to the group about comets: "And another thing. They are starting to worry about asteroids colliding with the Earth. They think a huge asteroid colliding with the earth is what made the dinosaurs extinct. Whole species wiped out in a year. They claim that one asteroid 6 miles across landed in the Gulf of Mexico and created such an explosion that it covered the whole earth with a layer of soot and fallout that lasted years. It created the original nuclear winter and all the dinosaurs died out.

"Yeah, so what?" someone said impatiently.

"Well, they have this plan. If an asteroid is gonna crash into the earth and kill everybody, they can send up a rocket and detonate a nuclear bomb with enough force to knock the asteroid out of its path so that it misses the earth."

Wow, they were all shocked about that.

"I mean it's kind of cool," Walker continued, "we might be able to save our planet, we might be so highly enough evolved that we would not have to die out like the dinosaurs, but could save ourselves by using nuclear bombs."

"So it is necessary that we have the bomb," he concluded quietly.

A bunch of people were smiling at Walker. The logic of that was inescapable. They were giving him a kind of — *here's the Berkeley dude*, always disrupting the flow of things — look.

Walker looked at the tankhas. What a stable picture of the world. He thought about the girl crying in the grass, and he just got sadder and sadder, thinking we really are at risk. And it was then he decided, I may as well throw my lot in with these people if they will have me.

As they were filing outside into the crisp clear night, tall Theo from the House came up to him shaking his head. He said, "People from Berkeley . . . always got to argue, always got to mistrust authority," and smiled.

Group Mind

12

Kalachakra Initiation and the Dakini

The second night Walker spent at the Loft was the night
they went to see a holy man whom Dahlia admired, the Very
Venerable Kalu Rimpoche. The Kalachakra Initiation is the
granting of authority to practice the Tantra. Walker felt
grateful to his inamorata for introducing him to this material.
She seemed angry and out of sorts when he picked her
up. As they drove along he looked for signs of cracks in the
armor of her bad mood like a crossword puzzle he might
take apart with wit and put back together whole. He noticed
the little wrinkles at the corners of her eyes, and the way her
mouth turned down so glum and resigned at the series of
unkindnesses that is life. Walker suffered, knowing things
could be different. Walker was having a tough time
remembering how to drive across town to Fort Mason, and
Dahlia got impatient with always being the guide, and
snapped, "Haven't you ever been here before?" For Dahlia
this lack of independence meant Walker was projecting his
mother on her.

"Yes, we met here," said Walker. He couldn't conceal a
defensiveness and exasperation in his voice. Men are a lot
more sentimental and romantic, he thought; women
sometimes didn't seem to remember what went on with their
lovers. Walker sighed. I wonder if she can even tell them
apart. He felt like getting into it with her, so he said, "and
then we came here for a date, once," knowing the word
`date' would press her button.

"Date!" she sneered in derision. "O, yeah. . ." She
paused for emphasis. "What's your name?"

In theory, the communards do not like thinking about
going out on 'dates'. They are really one-on-one spin off
sessions from the main group. Therapy is a frightening and
at times terrifying enterprise, and the House saw frivolity as
a kind of avoidance. Which is not to say that they were not
joyous. When one is liberated to feel again, one becomes
joyous.

"OOOHhhh. That hurt," he said.

They both laughed at this cruelty toward his romantic concern being treated with scorn. But it worked, the laughter seemed to bring her around.

The Kalachakra Initiation Ritual was being held in a big hall, normally used for trade fairs. Since there was already a large audience when they arrived, Dahlia and Walker sat on the carpeted floor in the front. Walker didn't have any idea of what to expect. The scene was festooned with a profusion of bright and gaudy colors. Stout monks with shaved heads and wearing orange sheets wrapped around themselves looked almost like benevolent bouncers of evil.

In front of the audience was an altar not unlike one in a primitive Catholic Church. There was a little tabernacle draped in brocade and a throne for the priest. Large silk tapestries of the Buddha, the Kalachakra (the Wheel of Time, Karma and Evolution), and various protector deities had been hung around the altar. There were scarves and prayer wheels and sacramental instruments. In an alcove at the far end of the room, behind the alter, monks had painstakingly, over the last week built a huge mandala out of colored sand on the floor. The mandala was roped off and people could mill all around it. It appeared to be the plan of a fortress.

When His Eminence the Very Venerable Kalu Rimpoche entered the conference hall, fat, cool-cat monks off to the side of the room let out a huge clash of cymbals and loud long lowing blasts on a pair of ornate 10-foot metal straight-horns. The immense wall of sound shook the floor and vibrated windows and was frightening. For indeed that was its purpose: to expel any lurking demons and to create an immaculate environment for the transmission of the Dharma. It was meant to vibrate a listener's body so that he could resonate with the holy presence of the Rimpoche's 'light body.'

The Kalu Rimpoche looked old and frail. He was dressed splendidly in yellow silk over orange, all swaddled in a wine-dark robe. To tell the truth he looked like an impish lemur, his eyes were soft from a lifetime of being present in clarity for the divine mind, of being a man who always lived close to his core self. His skin seemed almost transparent, and a radiance emanated from him. Walker thought he could almost see right through the ancient priest's earlobes.

Those people in front immediately leaped up and started doing elaborate and athletic "obeisances" which started out in a standing position looking like a mendicant with prayerful folded hands. Then they dove hard into the floor, palms flat. Then they threw their legs straight out back, getting into a push up pose, except then they arched their back way up like a cat stretch. Then they leaped up again back into the prayerful pose, repeating this over and over. Many got behind and out of step; it looked like a bunch of wild people jumping up and down.

Walker was quite surprised at all this. Dahlia, who was quite adept at these yoga moves grinned at his chagrin, and he just got down kneeling on one knee like a football pose and stayed there. Dahlia moved through the moves fast and wonderful, her wild mane tossing as she dove to the floor and arched her back. The powerful sound forms from the horns of the monks were continuous — they could inhale while still blowing out — so that there never appeared a break in the wall of sound from these half brass, half woodwind instruments.

After things quieted down the Rimpoche spoke for a long time in Tibetan. At first it was interesting to hear the language; it was powerful and rhythmic, and even though it was a divine poetry (in Walker's imagination) it sounded like a bunch of disgruntled people in a madhouse doing a high speed mumble muttering under their breath. But they were all doing it and it came through like a freight train blowing through the mind. Big wonderful low low sho chu drog chang tcho. The purpose of the initiation is to plant certain karmic seeds called bindu in the mind of the recipient. Walker was delighted to hear this ancient language down on San Francisco harbor. He made a mental note to write a choral dythyramb like this sometime. But after a while Walker began to want some meaning. By then he had enjoyed about all of this he could stand. Finally a very astute, crew-cut translator started to translate the words of the Milarepa Initiation.

The audience was asked to visualize various scenes of apparitions of gurus to rimpoches down through the lineage, the generations of transmitting of teachings. This was the oral transmission tradition with a directly traceable line going back to Naropa, Marpa, Milrepa. Walker had read a book about Milrepa, who is supposed to have achieved enlightenment in one lifetime, and who practiced black magic and could throw storms. Walker spent days bike riding in the hills of Berkeley high over San Francisco thinking about throwing storms. At one point during the meditation, the deep, earth shattering fog horns from Alcatraz and elsewhere around the bay, pierced the mist enshrouded night, and blended with the continual outpouring of sound forms coming from the fantastic horns of the monks and the chanting and OMing people.

The Kalu Rimpoche thanks the spirits and deities for their co-operation by making offerings to them. The monks play sacred music with bells, gong, cymbals, drums and 10-foot long horns. The Kalu Rimpoche asks Kalachakra to open the students eyes.

Who is the Kalachakra? There it was in a large tankha, the same one as the one in the Loft, a huge dark purple entity in standing intercourse with a beautiful stacked beauty wearing only a necklace around her waist. The center of the tankha is right where their two sexual organs are stuck together, 'where the rubber meets the road,' thought Walker. This is supposed to be the intercourse of method with wisdom. The spirit of the tankha flowed into him. His mind opened to an ancient religion which was not a religion but a critique of religions whose science applied to the study of mind. The Kalachakra is the time machine, evolution. It is usually depicted as the Wheel of Time, in a sand mandala. The great cycle of time and seasons. Walker thought of the Kalachakra as that place right at the still point between the centrifugal forces of dispersion, destruction, entropy, and the centripetal forces of concentration, distillation, amplification —the gate through which things come into existence. Yes. Now *that* was a good deity to pray to. The Kalachakra is something moving through the ages. It gets outer and inner. Outer has to do with the study of cosmic time cycle, astronomy, astrology, geomancy, geography, the evolution machine. Inner is about the number of breaths a person takes in a day and the number of heartbeats in a lifetime.

The creation and ritual scattering of sand mandalas is a magical act aimed at radiating universal harmony and bliss, while helping straighten out the interlocking 'wheels of time' that link *our* space-time universe to the infinity of other universes. This aspect of Buddhism reinforced Walker's intuition that there were other intelligent evolutionary advanced cultures in the universe. At times he thought he could almost feel, if not their presence, at least the ubiquity of emergence. And now here was a religion that not only recognized their existence but claimed to be able to intercede with the forces that touched all of our lives - sort of like when the mechanic balances your car's wheels only a whole lot more elaborate. (Tibetan monks are reputed to be quite adept at karmachanics.)

Next the initiates were invited to take a vow to have compassion toward all living things and to work for the benefit of others. Walker went up and got some righteous ritual done on him, part of which had to do with symbolically drinking some concentrated brain tissue out of an inverted skull. This is my kind of religion thought Walker, powerful and fantastic.

After this eucharistic consummation, when they moved from the hall to an external foyer, Dahlia got into a receiving line, for the blessing from Cinque, a monk she had known before in Hawaii and whose sharp presence could be very much felt during the ritual. All this left her in a much better mood. Thank god we have this interest in religion in common, thought Walker.

Driving back to the Loft on Mission, Walker pulled into an all-night taco stand to cop a coffee. It felt incredibly weird to be in this parking lot awash in bright ghastly yellow helium-vapor light throbbing through transformers below the edge of human perception after having spent hours with these religious people. Walker was having trouble looking at her —he felt like she was changing in front of his eyes, she was like this incredible Madonna of the Burger Joint Parking Lot. She seemed to have a halo of light emanating from her. They were warming to each other, though Walker was still sore from being treated like furniture.

He turned the engine off in the lot in front of her building. She asked him, "Why don't you come up and stay with me."

He looked up at the tall brick building silhouetted against the moonlit sky and thought about all the people in there who would hear his every going on and he theirs and he shrank from it, for it was a weird situation. He was not used to making love with so many other people in the room.

"No, Ah don't think so," he said in a fast clipped self-righteous, redneck way.

He was just into kind of liking her as a sisterly person, but she persuaded him in a deep, throaty sigh, "Aw, come — on."

"I probably better not," he vacillated.

She pulled his sleeve, like an encouraging wife.

"Come onnnnnn!" she said and kissed him deeply and passionately.

Still he shook his head.

"God this is weird," she grinned. "I have never been with anyone so reticent before."

She looked a little exasperated. Looked him deep in the eye.

If she could see down the eye tunnel to the inside of his head she would have seen a very scared little boy down there. Walker knew he must tell her about his sexually transmitted disease problem, it was his duty. But around doing that he was like a scared animal trapped in the cave of his own guilt. If he had any respect at all he'd tell her. And he would if it was ever necessary, if it looked like they were going to ever go somewhere. And at the moment he was astigmatic. At least on the physical plane; on the mental plane he was branded with the scarlet letter right in the middle of his forehead. Yet he so wanted to hold and cuddle up with and kiss this beautiful woman. Finally with a blush he allowed himself to go with her. They walked up to the door, and she opened the building, they walked up a landing, and then higher up into the Loft.

It was dark in the loft, most everyone appeared to be asleep. She brought down a futon, went off, as he sat down beside a column to await her. In a little while she came waltzing into the room, riding on the shadows, her perfect bare ass gliding like a deer running in the forest. She was like some natural creature totally at home in her own body.

She turned and was a little startled to see him there behind the column. Walker wondered if he didn't look a little rigid among all these loose Californians. He undressed and lay down in the sleeping bag with her.

They got into a hug, the full on hug — OMing and breathing in rhythm. Then he caressed her for hours with his hands. He was not an oral lover, not genital, not anal, but manual, and she was coming to know his hands. He had slow sensual hands. Now they were hot, shooting out Kirlian energy enlivening the tissues. He slowly let them range over her entire body even the soles of her feet, playing her like an instrument. For a moment, Dahlia recalled noticing his hands first parting and touching the petals of a flower in La Boheme. "You've got wonderful hands," she said.

A white Tara he thought. Maybe she is my dakini. The beautiful female principle of the tankhas. She has many eyes, for she never misses a trick. When he is trying to avoid feeling trying to get out of the divinity of himself.

He had two eyes: one male; the other female.

She had 7 eyes. The male and the female, a third in the middle of her forehead. And 2 in the palms of her hands and 2 in the soles of her feet.

He felt like he had eyes in the palms of his hands, and she had eyes in the palms of her feet and when he touched her he was looking inside of her.

She said, "I like the way you touched me all over."

He swaddled her in his strong embrace. But, like the last time he couldn't bring himself to penetrate her. It had become a matter of honor with him; he would not penetrate her even with a condom until she had been informed enough to make her own decision.

"But why, we do everything else," she said.

"Just too inhibited," he said. "It goes against my upbringing."

The next morning was not so bad, and he had a little gruel in the kitchen with strangers coming and going. She went with him over to La Boheme, and they had a coffee, for no coffee was allowed in the house and she kissed him like a wife sending her young husband off to work.

13

Diary of a Commune Nympho

In the fall of 1982, there was a lot of excitement and hope in the air. It was like the 60s again. The Nuclear Freeze talks were going on in congress; a referendum was in the works. And big changes were happening for Walker. Slowly things were coming into his life. He had an apartment and a phone now. He even had what he thought was a "girlfriend" though the sexual tension between this man and woman was quite unsettling but then, when was it ever not so. He wanted to get her over to his place and throw a good fuck into her to inaugurate his new bedroom. A man deserves a little pleasure in this life, god damn it! He didn't want to do it on the floor in front of a cast of 1000s and he did not want to do it in the van.

But asking her out was really problematic. For one thing he knew he must tell her about his incurable VD, —not a very inspiring enterprise; yet it was his duty. Plus in his mind dating required him to be elliptical. . . he couldn't just come right out and ask her, "Come on over to my place and help me break in my new bed." That wasn't done in the normal dating situation as far as *he* knew.

Dahlia too wanted to get to the root of the matter. She decided — give the guy a break. She had written in her secret diary, (Dahlia kept a second secret book in addition to the journal of personal development required by the House that she called her Diary of a Commune Nympho): *Advice to commune nymphos. Things can get dicey with an outside man. He just can't deal with the House, who in their right mind could? It might be better for him if we were to check him out on his home turf.*

That Friday, Dahlia's 'session person' had turned up ill and that left her free to hang out with Walker. Though he wanted to, he couldn't just come right out and say, "Let's go to my Berkeley pad." He had to continue to play it cool. "Lets go dancing somewhere," he suggested. He liked dancing with this cute babe.

While they circled North Beach halfway looking for some saloon to get into and dance, Walker's mind was machinating on how can I get her out of town across the bay. But he was being cool, letting it gel. Abruptly she brought the moment to its crisis and said, "Let's go over to Berkeley and check out the scene over there."

Yes! At last! he thought. We're going to achieve escape velocity. He caught the Embarcadero freeway, soared through the canyons of the skyscrapers on the upper deck and shot straight across the Bay Bridge. Still he thought it was way too early to take her directly to his newly spruced up crib and they cruised the Starry Plow on Shattuck and ended up at Larry Blakes on Telegraph Avenue. These catacombs were popular with Cal students. Walker and Dahlia drank a lot of wine, danced to a hot band of Pete Escovito and his daughter Sheila on the drums.

There was a vampy insouciance in the predominantly lesbian turnout for the great lady drummer — Berkeley is the Saphic stronghold of America. There was much cruising going on. Butch dykes in slicked down hair or mohawks and wearing leather jackets were cruising ultra femmes with long wavy hair wearing slinky, glittery, glamorous evening gowns with thin straps over bare shoulders. Coming from Texas, Walker was having a little trouble with the open ambivalence to sexual type in the Bay Area. He began to get the uneasy suspicion that he was being studied. It actually occurred to him: I'm straight, I'm a straight male and I live in Berkeley and perhaps some of these dykes are observing me — learning male behavior from me. On the other hand, in San Francisco I feel like an oddity — the last straight man on earth.

Finally the couple got to his small efficiency apartment across the street from the hospital on Dwight Way. The apartment had 12-foot high ceilings. The walls were a warm color of sepia cream. The wood trim, wainscotting etc. was dark blue. The walls were covered with maps and charts. Walker had a double mattress on the floor near the very large metal office desk and that pretty much filled up the room. He brought out an elegant tray made of inlaid wood and crumbled a bud of sweet smelling sinsimilla into it.

"This was sent to me by a friend who grows in it New Mexico," he said. "It's a nice dry, high-mountain smoke." And in his thoughts he added 'not like that killer California weed that you keep coming up with.'

Dahlia stretched out her arms and twirled in the center of room, put her head back and twirled faster like a dervish or a ballerina. When she stopped she stretched her arms out further like she was feeling the walls of the Taj Mahal and said, "It's kind of weird to see so much space for a single individual."

She looked classically hip in her boots and long skirt and long straight hair. They smoked the joint out of a length of slender bamboo stalk Walker had cut and modified into a cigarette holder. He was proud of this piece of folk technology. Natural simplicity. Walker smiled: "To travel the smoke and make it mild."

Then Walker stretched himself out on the bed on his side with his head lifted off the bed resting in the palm of his hand looking up at her. He smiled a come-hither smile. She sat down on his desk chair, and took off her boots. Walker enjoyed watching the skirts flash a little bare thigh when she crossed her legs. She lay down beside him. You could see her hip bones protruding from under the taut waist of her jumper.

Her Latin beauty was alluring. Her lunar stoniness was easy to be with. Her anima invited him to look into his own mind.

For Dahlia it was extremely important that sex was not mechanical, that it was connected. She had to feel the psychological connection. Things like provocative dress — because it allowed the lovers to be in a fantasy image instead of the real world — any kind of subterfuge, dominance or submission, of not taking responsibility were considered 'dirty sex' by the house and not to be supported.

They held each other close in a hug and began OMing in long relaxing exhalations that got louder and louder as the fear evaporated and more presence came into their bodies. The expression on Dahlia's face changed from being a monalisa smile to a lascivious grin as she felt herself getting excited and let herself fall deeper into the experience. Later she would write about it in her Diary of a Commune

Nympho: *I felt myself wanting to really open for him. Relaxing my pelvis and relaxing into the mattress I noticed: I can feel the blood rushing to my loins. I feel my pelvis relax and my cunt opening like a flower.*

Walker loved how her tongue pushed out from between her lips when she throws her head back and allows herself to feel the pleasure. Wow, he thought. This is hot, like being up close and personal with a beauty in a girlie magazine. But then deep OMing and long sighs took them into a totally loving connectedness freed him from being in some sexual fantasy. After a long while of this his fear and anger began to subside. The wariness and Walker's lifelong tendency toward isolation and interminable shyness seemed to drift away in this more spiritual embrace.

Dahlia was very sure of herself. *A good tantricka is able to prolong these feelings from years of tantric practice of deep breathing in sex.* The sighing exhalations caught the rhythm of the two lovers and discharged the fantasy energy and fear, and helped the couple go further into feelings. They took off their shirts and rubbed bare skin on bare skin. She showed her excitement with an involuntary shiver that caused her to wiggle and squirm all up and down and brought a smile to her serious face. She rubbed up against him more.

Walker was feeling tremendous empathy for her. A moistness appeared in each eye as his empathy for her grew into emotion welling up the salt ocean of tears and fell feeling as Walker rubbed his torso back and forth across hers, as pairs of his and hers nipples erected— mashed over each other and sent glissandos of feelings shuddering through them —concushioning to the pleasure centers of both.

"Make more sounds," Dahlia said.

Walker's hands ranged and played over her chest and neck and lovely girlish face, as though playing a touch organ of joy and relaxation. As he teased her frame, sweet sighs and energy streams of relaxing muscles breaking down walls and squalls of feelings blowing up into squeals and OMs came up from her breathing and resonated in her mind with closed mouth OMmmmm sounds.

Kissing lips to lips they transferred OM vibrations. They

penetrated into each other through vibrational affinity.

They looked deep into each other's eyes; hers were glassy, far away, like the moon setting over some deserted hills. He looked at her breasts from the side. He thought of Mt. Fujiama or Kilamanjaro or mounds of vanilla ice cream with a cherry on top.

He smiled and imagined he was tribes of little men — horny monks on speed — scaling the mighty Matterhorn of her side. Or the little fishermen in the ravaging sea in the famous painting of Hiroshike of Fujiama, seen through the swell of an angry wave.

His mind wondered how it would feel if he were a woman. What must it feel like inside a woman's body. When he touched her, she felt like all nature, moving and responding to his touch.

"You sure are fun to play with," he said.

"I feel so much coming out of you," she said. Her eyes were opened wide in surprise. She looked like an excited school girl and said, "I really feel a lot of love — that you really like me — coming out of you."

Walker slipped down between her legs, spread the lips of her pussy and flicked his tongue back and forth across her clitoris. That got her juices flowing. The mild scent of her little cassolette tickled his nostrils, and set a fire going in the pheromone sensing neurons of his mind and excited him rigid down deep.

The commune nympho knows when to submit to her lover's caresses, when to relax and spread her legs open wide for him. And I could do that here, and not bump into another sleeping Lofter.

Dahlia took the opportunity of being in a strange bed to spread her legs wide for her lover.

I could feel my pussy is wet and dripping. I could feel energies damming up to burst out of me. And they did, running out as sex juice as I flowed nearer and nearer to the edge of my own wildness in intimacy. I came and I was all wet between my legs, I could feel it flowing into my asshole! My eyes were closed into little slits, my eyeballs were looking up somewhere way up in the back of my mind. I remember having my mouth open wide gasping. I could feel heat in my body rising, and I thought: he is going to take me over, . . . again. No he is not! I won't let him. I want to experience that intensity in my body without going over the edge. I lifted my hips up to jam my cunt into his face feeling his lips all over the soft outer lips of my pussy. My slit is warm and very wet pressed to his mouth. My lips to his lips.

Walker used his two index fingers to push back the hood and expose her little pink clitoris. He lapped his tongue over it in long cat-like strokes. She came again flooding out to wash over his lips.

It was really shocking and wonderful the way Walker looked up at me with his lips glistening wet with my pussy juice and smiled a most loving smile.

Dahlia propped herself up on her elbows, had drawn her knees up in the air and spread her legs open wider for him.

"I want to feel you inside me," she said.

Walker sat up reached over the chair and got a condom out of the desk draw and quickly put it on. He knelt in front of her holding her legs spread apart with his body. Walker gently touches his fingers around the outside of her pussy. She felt herself relaxing in his gentle touch. Her clit pushed into Walker's fingers. Yes!

The sensation flooded her pussy, legs and feet. Walker pushes his two finger deeper into her pussy and swirls them around in the juice. Softly, deeply. She thinks: It feels as if he is inside my body already, like a cock in my pussy. It is so sensational, warm, full over my entire body.

He brings out fingers of juice and rubs them on the head of his cock making it slick with her lube. Then he puts his fingers up her again. Dahlia struggled and squirmed against his strong probing fingers.

I want to experience the intensity of DOING HIM, *fucking him, sucking him. Then I become the do-er and he is the do-ee and he has to take it as I am taking him higher than he thought he ever could go, overwhelming his defenses with sensation.*

Dahlia said: "I want to feel you with my mouth."

What he saw next was Dahlia slithering down and closing her mouth with its razor sharp white teeth around the head of his penis. His monstrous penis stood rigid in front of her eyes. She could see the veins bulging, felt the smooth cap even under the condom which glistened with her pussy juice and spit. She lowered her mouth on it. She shook the man's rigid member. His horny ego towered over his empathic transpersonal spirit body, as the moans and bellows of his delight echoed off the walls.

Dahlia let herself enjoy these powerful moments being an instrument of joy:

I sucked his cock very slowly. I let the head of it nestle into the back of my throat. I impaled my throat on his cock! When I got it way back in there I relaxed and swallowed, gagging a bit and made his cock twitch and flare! My mouth watered and I let the saliva flow out over his cock, a juicy blow job to quench the heat radiating down my throat to my pussy.

Walker was moaning in exaltation. Dahlia was enjoying her triumph. Walker had this thought: Dahlia is a Compassion Artist. She first forces her mates to make sound, by making them moan in ecstasy. Dahlia laughed and tittered into the cosmic mike making it wetter. He sobbed and sighed. He felt caught between two mediums, he was in metamorphosing from a nymph into butterfly. He was simultaneously inhabiting and inhabited by all the niches of creation going from water into land and land into air susceptible to thoughts from all sides, sprawled out, vulnerable. Suddenly it dawned on him. Perhaps this is how a woman must feel.

But even more than her mouth the commune nympho knows how to use her eyes. Be like an unlicensed hypnotist, a snake charmer at a country fair.

His cock contracted and engorged to explode. This rigid shaking snake threatened to blow its top. He stopped her, cupped his hand around the back of her neck. He could feel her arching and straining against his interrupting her, relinquishing her power to his control. Sweat trickled down her neck, matting her long hair around her ears. The male ape's ego demanded he mount and dominate.

He got on top of her and entered her wet tunnel, got her pinned and writhing under his weight. He had better control on top. And her cunt reached up like a hand to grab him in and swallow him up, placing all of his little man in her snatchel.

He watched the bitch staring up at him, challenging him,

her compassionate eyes piercing his soul, made him frightened to look down into hers, lest she see who he really was. Yet in that eye contact he felt truly loved. He looked into her eyes and smiled, his baby blues clear and bright.

As Dahlia lay on her back Walker pinned her, pushing her legs back so her knees were back by her ears. She felt her labia spread open and her clit stuck further out. He slowed down his stroke, feeling the head of his cock getting pulled in by the sucking motion of her pussy. After a while Walker stopped moving and rested his body on top of her. His cock was up inside her pussy its full length. She felt fluttering waves of contraction flowing from the back of her pussy to the outer lips. His cock twitched the underside of her clit. She said, "Ah. Bulls eye, baby." She felt so relaxed, so in control. All the movement and sensation emanating from her pussy, surrounding the contours of his cock.

He gasped.

Dahlia asked him, "What is it."

He whimpered, "Oooh I'm so close to the edge."

"Wait, wait. Hold it," she said. "Your cock feels so good in my pussy. Don't move. I'll do all the work from down here."

Walker wondered about what was the spirit that came alive behind that face. She opened her body and showed him his own soul plugging into a cosmic energy, plugged into the ultimate genetic socket, as she pulled him tightly into her loving body. Her pussy squeezed him, milked him and he felt the corona of his cock flare out in another contraction.

All he could do was ride it out, bucking all the way, the Great Mother Rhythm as the lithe peristaltic movements of her muscles contracted and clung and hung around his huge manliness pulling so close, so sure. Sensational.

"I felt like we could go higher and higher," she said. "Let the energy built up more intensely." Their eyes locked onto each other, there bodies sweating under an enveloping orgasm. "I can feel our orgasm circulating through our bodies," she said. Slow, easy and . . . And he couldn't hold it any more and roaring came and came and came into her hot hole, not caring, letting it all flow out. And him with it.

What Walker felt left him afloat in a black void. Beyond the black hole. The couple lay there intertwined in heavy breathing, sailing out on a sea of saturated sensations.

Dahlia later wrote in her Diary of a Commune Nympho: *The men of the House would most likely not have come the night before. They would have carried forth this potent sexual charge for another day. Or several days in some cases. That was the ideal. It keeps the men turned on and beloved. Until of course the blueballs became unbearable and then that night the girl in his bed is going to have her hands full. Advice to commune nymphos: A woman in a group marriage has to kind of keep track of where her husbands are on the blueball scale. A commune nympho might tease a man for days. And you might think that it would be hard to be sure if the erection at hand was really an extension of the one the day before. And it would be hard, but in our commune it is required to engage in much, sometimes very explicit, verbal communication about what went on in a couple's session during small group meetings.*

Walker's post-coital ideations were much less formed. He was proud of his performance but confused. This was all new to him. His set of beliefs on the subject of sex were pretty much the standard issue American male sexual character views. Everything was rigidly structured. Morality was stacked vertically in steps from here to heaven and hell. The paternalistic society, brutal, selfish, macho, where men ruled by hard looks and an iron hand. And it felt weird to let the woman have so much control over how he felt. For your standard-issue Texan, sex is a lot like violence. He knew how to love on a chick. But this was not your average grab her and wrestle her down and throw a good fuck into her! We're not in Texas any more, where the men are supposed to be like stallions, and the women like mares. He thought women expected it this way; it was a man's duty to wrench the earth moving Orgasm out of a woman's body, out to meet the male ego, and then it was OK for the two intertwined lovers to dissolve in their minds like the zero reset button.

The next day was a warm Saturday and Walker asked Dahlia to go up to Lake Anza in the Berkeley hills and have a relaxed day soaking up some rays. Dahlia needed some kind of bathing suit, for she had only the clothes on her back. She put on one of Walkers blue T-shirts over her little panties. And well, Walker thought that looked pretty good. He said, "You'd look good in a wet T-shirt," She opted for stopping at the drug store and picking up a sweet little Danskin while he waited out in the van.

Lake Anza was already closed for the season. "I'll make a scofflaw out of you yet," he said, showing her how to climb over the fence.

"What's a scofflaw?" she asked.

"One who scoffs at laws."

They stretched out on the warm sand, beneath the little hill off to the side where they could not be seen from the road above. It was safe. He took a last swim of Fall, in the cold water, then came and lay down beside her on the towel.

"Don't get near me with those cold trunks on!" she shrieked.

He tried to get close to her and she kept him at bay by putting her foot into his chest.

That was understandable, but she seemed withdrawn for deeper reasons. He drove her back to the loft, had a bit of dinner and left.

In a letter to an old friend he wrote:

> They are some of the most real people I have met in a long time. Actually they are like a big bunch of kids romping all around with each other in a huge, never-ending slumber party, just a big bunch of kids so high on life, so whacked out on tantric Buddhism, and the awakening psychedelic of their own psychology.
>
> And the women! They look especially beautiful! They have strong bodies and are used to hard work. They, the more superior sentient beings, stand up and stretch their sweet anatomies in the morning, naked guiltless....
>
> They believe the mind is like one of the senses, like sight and hearing. What is happening comes to them in feelings, like the wind in one's face, which can be interpreted like reading and understanding...
>
> But I don't know, I fear it. It sets up these chain reactions being confronted with their micro culture.

Poor Walker. This term "chain reaction" had a special significance for him. It described a causal link (in his mind) between sexual pleasure and punishment by VD. And within a couple of hours he started getting that creepy feeling, herpes brought on by sexual agitation. He couldn't even speak of this to himself in his private diary:

```
     Chain reaction. Chain reaction. Set up a chain
reaction. It started a chain reaction. Like one
idea, or image of feeling gets hitched to another
shooting sensation and pretty soon you are really
rocking and unreeling, and pretty soon you are
picking up the parts of yourself.
     What a mess you are you realize. Diet bad, not
ever getting enough exercise, weak, short of breath,
false teeth, glasses, seems like no amount of loving
could ever get you back to feeling good the way you
like to be feeling. It took a confrontation with
Death to really make you shape up, to give you the
big wake up in your adult life. It took those primal
screams, those merciless screams down to the bottom
of your being to get release. An emotional
impossibility for your average cowboy.
```

Here It meant the virus. The chain reaction he was writing about in this veiled way was the onset of a herpes outbreak due to such vigorous sexual activity. Poor Walker couldn't even confide in his own private diary! —let alone another human being. For him, the idea of the translator inherent in the virus was that impetus in human nature to manage a spoiled identity, to make lemonade out of the lemons that life deals you. It began to take on the meaning of the virus which is the most ancient code-changing entity — been around since the dawn of life, part of the basic building blocks of life. It is the genetic machinery that sets life on its evolutionary way. As the old familiar creeping weepy feeling came over him, Walker listened to the same song on the tape player over and over, sinking into a mixture of maudlin dispair, mushy sentimentality and guilt. She did not know what it was that bothered him, yet still she was there with him in it, trusting him, and there he had been wrapped around her tight, like a drowning man hanging onto anything that floats. Tears started to run down the side of his face listening to the words. "It's my heart, it's your heart."

He thinks: the woman in me is coming out.

No it wasn't. I won't let it.

It was the band Translator.

"It's my heart, it's your heart. On my mind."

14

Tantric Sex Secrets

Walker was more scared of rejection than a cat is of
taking a bath. He went to the loft for a Friday night session
filled with the fear of losing her because he knew he must
divulge himself to her completely — tell her about the
herpes and risk losing her. Like all "guilty" people who lived
in the netherworld of odium, he wondered how any one
could like him. The cave of odium was in a mountain of
shyness on an island called loneliness across a sea of
isolation. He was wary of meeting new people and feared
being himself in their company. Over the course of his life,
starting with severe acne as a teenager, he had become a
lonely, isolated, ugly-feeling person. He had learned to be a
shadow seeking heliophobe and just fade away and not deal
with anyone that he didn't have to deal with. Subsequent
years as a dope addict and writer didn't help that. Yet
somehow he felt he could trust in Dahlia; she would help
him to see himself and to see himself in the others, in
relationship and to see himself in the group of the spirit.

Walker was trying to work out some kind of
compromise, and they were trying him out in group. Due to
her authority in the place he had been given some kind of
preferential treatment; Walker the interloper had been given
a semi-official designation as something of an "outside
husband" loosely affiliated with Dahlia's group marriage.
Walker had been assigned a 'person' —of course Dahlia
couldn't be his person because that would mean a complicity
could occur.

The phone rang. It was Walker's assigned "person,"
Jesse. He was trying to arrange a get together with Walker.
Walker was somewhat reticent until Jesse sweetened the
deal. "Lucia and Dahlia are coming along too," he said. "We
can go out to eat at Little Italy."

Walker had met Lucia and Jesse the night of the lecture
on Psychic Numbing. Lucia and Jesse had just returned from
spending several months up on some wild land that the

house owned near Mount Shasta. All the time on the land had given Lucia a wild beauty, in her energy and the clarity of her eyes and her complexion. He sunny face had a freckled, healthy aliveness to it. And her smile was mirthful and mischievous, dangerously knowing and alive. Walker had never seen a human being so clear and real as Lucia. And to him it looked like the House was letting Jesse and Lucia be a couple; maybe there was hope for him and Dahlia.

Walker met Jesse on the floor in the big room. They had a nice talk about Jesse's profession — civil engineering. Walker made some kind of joke about studying soil mechanics in college, "a class they called Dirt 101". Jesse was a very accomplished woodsman. He pulled out his super deluxe Swiss Army knife and began cutting a bandage for his feet. He had walked large blisters on them.

Dahlia came and talked to them, and Walker scrutinized her out of the corner of his eye. There was this far-out angry look to her face, and Walker became afraid that once again it was all over for them.

"You look really depressed tonight," she said coldly to him. Walker stared blankly at her. After a while she wandered off up into the loft to get ready to go out.

Then some group grope machinations ensued, in the tactic of straight-on linear confrontation. Walker, already trying to supress a mounting anger thought they were getting him onto the hot spot over some issue. He withdrew in suspicion. Simultaneously while Walker was being the focus in Dahlia's small group, a larger group had convened a circle around a young boy who was a friend of Luke, one of the pre-teen children at the loft. The boy in the circle was talking about a lot of things that were troubling him in his home.

"My father thinks they are brainwashing people over here," he said.

Walker overheard this and thought: The truth of it is they ARE brainwashing people over here! And they wonder why I'm depressed. They are starting to make me depressed. I just want to go out dancing and drink with my drinking buddies.

Walker was on the verge of taking off, when he decided to hesitate a little and said, "Let's change the energy a little, let's go out." He wanted to split. He was shaking his head: I just knew I shouldn't have gone out on this 'date.' Walker was just about to tell them to shove it and split, when Dahlia came down wearing the cutest little leg warmers, which set off her gams nicely. They leg warmers covered her slender calves; were pink and fuzzy and flaunted her sexuality without any coyness or teasing. Walker thought she was probably unaware.

Maybe I better try a little forbearance he thought. Finally Lucia came down and they got out the door. Walker concluded he would try to make the best of it with these two chaperones. Striding ahead of the others, he jumped into his van and prepared a comfortable space in the back for Jesse and Lucia. He placed a large comforter on their laps for a knee warmer.

They went to Little Italy in Noe Valley. In the restaurant, Walker could barely stand to look at the people, he was so uptight and tense, but after a while drinking the good wine and getting loose, the conversation turned to aspects of the mind. The two styles of meditation the Zen style and the Tibetan Buddhist visualization style were discussed.

Walker had recently been making a study of of meditation began to pontificate, as if he knew. "The Zen style was where you tried to erase all inputs into mind to achieve a state of matched impedance with the world. Like the body is as transparent as air. In Zen, you don't want to see any visualizations of the world because they represent hypnotic enticements, and you want to get to that white white screen of the mind where there is nothing, and you are just yourself watching the feelings and ideas flow on through."

"The Tibetan style," he said — continuing his pedantic performance, "of meditation is visualization, where you visualized in colored detail the embodiments of mental states, clothed in raiment of psychological texture."

Lucia and Jesse and Dahlia who were very experienced meditators tolerated the academic exposition and read it as Walker trying to belong.

After that they went outside totally bloated, had a smoke on a side street. *They* smoked dope; Walker didn't —since he was the driver. *They* hugged; Walker didn't — since he was the outsider. Walker still wasn't clued in that they were in a group marriage.

Later, on that autumn eve in North Beach, the men were walking behind the women down the Broadway promenade. Walker watched the way Dahlia's dark hair fell and swayed across her back. He liked to watch the sway of her behind, the movements of her looseness as she walked with Lucia. He was very proud of her. She was a flower that had grown up in his life. He was the developing heart. He tried to share this male perspective with Jesse, saying, "MMM, don't these women look fine from behind."

Jesse took this as you might expect, a man not in his tribe was commenting on his wives. Jesse frowned at him as if he had made some major sexist *faux pas*. Jesus, thought Walker, as he sped up and got into step beside Dahlia. Then as they were standing on the corner of Broadway and Kerney, waiting for the light to change so they could cross and Walker was casting his eyes about looking for somewhere to put them, he looked between the double swinging doors of a tavern and saw a boxing match on a TV. A crowd roared as two young Asians were duking it out. And an old, anachronistic, perverse element in Walker's make-up asserted itself as he leaned over into Dahlia's face and said, "Do you like boxing? Do you like to watch face-punch?" Walker didn't know it at the time, but it turned out to be the very fight and the very punch in which Dee See, the young Korean boxer, was killed by a punch in the head.

"What do you mean?" she said, looking arch and shocked. You don't say things like that to Dahlia. She got real pissed off.

"I think it's kind of beautiful myself," Walker said, "I mean to see two trained athletes going at each other. The human animal is a fabulous fighting machine."

They came to the front of the Saloon. Dahlia walked in and was looking for her friends. She came out and looked up at Walker and said, "What do you mean by that. I don't even want to go in there now." By now Lucia and Jesse were scrutinizing Walker giving him fearful looks.

"What's supposed to happen now," Dahlia said, "are we supposed to have a fight, and you are supposed to split, is that it? Or what!" She had a pouting pugnacious look on her face, like she might slug him a good one.

Walker then looked over a Lucia and Jesse and said, "But I do like to watch boxing, I find it beautiful. The human animal is one of the most well made animals; given a knife it can take on any predator and stand a chance against any animal on the face of the earth."

"I don't even want to go into the bar now," Dahlia said with exasperation.

"Let's go across the street to that coffee shop and talk about it," Jesse suggested. They entered Cafe Trieste and found a table up front among the beatniks being beatific. Dahlia was almost in tears.

'A day in the life of a fool' was playing on the sound system, and Walker kind of hung his head, and later slid his hand onto Dahlia's knee as she spoke of the violence in her past, especially from her mother. The idiotic Walker was still defending his position, and so the conversation shifted into confrontational group therapy about how he spoke in conversation.

"You are like a boxer," Lucia said to him, "constantly being defensive, ducking — it really requires a lot of energy."

In further groping it was brought up about Walker's father being a good fighter around pool halls, and how Walker wanted to be a good boxer, to be able to fight with him. Then each person of the four talked in turn about beatings and whippings they had withstood as children, and this commonalty of shared pain led into a discussion of how this pain really does affect your life.

"But I forgave my daddy," Walker said, "when I turned 30 because I realized how difficult it must have been to bring up 4 kids, and no wonder he was alcoholic, being married to my mother.

Walker thought privately about his mother, and how early on it was her that always seemed to disrupt their happiness, she always felt stuck and could never do anything, helpless, always only half there, while his father was vigorous and robust, but somebody you could never get to know either.

This talk, which lasted for a few hours, greatly disturbed Walker. Images from his childhood started "coming up". He saw himself running down sunlit corridors in the city. He was always running. He had always been in flight.

"One of the first experiences of sex I can remember," he started telling the others, "was this little girl in the apartment house in Montreal. She took off her panties, under her little dress, and so I took off my little short pants."

"I was a lot more exposed than she was, for she was all tucked inside, and had the dress falling down over it."

"My father got hold of me, and pulled me upstairs by one hand and spanked the daylights out of me for that, and I guess I somehow got the impression that sex was dirty, that the penis was dirty. I suppose that this incident and its associations (I couldn't have been more than 4) has colored my impressions of women and my ideas about sex ever since."

Rather than feel the pain of this, Walker began to wonder about and appreciate the way intimacy with these people had tripped his mind out. Having words with people sends you swimming back into the field of associations, into your own mythology.

Finally, they split for the Palladium disco. Walker was still standoffish, just wanting to be out in a friendly platonic fashion, especially having seen that look of anger and dejection on her face.

The sound system was EARTHQUAKE SOUND, reverberating around in bunker walls. Loud and relentless. At one point, all four of them got into a hug dancing on the brightly lit floor, Jesse and Lucia, Dahlia and Walker moving to the Grandmaster Flash rap tune 'Don't push me cause I'm close to the edge.' Walker thought: Yess I have rolled all the way across America and am now on the edge, about to jump off into somewhere. Maybe I should go with these people.

They were all piled into the front seat of the van, a jolly crew, when Walker pulled into the parking lot of the loft. Dahlia asked Walker, "Want to come up?"

"No, I better not," he said, backing down. He had vowed not to sleep with her another night until he had told her. "I've got a lot to think about."

Lucia looked at him with scorn, for not jumping at the chance to get into feelings. "Do you have to work in the morning?"

"No."

"Then why don't you come up with us."

"Well, I've got a lot I want to think about."

—

Feeling kind of sheepish for being such a cop out, he went out and bought her a gift. The only thing he could think of was a Swiss Army Knife. He told her about it when she phoned to invite him over for dinner. She of course refused. All gifts are considered coercive in group therapy.

The next Wednesday Walker crabbed, waffled and hedged his way to the Loft, a secret society, gradually. It was as if he was trying to move around in the city which was really his unconscious and somehow end up finding himself at the loft. First he gave himself the excuse for coming to San Francisco to see a film festival playing at the Castro. Then his itinerary was to take him to a salsa festival at Ceasers, on Mission Street, with its enormous cavernous ballroom, and rotating mirror ball. Slowly he was getting closer. Finally he plucked up his courage and went up to the loft feeling a little ridiculous about a) the letter he had sent her, b) some of the things he had said, and c) wanting to give her the gift. And also he felt really good about her now.

He buzzed the loft, a voice said "Who is it?"

"It's Walker."

"Walker?"

"Uh... Dahlia's friend."

Malcolm let him in, met him at the landing and was now walking him up, talking to him and saying that yes they did take visitors on a Wednesday night.

Dianne, the shy one in the group, a quiet person, a person who listened to other people, who had never spoken a word in all the time that Walker was there, was talking about a man she was keeping time with outside the commune. "He is into theater, has a degree in Physics, has moved to California to start a new life," she said. Then she casually looked over at Walker. "He must remind you a lot of yourself."

This quickly made Walker the center of attention. Malcolm made the transition: "You obviously have something to talk about tonight or you wouldn't be here."

Walker started talking about what had happened around

the boxer when last they were together, and more things about violence came up. Then Dahlia humorously brought up about the knife Walker had wanted to give her.

The group made a big deal about this and wanted to know what was going on. Walker told them, "It is a medicine knife. The concept of medicine knife is you can't buy a medicine knife, you have to be given one." He mentioned that he had never had much money to give people anything, and now he was making good money, and he wanted to give somebody he liked a good thing. "The Swiss army knife is one of the neatest little things I've ever seen. And there aren't that many good things in the world. Well — there are good boots, and good sleeping bags, good pens or a good bike."

"Or even a good beer," Lucia said.

"Yea, it's a pleasure to own something you dig on."

Malcolm wanted to confront him. "You're a writer, and presumably you know about symbolism, did you think about the symbolism of the knife before you gave it to her."

They all looked at him quizzically, with honest curiosity.

Walker knew they would be looking for the obvious, and he said, "Well a good knife does feel like a pecker in your hand."

That broke everybody up.

Malcolm, his proper British demeanor kind of shattered in confrontation to the southern dumbass, was astounded, "I'm sorry," he said, "I didn't hear you."

"Pecker, a good knife feels like a pecker in your hand."

This scene really broke everybody up, people giggling all around if not totally falling out of their lotus, and Malcolm kind of stumbled and laughed and said, "You wanted to give Dahlia a pecker?"

Then Morey came up with the idea: "The knife really represented castration, and that you are in the habit of giving your feelings away."

This struck home because Walker immediately got defensive and said, "I don't know about this amateur Freudian psychology."

"Wait a minute, let me finish," insisted Morey with an authority that was not to be denied, "You were so beat up that you don't even own your own feelings as a kid, and you grow up not even owning your own self." He let that sink in a moment and continued: "The knife represents some kind of symbolic bond. . . to someone you are close to. Your brother gave you yours."

"I once gave my brother a Swiss army knife . . . ," Dahlia interjected, ". . . to protect him from my mother."

"And you wanted to give it to somebody you felt close to," Morey finished.

After more discussion the group session was over Walker left.

A few days later, Dahlia called Walker.

"I'd like to get together, spend some time with you. Maybe come over to Berkeley," she said.

Walker was feeling low and this got him out of the funk. He spent the next day picking up the pad, mopping the floor. The kitchen and the bathroom were immaculate. He had scored a tape, of a band called Translator, and played it on a little portable AIWA machine. He got some tiny little speakers to plug into it at the Berkeley flea market. He played the tape a lot, in his small apt and as he drove around the city. Walker was especially touched by their song: 'My Heart, Your Heart'. For him it really spoke to the times. "It's my heart / it's your heart / on my mind / on my mind." Walker thought: the boy has such a beautiful voice. He sings that "on my mind" so plaintive. Some music is just Zeitgeist music. We are living in a time trying to bring about a revolution: the nuclear freeze, the possibility of communal living, but more important, this was a revolution of the heart. He was caught up with Dahlia in a revolution of the heart. He began to think of the song, as 'our song'. And too there was a great freeze chant: Stop this missile building.

Walker, a little older than some in the House, had yet to really warm to punk music. Walker found it clashing and repetitive but this band Translator seemed to combine the best elements of the punk music aesthetic — its frenetic, driving, steamroller energy that refused to be duped by manipulation — mixed with a strumming, jangling chorus of guitars that sounded as sweet as the Beatles. The result was a sophisticated big city toughness mixed with a tender, self-aware cynicism.

The song before'My Heart, Your Heart' was "Something changes when I leave my room.' To Walker it spoke of a hip sensibility that was also reclusive, beat-down, furtive, hiding, protecting — as if the narrator was surprised that he had the courage to leave his room at all. It showed Translator had a sophisticated sense of humor. Walker would spend hours wandering around in his room trying to think of the words he wants to say to Dahlia, "I know the world's on fire / we feel the flames again and again, / It's my heart / it's your heart / on my mind / on my mind. / it's not money not revolution / not this time / not this time." 1982 felt like the 60s again, but this time it was not about trying to be a hippie, not about seeing how much sex and drugs and rock and roll you could be into or how politically active you were, it was about the heart really opening this time. It was like being part of the last stand of love. Moreover, for Walker there was a deeper level: the term Translator was like the operation of the virus, it interjects a code modifier to get the cell replicating machinery to make copies of it.

But at the last minute she canceled on him, saying something had come up with House business and that she had to attend to it.

Walker went to the loft for a Friday night session with Dahlia as had been scheduled by the group. He felt like he was some kind of great anxious brute interloper determined to carry on the campaign to hold onto this princess in her castle. He was truly in love with her. He had never experienced such an intoxication of love, and he was filled with the fear of losing her. Yet somehow he felt he could trust in where she was making him go; she would help him to come to know himself and to be known by others, to see the group of the spirit. He had to have her. Dahlia was responsive when he touched her. He recalled of a nasty line from Burroughs: "best deep trance medium I ever handled" She was a girl with a woman's body, a dancer's body, lean, expressive, attuned in sympathy of feelings with fluid dark eyes penetrating to the heart. She *was* like some deep trance medium, a space ship to travel in, past the here and now to the constellation of the group. To the heart of hope beating in all humanity.

This kind of romantic sympathy is not the kind of presence needed in group, but Walker didn't know that. She certainly seemed to have very high highs and very low lows. And he somehow took it upon himself to lift up her spirits.

At the loft after meditation, they got into small groups. Things seemed to be going all right. At this point group was something he had to put up with in order to go out with her. They all had to be invited along like chaperones. Nevertheless, Walker tried to be charming about it, made Dahlia and the women in her group laugh when he said, "Well we could go to that vegetarian restaurant near Dolores Park, the "Nothing - Strikes - Back" restaurant, or we could go to the "Karma of No Return" restaurant on Church. When Dahlia came down from the Loft upstairs she was wearing a stunning red velvet high-necked Chinese shirt. She had on tight black pants and black suede pumps. She looked real good to him. The others had other plans and he and Dahlia were on their own.

This was it. The moment of truth. He was going to open his soul to her. Tell her the worst possible things about himself, put it on the line. He took her up to the revolving bar on top of the Hyatt Regency hotel downtown to frame the auspiciousness of the occasion. Even though in his own mind he looked like some kind of tall wild man and always did, he tried to feel part of the privileged crowd there. In line he started singing a popular song: "Everybody was kung-fu fighting, kicking butt fast as lightning," because she looked like a sportswoman ready for action. She left him to wait in line, and went to the girl's room. When she came back, he couldn't keep his hands off her. Slipping his fingers between two buttons he discovered she had taken her silk undershirt off! He pulled away for a second, to make sure nobody was looking, spent a long time thinking about it, then gently slid his hand down her front and felt bare breast. She just let him.

"I felt you pull away," she teased, "then the thoughts going through your mind, then you decided to go for it. Good for you."

It was a Friday night, there was a large well-heeled crowd. Tres chic and elegant couples and groups in bankers clothes and women in hose sat at tables near the window drinking mai-tais and singapore slings. Rich old ladies with pink and blue hair sat together without husbands. The whole restaurant rotates, giving a changing view of the Bay and the City. "I can't tell if it's us moving or it," Dahlia said.

After they ordered drinks, she put the onus on him: "What kinds of changes have you been going through since the last time we were together?"

He had a hard time getting started, then blurted it out: "I really care about you and I want you to know the truth about me. I've got to tell you my big secret. . . I've got herpes."

There was a pause.

"I have it too," she smiled. "I'm lucky. I have the kind that shows up only every year or so."

Heavenly God! Walker exhaled a profound sigh of relief. She understood perfectly what he had been through. And it was no big deal for her. His mind raced: or at least she had the antibodies so that he didn't have to be afraid of giving it to her; or at least she stood about the same chance as him. Was she just cavalier, or had he blown it all out of proportion in his life. He sat their in silence as the awful truth evaporated. They watched the full moon passing over the city and long sinister black submarine cruised past Fisherman's Wharf. She said, "I don't really feel much like dancing. Why don't we just go over to your place."

Walker began to see that his body was something to feel with. That it was time to put up the first of his flowers. He had bloomed! He had disclosed some of his darkest parts to a person to whom it really mattered. He felt so much in the acceptance. He wanted to feel himself, wanted to make love to this all American beauty. She was beautiful in her soul as well as in her body. He didn't from the outset feel a whole lot of jealousy. But he did feel a whole lot of need.

Back in his Berkeley apartment the stereo played the song, 'My heart, your heart. It's not money not revolution, not this time, not this time.' They laid down on the mattress on the floor, and Walker got to feeling really soft and loving in his person, and in a hug, a full-on hug, felt her heart chakra through his own.

He felt unbelievably soft and resilient with her, felt himself dissolve and he closed his eyes and hugged her to him and began to feel tears of joy streaming from him. This was what he needed. This was the step up to the next realm of being, the one governed by the heart, not money, not revolution, not this time, for this was the time of the heart.

Beating to the beta wave awareness of rock and roll heart to heart, Dahlia and Walker became a flying thing, beating its wings down past where they are now, able to make a promise to transmit it to the future.

They got undressed then and hugged each other kneeling, their nude bodies providing warmth in the winter apartment air. They made beautiful love for hours and hours. She was auming a lot and making long sighing sounds. That night Dahlia showed him the innermost secret of Tantric Love while she was giving him a most slow and exquisitely tortuous blow job.

She began auming and humming on the head of his cock. It turned his thing into his cosmic mike, and it resonated down through all his being. It was the most wonderful thing he had ever felt.

Oh blow job Oh / ummmmmm mmm she goes
auuummmmmmm
ummmmmmmmbuszzzzzzzzummm lick lick
auuummmmmmm / giving her maniac a lobotomy
the head is in a hummm job
the blow job is wild is wild is wild is wild
hummmmm mmmmm hummmmmmmmmmmmmmmm
the head is in the hummmmmmm of her mouth
HHHUUUUUMMMMMMMMMMMMMMMMMMM
the head is in the hummmmmmmmm of her mouth
the lovely blow job, the lovely blowjob
she pushes back her cascading long hair so he can see
her better hummmummmmms and squeezes
the ultimate aummmmm / the blowjob hummmmmm
the blowjoy hummmmmmmmmmmmm
the blowjob hummmmmmm / the blow joy hummmmm
HHHUUUUUMMMMMMMMMMMMMMMMMMM
the pressure is building up behind / the pleasure centers
are scrambling / the pleasure, the pressure, the pleasure, the
pressure HHHUUUUUMMMMMMMMMMMMMMMMMMM

In the morning she leaned back against the desk and said, "Walker you can put your pecker in my hand any time you want to, or any place else in me for that matter."

15

Tara the Bodhisatva of Compassion Rising in the Great Mandala Calendar of Days in the Dome of Stars

In early December, Dahlia spent a week by herself in a tent, pitched on the snow covered land that the commune owned in the Siskyou forests of northern California. It was in sight of Mount Shasta and she was looking forward to using the slow time to meditate.

She took the Greyhound bus up to just a few miles below the Oregon border. The driver let her out with her big pack and Gor-tex jacket, and snowshoes and gaiters right off to the side of Highway 5. She made sure she was out of sight of Franklin's farm house. She got off the road down the embankment and started walking along the right of way. The easiest way into their land was a surreptitious sneak along a creek, across the mean old rancher's land. It was intense, because they had had altercations with Franklin before. He wouldn't cut anyone an easement. She waited a while listening, looking where the creek came out of his property and went under the highway. She took a deep breath, ducked under the fence and headed in. She was scared to be caught trespassing and it made her angry.

The snow started falling but she was warm working her way up the frozen creek bed, careful not to be seen. And very careful not to fall and sprain or break a leg, she would be hell-pressed to get out of there then. It was a four-hour slow motion scramble over frozen boulders and rip-rap scrabble. By the time the sky was starting to glow red she was finally on her own land. She was in a hurry and wanted to get to the tents before it got dark. She was ever so glad to see their camp. The tents were two very large army barracks wall tents butted together. They had a layer of snow on the roof. She knew this would be good insulation if it didn't cause the roof to collapse. She was glad to put her pack down. She untied the flap and opened it wide to let some light inside. Each tent had a wood burning stove, set in a firebox with a proper flue out the roof. Someone had set up a platform on milk crates for a bed to keep off the floor, which was frozen ground covered with tarpaulin. There were some shelves. From fear of bears, and other animals no food stores were kept in the tent, but stored in a mesh pantry shed 50 yards away under a low tree. With the flap open to let in the setting sun she quickly got a fire started from the woodpile in the other tent. After getting warmed she did a few chores.

In the last bit of light coming through the tent opening from the setting sun she laid her sleeping bag out on top of her thermarest on the platform. She found the camp logbook on the shelf and started a new page.

Day 1
When I first got into camp I was tired because it is a long hike in. It brought up a lot of anger in me to have to skulk around on Franklin's land, creeping up the creek. But after I got on our land the anger dropped off and it felt so good to be back out here. There were only a few snow flurries around and it was quiet.

It felt glorious good to get into camp. I was looking forward to being alone. No distractions to meditation.

I got a fire started, to warm up the tent and me. I got the guinea hens some more feed and set them up with new straw. I decided not to use the Coleman lanterns because I had heard they were dangerous.

She banked up the fire in the stove for the night, then leaving on her long-johns crawled inside her down bag. It was strange and scary in the dark watching the flames from the grate throw shadows on the sloped tent walls. She drifted off to a restless sleep getting up a couple of times to stoke up the fire. Once she looked out the tent at the trees in the moonlight. They seemed to be reaching up their denuded twig-tips into the cold dark starry sky as if trying to grasp at the passing moon.

The next morning she stayed inside her sleeping bag 'til she saw light through the tent panel. She got up and stoked up the fire again with fresh wood. Outside she filled a cooking pot with snow. She heated it into water on the stove. She dropped three big pinches of lyche black tea from Chinatown into the water and made a billy-boil tea. Her day was filled with basic camp chores and cooking and cleaning.

Day 2

I set up a schedule where I worked only during day light and didn't use the lights because there was natural light even though the days were kind of short.

There was a lot of snow on the roof, and I was afraid it would weigh in so I swept it off. I brought a bunch of wood into the tent, for it to dry out and to have a stash. I cut the wood.

Though there is the sump and lines, I broke ice and drank the water outside because it was more fun.

I washed dishes. People ought to do their own dishes.

The next day she took a long hike over the hills up the road through the rolling timberland of their property. She imagined herself to be a woman of Tibet, a nomad living in a yurt on the windswept plains. She was away from her tribe tending sheep. It was a glorious clear sunny day and her walk was perfect.

When she got up the hill a ways and looked back at the camp she could see the lake they'd dug out of the low-lying basin at the bottom of their property. Since there was enough creek flow it was not frozen and in fact there were gold fish surviving the winter in it. Being in the mountains made her recall a trip to Nepal she took with Eric and Frieda and Denise and Greg and Jesse and Lucia a couple of years ago. They had stayed in Katmandu and done the Anapura trek. She remembers the great affinity she had with the women she saw. She had enjoyed their lean dark looks and out of respect wore sturdy skirts that she bought there. She wished she had one on right now because she had to take a pee. She remembered the necklace she bought there, lapis and silver, but she never wore it. She wondered about reincarnation. It was very hard for a westerner to accept, unless you took it in the Jungian sense of being reborn many times in this life.

Climbing the hill made her warm enough to open her down jacket and take off her toque. She shook free her long black hair and felt free and wild and breathed deep the clear country air. Further up at the top of the hill at the fork in the road leading off to their orchard she saw Mt. Shasta away in the distance shimmering in a shining snow field. She said the mantra, "Om Mani pade hum," to help her feel the immense presence of the creative source more. She dropped her trousers and long johns down to her ankles and squatted ignobly to pee.

Further up she came to the high intake of their water system and inspected it. It was there that she saw what was a large cat footprint. A cold chill ran through her as she realized a mountain lion was about. This snapped her out of her fantasy, and she started back to camp. She had not realized she had come so far. It got quite dark on the shady side of hills away from the sun. There seemed to be animals looking at her out of the hollows of shadows. She imagined there were deities in the forest. And demons too. She felt watched.

She kept a stout walking stick someone had left in camp beside her at all times as a weapon. After much trouble priming the carburetor, she got Kong (the giant army transport vehicle the house owned) started in case she needed to drive out. That night she set her Swiss army knife open by her bed and club within reach. She awoke in the night and thought she heard footsteps crunch through the snow outside the tent! Dahlia grabbed her stick. "Hello!" she shouted, with as deep and fierce a voice she could muster. "Who's there!" After a long moment the footsteps crunched away. She spent the several remaining hours until morning being afraid, unable to sleep. She started Oming and chanting mantras quietly and then more loudly to calm herself. Finally she gave herself over to the flow of Big Time and slept.

Day 3
I saw mountain lion tracks!
I had gone for a long hike. At first I was pretty scared. I high tailed it back to the tent. All the while I felt the presence of the cat, don't know if it was just my imagination or what, but felt something trying to out-circle me before I got back. It seemed to take a long time.

It was almost dark when I finally got back to camp. I was thinking I might have to try and drive out in Kong if it came to that. I started Kong, had to prime the carburetor, and charge the battery with the generator. It started to snow and get wild.

I heard some wolves on Mt. Shasta off in the distance.
It helped me a lot to do some chanting and make sounds.

The next day, some of the guinea hens had disappeared.
Dahlia didn't know whether they had just wandered off, or
whether the cat or a wolf or a dog got them. But, she
rationalized, the cat would have to be awful hungry or awful
sick to attack a human, and that put her mind at ease.

Day 4
It felt good to make radio contact with the loft.

A few days after she got back she met Walker in La
Boheme, as she was emerging from a dance class in the
studio upstairs. She felt like warrior woman doing leaps and
pirouettes and even a *tour jete´*. She was looking real good
and her energy was real good from being just back from
spending a week by herself snow shoeing and fending for
herself in the woods. How clear and simple life had been just
doing the daily things necessary for survival. To Walker she
looked cute and girlish, with those knee-high leg warmers all
the girls just had to have that year. You could not *move* in the
world of dance without a pair.

She was feisty, and wound up, and agitated and beautiful
and Walker became astounded at the profundity of her
beauty. A real deep psychological beauty.

"Dance class brought up a lot about moving and looking
like the other girls," she said.

"What does it bring up?" he asked. "You look tall and
slender like a ballerina."

"Well, you look at your body in the mirror, and I have
always felt so estranged from my body, I mean I feel a lot
less so now that I have been in the House, but it used to be
like walking around inside a foreign movie."

Walker had made the plans for *this* evening. He wanted
to take her to a movie about his birthplace, Montreal, and
maybe get into a discussion to give her some idea about
where he came from. Walker argued, "Since I picked the
movie you can be my guest. It'll be my treat." Before going
into the theatre, she had to have a glass of eggnog for her
supper. It was delightful to be in a swank restaurant in San

Francisco. They felt more like colleagues than lovers.

A girl in a sweet mini-skirt sashayed through the restaurant, turning all eyes.

"I knew they'd come back," Walker commented with appreciation, "and I'm glad they did,".

"Yeah, I don't dress like the other girls do either," was Dahlia's reply.

Walker thought Oh, god now I've put her on the defensive.

This vulnerability on her part struck him. Poor Dahlia, he thought, smiling tenderly at certain things picked up here and there during the evening's conversation. Walker felt a wave of tenderness wash over him at the idea that Dahlia who was so beautiful, a really strong, wise woman, should be so caught up in the high school popularity syndrome. So there *was* a network difficulty in her own self image as a woman. She's afraid of not looking like the other women!

Walker tried to reassure her.

"I think you look really good in that long dress you wore out dancing at the Saloon one night. I like the way it swirled around you, and I like your long hair. . . You have a real smile and you look approachable and interesting."

The film, *Suzanne*, brought up a lot for Dahlia as well as Walker. Dahlia talked about her first sexual experiences. "It was so awkward being in high school. I remember this boy I really liked, and I wanted him to touch me so bad . . . I really needed to be touched, because there wasn't any love or touching going on at home. Yet it was impossible, there was so much of a guilt trip going on."

For Walker the film revived a lot of painful memories of how he lost his virginity. He told her about how Edouardo Mendez's uncle took them down to visit a whore in the boys town area of Neuvo Laredo, which is how most Texas boys did it in the days when he was coming up.

They drove up to the top of Twin Peaks. It was a clear night. Strong winds had blewn the clouds away and now were felt as hearty gusts rocking the car and whistling under, over and around it. You could see the whole bay, all the way down to San Jose. Incredibly deep light-profusion clarity.

It was a beautiful spot. Walker really wanted her. That was clear. He slipped over into her bucket seat and held her close and they sighed. Holding her tightly they looked at the scene. Many small lights circle the bay and the bay wears them like a garland of lights around its cold darkness. Softening his gaze and opening his heart he let the goddess enter him on the lights. And the geology undulates them, string of lights, lights at sea, rocking, floating. Like ideograms, it appears as a giant electronic arcade game or cave drawings of a new tribe. A tapestry of woven optical fibers.

Who manipulates, who plugs them in. The great string of lights, seen from the peaks, seen from the high satellite eye in the sky.

The Golden Gate spans the cut. Through this gate the East enters.

Through long adaptations the beings have set out lights in the dark around the dark waters.

And the geology undulates them.

By day demography snarls traffic in a non-stop rush hour.

Safe in dreams, the little lights drift in and out of the demography.

Radio towers rise on the peaks, altars to the sky gods.

And in his lap a woman, she draws you in, leads the way. Compassion is her art.

Tirelessly she works at it, ever in focus, she enjoys long days in its embrace. She floats above the manic depression rhythm of days. A light flight over the hills, circling the bay.

Men run wild, saturated in the hormones of aggression. She moves easily from one bed to another takes men into her arms, frees them from their mother, so that they may return to another.

The great mandala calendar of days in the dome of stars. We didn't ask to be born. We are rarely synchronized with the natural clock, never at one with ourselves, always at odds with the moment, not this time, not this time.

Radio towers are flowers that bloom in the sky. Their fragrance is music in the air waves. They produce pictures and sound and sell life styles, the external language of persona, the electromagnetic culture, the highway, the houses, the neon lit bars, the restaurants, the telecommunications business. The whole scene manipulated by the visible and invisible wires of this all powerful dynamo. The city sends out great spans across the bay, bores tunnels through mountain, floats ships like toys in the bath.

Dahlia smiles her shy sexy grin, wiggles around on his lap, looks into his eyes. They kiss. Swooning, he hovers and zooms like an astronaut down from his high place in the sky to race along with the traffic below.

Daily the people migrate on highways through valleys winding down to the sea. Thus the hill people do commerce with the flatlanders.

Thus has it always been.

The small lights hang like bright fruit from a large vine, intertwined around the bay like a garland.

The geology has gathered them into its folds.

Headlights blur into streaks.

The geology draws the headlights to and from the city in necessity like signals on a large switchboard.

The big dipper scoops out some black sea.

Walker sighed, "I look at all this and think about it all, all the forces that got it started, down to the evolution of DNA, and I am swept away by feelings. That's probably why I got into science, for fear of feeling too much."

He disolved into her bucket seat.

Wild winds did blow, and rock the car to and fro. It was a strange night with the powerful city below.

She asked him to stay with her in the loft.

He became agitated and looked around at the sinister shadowy landscape, unable to sustain the feelings of the moment.

"What are you looking at out *there*?" she asked.

He didn't know, made something ludicrous up. "You might look up and see the Son of Sam standing there pointing his big bulldog 44 at you."

She laughed nervously. "You sure do have a weird sense of humor."

"Yea, but I make you laugh," he smiled.

"Sometimes. . . but I wonder what I'm laughing at."

Back at the loft, they bedded down for the night. She was having her period. He held and caressed her all over for a long time. He felt every inch of her. Her soft womanly tissue was so relaxed, so well connected to the loose joints. He turned every part of her into an erogenous zone.

"I can still smell the forest in your hair. Can that be?" he asked.

Late in the night she sucked him off. It was an exquisite torture of an orgasm.

"What was happening in your mind, right before you ejaculated," she asked.

"Uhhhh, ha..ha, I don't know."

"It's just another way of not wanting to prolong the feelings, when you come too soon," she said.

Walker didn't say anything, but he knew she was right.

Instead he asked her, "Do you like to be penetrated when you are having your period."

"Yes."

They talked some more about her week up on the land. She seemed a lot stronger.

He asked her about the tantric lovemaking. "Do you think I'll ever get the hang of it?"

"You're amazing," she said. All the while she had this delighted grin on her face. She liked his touch.

The next morning she was putting on a pair of fine Indian mukluks, all set about with beautiful design. She had made it a point of situating herself lower than him. She was looking very girlish, wifely and being attentive and sweet.

He was ringing with her presence, feeling the imprint of lying next to her body all night long. He was always feeling her presence now, in his mind, in his heart, feeling all that womanliness that had come through her.

Women really are at the other side of being in some ways. The being that was solidly there, in the body, waiting, receptive. Is there a Tara in the Tibetan constellations?

16

Group Shower Authority

Walker began spending more time at the loft. The first time he saw Chase working was pretty scary. Walker had never been in therapy, had never even considered it, knew nothing about it. He had the standard American idea that it was pretty ridiculous to pay money to talk to somebody when you could talk to a friend. Nor did he hold much truck with religion. He didn't have much respect or trust for authority either, instinctively finding cops, lawyers and men in white shirts with ties untrustworthy. He had seen Chase around the loft, and at various of the talks that the Center for the Study of Consciousness put on during the freeze. He thought Chase looked fierce, like an Indian chief; he had a powerful red melancholic aspect. Walker already felt defensive and immediately felt like he would get into a big hassle with him.

Having slunk in, Walker made his way around the back of the Big Group, and leaned up against the wall. He was behind Lucia, because he felt he could trust her most.

He was shocked at how Chase kept on trying to penetrate the passive, depressed mood of Dianne. She kept retreating into a blank stare. When she did that Chase attempted to prove an anger response with: "Come on, dummy! Wake up! Where did you go just then."

Again and again Dianne would go off inside her self, and just stare and not respond. Perhaps the beginnings of a catatonia? Chase was using shock and love to break into her passive depressed mood. When one of the communards freaks out or has just had enough and can't stand it any more and begins to start to leave, the Group circles its wagons and becomes like the army trying to deal with fight-flight phenomena.

Later when they were all around her in small group, Dianne kept on leaning against the wall.

"Hey," cried Lucia, "why don't you move into the circle." She motioned toward Dianne, drawing an open palm up towards herself.

"Yea, move in close," said Jesse.

Walker was freaked out by his first taste of group therapy. He didn't know what to make of it, had no one to ask. In these cases sometimes things get so bad all you can do is hug your diary and play it cool.

Sun. Dec 11/82 Started to get more in touch with myself. It was good at the loft last Wednesday. A simple thing about Dianne leaning against the wall, instead of being in lotus position. The people in our small group started talking to her about not supporting herself.

— —

"One takes strange gains away," he said to Dahlia once when they were opening the door to her building together.

— —

One night after group Dahlia said, "Let's take a shower together."

She expected him to have the same ease, warmth, compatibility and looseness that she felt with her female and other partners in the loft.

A nervous response ensued. Walker smiled and said, "I don't need one."

But Walker was feeling like he had copped-out. He knew he was here to confront himself. One of the main efforts of the group is to confront the well-established false self and to uncover the real self which has been rejected and suppressed.

The loss of privacy involved in communal living is obviously one of the most difficult things about it and the House used this to attack narcissism and confront unreality mercilessly. Having to go to the bathroom in a public toilet with no stalls was a kind of mortification exercise. Life in the House was like being in a nudist colony most of the time. They all really were married to each other and all together.

The bathrooms had three open toilets each, side by side. Walker was terrified that if he followed Dahlia into the bathroom he would embarrass her or another communard sitting on the throne. However, he told himself, they had chosen to live like that without privacy. He decided to take up her invitation.

He follows her through the door. Thankfully they were

alone in the long bathroom, with 5 sinks and mirror stations, the three open thrones, and facing them two porcelain contraptions he had never seen before. They were not urinals, not toilets and they had nozzles point up. My god he thought, that must be a bidet! He had heard of them. Read about them in a French porn book.

After turning on the water, Dahlia gracefully climbed into the shower as Walker casually undressed himself in the steam-filled room. He hung his clothes on a peg in the wall mounted rack provided. He can see Dahlia's silhouette through the semi-transparent curtains. Immediately the friend set free in-between his legs begins to awaken at his owner's thoughts. He pulls back the curtains and joins her in the shower. Dahlia is all wet and facing the shower. She is letting the water run down her shapely golden brown voluptuous skin.

Walker tried to be casual. "That's a bidet, isn't it."
"Yes it is."

He played with his redneck persona. "I've heard of those things but never seen one before. I hear tell you can make 'em shoot water where the sun don't shine."

This made Dahlia laugh. She turned and looked at him smiling, then got more serious in her eye contact. He looked back, embarrassed. She smiled and steped aside, motioning for him to enter the spray. As he moved forward his wang is startled by the water, and accidentally brushed past her slick soapy bum. His penis elongated to the semi-hard-on position. He turned to hide it from her and any communards who might have entered the bathroom. She reached out to soap his back and absently-mindedly lets her hand graze across his bum. This brought his cock to fully erect position.

As he stepped back to let her get under the shower, his rigid cock sticking out of him accidentally brushed her soapy wet bum. She was shocked by this. Because the men of the house are so used to nudity and innocent purposive bathing activity in the shower that they don't get turned on any more.

She smiled up at him, but is a little bit freaked out because if others see him like that there will be some explaining to do about provocative behavior. "Get away from me with that thing," she laughed, and Walker, turning beet red all over because he is not like the other guys in the commune, tried to think of garbage and maybe lawns, anything boring to make the boner go down.

His shyness was something she decided needed changing, something she decided to take on and overcome. When they laid down on the floor on her futon, there was a woman right next to them, almost touching, casually reading a magazine in a small light.

And Dahlia expected to get into sex!!

Walker just could not do it. He became very discouraged at himself because he had too much control to make love in front of a someone else. This was very frustrating. He got pissed off and started putting himself down for being such a prude.

He started to bolt, get dressed to stalk out in humiliation, when Dahlia grabbed him across the shoulders and under the arms and threw him back down on the futon as he halfheartedly struggled to get up and leave.

"I don't even know why you hang out with me!" he said deep in self put-down.

"Because I like you," she grinned.

17

The Husbands of Acid House

Walker and Dahlia had been talking about tripping together. He came over to the loft in the daytime one Saturday morning. As he came up the stairs to the upper level of the loft, she came half way down to greet him, her hair wet and wild from just having been washed. She looked tall and especially lanky, a country lady in a red checkered flannel jumper. This was over a crisp pink frilly blouse. She looked like a tall, willowy English school girl. It was the first time he had seen her legs in the daylight and they were unshaven. She looked warm.

They hugged and looked around. It was a clear day, sunshine pouring through the windows that went below the floor of the loft, making the waxed wood shine like a huge ballroom.

There was another woman sleeping in her bag on a futon on the far side of the room

"Who's that?"

"Loretta."

There were some 35 futons in the pile of futons, it was as big as a car. They looked so inviting. "Can I jump into that pile of futons?" he said.

Soon she joined him and they were rolling around like too kids in a haystack. As he hugged her and kissed her, his hand moved down her spine, until he encountered her bare bottom beneath the hem line of the chemise, which he instinctively pulled down to cover up her perfectly well-rounded derriere.

This husbandly reaction provoked her scorn.

"Are you afraid somcone will see?" she chided.

His easily embarrassed demeanor, embarrassed him even more. Walker was always having to feel his controls confronted by Dahlia's easy looseness. But he kept hugging her, holding her, rolling around with her. He put his leg between her legs, and kept feeling her little white breasts making the nipples poke up against the starched cotton ruffles of her blouse. The girl-woman in her provoked protective and lecherous thoughts. It was an exquisite fusion of roles. Sometimes when making love to her he felt as though he were comforting an angry child.

She showed him a large rectangle of 4-way blotter acid with a Sphinx on it.

Walker could see that now here was a young college graduate woman who just wanted to get down with her man and talk it all out, to get down and do some psychedelics with him. To be sure, he had taken LSD but much preferred the organics — peyote and mushrooms. Too, he was a day-tripper, felt compelled to move and walk a lot especially into the great fractal convolutions of nature when surges and rushes of energy got ahold of his being.

Dahlia had taken hundreds of acid trips. One year Chase had the whole House drop every weekend. These acid trips would convene in huge group meetings and sometimes group sexual encounters. Often a member of the house would drop acid and spend time with their parents, to get a different perspective. This was a really frightening experience, but insightful.

The LSD excursions into phenomenology often took place in nature, on their land in Hawaii, or now in California. It was a marvelous sacrament that let them find their way into things, because it helped blur the boundaries of self and other and past and now. With experience the trips deepened from epistemological play with the colors and sounds and attributes of phenomena. They were able to admit and observe into consciousness the repressed and hidden aspects of their nature, and though this was terrifying at times it helped build the strength of ego necessary to handle even deeper energies, the mental objects and constructs and projections. It allowed them to have out of body experiences, to experience the 'light body' —the form of forms which allowed them to get, for moments at a time, into the transcendental source from which all things flow.

When they went down to the lake, they were so high and together and in love and so vulnerable and sensitive to it all that they thought they were able to see through the eyes of the swans in the lake. And they were able to see through the eyes of each other.

LSD let loose the magic in the world that broke down the sense of separation which lead to dualistic grasping. Indeed the sacrament of LSD was considered the shortest path to Buddhism because it showed one how the fabric of his reality was a construction of images floating on fields of the imagination. LSD as much as Jung, the Beats, psychotherapy, the reaction to the selling of indulgences in the temple, or the turmoil in Asia was responsible for bringing the swans to the lake. But Walker was not at all used to tripping with other people. He felt too stiff, too weirded-out by the general environment. He demurred.

Now, it is a gross breach of hip etiquette to not drop acid when offered. Dahlia questioned why Walker didn't want to drop the acid with her. Walker thought about the one or two women he had tripped with — Terry, Colleen. It had gotten very mystical and he knew he was not in a place like that with Dahlia yet. Walker was beginning to feel like he was being a drag, and offered to leave, so that she could drop.

"I suppose I've set it up, so that you don't trust me somehow," she said, sadly.

She carefully tore along the perforations of the page, separating out a quarter pane of the 4-way.

"You won't leave if I drop it?" she said.

"No."

And sticking out her tongue, she coolly placed the hit in the center of it.

Walker thought about the women with whom he had dropped acid. You have to really trust them. There is a sacred pact among people on psychedelics when the boundaries between self and other or the constructs separating past and present have been dissolved by acid: you should not do anything to scare them while they are in that very vulnerable state.

After a while they got into a conversation with Loretta, who is perhaps a godmother of Loft liaisons. Dahlia was having a hard time with the idea that he had not dropped with her, but Loretta smoothed it out.

Walker wanted to assure Dahlia of his feelings for her. "You're a strong, wise woman, and the world needs more people like you." The two women thought about this statement for a while.

Dahlia was hugging her knees, like a waif —little Alice — and Walker felt that kind of protective feeling, that kind of catcher in the rye feeling, when you are the keeper of people who have taken a psychedelic. He was always having to be the responsible big brother. He had usually been the driver in long-distance over lonely-highways drunken escapades you get into in Texas back when he was a teenager and gas was 19 cents a gallon.

"Sounds like he really wants to go somewhere with you," Loretta said. That opinion from her old friend relaxed Dahlia. Walker breathed easy, grateful for the support.

He and Dahlia retired to Chase's room. Since he was the house therapist and head guru, he had his own room for privacy in sessions. "Sometimes when you're on acid, it is helpful to have a mirror to look at your eyes," she said. Struggling, they lugged in a huge full-sized mirror, positioning it along side the futon so they could look at themselves.

They started hugging and chanting, OMing, making sounds. Walker had learned from this practice, that a certain kind of breathing, a sort of fairly fast almost slow panting breathing, with audible involuntary sighs, that sometimes felt almost like a shudder of awakening or a sob —but not that far — from deep in the lower abdomen, caused him to go into a relaxation response, where a lot of his fear dropped away and he could drop inside his body and feel more of himself. Walker was delighted to watch his hand on her perfectly rounded bottom reflected in the mirror. She had her back to the mirror and was running her hands over him. He felt like an artist stroking the long curves of a women's body like one of those nudes with the long shapely torso in an Ingres painting. Or like a belly-surfer running his hand over the waxy surface of his board before the big ride.

"You certainly are lean," he said.

"You are too."

When someone is on acid it's easy to get saturated on physical feelings. Walker certainly knew this in himself. When he did psychedelics his mind would get speeded up so fast that he became too distracted to focus on sex. He was perhaps coming to see this as his mind manufacturing thinking to distract or intercede with deeper feelings that could be threatening to the ego. Walker felt it was necessary to check in to how she was feeling, because for him, if he were the one on psychedelics, it could be very frightening to contemplate getting into sex. She on the other hand might have different expectations. Walker didn't know about Dahlia's extensive experience as psychonaut. She was very adept at it; it was like a sacrament in their religion. After a while Walker decided to take some risk, change the energy and get them started talking.

"I'm embarrassed about the letters I sent you."

"Why? They were thoughtful."

He started teasing her. "I cried when I wrote that letter."

She could tell he was teasing her with his seriousness and she laughed, "Ohh boo hoo. It's all so serious with you."

Then he told her about how the other night when he inexplicably cried on her breast while listening to the song by Translator. And he was trying to get it out about the heart chakra and she laughed at this great deep felt admission of learning what the heart knows. And she generally kept on giving him a hard time, so he gave up and went into his joking mode.

"I bet you got down with your sisters, like in a sorority, and read that letter to them, and had a big laugh and a guffaw, and a few titters as well."

"No I didn't," she said play-acting arch, defensive.

Walker inhaled a sharp gasp overdoing fearfulness. "I was really mortified, when I thought I saw Morey bring it into small group.

He waited to see her smile at the mock hysteria. "I thought he was going to read it to the whole group."

She smiled in the warm yellow sunlight coming in and angling off the mirror onto the tankhas, bouncing off the paraphernalia of a shrinks shop like light undulating in a swimming pool. He was picking up some kind of contact high from her. She appeared to be looking younger right in front of his eyes, then she would shimmer and be back to herself. She was traveling in and out of time.

"It is really beautiful," he said. "Here you are. Changing right in front of my eyes, from being a 32 year old woman, to being a 16 year old school girl. It is wonderful for lovers to be able to exchange fantasies that way."

But the word 'fantasy' ticked her off and she would have none of it and wrinkled up her nose in disgust at his romantic fantasies and began to quickly undress.

"O god no, let me get out of this ridiculous get-up."

She stood up, bent all the way over, caught the dress by the hem and lifted it over her head like a long shirt; dropped it, then quickly unbuttoned the blouse and laid it gently aside as she knelt down beside Walker. He got up on his knees and there kneeling they embraced. Then he gradually laid her down on the futon.

He said, "You just lay back and relax. Let me feel you. You don't have to do anything."

Dahlia sighed and relaxed back in the afternoon giving herself over to the pleasure of his touch. She thinks, Walker is doing me, yeah.

He asks, "How do you feel. Do you feel high?"

He is petting my pussy lightly. It is easier for him to moan and OM as I am whimpering softly now. I am lying back, not doing anything, letting him do me, not feeling like I have to do anything.

Walker slowly, sensuously stroked her clit. She gasps and inhales. "Yes like that. . . slowly." Dahlia took his hand and his finger, "Here let me show you." And in a very small movement rubbed his finger over her clitoris and then down just inside the lips of her cunt. Then just a very slight movement back and forth. It quickly brought on that tingly melting expanding feeling she liked. It was electric.

She said: "Wow that is wonderful, just what I wanted." She thinks: I am sliding . . . running out. Slipping into the stream. I am going to go over the edge. He slows down his strokes. Not now, not this time, not this time. I love it that he keeps me high. He slides his fingers in my vagina. My pussy feels so warm and soft. I sense him getting undressed, I just lie back feeling warm and happy. He lies down beside me. He gently rubs his hand all over my ass and pussy. He lifts my hand up gently by the wrist and drops it on his cock. I grasp it. With one hand he opens my pussy and gently pushes his fingers back into my vagina. My pussy contracts. I am holding his rigid cock in my hand. It feels strange and hard, like I am holding a telephone. I squeeze it. He gasps. Oooh who. Baby. Oooo! I get this image of putting it to my ear and talking into his balls — the com-phallus. It makes me laugh out loud. It feels so good to laugh. Giggling, I lose focus. I feel the slow stroke of his finger in and out of my vagina. I began to stroke his cock in the same slow intentional manner simultaneously squeezing his cock. I could feel our heat and energy circulating through our hands and bodies. It was emanating in heat. Surely this must be the enjoyment body of awareness. Slow, easy and sensational. I felt like we could go higher and higher. I feel my clitoris long and relaxed emanating beyond the body, tumescent. The energy in my body is begging to fluoresce. Yes! This is a kind of enlightenment.

Dahlia said, "Just hold your hand there and don't move it." By moving my hips I start to rub my clitoris even more slowly against his rigid finger. I feel the walls of my vagina start to vibrate. She said, "I want to feel your penis in my vagina." I moan, my pussy is contracting, as the warm sensation spreads all over my body.

Gently, both of them sweating now, he slides into her hot tight slit. He fucked her with the short, slow stroke -- barely moving, filling her.

I could feel our orgasm circulating through where his penis was inside my body and I squeezed his cock hard with my vagina to hold him there and our bodies stopped, suspended there. And he pushed slow against the hold. And as he slowly pushed, a blast of orgasm, powerful, like a rush of water from a fire hose, poured from my pussy.

Her orgasm lasted about 10 minutes. Her body flushed red and hot and melting all over. She was yelling and moaning at the top of her lungs. Her eyes are burning as she slid over the edge. He pulled out. He'd save this one for later. Walker just held her.

And in that short time she came floating back to our world she felt she was made right again, her head clear, body relaxed, smile on her face and a sparkle in her eye. Lucy in the sky with diamonds.

They played like this for hours. She'd lie on her stomach, with him relaxing on top of her, his semi-erect penis between her thighs. After a while she'd start to wiggle and make him hard again, then they'd roll over and start hugging and AUMing, and build to another penetration and wet blasting orgasm for her, him holding off.

As the people from the loft started coming home toward the end of the day, Walker felt conspicuous and ludicrous with this woman changing ages in front of his face and screaming in his ear. Surely they must know we are in here.

Dahlia and Walker decided to go outside for some food. Outside on the street Walker had the feeling that people were all the time smiling at him now. They went to a vegetarian restaurant on 18th and Dolores called Real Good Karma, and had a long feast sitting cross legged at a low round table made out of a telephone spool.

"I would do anything for you," he said, at one point in the evening's conversation. "Is there anything you would like me to do."

"I'd like you to drop acid with me," she said.

Later that night when they returned to the loft, it was dark and not too many people were up and around. It wasn't that late. Dahlia and Walker were in the kitchen making herbal tea when in strolled the beautiful Jade with a top on but no pants — she had nothing on below the waist. She stood casually at the sink doing the dishes. Walker casually admired the moons of her ass.

Then a little later in walked the handsome Greg, totally naked. He prowled around a shelf and walked out. Walker was impressed. All these good looking young men walking around with their penises dangling, just as natural in their sexuality as they could be. How do people get to be like that. Maybe I should go to the Amazon and study anthropology, thought Walker. Then he realized I AM in a tribe. I am living among the wild Urban-utopians of San Francisco.

Dahlia and Walker went upstairs to sleep in the upper loft. While he just wanted to be cool, and blend in and not be seen, Walker knocked a metal bowl and spoon up into the air, making a big racket and drawing a bunch of attention to himself, as he stepped over to her futon. Some of the women looked over at him and grinned at his sheepishness.

"Got caught in the tin bowl trap?" Dahlia grinned as she came over to him.

They got down under the cover and made love this time for the first time without a sheath. It felt incredible. They kept at it until way late in the night.

When Dahlia and Walker's breathing had become tight during fornication, someone in the room shouted "Make more sound!" This caused Walker to shrivel a bit and gave him pause. He and Dahlia looked at each other a little startled and said together, "Are they talking to us?"

Walker said, "Looks like we've even got a cheering section."

The next morning, Sunday — Big Group day, was spent in doing work around the Loft. Walker was doing what Dahlia wanted, trying to blend in. Everyone was doing chores around the Loft. Walker met Dahlia's husband, a nice young Scottish chap, an electrical engineer named Kevin. Walker learned a bit about room wiring from Dahlia's husband. Kevin was gracious enough to tell him the story of their marriage: Chase had them get married to insure his commitment to staying with the House.

After Big Group had broken up and he was leaving, or getting ready to leave, Dahlia jumped on him right there in front of 'god' and everybody. She was wearing her pink sweater and tight black corduroy pants, and they were sitting there on the carpet and she grabbed him in a big full-on hug and they fell over on the carpet and started moaning and sighing and carrying on under the lights with everybody standing around them looking. This made the shy Walker very embarrassed.

"Are you sure this isn't an inappropriate display of affection?" he said. This quite pissed her off, and took some of the ardor out of her embrace. She seemed to steam (lower jaw protrudes above upper, air raises hair off of forehead). Yet they continued to hug.

He felt immediately embarrassed by his reaction. It was a typical thing he had done, not being aware of the spontaneity of the moment. To be untrusting and to suspect the motives of a lover. He couldn't get past his fundamental belief: Man wants woman, but woman wants man's want of women. So the saying goes in our culture. Or so Walker thought; it may as well have been true. But on thinking about it he realized that this was real love. And, god damn it, I've blocked it. I couldn't let myself accept it.

18

The Ineluctable Reluctance
of Permeability

Kevin, Dahlia's husband, was taking a class in Digital Signal Processing at the UC Berkeley extension night school. He was an engineer at Audiomedia down in Silicone Valley. Walker and Kevin had Dahlia and nerdulency in common. They started hanging out in Berkeley before or after class, talking and sometimes smoking a small bowlful of the herb. Walker was fresh from teaching his class in electronics at the trade school and they had many interesting technical discussions. Kevin found this refreshing from all the analysis that constantly went on at the House.

For Walker it was fun to be able to speak to an engineer and say things like, "The reemergence of Freudian material was causing his mind to flip-flop in and out of the smooth running state to a runaway state." And have him get it and both of them laugh in mutual confirmation. Walker also began trying to change his work attitude by applying a method or philosophy from the House, where you tried to treat work like a group, and used it to explore the relationships with people as well as the impact of these relationships on your self. Walker thought about these things as he drove up Ashby, over the hills and through the deadly Caldecott tunnel, flat out down the hills, and beneath the impressive Mount Diablo to Concord, pronounced conquered. Walker was glad to have the job to take his mind off himself.

Walker's reality was actually beginning to be quite shaken by the House. Reality as he knew it was dissolving due to the transference of love.

Walker was looking around for something to believe in. What he wanted was a quick answer, an intellectual answer. He didn't have a whole other lifetime to figure out how to be with these Californian Buddhists in the House.

Kevin was the same age as Walker's younger brother. Walker himself was the same age as Kevin's older brother and this symmetry in their relationship was implicit. In addition to being a hard working engineer and audio technician, Kevin was also a musician. Are all these Californians like this? Walker wondered, —they all seemed to be multi-talented, multifaceted, multiorgasmic.

By way of trying to relate to Kevin's Buddhistic proclivities, Walker told him about the study he was making of the iconography of the tankhas. Kevin, who really didn't care to bother his mind too much about the artistic details, likened it to commercial art he saw in advertising, and talked about the iconography of commercial advertising. "Budding Buddhists," he said, "are brought up to look for the currently operant Image. The Image of who you think you are or think to become at the moment. To recognize it as an image and to try and live beneath the image. This is hard to do. Especially as we are constantly bombarded with tons of images per second in the modern electronic world. We are so drawn to the image. And we create and recombine images all day long. But beneath the images to which we are attracted is pure attraction. The life force of becoming which is to be honored."

This started Walker into thinking about a theory of personality. He began working on it. It was built on the analogy to magnetism fluxing through your core.

Walker wanted to talk to somebody about his love for Dahlia, and what was going on at the Loft. He talked about the general problem of his shyness with women.

Kevin suggested that he see someone who can be objective and not somebody that he was intimate with, because people you are intimate with tend to lose their objectivity.

Walker recalled in small group when Dahlia was showing him some photos of her past, and he could not at all see what was going on, but kept saying nice things. Morey was able to plow into these images and see them for what was there. He talked straight with her. Walker kept denying what was there, letting his intimacy get the better of his objectivity and it was objectivity she was wanting now.

Dahlia had gotten miffed at his compliancy towards her.

"I can't believe you can't see what is going on here," she said. Thought Walker didn't know what she was talking about.

It had been a long time since a woman had been intimate with him and shown him her pictures. He began to see her through the eyes that were coming out of these images, through all the states and ages of being that had grown her up into who she was.

He selectively viewed reality, filtering through what he wanted, refusing to see what was going on. Were there many things about his own life that he did not see either?

"It is hard to be objective about yourself," Walker said. "That is why we need the help of teachers. Yet that scares me, because in many ways it is like looking for the father figure that will tell you what to do."

"Yea," Kevin said, "but if you don't you get caught in the hypnosis loops. Dealing with the symptoms rather than the root cause."

"I ask myself," Walker said, "why are you shy around women? What are you afraid of? Do you give off signals of non- acceptance? Is it some kind of fear from the guilt trip laid on us by our parents?"

Walker thought of his first sexual memory that had come up in Cafe Trieste in North Beach.

"Why am I such a one-on-one person," Walker asked. "Well not so much — I teach school. That deals with large numbers of students. When I am with people I get my consciousness so easily copped. I have always felt that I was so oceanic, lunar, mute. I always act like the big brother it is like the only way I know how to relate, always giving people permission and encouragement, rather than being there objectively for them. I am afraid to confront that in myself I guess.

"Being objective, on the surface of it," said Kevin, "sounds heartless, but it is about the only way you can be of any real help."

Kevin and Walker had a system of communication that symbolically allowed them to stroke each others intellect. One day they were talking about writing. Then Walker began imagining a story in which the characters were introduced on a psychic grid. He thought that the same grid applied to all personalities, and that like in a tankha, a visual artist used it to draw 'abstract portraitures' of people. Walker wanted to do tankhas that were science crossed with visual art.

The two men followed a path of reasoning by analogy to hysteresis curves and magnetic flux.

Walker said this abstract portraiture space, this personality space is was a 4-dimensional vector space, where the vectors that spanned the space of personality — were descriptors of a psychological nature. "The basic descriptors of personality were four: Permeability, the ease or difficulty with which someone considered new ideas; Reluctance, once ideas were accepted the difficulty with which one could let go of them; Coercivity, how much stimulus it took to overcome inertia to change in a character and Reminiscence (or retentivity), how much of the stimulus they recalled."

Kevin jumped back and gave a big horse laugh, "Wow, you've really thought this out. What a novel idea!" He paused and considered. "Hmmm, well I never thought of that. You are saying coercivity is how easily are people coerced, how reticent are they to new ideas."

"Right. Yea."

"And permeability, what would that be?"

Walker said, "Permeability, that's like consciousness, like the sensitivity of consciousness. Openness to being swayed by ideas and feelings."

"Yes! Exactly."

Walker continued: "And hysteresis is like people's programming curves, their destiny. People are way far along on their programming curves, therefore, they have a bias, and there are all these little eddies of hysteresis associated around all interactions, based upon what has gone on in their past. This can be reflected in the cells which go to make up the face and the body."

Walker opened up his eyes big with discover. He cheered. "Wow! Hysteresis as destiny!"

"Wouldn't that be more like magnetic flux?" Kevin challenged.

"Yes! Wow, exactly. Destiny is like magnetic flux!"

Thinking about magnetic flux, Walker realized he was walking around in hysteresis. Thinking about how all these beings and entities were on a voyage and they could not go back. Magnetism is like the colorless color, the color before color. The quiet force bringing things together, but also pulling them apart. Animal magnetism, Svengalli, cults.

"What would be the equivalent of Magnetic Flux?" Kevin asked, leading him on.

"Well, magnetic flux is tension per area, right?"

"Yea."

"We are trying to find what would be the analogy in personality portraiture. Tension is the pull between two opposite poles, tension is potential, like voltage. The place you are now, relative to where you were before, and to where you are going," Walker raised and lowered his eyebrows with obvious delight.

"Do you live up to your potential, or do you reach saturation, like most people," he added philosophically.

"Now current," he continued, is the output, or through put, or in life it is what you produce, what you do with the time you have."

This was good. Walker began to think of tension in the body, tension that is stored up energy, blocking area, due to nefarious stuff, this is my STUFF, he thought strong magnetic field, in a rain of elementary particles.

Later that night by himself after smoking a bit of the herb, Walker began to think of the concept on a more molecular basis, rather than the gross phenomenological level of macroscopic magnetic fields.

One thought about magnetic domains in material and the interaction of the spins of electrons. This got into NMR and the colors of radio pulsed flesh in a strong magnetic field.

Then he thought of the Translator which had to do with the Turing machine, the creation of order and Maxwell's Deamon which doth happeneth to us all. He began to think of himself and personality in terms of the gas laws, of molecules with their energies in a gravitation bias, percolating in space separating and recombining in endless combinatorics of platonic forms. And then out of this came the self-reproducing patterns, autopoesis, that began billions of years ago and still go on, life, and non- linear thermodynamics, a long way from equilibrium.

It was like trying to derive the weather, from

understanding an air molecule. Spaced him right out.

Walker had no manual of Tantric Buddhism, and wasn't getting that much help from the House. Or maybe he was but his resistance was choosing not to see it.

All Walker had to work with was his diary.

```
Fri. Dec 16, 1982
I thought of the iconography of the tankhas, and
how the figures are painted by the formulas of the
golden section. And how phi (φ), the golden ratio is
present in all life forms and perhaps in all the
pathways of our life, and that we really don't have
that much choice in what we do for all world lines
are curved arcs in this grid.
    And one can feel in meditation, the lines of phi
symmetry, informing the body, making the body grow.
It is the same transformation of coordinate space in
which an individual grows as the human archetype
evolves. One can visualize this grid, fit into it.
    This principle underlying tankha paintings, could
it underlie writing too?
    The pictures in the codices precipitated a
feeling of metempsychosis, in which I felt the
presence of all my ancestors at once, all the people
that I was in the lineage of, all the hunters, and
craft women, the shipbuilders, the farmers, all the
way back to the killer apes from which we are
descendent.
```

19

Keepers of the Flame

The House was making a trip up to the land over Christmas and Dahlia met Walker in La Boheme for tea to invite him to go along. But he panicked at the idea of spending a whole seven day week in a tent, using exposed public bathrooms with a bunch of people he didn't know very well.

Dahlia was very pissed off when he turned down the invitation.

She was especially angry because he wanted to spend the holidays with his parents out of a sense of being the dutiful son. She was almost outraged that he seemed to be wanting her permission, moreover asking her to help him with this family quandary.

She was disappointed. "Go where the feelings are," she said sadly, then stormed angrily out the door.

— — —

And that was the last he saw of her for three months.

— — —

He didn't know what was going on. After the first week he called and somebody told him she was out of town for a couple of weeks.

He called a couple of weeks later, and somebody told him she might be away for another couple of weeks. Finally someone told "We've all had a big shock here, Walker. Chase was diagnosed to have cancer and is undergoing a treatment down in Tiajuana.

"Dahlia went down south to be with Chase. We don't know when she'll be back."

Walker really missed her bad.

On Valentine's Day, Walker decided to go and be with these people who love each other. When he got there he found that Chase was fighting a losing battle with cancer and this put all other concerns into perspective. The people of the House accepted Walker with a quiet and real confirmation of recognition. And that night he would see that he was totally unprepared to deal with: a beatific vision.

It was a turning point for the House. Chase was still undergoing cancer treatment. The House was deciding whether to rent a house down there in San Diego, or a trailer, so that a small group of people could live down south and help out. Much discussion ensued about how to finance this and who should go.

Much group discussion went back and forth. Carlos decided to quit smoking and go down there and be with him. Chase's wife Serena was already down there. Morey had gone and was back, Dahlia was down there. Harv had fantasies about going, but he was hot to pursue his career as a architect. Finally he decided to go.

Toward the end of the evening Harv said to Morey, "I had a fantasy about getting into a hug with you." They looked at each other, and then they did. They lay down on the floor and started making sounds that got louder and louder, and pretty soon the whole House got around them, people up close touching them, and people further away, touching those closer. And the sounds of everyone OMing and screaming got louder and louder, and although Walker didn't know, the House had done this often. They were experienced. Many times they had taken acid together and gotten into a naked pile three people deep in one giant hug, and they had lots of experience in the circle meditation, but this was really focused on the two men in the hug.

Some kind of disgust from the primal screaming came up for both men, and Morey coughed up a little clear fluid, he couldn't help himself and it got Harv's hair wet. This was pretty shocking to Walker, and to Harv too. But when it was over, and Morey sat up stunned, white faced, everyone else had kind of a white drained face too and were very placid and peaceful, almost waxy in their demeanor. Walker saw the spirits that inhabited their bodies, like in a kind of El Greco painting, the one where the people are all around this dead person on a bier and the soul of the person is being sucked up from these real people into a tumultuous cloudy heaven through a kind of inverse birth canal, into a heaven of phantom-like saints whose elongated forms were even more stretched up than the people. In his paintings and here for a moment it was like Walker could see how we are flesh hung on spirits, spirits on the material plane. We are flames burning for a while.

There was much peace and unity in the House that night after all the turmoil around Chase's struggle. It was as though they had sent strong healing energy into the beatific ether connecting all beings in compassion. This gave the people of the loft a kind of soft drained, waxy appearance.

Keepers of the flame. Hands in the air, what a wonderful air, they are zooming in great religious mysticism.

Later as he was leaving he and Pia were in a kind of consoling way with each other over the loss of Dahlia. Though Walker didn't know the details he realized Pia was also Dahlia's lover. He said, "Yeah, it was quite a vision. It was kind of like that El Greco painting about the man laid out on the bier and the inverse birth of the soul of the dead man going back up into a heavenly host or choir of people. Do you know that painting?"

"Oh Yes," she said, thoughtfully seeing the painting in her mind. "It's in the Prado museum in Madrid. I've seen it."

They smiled at each other, brother and sister of the flesh.

20

Make love as if it is the last time

By keeping up his contact with the house Walker was able to find out when Dahlia was to return. He was overjoyed and terrified at the prospect of seeing her. Finally the Princess was going to give audience to her Brute. In his overweening enthusiasm to see Dahlia, Walker showed up at the loft too early. She was not overly enthusiastic to see him.

"I'm kind of busy right now," Dahlia said. "I'm working with a new diet. I want some time to be by myself."

Walker went for a long walk down Mission Street, feeling like a lost soul or a puppy on a short leash. It was a misty gray day. It was going to rain. He walked past the two *peliculas mexicanas* —the Hoy and the Mission, listening to the voices in his head telling him how put down he felt. Transparent forces that spoke in perverse voices guided his moves. Guided his mood.

He ran into Serena on the street. She was brightly dressed carrying a paper Chinese parasol. Serena was once married to Chase and was the mother of their 2 sons in the commune. Though in her 50s with two teen-aged sons, she carried her wealth and her power well. Walker found her very attractive.

"There isn't much money flowing down Mission Street anymore," she observed.

Walker was delighted and proud of his social self. To think that he could be walking down a major street in a famous city and to run into someone who knew you! Walker felt that his life was so lonely, he really needed and wanted the kind of intense intellectual and emotional interaction that he saw going on with the people of the loft. And later, on the way back to the loft, he smiled and said hello to Beverly who was waiting for a bus on Mission Street.

When he got back, Pia whisked him off to dinner at Real Good Karma. Apparently some subterfuge had occurred for Dahlia to ask Pia to substitute for her for a while. It was raining by then, and Walker got his lank frame — in stocking feet — under a low table made out of an old telephone spool. He got into the cross-legged position, his wet jeans feeling tight against his leg.

"It sure rains a lot here in California," he said. Seemed to Walker that every time he drove the van over from Berkeley, he was navigating a lashing storm on the bridge.

Pia reached over and patted him on the thigh as they scanned the menus.

"I'm really scared about being hired by the house to start building the indoor landscaping business," she said. "My mother was a real castrating bitch, always wore pants. . ."

Walker wanted to talk about Dahlia but knew he must be present for the others. "Oh, yea? What did your father do?"

"My father was a gambler, I remember. . ."

"Did he ever lose the groceries?"

"No, we were well into upper middle class. I remember being with him one time on Nassau and seeing him win about $19,000 in one night, which was in about 1954, and that would be like $60,000 today."

"Wow."

It was nice, Pia and Walker spending some time together, trying to get into a relationship. She said, "Everybody in the House is taking these Chinese herbs, boiling these huge piles of mushrooms and plant matter concoctions in glass kettles. A bunch of people are working with this new diet which requires lots of juices and potatoes for potassium, to balance the potassium-sulfate polarity ions in the cell."

After a while Walker began asking her about what happened during the time when Harv and Morey got into a hug. This seemed to put her on the defensive.

Walker thought to try disarming her with his southern drawl: "Does that make y'all defensive. . . if I ask questions of an anthropological nature?" The incongruity of this redneck trying to be scientific cracked her up.

"No, I don't mind," she smiled.

"OK. You believe in — what do you call it? What is the word? — non-preferentiality, don't you? Do you guys use the term 'polyfidelity'?"

"Poly-fidelity? Where did you come up with that term. That's good."

"I read about it in one of those free newspapers you find

at the laundrymat."

Pia ran it down for him —the House position about Non-Preferentiality Among Communards. Walker listened to this; then asked, "What do *you* think?"

"Well, some people you can grow with in a different way than with other people," she said. "What did *you* think about what happened that night?"

"It was like some kind of a meltdown," Walker observed in what he thought was a sincere and astute manner. He noticed himself being able to speak with increasing psychological sophistication. "It seemed like some kind of turning point for the loft. It seemed, to me anyway, that the crisis of Chase's bout with cancer, seemed to bottom out at that point."

"Yeah."

Walker continued. "And then after more decision, Carlos decided to quit smoking and go down and be with him. Harv decided to be more true to himself, and wait a while on getting his career together, not being into filling the void of his life with image and instead going down to Mexico to be with Chase. Also Morey was having to run the business by himself. . . Wow. It was quite a vision. Like that Inverse Birth painting of El Greco I mentioned the other day you recalled was at the Prado. It's got the soul being assumed up into heaven. You can just see all those mystical spirits inside people inhabiting this material plane.

"Yea, it is quite a vision."

"Wow. . . You've seen it!" Walker said enviously. "It's his style, all the people have these elongated faces, and they are all standing around looking pale at the dead one, and up in the sky is this whole heavenly host of spirits in the clouds assisting at the delivery of the soul up through a channel into heaven."

"It felt like that at the loft, all of us around. . . I have never seen people look so angelic, it really made me see how beautiful people are, and we were all touching each other and it was all right."

Then they talked about one of the children of the house who had charmed him, Dhyana. "I really like her," Walker said. "I never get to spend any time around children. I'd like to."

"Yea, those kids really speak from the unconscious," Pia said. "She once called me on my shit when I was heavily into a little girl trip one day. She came up to me and said, 'My you're a little cutie aren't you'."

Then Pia said, "I spent the night with Dahlia last night and a lot started coming up about cancer and illness."

Then an adult conversation about disease ensued. "Jesse has to have an operation for some fistula near his asshole," she said. "I thought about a similar operation I had because I got gonorrhea once and it got all up inside my tubes, and it was because I wasn't taking care of myself. You are so divorced from yourself and used to so much abuse that you abuse yourself."

"Yeah, it's a real sexual jungle out there."

Though the conversation and the weather depressed him it was a kind of adult maturity Walker hadn't faced in his life. They went back to the loft. Walker was driving Loretta, Nancy, Lucia, Pia, Denise and Dahlia to a solo theatre show of Whoopie Goldberg at the Valencia Rose. He felt quite paternal pulling up to the club with a van full of women. Whoopie had some wonderful sketches, powerful and true. Walker felt real important when Whoopie recognized him in the crowd and said: "Hi, Walker. Wow, you drove all the way over from Berkeley in the rain to see me."

At last Dahlia and Walker lay down on her futon, and he could resume the intimate talks with the remarkable woman of his heart.

"The show was very sad," she said.

"It was also very funny. Don't you think that things can be both funny and sad at the same time," he said. "That's poignant."

"Yeah. . ."

"Tell me about how it was down south with Chase."

Dahlia began: "He had gone down to Mexico while the rest of the house was up at the land. Thinking it was the pollution that was bothering him. Came back, things hadn't gotten any better. Went to some better doctors, and x-rays showed a tumor in his chest. Further tests were: they took a biopsy, and a sample of the lymph system, to find out that it was cancer, and that it had spread to the immune system."

"The doctors didn't think then that it would do any good to operate, and they gave him a year and a half to live. Then we started calling all over the states, and in Europe and talked to a lot of people and did a lot of research, and decided to go with this metabolic cure in Mexico, called the Gurnsey system.

"See, they see cancer as a failure of the immune system. And they really try to attack it with metabolism, they try to use this system that is called polarity, where they want to get the cells polarized correctly. Eat potatoes for potassium and drink these juices, which are a mixture of carrot juice and pureed liver. Then you take all these coffee enemas, which open up the bile ducts, and forces you to get rid of the bits of tumor, that now are broken up and in the blood stream and are threatening to poison the individual. See, they give you all this predigested stuff, so that your metabolism can work on the tumor and not be taxed with any other task. And when the tumor does break up, it can poison you, plus you are very susceptible to all kinds of other diseases, since you are in such a weakened condition.

"This really started me into understanding my own health," Dahlia said. "I had a tumor diagnosed in me too, before, right around the same time." At that Walker recoiled and gasped, "Oh, my God."

Yet Dahlia, barely noting his alarm continued, "And all this stuff was coming up. Like we really had to be there for him, had to be at his beck and call, running to get him the freshest juices, because it was hard enough to get the stuff down, and he was very much attuned to his body, trying to fight it."

Walker was shocked, looked at her aghast. "You've got a tumor?"

"Yea." There was a long pause. They looked at each other in recognition of mortality and confirmation of now. "You can feel the tumor up inside me," she said, taking his hand and pressing it on her abdomen near the ovary. In spite of being stricken with dismay, Walker fought off the reaction to recoil and pull his hand away in shock. He let her take his hand and place it on her side. He could feel the knot inside her.

"It made me realize a lot about why," she continued, "I

was coming to have this. That it was my anger that had done this. I was always brought up to be ashamed of my body, that men only wanted one thing, and that they wanted to take advantage of a girl, and that women were weak, and they just had to always keep everything under control, and not feel anything. . . And it leads you to think that you don't have a good sense of your own self."

"This repression leads to a lot of anger," she continued. "Someone who just can't get angry. Illness is metaphor! You do punish yourself for excess, and the illness is another way of allowing yourself not to feel. It keeps you from feeling."

"And yesterday, when I was talking to you, I was in a lot of projection, and probably you are projecting a lot on me. Malcolm and I can identify with you so easily. Sometimes I act like the Big Sister. Or I wonder if you don't think of me as your mother."

When Walker had visited his parents over Christmas, he had managed to get his van side-swiped by a crazy poor woman with a child in a car seat on the freeway near Tejon Pass. Walker had not bothered to exchange insurance data. He had avoided telling the House about this because he knew they would make a big deal about suicidal tendencies brought on by parental visits. Even so when Walker told Dahlia that his parents were coming to visit the next weekend, she started giving advice. "You should tell them that there is a lot of work, that you don't really have the time off. You ought not to see them, where you have to maintain the roles of being the dutiful son."

"I couldn't say that to them," Walker said in dismay. "How am I going to say that to them on the phone."

"It would be interesting to see just what they come back with over the phone."

Since Dahlia was going under the knife, Walker knew that it might very well be the last time they made love together. She might not come back to him from the operation. He made love to her for the last time, trying to sum it up, trying to take an impression away from her that would last him forever.

That night he ran his hands over her arms and legs and massaged her feet, and he felt into her joints and tendons, and played with the skin that enveloped her being as though her flesh were all one erogenous zone like her sex. His hands played over her with little caresses the way clouds moving through the sky caress *it*.

And playing with her lightly from a distance, he saw arise in her smiling face a tantric field, a tacit understanding, where you see each other as though your sex was an eye. He could see with his sex, he had a kind of tactile eye to touch the beloved body of this beautiful woman, perhaps for the last time ever. She felt it too.

It was something like seeing beyond the girl in her to the girlhood that she had come to understand in herself, and then to invent and play with that.

The hands that touched and the arms that held became like sex organs.

She was the remarkable woman of his own mind, the female part of his own psyche. It was as though the progress he made in his mind, the large steps he was making in his mental growth, were ratioed to the little spaces he touched on Her, and the way he came to feel Her through his skin.

This is what came to him, and he longed to whisper it in her ear, to tell her out loud, but he dared not: *For it is at night that we are totally engulfed by sex, the poor man's tantric heaven, heavy breathing and deep hugs. We are taken up into it. Sex carries on its surface a gush in the form of a double helix which reminds us that we are involved in the tournament of matter. He cruised his longevity, and fell through a hole in the earth just larger than the size of his body, and in this cavity began the long voyage through the void. The body was quickly forced to stand, sailing as though the earth suddenly became fluid. Transparent fluid. Having sex pushes through the front that we represent.*

For Dahlia had eyes in her hands and in the soles of her feet, all of which he touched as well as her vulva, and she his member just to see if they could make the fluid flow.

Wasn't it true that under her gaze their sex had grown like a baby and their playing in front of the eyes of everybody in the house in the way of the house had given him new life.

Have you ever looked into your lovers eyes?

When you look into your lovers eyes while having sex it

is a kind of play that takes you over the edge of nothing and around the community of sex to somewhere beyond the armor, to the person within.

The eyes are open only to your lover's eyes, just as their sex opens to surround the person within, for the eyes of empathy can see way down deep inside. We look up inside as far as the eyes can see.

When she lets her legs fall open and separates the fur and lets us look inside the lips as she opened her sex soft and warm, moist and slippery her body completely opened—legs spread, arms flung carelessly over her head. Or when she turns over doggie style it's as though her hands became feet and her cunt that she hoisted up into the sky was like another eye, and the legs flailing about in spaces were like long lashes and he could see through all the parts of her body, as she touched the world gently like a child with no anger, just curiosity.

Curiosity and compassion poured out of her. She touched the world through her skin like the pores of her skin were eyes. And the eyes on the soles of her feet touched the earth with nimbleness. And all hooked up in sexual intercourse it was the way they walked in this ancient newfound void and covered distance and movement in a space penetrated with their walk. The eyes — the feet. In this way the walking was a walking with the goddess.

He felt his cock become like an eye that could elongate itself and press into her darkness and go falling into immense distance. Because he could, he would, penetrate into her eyes with his eyes, as though he could burn the tumors out of her with his penis.

Later after making love and hugging he started asking more questions: "So why did you end up with me?"

"I could tell you had potential."

He asked more questions but she silenced him with, "That's enough analysis for one night."

And they hesitated to get up in the morning, because the bed was soft and warm and comfortable beneath them and they still felt the warm imprint of the warm body they have lain with and because they knew the kingdom of the day is ruled by the eyes while the kingdom of the night is ruled by sex.

21

A Chiaroscuro of Jealousy
Moving through an Oblique Light

It was a sad situation at the Loft that Monday night. The small group was focusing on Dahlia. She was getting ready to go into the operation to remove the tumor. Dahlia looked scared but composed; Morey, Malcolm, Pia, Lucia, Jesse and Walker were close in around her. They were aware there was a probability that when they opened her up and saw what was there that they might have to take the ovary as well.

Dahlia looking forlorn said, "A lot of images of the knife are coming up. . . A lot of images of being opened up. . . I imagined my mother wanting to reach inside me and tear out my internal organs, to give me a hysterectomy. . . Hysterectomy. The very word sounds so horrible."

Walker was shrinking away from these feelings of fear that she was having. He was trying to maintain his composure and sit in good focus but was feeling also ashen. He was having a lot of jealousy for it had been decided that the two men, Jesse and Malcolm would take her to the hospital the next day and that Malcolm was sleeping with her that night. Walker kept telling himself: Jealousy is another way of not feeling, jealousy is another way of not feeling.

Dahlia was having a lot of fear about loss of womanliness. "There is a lot of man hating in it," she said. She started talking about images of her father. "He used to stand around and watch while my mother gave me and my brother enemas."

"I always had the feeling that he was enjoying our pain. Once when I was with him, while on acid, this fear came over me, about how he wanted to rip me up and hurt me, so that I would be totally dependent. There was this conspiracy between my parents to have the women staked out, totally dependent."

"A lot of man hating is coming up," she said. "Maybe I should go to the hospital with a woman."

Much discussion ensued and they talked about how she was projecting her fear about her father onto the men. And it came out that the men were feeling very protective about her like they would for a child.

Walker had never seen anyone express that kind anger at a parent. It was totally foreign to him. He was empowered to revisit his own anger at his father. The next day he wrote in his diary.

> Tues: March 15, 83 Images started coming up for me today about my own father. I guess I was emboldened by what Dahlia was saying last night.
>
> It made me think of how at an early age I had this incredible fear of my father. I remember I externalized it to be <u>out there</u> in the city. I projected it onto these black leather motorcycle gangs that ran around our neighborhood. They had these malevolent powerful engines plugged into dark night. But it was really a fear of him.
>
> Then much later the memory of my father, coming in the night, into my little brother's crib, we shared the same room, he was in the crib right next to me and he was crying and my father slapped him across the face so hard the next day outlined on his cheek were the long bruise marks left by the four fingers.
>
> After that I started to really hate him. A few years later I came within inches of killing him with a gun.
>
> That really raised a lot of fear and anger in me. It made me repress this anger, for I feared what it would make me do.
>
> And it wasn't long after that that I dropped out of school and hitchhiked up to New York city to be with beatniks.

That morning Walker called into work and told them he wanted to be with Dahlia when she came out of the anesthetic. He went up to Telegraph Avenue and bought flowers from the sidewalk shop next to Cody's Books. A beautiful bouquet for Dahlia, with one red rose.

Then Walker drove over to S.F. to the Franklin Hospital on a hill looking over the city, on Castro Street just before it changes into Divisadero. He looked like a hopeful young husband walking around the various corridors, with a really beautiful bouquet looking for her room. Lots of nurses and people smiled at him, for it really was an outstanding signifier of his love. Lilies for her purity, rose for blood lost.

He was relieved to find that the operation was a success. He left the bouquet in her room, for she was still down in Recovery. Not finding any other people from the Loft to hook up with, he hung out for a while and felt the anxiety of the place. Walker found Malcolm in the Operating Reception room. Walker felt intimidated, guilty and angry all at once trying to talk with a husband of his beloved.

Malcolm seemed kind of bored and imperious. This drove Walker into intellectualizing about Julian Jaynes' *The Origin of Consciousness in the Breakdown of the Bicameral Mind*. Malcolm seemed to have his own agenda and was not entertaining the intellectual sound bytes. It set Walker to wondering about his own motives: am I just blathering, trying to feel him out about Dahlia.

They walked over and got a slice of pizza at a parlor on Castro Street. Malcolm left the restaurant saying, "I want to be there when she wakes up," leaving Walker still eating the sad papery pasta. Walker began to sense he was making it a bit awkward for him. He had to admit his jealousy over the closeness Malcolm had with Dahlia.

But then a change started to occur for Walker. He found himself admiring Malcolm's sense of self-containment in a social mileux. He went for a walk around the outside of the hospital on the sweeping marble terrace. Some kind of a change in feeling from the awkwardness seemed to put the whole world, for a moment, into a kind of clear relief like looking at a painting. Walker saw his jealousy moving in the wind across the hospital terrace, fleeing with the shadows pursuing the setting sun in the afternoon glow of slant spring light evaporating. Walker decided that Malcolm didn't need to have his hands occupied with a jealous person right now. Like him, he was probably feeling a lot for Dahlia. Let us be in our feelings.

Walker picked up his books from the car and sat down beside Malcolm in the lobby. Malcolm had fallen into a fitful sleep in the overheated room. There were lots of anxious husbands walking around in that shuffling, hands-in-the-pocket beat, musing, with that special waiting walk people have when there is nothing to do but wait. Finally Malcolm went up to her room, while Walker waited some more. He went outside once, the lights of the city had come on.

Finally Walker went up to Dahlia's room then and peeped through the door. Blue room, blue covers, legs in an unmade bed. Two pairs of legs! They were both there in bed, Malcolm was holding her and Dahlia had her back to him, lying on her side.

Walker had to admire the guy. He was doing the most perfect thing right then. Just got into bed with her and held her, after the terrible trauma she had been through. The other woman in the double room was shuffling around.

Walker realized: I wouldn't have had the loving courage to do this. To get into bed with her. I would have bowed to the propriety of the shared room situation.

Without letting them see him, Walker left the beautiful bouquet standing on the night stand just inside the curtain. He turned around and left them to each other. He moved down the hall, his mind a chiaroscuro of darkness and light, his jealousy turning into its opposite: a kind of cross between compassion and self-personification into the other person. It was good that she had Malcolm, and that Malcolm was who he was, and had the good sense to do what he did. She was in good hands.

Outside on the terrace, there was nothing but the vast sweep of the cityscape below, into which the wind blew the fleeing, possessive, troubled figure of his jealousy.

In the meantime, Spring had come to San Francisco. Freak weather conditions from the ocean current called El Nino made it like living on another planet. Storm after storm rocked the van as he crossed the bridge week after week to be with his tribe.

Walker wrote in his diary.

3/21/83 I visited Dahlia in the hospital and she liked the flowers. She is back at the loft.

Last night at the loft, Lucia asked me, "Do you want to have a session tonight?"

"Yes I think I'd like that," I said, trying to be cool and not look too over eager. "What would we do?"

"We could get really close and talk, and maybe get into a hug."

At Big Group there was much talk about cancer, a

lot about the Gurnsey treatment. Also Kelly and
Rhinheart, who had been called in as consultants.
Rhinheart had the most up to date research.

When I got into bed with Lucia, a lot of fear
came up. I talked about the fear that something
would harm my face.

"Maybe it is some way of not being able to show
facial expressions," she said. "You know the way
kids look at people, they look with their feelings,
they have this wide, wide open stare, and they don't
always have the social smile."

We hugged and aumed for a long time and then she
rolled over and we got into a spoon. I started
telling her about this novel I was reading called
Dry Hustle and I guess she took this as some kind
of a challenge because she turned back over and
looked at me and I started touching her vagina. It
immediately became running sopping wet. I became
wooden; rolled a condom over my love-log. We got
into sex, and I came really quick. Too scared I
guess.

I feel pretty good about it, though guilty as
hell. There Dahlia is on her sick bed in the office.
I'm starting to build multiple relationships with
several people. Learning how they are, getting into
their stuff. Everybody is a little crazy.

I slept with Lucia to prove to Dahlia that I am
not that attached, and thus alleviate her fear of
my dependency on her. Dahlia's always saying I'm too
dependent on her.

It feels like I'm being accepted into this group
identity cluster, and I've got to get committed to
that.

22

The Things We Need to Do for Love

The next time Walker was over,he watched Dahlia slwoly descending the stairway to the Loft, by one step at a time by putting her right fot down, then her left foor over and over slowly. She looked drained. Yet she had been strong enough to make it to small group upstairs in the Loft.

Jesse got things started as *he* was having an operation the next day. They were going to remove a fistula from his anus. He was in a lot of fear, feeling the fear, going with the fear.

"I've got my father's asshole," he said. "He had a hemorrhoid operation when I was little, and my mother said they had hurt him."

Walker recognized the mechanism Jesse was talking about although he didn't want to admit it, for it seemed so rooted in that pessimistic Freudian determinism. This ominous transgenerational hand me down of diseases—he had felt it and feared it when he was with Lucia last time, his mother had face pain and he feared that he would get it.

"What is the mechanism?" he asked Jesse.

"I have their genes," he said. "They brought me up. I have their programming. I react to things the same way they do."

Walker was both bored and intimidated by how self-absorbed some of these people were. His mind wandered into a big transgenerational fear. He thought about autopoeisis and thermodynamics. Of how living beings were evolving chemical systems, who were still undergoing chemical reaction a long way from equilibrium. And with our minds and upbringing we can influence these things. There seemed to be too few barriers, and perhaps the ego was an attempt to interpose more barriers. It is only natural.

"I used to go hiding in the woods a lot when I was a kid," Jesse continued. "And I got poison oak. My mother was always grabbing me and pouring Calamine lotion on my penis. It was very castrating. She was always grabbing me and sticking needles into my boils and pimples."

"That's why I'm so afraid doctors might be like that. When I went to the examination by the proctologist, he had me all splayed out on this moving machine that made my asshole totally accessible to him. He started to stick his finger into my ass, saying 'Relax! , RELAX!' and I would say, 'wait a minute! Stop, so I can relax!' Just like how my mother would just say 'hold still! god damn it!'"

Then Dahlia started about her operation. "My mother would grab me and turn me around and hurt me and do whatever she wanted to me. I had these fears when I was a child, and they started coming up with the doctor. I could remember some place where they wanted to hurt me, where I was really afraid that they wanted to hurt me and that I had to be really fucked up, like a broken leg, to be able to ask for anything. I didn't even want to know about the tumor. I stayed down in Mexico with Chase for 3 months after it was diagnosed before I came back to do something about it."

Then in the round, the group focus fell on Walker.

Morey asked him, "What about the way you took the day off from work. Just called them up and told them you aren't coming in."

And Walker said, "Yeah, a couple of days later I was trying to drive through the tunnel in the rain, and there was an accident, and I got the fear, and just couldn't make myself wait about 2 or 3 hours to drive through the tunnel and called them up and said I couldn't make it in today."

Malcolm saidm "Yea, well. They are going to think you are a real flake on the job. You told us that they are only going to offer you teaching in night school — and THAT will interfere with your coming over here during the week.

"The Loft is the best thing happening in my life right now," Walker said.

They all looked at him.

Dahlia said, "There is a lot coming up for you, you have really changed a lot in the time I have known you."

"You need to slow down," Malcolm said, "you are dealing with some very powerful forces here. Your ego might really try to destroy you right now, a lot is coming up for you. The job seems to be something you ought to go through."

As the group broke up, Dahlia said "You should get into a session with Morey and Malcolm tonight."

Everyone agreed.

Walker demurred. He hesitated, he dug his heels in, he practically ran out the door. He put his shoes on and was standing ready to go when Morey came up to him and asked him why he was leaving.

"Well isn't your session with Malcolm? I don't want to violate the sanctity of the session."

Morey looked sad and said, "Man there are a lot of forces pushing you around right now, you ought to stay here tonight."

"Nah, I don't think so man, I better be getting on back."

"What do you think goes on?"

"Well I don't know."

"All we do is lie down on the futons, and talk and hang out and go to sleep."

"Well I better be getting back on over to the East Bay," Walker said as he crabbed, waffled, and hedged his way out the door.

23

Egodeath

The bureaucrats running the school put Walker on the night shift. He knew this would cut into his time at the Loft and so he got pissed and quit. This was typical behavior for him. At the ripe old age of 34 he had yet to hold down a job for longer than a year. That day as the realization sunk in, that once again he would be cast adrift in the economic sea without a paddle, Walker went over to the Loft because he knew the meditation and chanting helped quiet him. He was not going to tell people about losing his job. He was distraught and hiding it bravely. I'm feeling bad he thought but I'mH not going to let anyone know it. I don't want them to get on my case. I'm tough. And I can handle this.

But at the Loft he found himself confronted with an even more calamitous change occurring. It was time for the periodic restructuring of the SOCIAL CONTRACT!! The House just sprung it on him: The big group recombination of the groups was occurring. Even though Chase was not there to facilitate, the House was moving ahead as scheduled. The small group marriage contracts to stay together for a year or so, were being vacated and the small groups dissolved and reformed with other small groups. Dahlia's marriage among Lucia, Jesse, Morey, Malcolm, Pia and Dianne and the interloper Walker was being disbanded and reformed by an extensive process of group discussion.

And what was even worse was that he and Dahlia were not going to be in the same marriage! After much discussion and deliberation, everyone had been assigned to different groups. The survivors of Walker's old group, himself, Malcolm, Morey had formed an alliance with Aaron and Adrienne and Rachel. Jade was assigned, too. Walker had thought that Dahlia was coming to this group too, and his fear was at least tempered by the fact that he would be with her. But she eluded him at the last minute and betrothed herself to another group. He had to respect that she did not want to be in a group marriage with him. But he felt extremely put down about it. It did cross his mind that the hurt could be assuaged at least potentially with the prospect of sleeping with some other women, the lovely Jade and the beautiful but melodramatic Rachel, and Walker took some consolation in that.

And as if getting divorced and remarried in the same day wasn't traumatic enough he now had the sinking realization that he would need to tell the women in his new group marriage that he's got eternal viral VD. Shit! Plus he couldn't tell them that he lost his job because they would jump on his case with a thousand I-told-you-sos.

There was a lot of chanting and a good supper but the air was thick with tension as the big group disbanded to go into small groups. The new groups were going to begin and Walker's group was to have a double group with Morey and Malcolm's group and Aaron's. Even though Walker was mad and hurting about it, he couldn't stand up and protest. What am I going to do, he thought. Quit?

He set himself the task of hanging on. Try to be in your own thoughts, he kept telling himself, try to maintain and contain.

While Walker was feeling this enormous hurt over losing Dahlia in the small group he was trying to be alert and present in the new group. Many of the people in the new small group marriages — some of whom were quite knew to each other — were getting acquainted by bringing out their photos and starting to fill in these new husbands and wives about their past. Aaron had laid out many of his pictures from an album on the carpet in the middle of the circle of new friends.

Aaron was coming to grips with the meeting he had had with his mother recently, after not seeing her for 7 years. He had done the encounter on acid. Adrienne, a therapist who was also a new recruit to the House and had gotten involved through Malcolm, picked up one picture of Aaron's mother. She looked at it and said, "The persona has fallen here."

Aaron said: "Yes her face is. . . It often looked to me that it is held up by the superstructure of her smile."

Walker looked at the picture. There, was this huge fat gargoyle! He looked at the picture of this woman's face and the smile was *holding it up, and the rest of the face was sagging down around it!* Even the inexperienced Walker could see that the persona had fallen: the fixed smile disappears, the facial bones stand out, the color drains from the face, the eyes seem to be hollow sockets. It is a ghastly expression and strikes him as the look of death.

"She looks like a pariah," said Malcolm.

"It looks like her whole face is falling off and there is this person behind it, this dead person," said Jade.

In another picture, all of them actually, Aaron really looked like an alien near his mother. He looked real remote, smoky-eyed, terrified.

Aaron smiled and shook his head. He kind of admired her though. He said, "She has wrists bigger than mine."

At one point Malcolm said: "She looks like a hooker!"

Aaron said: "I think she always wanted a girl, it came to me when we were together the last time."

Malcolm said: "This is really your fear of castration, and that is your way of saying it, by saying that your mother really wanted a girl, but what is really going on is that she couldn't have any male energy around, and that she really was a castrator."

Malcolm looked over at Walker and said "Your mother looks like this too. And so does everybody's mother."

Are they all castrating? thought Walker. Voices of protest and propriety objected from down under the substrate of his being in collusion with his persona. Shore up, shore up, my mind is coming apart. And I have all these guilt voices. . . But these voices are not real. They are trying to sabotage me. . . But they're not real. I'm afraid that I'll lose control, afraid that I'll break down and cry in front of people. I don't have any frame to reference this to.

He saw the image of Aaron's mother again. Like it was just some kind of covering over a corpse, and she was with this man who also was going to be dead in a couple of weeks.

And Aaron was talking about trying to be there with it, (on LSD) and he really looked scared and horrible.

Morey brought out his pictures and Malcolm talked about how these mothers really didn't want the male energy around, that they were castrating women, they wore the pants and were really out there.

Aaron talked about how his mother embarrassed him this time by talking across the dining room at a restaurant to total strangers. "She is outrageous and flamboyant."

Malcolm told Morey: "Your dominant mother gave you the big-shot images that you had to live up to."

Walker just tried to be into his own thoughts: Trying to maintain and contain. But god damn I am mad and hurting and mad about it. Yet I can't stand up and protest! I just had to suffer in silence. No place to run and no place to hide in an unlimited expanse. Squirm thou vermin worm!

When Aaron talked about taping the phone conversation with his mother he used the word "stream of consciousness" in the context of how, in the interaction with his mother, she controlled the stream of consciousness, meaning the free association of ideas, and the ability to know and discern. What are you feeling at the moment to be in the flow, going with it. Walker was astounded at how perceptive that was.

Walker felt sodden. Physically he felt like he was going to die. He was actually nauseous with despair.

Somehow Walker made it through small group and in the confusion and transition he slipped away from the House and got back into his sad cell of a room whose walls were colored a light tan with blue trim, across from a hospital on a busy street in Berkeley. He has a mattress on the floor, a ten-speed bike in the corner. The whole room looks like a boy's top drawer, —a bachelor is a big boy who won't grow up. Funky stereo, hand calculator, various ohmmeters, bags of parts, and everywhere you look, books open with sheathes of paper in them.

Walker's mind was really in a turmoil. Ego-death thought Walker. This must be it. This must be egodeath. Less and less things are making sense in my world. Meaning is draining off. I am torqued to the point of hysteria. Entering an epoch of great instability. Is this a kind of hysteresis in the engineering account of consciousness I am toying with?

But whatever you call it, his ego was dying. Is that what this is? he asked himself, ego death? He was being confronted with a totally alternative reality. The ego just gets mortified and becomes crushed from being confronted with a whole other reality. Really makes you see how different we all are. We hang out only with those we like and know, don't sleep with the boys, are mistrustful. This microculture of the loft is a totally different reality! It is the reality of the self over that of the ego. Being crushed under immense hurt.

Ego death and alieness, starting to feel the other, the translator, the personality, the persona is falling . . . falling here. Ego death, mind floundering . . . Keep generating hypothesis. . .

It is a terrible thing to watch consciousness shatter and rebuild itself. It happened to Walker while he was alone by himself in his room. Luckily he was able to smoke some pot and sleep.

Next morning, Egodeath was standing inside his room like a shroud of emptiness with the hood of its anonymous jogging pullover covering a vacuum where its head should be, thick rubbery lips grinning, sucking on a life saver. He is Walker. Here he is getting ready to go back to a job he hates. He still has to finish out the semester, out of a sense of professionalism and duty to the students, but he feels like a lame duck. He has not changed from his work clothes from the day before. He was nicely dressed in dark pants and sports jacket, blue and black spotted tie. Not your three piece IBM junior executive off the shelf nerd, but decent enough. Now much the worse for wear. He's unshaven.

Walker paces around the room some more and talks to himself. He makes a cup of coffee by boiling the water in a stainless steel pot and pouring it through an unbleached filter in a little plastic cone. The aroma of Celebes Colossi fills the air. Walker likes his cup of coffee, for he found his life lonely, and at least there is that in the morning.

He is pacing back and forth and talking to himself about ego death aloud. "I quit my job so I could spend more time with Dahlia at the house, and now she's off in another group."

All these voices rise up like ghosts and crowd into his head. He feels like an alien has taken over his body. He is starting to get in touch with his own programming. "OOOOOOhhhheeeeoooeeeee . . . I'm really shook up today. I wonder what I'm gonna do. Feel weird, really shook up. Wild. Like dread."

There was a burning sensation in his penis. He looks and horror of horrors his herpes was back. "God this is all I need!" He is at least a *little* relieved that he could not have given it to any body at the House, because of abstinence. And he always wore a condom.

In his mind he started to go down a litany of lamentations to see if he could pinpoint the stressor that put him over the edge. Got fired off my job. Lost Dahlia. Got divorced and remarried in the same day. And this incredible thing came up in big group with everybody looking at Aaron's pictures. And now the stress has brought on a herpes attack. And this nameless dread is coming up. I wish I could at least define it. I feel incredible guilt.

Aloud he cries out: "I've got to quit hanging out there! Either that or open up to them and move in there. Cause I just can't go on, can't go on being this vulnerable and then just coming home to this place every night. Man I'm just so fucking SHOOK UP!"

Walker got out *his* pictures and started looking at his own face. He had his mother pull them together when he saw how useful they were at the House. The pictures were like slow still frames of a fast, in-memory, flashing movie before Walkers eyes. He had seen his face go from an open face of a child, through school, a little Humphry Bogart existential man, to bearded college student, to long-haired knight of the road, to night cook in an Austin diner, to guerilla pot farmer to mild mannered college teacher. The face still had these starry eyes, but the eyes had turned to pinwheels, and now looked inward for truth.

He looked at his visage in the bathroom mirror. He looked his age or younger. He had been wandering alone for a long time. He smiled at himself. He spoke to himself of himself, as if reading in his own obituary: "His mind was an artfully contrived union of science and art, standard for his time. His teeth were well taken care of."

In his dank carpeted closed room Walker lights up a joint after carefully breaking up a beautiful bud out of a small gram, rolling it into double papers, and put the slender joing into his long bamboo air traveler.

He sees how his father gets bigger and bigger and more powerful looking in the pictures. There is one picture of his father with his shirt off looking really stocky, as squat as a cigarette machine, and powerful. Another of his father looking all sheepish, obtuse, bovine, drunken.

He argues with himself: you can't really be saying this about your parents. The loft people had spent a lot of time running down each other's mothers and it was just a kind of 'signifying' they got into. Wasn't it? Something that close friends can do with each other.

To tell the truth, his mother did have a queenly bearing. His father held down a job, smoked and drank a lot. He could hold his booze though, and always made it to work. They stayed married and they were pretty happy together today, or at least their neuroses meshed.

But what has happened to MY face. It had started off the relaxed face of a child, and been shaped by the expression it had seen from other people's regard. . .Walker starts mumbling about his self in the third person as though he were observing and commenting on someone else. "He was like a little robot, man."

Walker began walking around talking out this monologue in his room, as if he were addressing maybe some kind of an audience —out there beyond the 4th wall.

"He was like a little Robot . . . I felt like a little robot out in my home growing up."

Walker gestures two hands pointing into himself as though a lecturer making a point to an audience. "I have a threaded interpretive language, that is — there is a core program that keeps me functioning, and a body language that allows me to manipulate things in the world as they come up."

He steps around mimicking stiff legged robot moves.

". . . Who *am* I, what *is* under this body . . . I have a head haunted by ghosts, or aberrant programs —these are lies I tell myself. Lies I must live by."

Walker paces about the room. He sits down on the mattress and stretches out, covers his head with a pillow, rolls around and moans: How could I tell them the big secret, about herpes. I had to keep it inside myself, live the lie. How nice it would be to unburden myself of this responsibility. And of the personality . . . that haunted every action, that rode on my body like some kind of mind parasite.

He was on the great horns of a moral dilemma, and there didn't seem to be any way out. He knew he needed the love and human touch more than anything, yet how could he trust himself with these people and how could they develop trust for him.

The people at the loft had a totally alternative reality, that he had entered, and now carried with him in his mind, in the form of ideals realized. The had discovered utopia in a corner of our world. They were coming to know the divine within themselves.

Walker is walking around like he is in some kind of solo monologue addressing an audience. "There is a growing panic inside him. That he will end up lonely and alone wandering around trying to get on SSI, or food stamps, because there is no one who will be with him."

"He could see it happening."

"His ego was dying. It felt like a kind of nausea, like before you vomit, with a feeling of the sweats. "

"Ego death."

Walker thought of examples of ego-death in western lit. Intellectualization was always comforting for him. Like in Sartre's book the existentialist goes into a state of nausea at the recognition of his own being. God was that going to happen now? Or When Casteneda *sees* don Genero suddenly sprout tentacles of luminous fibers from his stomach and walk up a waterfall. He makes a note to himself that he must write a paper on ego death and the stream of consciousness. Thinking of writing helps him feel a little better.

He saws the air with a bristle of gestures. "There is much confusion! But it is clear," he said heuristically - trying to mollify his increasing concern and fear. "It is a clear confusion, in the sense that more and more bits of information from the world are trying to get in."

"There is a hysteria, a magnetic hysteresis."

"What are these forces that go through us, god, what is COMING UP!"

He falls to his knees on his mattress, "And my own self. . . Aww shit, I'm having a hard time." He collapses all the way down to his mattress on the floor. He says, "I'm so afraid. My mind is just running away from me."

He thinks a little more, "Not to mention the weirdness

over loosing that job. Keeeee-rist!" He collapses further and tries to sink deeper into the bed.

Walker calls up Dahlia and cries over the phone, talks about being afraid of breaking down in front of the people. And she tells him: "I remember the first time it happened when I was back in Koana and was walking back for the bus. I walked around in the forest and saw this little tree growing. I sat there and cried for all the new things coming up. But I felt like I was dying. My guts were smeared all over the outside of me.

"I went to Chase's office and said 'I'm dying.' He told me that I was present at the death of my own ego, it was coming apart."

"I never had any real friends," she said. "I mean there was people I knew and had a common interest with. Like politics, and work, but I never had what you might call friends. Real close intimate friends that I could be in love with."

"I haven't had that many friends either," he said, "just lovers and other strangers. Lovers who had not stuck around long enough to be friends."

She said, "You ought to come over and be with your group."

After he hung up he started reacting to the phone conversation immediately. He began thinking of reasons not to take this hand reaching out to him: For her, friendship was platonic, loose, like the way she was with her girlfriends. Then he argues with himself: I could play it that way. On the other hand this possessiveness and jealousy, were completely inappropriate in this scene and would soon be pointed out with derision.

Walker shouted out loud in defiance: "I mean, what is so weird about wanting to be with a woman you love! So what if she sleeps with a lot of other guys. So could I, sleep with others —women! I mean. It is all part of sharing your feelings. Of having many close intimate relationships with more people."

He reasons: They were making it quite easy for me. What would be the real cost? I would have to give up writing? NEVER! And it wouldn't be necessary. I could take notes, really have feelings, be like a kid in a new family, that discouraged collusion and dependency. In a place where there was a lot of touching. A lot of love, a lot of support, and I could get committed to them, be protective of them. It just takes vigilance. I couldn't have a little writing table, but maybe I could have, in the sense that I would just have to put more concentrated time into my writing.

It was like the robot I'm programming at work. The threaded interpretive language. Am I language? I am a being that has been programmed, and now the interpretive programming is interacting with the core programming through stress.

Then Walker launched into his walking monologue again: "It walked around with little TV cameras in its head, looking at the world through them." Walker tilts his head like a dog looking at his master's voice, "through some FM transmission to another room. Like you are not ever really there."

His persona was falling away!

He was being confronted by a world in which everything he had believed to be true had changed. A kind of wild panic set in.

Where before he had led a wild and chaotic life, drifting from job to job, hating authority, projecting his parents into the work situation, and one day he finds that the reason for all this is in his family, and the program of guilt and aversion and obfuscation of feelings that forced him to go through life posturing and gesturing in roles because he could not deal with his mother trying to fall in love with him, his father hating him and his sister making him feel guilty and ashamed of his sex.

Where today, he was really there. Really feeling everything and it scared him, not to have his ego program buffering him like layers of plumpness.

How would it be, to be there with those people and to be seen by them. To just be in your physical self. To get up and go pee in a communal bathroom. Would they spend a lot of time looking at you?

He began arguing back and forth with himself, one side taking the Utopian and the other side his nay saying ego.

Ego of Now: What kinds of phases do you get into?

What would you expect to happen to you, and your intersections with them in Utopia?

Utopian of the Future: You might go into an embarrassed grinning phase, but that could be gotten over. Negativity? A lot of that.

Ego of Now: They are so argumentative! What about having to have all these consensus discussions every time you tried to do something?

He was trying possibilities on for size, trying to psyche himself up for the big change.

Utopian: You could become a participant as well as an observer in an experiment.

Ego *(in a self mockery):* —It is really time to enter into this type of life-style. *(More earnestly)* I mean I'm a good guy! I have a hard time with authority, been having a lot of trouble holding down work, but I'm basically a GOOD guy. Have been out of touch with my real feelings, but maybe this could really help me get in touch with them. It is a well designed life style. One that keeps people active, keeps them moving, keeps them honest.

He pounds his fist as if making a point. "Good old fashioned Lutheran fear of idleness. Tantric hedonism."

What would you like to tell them. To beg the Utopian to let you go. But it is really a technique of how the ego argues the self out of feeling.

Utopian: So lets get a look at it. The Utopian looks at you from the future and says why not now. He looks at you with these big eyes, as if to admonish you for not hooking up.

Ego: I could start crying, I could get busted up, could crack up in front of people. I'm just an ordinary guy. Trying to get a little nookie. Needing a little tender loving care. Wanting a family, wanting tribe.

I'm not that heavy. And I'm afraid to keep my life in

such sharp focus, such scrutiny. Total lack of privacy! It boggles the mind.

Utopian: It's kind of warm and cozy. These people could help you out.

Ego: I could just move myself in, and be in my self, and maybe sometimes the ego would come up, but I could keep the deep sickness in me to myself.
"Persona falling here. Even the superstructure of your smile, can't keep it up. I am dying. I fear this. There is some alien being who has taken over my programming."
"Is the code genetic?"
Maybe these people would be the ones to live with.

Utopian: Egodeath is the way to get to Utopia, the tantric heaven. Take the *nuit blanche*, turn right past egodeath, and continue straight away till mourning. You perceive the world on many levels. Maybe at last you could inhabit the world through your body. Maybe you could just stand there as naked as a tree, under the cover of humility, in the expression of openness.

Ego: Maybe in Utopia, he could walk the ground grounded, feel the world through the extension of his body, revitalize the dead spots.

Utopian: No more myopia, no more shit eating grins of embarrassment. No more emotional blackmail, and to lie down with some real women who really did like men as equals as part of a whole, as part of a belonging to, and mutual longing for, and giving of what people have longings for. To be really accepted by some people, not for what you produce, but just for who you are.

Ego: Maybe he could escape the karma that had been laid down for him before his birth, that was a kind of rape that he had suffered wasn't it? Maybe he had burned off enough to . . . to really let himself live now.

Utopian: It would be wonderful to have those childlike

eyes staring at you for the rest of your life, and for you to look into them. They were vulnerable people too, they have feelings too. There are not robots, but seemed to live beyond, in a bigger sphere. The neurosphere of numinosity.

Ego: They seemed to know a lot more about this than he does. Although some have much more authority than others. This authority was like a wall he could not get through. He felt like pounding and pounding on it, shouting Open. Open! You son of a bitch!

Utopian: He had read about it. It was like some kind of aphasia, the inability to distinguish words, or communicate them, but it was in the right side of the brain, aprodosia, or alexithymia, the inability to feel or communicate emotions.

Ego: It is like I am communicating to the impression that my parents have left inside my brain, like they are always there, watching me, they are the ones that are carrying on the experiment I am just a little robot, plunked out there, that has been programmed. Sex brings up the two aspects of my nervous system. Sex with more than one person brings out the multiple aspects of my nervous system!
It must make you feel really weird, because the way they are living is a great indictment of the macroculture at large. The people like me though. I wonder. After a while people on the outside must seem practically like sociopaths, compared to them.

Utopian: All this lovely physical sex would make the male and female merge, and a new sensitive s/he is reborn.

Ego: Somehow my past has been opened, and I have gone back there and I am looking for myself. I am this alien being, that has been programmed to be sociological. I am this self that has developed this ego. There is this potential inside me, that I have got to control, that could come out at any moment, this curse, this translator, or it could be translated into something bad.
Surely these people must see it, they seem almost brutal in the way they see. They look at me with the eyes of

children, curious, accepting, not filling the face with a shit eating grin.

I could just get with them and ride out the waves of manic depression, maybe get to a state of being where I just hovered above it all. I could be all that I can be, or would be. I find my mind sound, and my capacity for feeling still large.

Utopian: Why not go for it?

Walker looked out the window, and saw the wind rustling through the trees and the tall grasses. That was the way feelings were, they just came up, invisible, outside like the wind, don't they? Or are they all inside. It is you that generates the feeling, and you can have them with anybody, who is having them too.

Feelings swirling around, like ghosts in the forests, projections of past lies, past lives, holding control over us all. Hands that reach out of the grave into our minds, still manipulating the controls, like the moving hand that moves the economy, that writes our destiny, our fate.

The translator burgeoning out of some All-mother.

Walker wrote in his diary:

```
March 27
Trying to decide to move into the loft.
Maybe I should move in there. It is the most love
I have ever felt in all my days.
If I didn't have my problems, I would move into
the loft immediately. But maybe that is why I should
move in there in the first place. Because I do have
problems. Like Herpes god damn it! Out here. It is
going to be nothing but loneliness.
This snake my cock is a snake wrapped around my
reason, will not let it have its way. It has
betrayed me many times, but no more.
```
—-

On April fools day he decided What the Hell. And he went over to announce his intention to move into the House. But when he got there he could sense Dahlia didn't want to see him and he got cold feet left.

Once again he slipped away from the house. Went for a walk down Valencia Street. Saw a fight, in which two young *cholos* were bating three big dykes. One of the hoodlums got his head slammed into the pavement of Valencia Street. He got thrown over a car. Right in front of a tourists car, almost got run over. Man, she could really fight this one.

Meanwhile a bigger dyke, got worked over by this other young *pachuco*. Both of them flailing the daylights out of each other.

One of the women asked: "What started it?"

"One of those assholes called her creep. That's what started it."

The punks kept taunting, and they almost got into it again.

Her partners had to keep pulling the big one off saying, "It's not worth it! It's not worth it!"

```
    4/1/83 April Fools Day.
    The rules I have to play by, are to get going in
the house, or she won't see me any more. No I can't
bear to be without her, even if it is from afar, so
I need to get with the program over at the House.
Either that or lose her. Hey, it's a good
opportunity to find out how people make friends with
each other.
    It sort of dawned on me when I went over there
tonight. Dahlia didn't want to see me, so I split,
and didn't come back.
    There is so much of the way that we hover around
closed doors, and hide so much from each other.
```

24

Jade, Cool as Green Ice

Having slipped away from the House twice, Walker knew that soon he would be required to confront his panic around facing Big Group. Walker's plan was to get involved with the commune in hopes that down the road he'd be able to get together with Dahlia again. I'm not obsessed, he kept telling himself, I'm determined. I'm not a stalker. I've just got to have her. She is the woman of my soul.

Monday night started off with Big Group chanting and meditation in a large circle as usual. Strawboss was Denise After some other issues were discussed, Denise casually looked across the assembled powwow at Dahlia and said, "Was there something you wanted to bring up in Big Group about Walker?"

In front of God and everybody Dahlia looked across at Walker and she said, "There is some way, that you come and go around here, which —like for example—you came by here last night, then you split.

"Then you call me on the phone and talked to me for a long time about how you were feeling in the group last time."

Walker looked up and everybody was looking at him. He was struck dumb with panic. There he was sitting in lotus position on the floor surrounded by some 35 people in one-point focus looking at him in his flimsy blue T-shirt feeling vulnerable. Luckily Rachel cut the tension by sending out a grope that spoke to everyone's concern with the new groups: "I'm really scared about getting to know you."

"That makes two of us," Walker quickly replied, relieved.

He knew everybody was freaking out from the group restructure and in a way it was a perfect time to start with everybody else starting off more or less at the beginning. "We are all in the same boat." Walker interjected. Everybody laughed.

Dahlia was setting him loose into the group. Kind of

232

introducing herself to him and him to the group, where here she is her own person. She will not be pursued into her group. He didn't try.

More discussion ensued about how the group was to handle new people. Dahlia said: "Chase isn't around to help you. You should get some help from your group."

They were having to go entirely on group processes that they had learned the hard way from some twelve years of intensive group practice. The gist of it was, that Walker should stay around and have more sessions.

A lot of people were smiling at him, and making friendly overtures to him during the evening. They came over and talked to him during clean up. Some people mentioned times they had encounters with him before. Walker could feel their goodwill under the ackwardness. Serena came over and asked him to have a session with her sometime. Walker was both thrilled and scared to be invited into this older woman's bed.

In small group when it finally got started, the group talked with Rachel who was having a hard time. Her fear was reaching a level of panic. "I saw my father's face dissolve in front of me," she said," and it almost made me crack up. I'm feeling like that now."

After dealing with her issues it was decided that Jade and Walker would have a session. Jade was a very attractive woman, she had these half-wild cat eyes, and Walker was excited at the possibliites. She looked kind of wild and mean, or angry all the time. Almost boyish. Walker had learned from her that she was from New Orleans. She was not as tall as the other women and she was southern, he liked that. Jade dug up a couple of sleeping bags while Walker talked with Morey and Luke, Chase's teenage son. They were looking at this big kit for making electronics devices. It made Walker feel good to give a child of the house some pointers in electronics.

Then Jade and Walker lay down on top of the sleeping bags in their clothes and talked. It was awkward and he didn't know how to be there, with everyone else around making love and groaning and moaning in tantric sex. Jade's mood slipped into one of darkness and negativity and her brow became wrinkled in consternation. She spoke about things that were bothering her -- sad things -- most of the time, until he started kissing on her. He kissed her forehead and cheeks with compassion, kissed her lips with love and she smiled. Yes, that finally made her smile. Walker didn't try to get into any sexual activity with her because of his sense of guilt over having herpes and responsibility not to have sex with anyone he hadn't informed. and he couldn't bring himself to speak of that. His diary the next day read:

Tuesday April 4,83. Monday night was quite a night. It started off with meditation.
It was a rough night. Didn't have the right pillow. Jannett started crying, right next to us on the floor.
She has some terrible eczema all over her body, and is taking a primitive cure where she doesn't use anything, just relies on her own immune system and it is very painful and keeps her up all night. She plays the radio.
She tries to get some relief in a little smoke.

God damn the infernal irony of this though. Here I am in tantric heaven, a bachelor, horny, constantly on the make, and yet, I am wanting to be with Dahlia, wanting to pursue only her. It is crazy this idea of romance. An opportunity to engage in all the sex I could sweet talk my way into and yet blocked by this eternal venereal disease that frightens partners. I'd have to laugh if it wasn't so pathetic.
This is utopia, this is tantric heaven.
The next day I was all shook up again for hours.

I wonder about my relationship with Dahlia.
A lot of things went unsaid in our relationship. Like why are we are even hanging out with each other. It feels like the first time every time. This awkwardness. It must make her feel like that too. Not to take anything for granted.
Maybe I can make this group of people who are here to help me, my group. Maybe I can make it work. Maybe I can get rid of this negativity, and be of service, become a committed friend to this group.
There are a lot of parental guilt figures hovering around. Like harpies: a foul or malign creature of Greek myth , part woman and part bird. Leech. A shrewish woman.
Voices of guilt, like nuns, school teachers, the mothers. Voices of pain. Sad voices, hollow voices. Faceless voices. Voices with strange faces!

Yes we begin to see these ghosts. And they really do try to castrate you.

The little mother, who puts spaghetti dinners down for you, who sat up with you all night long when you were sick and who read to you, saw you growing up and felt sapped of her energy, and so saw you leaving and taking away her main identity, and thus wanted to cripple you, so that you would be dependent, and want to stay with her. So she castrated you. They all do it.

It should not be too uneven in a relationship, or people will be uncomfortable. I wonder what Jade thought of me. It is a way I can study myself. And I can keep this sick point in containment, not let them push me around.

Next time I go there, I'll ask Pia, "When men have sessions do they actually get naked and hug each other!?"

Yes, there are harpies floating around the bathroom. Harpies floating around the bedroom. I know, to be loner and a monk is to flee from this power and feeling this power. And to be a flake well, one reason is because I have been doing a lot of things to punish myself, to hurt myself, but haven't managed to do it totally, and I'm starting to see it now. And another part of the flakiness is because people don't get to see me do what I do best. Writing. I have to hide what I'm really passionately interested in.

25

Memories like Blossoms on a Stream
in a Japanese Tea Garden

On Saturday Dahlia called Walker and they decided to
go to a movie. Walker came over and they had a little dinner
at the loft. She looked skinny in a blue flannel jumper dress
that was just hanging off her. Smiling though. . . and coming
along.

"It never stops," she said. "Now I've got this infected
spider bite. I'm taking antibiotics for it. They make me kind
of nauseous."

She took him up to her room. Some House men had
fixed Dahlia up with an actual bed made out of plywood on
top of blue plastic milk crates in Chase's room —to keep her
from having to lower herself up and down off the floor with
her stitches. As soon as she could she was walking up and
down the stairs, working for the commune, fixing her own
meals.

Everyone was out of the House. She had to keep the
infected arm idle, tied up in the air with a sash. Someone had
shown her how to tie the knot with one hand. She looked
pathetic, quite the hapless waif. Not skinny, not white but
lean and Scandinavian. Thoughts of taking advantage of her
while trussed up like that drifted across Walker's mind and
shocked him. He started wanting to get this show on the
road, to get her out, get her walking around. And it was
turning out to be a beautiful day. It would be their first
outing since the operation and she wanted to wear something
spectacular. She went to her closet and put on an elegant
cream-yellow full-length summer dress she had picked up
cheap at the consignment store on Mission. It had con-
trasting white collar and cuffs on the short sleeves. It had
black buttons down the entire front which she had buttoned
about halfway down. She also put on a floppy straw hat with
a little fake corsage in it. She looked like an elegant young
rich white fox, a lady who had forgotten her gloves on her
way to a Marin garden-party wedding.

He gasped with amazement, he had never seen her like this. "I want to go where a girl wears a yellow dress . . ." he said with breathy gusto, smiling at her in appreciation.

She smiled a knowing smile back at him too.

Before going to the movie the couple went to the Japanese Tea garden in Golden Gate Park since it was turning out to be sunny Spring day. The cherry trees and the almond trees were in bloom.

Walker was solicitous. They walked slowly, his arm around her the whole time. White petals drifted through the spring arbor dancing in the shimmering air. They looked at the Buddha which stands for freedom. Looking at the blossoms, breathing the spring air Walker remarked, "It's a buddhaful day."

There was a little stream floating by, with almond petals floating in it. He observed the white petals fallen from the air into gently murmuring waters of the little irrigation streams fanning out through the garden running fast past each other in parts of the stream then twirling around and getting hooked up again. He paused a moment and thought: God I'm glad she's alive in this world and we met and she is returning to me.

When they sat down people couldn't help looking at the attractive couple. She looked so fay. A cute Japanese woman took their order for tea. Walker displayed his tourist status by saying, "Don't forget the cookies."

He quickly turned the topic over to their mutual interest and passion —the House and its psychology / religion. Walker wondered about the Primal Scream aspect of the House.

"What are these images that people talk about seeing when they get into a lot of screaming?" Walker asked.

"I recall how on the wall in my room when I was a kid," Dahlia said, "there were all these images of Disney characters on the wall. I remember looking at them with great anger, just standing in my crib and looking at them with great anger. These images come up now when I recall the great anger I had and I know it relates back to what I felt when I was a kid."

"I've seen them on acid sometimes," she said. "When you've done a lot of acid, you find that the earlier trips are very visual, but later they become more dramatic and more personally involved with past memories, and projections with people in the present.'

"We sometimes take acid when we visit our parents now. It leads to a lot of insights."

"Yes . . . That would be totally terrifying."

"Yes, and why you might wonder."

After a while he asked her, "What about sleeping with men? I'm having a hard time even thinking about that."

"It really breaks all the rules," she said. "It's not even homosexual with all the women-hating that *they* are into."

"It's easier for women to sleep with the same sex," Walker challenged, "—because they hug on their mothers."

"Not for me," she said. "It really brings up a lot. The only time my mother ever touched me was when she grabbed me and wanted to make me do something I resented."

Dahlia reminisced about her earlier experiences with the House. This helped Walker greatly.

"I had a real hard time with Malcolm," she said. "We were so much alike, I thought we'd never sleep together."

Then they drove through the park to the ocean. Parking on a bluff overlooking the sea. They watched the sun set. He got into her seat, knowing that it made her feel better to be touched and hugged.

He held her to him. They kissed. She pushed her lips into his, pressing into him. He pushed his tongue into her mouth and touched her tongue. She stuck hers out between her teeth in the cutest way and teasingly flicked it over his lips. Swooning them made out heavily like that for a while.

And their hands began to very slowly roam of their own free will all over each other, touching squeezing feeling. He felt her touch; her fingers reached under his shirt and touched his nipples. Her fingertips were hot and tingling, as she raked the nails briskly over the sensitive male buds; he gasped at her touch.

Her hand felt hot as she felt the muscles in his stomach. Then, much to his surprise, she maneuvered her small slender hand down under his belt and snaked it slowly down to meet his cock which was inching up to meet it. When she closed her hot little hand around his cock it engorged and immediately stiffened. She pulled his cock up toward his navel elongating it, stretching it out and massaged it and pulled on it, till he thought he was about to come in his pants.

He started squirming away from her and she said, "Breathe, make sound." He exhaled a loud moan and pulled away.

Then she squirmed in her seat to rearrange herself. The long yellow dress opened revealing her long slender SHAVED! legs more. The dress opened way more to reveal her soft white inner thighs.

He opened a button at the top of her dress. He reached his hand in and cupped a breast. His thumb played with her nipple, which began to harden. She rounded her shoulders so he could get a better view down at her creamy white tits.

Then they both smiled at each other as he opened a few more buttons further down opening the dress up even more to reveal her lovely pink cotton panties. She rearranged herself again throwing the open skirt over his hand hiding it from view. He reached further up into the dark canyon gently touching her crotch through gauzy panties. He could feel the outline of her pussy lips. He gently played his fingers over them until they were swollen and hot and becoming moist. They made out hot and heavy like that for a while. She was panting hot in his ear as he bent unawares to his task. Then they pulled apart again and smiled at each other in chagrin.

"You're not bad looking," she said to him. . . "We didn't even look up. I'm sure everybody must have known what we were doing."

"Wow! I haven't done that since high school," he said.

"Me either."

Then they separated and got in separate seats, still watching the sun set.

"I had this dream the other night," she said. "I was being the Big Sister. I was out on a pier and these huge sharks were swimming around. Someone was standing on some rocks nearby. 'Let's go swimming' someone — who turned out to be my younger brother — said.

"Sharks came, there was this huge fin of death knifing through the water, and quickly, immediately dragged the person in the water down. Then all the sharks rushed the pier and when they leaped out, they turned out to be a blue marlin sail fish and a porpoise."

Walker began thinking the dream was about him, about the threat he represented to these gentle people. That somehow she was the guardian of the House, keeping the sharks at bay.

"I don't know why I didn't just run," she said.

On the drive from the ocean to the movie, they talked about how they felt like high school kids, with all the awkwardness and trying to get out of the house, and how they hadn't done that kind of thing since high school.

"How was it the first time you did It?" she asked.

Walker hemmed and hawed; he didn't have fond memories. He had told her about his first time with the whores in Mexico."s

"My first time was really awful too," she said. "It was really awkward. I thought the guy would think my breasts were too small, and just tell me to get lost. But I decided to just jump into it and if he was going to get rid of me, then so be it.

"After a few times it got to be quite enjoyable, and I started to really love it and want to be close. I had a really hard time with oral sex. Thought that I was some kind of whore or something."

"Then I married the guy, then got divorced and lived with this woman who was a prostitute, and hung out with her pimp. I hung out at a lot of rough bars, these Philippine bars in Hawaii.

"I almost committed suicide, when our car broke down one time in the rain," Dahlia said. "I was running against the light across a rain-slick street. I slipped and a car stopped just a few feet from my head.

"I had a lot of difficulty in high school, wanted to get into sex with people, but was afraid to go all the way. It must have been very frustrating for the boys."

"Yea," Walker said. "I remember having the worse case of blue balls. I would pet, and make out for hours. It's nice to hear what it was like from the other side."

That nigh,t after eating at a place on Haight Street called All You Knead, they returned to her infirmary at the Loft, and sat around talking to Jesse who was in there, too, recuperating from his operation.

Then they undressed and crawled into bed. Walker was inhibited with Jesse, only Jesse in the room. Walker realized, that when you are out on the Floor with the main population, you are more invisible. Although Jesse politely turned away, on the Floor you are more invisible because everybody else is into their own session and not paying attention to you. With just one other person in the room it is more inhibiting.

Dahlia pulled off Walker's underpants and began squeezing his hard cock, causing him to quickly come on her hand.

"Want me to dry you off a bit?" he wispered.

"No. I didn't get any on me," she said. "We should have made more sound."

As he was getting ready to go down to breakfast —he was brushing his hair with her brush — she looked at him with love and sympathy and said, "You look presentable."

He felt like she was his big sister, looking out for him always — really loving him. He also felt that he was not loving her back the way she wants. The way he wanted to really make sex happen for her.

26

First Time Again

That Tuesday Walker, having dismissed classes early, was with Dahlia in Chase's room in the afternoon. Jesse was gone. She was sitting up in the platform bed with her arm raised above her head tied at the wrist in a home-made sling.

"Would you give me a back rub?" she said sweetly. "My back is sore. I've been lying on it a lot." She looked so vulnerable and exasperated and staked-out in her blue slip with the thin straps. She undid the sling and slowly in many steps slid down rolled over and laid on her front. Walker got some massage oil off a nearby table warmed a dollop of it in his hands then rubbed and rubbed her body in a most gentle way. Soon she felt relaxed. Walker had such nice hands.

In bed they wanted to hug. Carefully, gently Walker touched his body against Dahlia's. "Lets take these clothes off," she said.

As she couldn't hardly sit up due to the incision in her stomach she said: "You'll have to undress me." This was a rare oportunity for Walker because the women in the loft always undressed themselves. They believed that anything else would have lent itself to fantasy, illusion and ego manifestation.

Walker knelt on the bed next to her knees. He put his hands on either side of the elastic of her panties, flipped the top edge over and slid them down slowly. His hands kept moving, revealing more and more of her perfectly rounded ass. "It is amazing how important the stomach muscles are," she said nervously.

Walker left the panties binding her at the knees for a moment, and gently rubbed his hot hands all over the cool cheeks of her fine ass. It was making him hard. He slipped the panties past her knees down to her ankles and he let his hand feel up her bare thighs to slip between her legs. She instinctively opened her legs, straining against the binding panties around the ankles to accommodate him. Seeing the panties binding her like foot cuffs like that made him harder.

He leisurely took them off her feet then tossed them on the floor.

Leaving her slip pulled up to her waist he gently maneuvered out of his own clothes stripping all the way down to nudity, trying not to shake the bed.

He lay down beside her, then gently began rubbing her back some more. She was in heaven with his touch. She cuddled and quivered in his hands, like a shy, young, cat-like connoisseur of pleasure being petted by an affectionate owner. He kissed her face and "third eye".

After a while she gently took his hard cock in her hand and was rubbing it gently up and down. Slowly jacking him off. With her hand she worked him up higher and harder. She felt his stiff cock by letting her fingers dance up and down its length. Reaching down she held his balls gently in the palm of her hand as if handling precious jewels. She had him standing tall.

"What does that feel like when I touch you here?" she asked.

"Where?" he said.

She closed her fingers and thumb into a claw and pulled it up the whole length of his shaft, giving an extra strong tug on the head of his cock.

"Here!" she said.

He felt the entire area between his legs had become one huge amorphous erogenous zone. He held his breath. He tightened up.

"Where?" he said, trying to get her to touch him like that again.

Dahlia fiddled her hand faster, her fingers playing an instrument causing Walker to gasp.

"Here," she said.

"I can't tell where you're touching, it all feels so good," he said moaning.

She smiled, getting up to his tricks.

This hand-job went on for several minutes.

Then he helped her turn over and sit up. Walker enjoyed lifting the clothes over her head —having her need his help. Then Dahlia reclined luxuriously into the soft pillows sitting upright. She extended her hand.

"Here we better put the sling back on," he said. He took

her hand and slipped the noose over her limp wrist. He pulled the sash up taut, looped it over the coat rack and tied it to the turn buckle. As he was reaching up working to do this his cock grazed past her soft breasts once, then bumped into her shoulder.

Kneeling, he leaned over, brushed her hair back out of her face, kissed her on the cheek and said, "I love you. I would never do anything to hurt you." He kissed her mouth, hot, deep, forceful. She kissed back. He slid his hand over her chest, caressing her breast.

She almost lost her breathing.

Then, getting up on his knees, he very carefully straddled her supine body. He moved his huge hairy engorged goat-like cock up toward her sweet precious mouth. She had her head propped up on a pillow.

She closed her eyes while he traced the outline of her lips with the tip of his cock. Finally she opened her mouth and let him slip his cock inside.

"Are you OK? I hate to take it out of a sick woman," he said in a teasing tone.

This challenging tone made her laugh.

"It feels pretty scary," she said.

She started breathing to make herself relax. She blew hot air over the head of his cock. It twitched and jumped around. She thought: his cock is the hardest I have ever seen it. She remembered what Chase had told her: Chase told me to give my lover the best cock suck of his life. Then I will let go of my prejudices whatever they are.

As she gently closed her lips around his rigid cock she thought: As I slide my lips over the head of his cock, I fall in love with his cock. I can only think about his cock in my mouth now, my lips are tingling.

She looked up at him her eyes staring wide, one moment they looking shocked and amazed; the next moment smoldering. She started using her lips and her tongue and looking up to see his reaction. She began running her free hand up and down over it.

Walker's eyes were as big as she had ever seen them.

Walker had a perfect view as her lips formed a circle around the shaft and she sucked it in as far as she could. He

244

could see the muscles in her throat making a swallowing motion. He said, "Oh, Baby!"

She thought: I get this mixed feeling of joy, sadness, excitement and peace as I stop arguing with myself that he is taking advantage of me.

And while she did this to him, he groaned in ecstasy, and prayed that he had not jostled her too much.

Walker said, "God, what exquisite torture."

After a while he starts getting overwhelmed with guilt: if she isn't going to have an orgasm he wasn't. He stops, pushes her away and pulls it out of her mouth for he was about to come. He kisses her on the lips, and her big hot soft pouting wet lips responded.

She made a mental note for commune nymphos: The quickest way to a man's brain is by giving him a blow job.

They got into a hug and began auming together, resonating their bodies. THERE was that feeling of power and love.

27

Looming toward a Phantom Love High

Walker is in his little Berkeley studio apartment walking stiff-legged as though up on stilts swaying back and forth, as though looking down on the world from some kind of fantastic love high.

"Looming toward some kind of phantom love high," he says aloud to no one. "Tilting there! . . . Shifting."

It is some kind of terrific up and down thing, mood swings, oscillating, spiraling, out-of-control, beating and pounding against itself getting into higher and higher feelings. Yes, that was it! Love was an escalating positive feedback situation where action and reaction enhanced each other producing stronger and stronger vibrations! He wrote incoherently in his diary:

Diary April 10 83
I want the perfect love. Who doesn't? I want both me and Dahlia to have our freedom. She and her beauty were always affecting me now. She was the big sister, I had always wanted. The woman who helps me out.

But I wonder, what am I to her? Sometimes it felt like I was a project she had taken on. Somehow I fell that I was involved in some projection of hers, that I was playing some fatherly role, or some brotherly role.

I have this fear of death. And I can't tell anybody about it! It felt like I was walking around on borrowed time. It is what drove me closer to people. . .

Dahlia is a brave woman, you can tell by the freckles on her back. She is a strong wise person. I'm afraid that my need might drain off her strength. And yet there is much strength to be had in what she made me confront. She showed me where there is a lot of paranoia, made me admit there is a lot of fear and guilt that comes up around sex.

I have seen this fear in myself before, and I always try to cover it up in a fit of impatience. It was a fear of being receptive, of waiting. That was why meditation was so beneficial and so difficult. You had to have a sense of timing where you are not so stoned-out relaxed that everything goes by, nor so avidly after it that you get ahead of what is supposed to happen making it impossible to perceive what happens.

I wonder if we might be able to speak of it in terms of communication theory. Ghosts in the line, harmonic aberrations, shadowing images. These came up and spread out of the organism, like phantoms and shadows into the interstices and other dimensions of time. There is a flurry of verbal activity always going on inside my mind. My brain is frying. Something there is that always translates my good intentions, my feelings into something else, some kind of avoidance, standing off like a British gentleman, hands in his pockets.

Dahlia is becoming a Bodhisatva of compassion for me. For brief moments I saw the world through her eyes, or eyes of the feminine, the eyes of compassion. Did she see people as transparent beings? Was it possible to see the source of these emanations.

Emanations from the human archetype. Ah it's all so deep, how could I ever understand it! I am always in my ego listening to the constant fears and arguments against feeling, against really being.

She had become a part of me. She had become the compassion artist within himself. She would liberate me, liberate my feelings, she was becoming my feelings!

At times I slip into these incredible moments in which I see how the human archetype really was a self-contained microcosm of its own, projecting things out onto the world. I saw the archetype as the crown of millions of forms of evolution, writhing out, in fluid and color. The chore data, — the spine that evolved from the plants and the trees. I am an experiment in the theatre of the world!

It frightened me how much I am ruled by my cock. I have no control over it!

Now how in the hell can I get over there? I mean what _would_ it be like to live there with all of them. After all those years of being with people who were unconscious of their feelings, myself included.

There is this bridge of hope and faith we build into the future, that is what feelings are, aren't they? They are the pattern that we follow, the road map. We have got to be able to trust feelings.

I came to the Fear, and wanted to know what this fear was. Wasn't the world my mother, my own autonomous nervous system that lets me live on even though I am weak and dependent in it?

How could I get out of this dependence? I had to be born again by a new mother, the good mother. A good mother that would nurture me. A good mother that is not something to be fought against, not something to be dominated, but something you just have to relax and go with.

The House is such a mother.

I must begin to know it as Gaia.

When I got into a full-on hug with Dahlia or any other member of the house, I would think of it as the embrace of Gaia.

28

Sisters and Brothers; Wives and Husbands

Rachel, who was now according to the House convention a wife unto Walker, was to him not yet even a House sister, called him up and made arrangements for their new small group to go out together on next Friday night. It would be like being in the group out in the world.

When Walker got to the Loft, Dahlia totally ignored him. He feigned nonchalance. Instead he got into a really hot game of tag with little Dhyana and Malcolm. It was a very vigorous game, socks off, shrieks of laughter; others of the house joining in. As they were in the thick of it, the beautiful Rachel walked in from her downtown job as a legal assistant.

She was wearing a full length dress trimed with brocade. The top, which had a stand-up collar with large bow in center, was white with a silver thread running through it. It had long sleeves. The full length bottom was a wonderful lemon yellow with lace panels that meet in the middle. She also was wearing a vest that made her look stylish and powerful. She was smiling because of a recent promotion. The way she was holding a wide brimmed hat in front of her made her look urbane, attractive.

Walker was so grateful that his friends and fellow brothers of the flesh, Kevin and Morey would be going out with them too.

Dahlia was keeping her distance, letting him know he was on his own. Walker saw her getting into a big hug on the floor with two other house sisters one was Lissa, a wild looking punk woman with a shock of straight hair in a barely acceptable mohawk, —she was also a new recruit — and Denise a nurse with massive pitch-black curls.

As they were all going out the door, Dahlia did a big sister number, inquiring about the image of Rachel's hat: "You must have made quite an impression with that big hat in the BART crowd, Rachel? I bet everybody stepped aside for you."

Rachel gave her a condescending Huh!? look.

They all ran into each other again at the restaurant
Amazing Grace, Dahlia and the other two women at a
separate table, Walker occasionally looking at her, she not
acknowledging it. Dahlia was being an observer from afar he
thought. — I am her experiment. She is trying to make a
liberated man out of me. I hope the experiments continue.

Walker was taking this rag-tag group of revelers to North
Beach in his van. It was joyous and weird like being in a
color Felleni movie. It was April 15 and they swung down
Market St. so Morey could drop his taxes off at the last
minute. There was a long line of cars in front of the S.F.
main post office, getting their taxes in before the midnight
deadline. And to add to the carnival atmosphere, the
Libertarian Party was out in full costume protest, one guy
dressed like a pig, handing out satirical literature. Rachel
was perked up, enjoying being driven around in a car.

The Saloon, a funky old bar with beatniks and hippies
and a stinging powerful blues revue, was packed, people
wedged in everywhere and grooving out on the small dance
floor.

The Saloon is definitely the kind of place you go to meet
people — you had to — because you are so crowded in
together like being in a party in somebody's front room. An
enormous man on stage, the lead singer of the blues band,
joked: "Welcome to the Drip Dry Lounge," through the thick
smoky atmosphere.

Morey danced with Rachel, and some other woman he
met in the crowd. They finally got Walker to dance.

"I really like to dance," said Rachel, looking fine
swaying near Walker at the bar.

"I guess humans are the only animals that dance,"
Walker offered.

"Bees dance," Morey mused aloud.

"Are bees animals?" Walker queried.

"No they're insects," said Kevin.

"Elephants like to dance," Walker said. "They like to
stand up and bump butts." He did a slow motion routine, of
sliding a massive buttock crashing into another and bouncing
off.

He said to Rachel, so that Kevin could hear, "Did you
know that the elephant orgasm lasts for something like 6

hours?" Walker waited for the smile to appear. "That's right. As part of the foreplay the female cow digs a hole and gets into it so the bull can mount her and they carry on for days. When the orgasm finally comes they trumpet wildly as it lasts for hours!"

Toward the end of the evening, the band shocked everyone by singing Herpes Blues.

I got sores / on my mouth and penis
it'll be a long time before / I touch your mons Venus
I got the herpes blues, yeah, yeah, I got the herpes blues,
It ended with the refrain:
It's only a cold sore!
Of course, this really got Walker's mind going.

As the group was leaving some women that Kevin and Morey had danced with stopped the boys and engaged them in long conversation. Rachel and Walker went to get the car to pick them up.

Walking down Broadway beside this beautiful woman, he said, "The men at the house must really be prized by the women that they meet. I mean, they are sensitive men. Just as the women are so approachable."

She responded with a question: "How did you meet Dahlia?"

"She came in and sat down beside me at a theatre and I felt from the moment she sat down she was approachable."

"I'm afraid of having relationships with men outside the house," she said.

"Why is that?"

"Because I'm afraid of what kind of fantasies they get into."

Rachel was his Session Person for the night. She brought down a beautiful down filled futon. She had a fine satin lined comforter to lie under.

"I like my bed a lot," she said as she, all undressed, plopped her perfectly round tush down on the little soft isle of dreams beside Walker. He, the scared idiot, had on his briefs and T-shirt.

And that's the way it was, for this their first session. Rachel was beautiful and strong and open, she handled the scared and up-tight Walker with kid gloves. She could see that he was having a hard time, unable to disassociate nudity from sexuality. And she just allowed the night to roll on, making it fun and casual.

Walker was too terrified and too mindful of his duty to tell Rachel of his eternal VD to be able to respond amorously to her cheerful physicality.

He needed to tell her but he couldn't make the decision, he was confused and didn't know which way to turn, he wanted to get into sex with her, but didn't feel that attractive to her, though she was a beautiful woman. She let him keep playing with her pussy and she seemed to enjoy it. For Walker, a lot of pain and guilt came up about punishment for nudity and sexual experience. He brought the lovely Rachel off with his gentle hands though.

Toward dawn, Loretta, who was a wonderful little pixie of a woman old enough to be his mother, and Ursu, a stout young fellow from Germany were getting into a real wild love making session. She was letting out with excruciating sobbing long drawn out moans at top volume.

OOOOOOHHAAAAAAAA
HHHHHHHHAAAAAAAAA
AAAAAUUUUUUUMMMMMMMMMMMMM

It was really something to lay there in the night and hear these wild human animals really baying for love.

OOOOHHHHAAAAAAAAAAAAA
HHUUUMMMM!

Man, what a sound. Completely blow out the bad electrons from those old engramatic circuits. Like somebody falling off a high cliff into a cold ocean. A tremendous vibrating drone.

"OOOOOOOHHHHHAOOOOOHHUUUUUMM
MMMMAAAAAAAAAAAOOOOOOHHHUUUUUUMM

Walker could hear the release of a thousand pent-up wrongs in there and the couple like dynamos generating electricity from huge roar of rushing waterfalls, or like some high cyclone airplane engine steadily flying through a tumultuous storm of passion.

"Hey! Use a pillow!" Somebody shouted from the floor.

Later in the early light, Walker could overhear bits of their post- coital conversation, coming in gulps and panting.

Ursu: "I can't believe we made such beautiful love."

Then later. Loretta: "Sometimes you make me feel like I have to seduce you. I don't want to feel that I have to seduce you."

Ursu: ". . . There is some kind of disgust that comes up."

Loretta: "I don't want to feel that I always have to be the one. . ."

Ursu: ". . .We just have to let it work itself out."

In the morning Walker and Rachel lounged in bed after everyone else had gone. She was warm and smooth and was very strong in her embrace of Walker. He liked that.

"Did you ever lift weights?" he asked.

She smiled at the compliment and said, "When are you coming over next?" she said, holding onto his big toe, and stretching out her long sweet dancer's body.

"Monday for sure!"

On Monday, Walker was there for small group. It was to be his first session with a man. O god, he thought. This is it. Now I'm going to sleep with a man. What *won't* I do to get close to Dahlia.

But several other men on the Floor had sessions with other men that night, and if they could do it he could do it. It would be just like sleeping next to somebody in a tent on a camping trip. Wouldn't it?

Morey laid out his futon, with sheets and blanket made of what appeared to be horse hair. Morey took off all his clothes and, naked, got under the covers. Walker knew he would have to get undressed somewhat, so as not to embarrass Morey, but he left his underclothes on.

The two men talked for a while, and were just generally reclining under covers watching the proceedings of the rest of the house, getting set up for the night's sessions. Dahlia came by and grinned openly with delight at her two lovers' heads poking up from under the covers.

Morey said: "Want to get into a hug?"

Walker said: "O.K."

And they did. They started making sounds, to expiate fear, like monks chanting together. They pressed body to body, and Walker was shocked to feel Morey's penis touch his bare leg. Walker quickly moved away. But didn't say anything. He didn't know what to say. Walker was quite surprised to find that a man's body, in a naked hug, could feel almost as soft as a woman's. All in all it wasn't so terrible.

The next day, being out in the world, he felt he had been given a tremendous knowledge about men, that very few other men had. He would look at them differently now.

Walker began to see that he could be there, and if he needed some space, just hide behind being sick like the others. Not have sex. It was cool, the atmosphere was so loving.

You just retire to the bed and let the aums turn into moans. Retire on the floor on a futon in a room with 20 or 30 people in it. Live with 2 feet of space to call your own. Easy. Every night there was the caterwauling Walker loved to hear, as night after night he heard the moans and the aums and the hugs of people relaxing into their own real body.

Sometimes he looked up at the full moon, shining down through the south window, against the hills beyond and knew this was a tranquil and innocent place, with little futon islands of dreamers swaddled in bright lively colored down bags and flannels and quilts— the carpet under them all.

And there are the various personified sub-personalities — coalitions in all of us. They come to the fore and speak at times. At times it seems that they only have words for each other. The continuous repetitions that each one does.

Walker is learning some tantric practices. He read in an ancient Tibetan yoga book about coitus reservatus: Orgasm without emission of semen by adult males who deliberately contract their genital muscles. The energy compressed by this practice is translated and emitted in making sounds. This is called the full-on hug. Sex for the women and men of the loft was among other things a test of each other to see how much outrageously pleasurable sexual stimulation they could withstand without ending it in orgasm. The experienced male could go on indefinitely... the multiorgasmic female could too.

The wild tantric women could really tease and test.

29

The Genius of Love Tries out her new Body

Walker arrived for a session with Dahlia, on Tuesday night, just a month after her operation. She was with one of the small boys. Dave and some of the other men and children got a wild jump rope session going. Several members of the house joined in. For some, including Walker, it was their first time jumping doubles. It was hilarious.

Even Dahlia joined in and Walker was scared that she would dislodge a stitch, but she looked good, wearing a long skirt of dark cloth and leggings (looking like a nun), holding the change in her pocket, jumping to the skipping rope.

That tired them out and they lay down beside each other on the floor and then went into the kitchen and she made him some orange juice. In the kitchen a big discussion about women in the works of Carlos Casteneda was taking place.

"You know in his later works there is a lot about men sorcerers being in battle with women sorcerers. They have a lot of trouble getting it together," Beverly said.

After a while Walker and Dahlia went upstairs into the Loft and he carried their futon, and placed it on the floor, after getting a few others to move over a bit. He helped her put the newly laundered flannel sheets on it, for this was her first time back to sleeping on the floor.

"Let's look at *your* pictures," she said.

They started with the baby pictures. They looked at a picture of him sitting in a perambulator. "Wow, look at that big old heavy rig," he said. "My mother told me they were made of hard-edged cast iron. It must have been hell to maneuver around."

Dahlia placed her hand over the mouth and nose of one infant picture, so that just the eyes could be seen. The first things Dahlia noticed was the fear - no - the terror in the undistracted eyes of the infant Walker.

"It is not natural for a child that young to show so much fear in the eyes," she said.

Another page showed earlier pictures, out of sequence,

of Walker's mother, holding the infant Walker at christening. She looked like she had bags under her eyes in one picture, maybe just home from the hospital? She was so young and inexperienced in the way she held him. There was a lot of trapped fear, yet bravery in her eyes.

The next picture that was really pretty shocking, to even Walker, who was still into defending his parents, still the good, dutiful son, was a picture of the 2 year old in a thick snow suit, tied to a leash, in this impoverished tenement yard in east side Montreal.

"That is probably where you get your fear of confinement, from being tied up," Dahlia said. "Look at that face, do you think he wants to be there? He looks like a dog on a leash!"

Then the next pictures showed how Walker had learned to develop a smile that covered this fear. There were inklings of it in his first communion picture. There in the second grade picture, it was a sprightly smile, beneath a portrait of the Queen of England, next to one of the Sacred Bleeding Heart of Jesus.

There was one with him and his two sisters and very young brother, next to another family of 6 children. These children were dressed casual, while Walker and his siblings were dressed up; he was wearing a natty bow tie. The 3 older children — Walker and his 2 sisters — had a look of phony smiles plastered on their faces, while their little brother looked really afraid.

Dahlia said, "Looks like the older ones can cover the fear pretty good by now, but the little one can't."

Walker said nothing. He was shocked and not believing this revelatory observation.

Then there were some really terrifying images, taken on a Christmas day. Times were hard then. Walker remembered a lot of poverty. There is a picture of his father looking really hung over and sheepish, because by this time he was a heavy alcoholic, and Walker's little brother was looking up at him in terror. This was after that horrendous slap. An occluded memory he had recalled with the group help.

Walker could recall that by now the family life was one without love, without touching, except when there was violence or punishment to be meted out. So not only was there a low-level noise of constant threat, it wasn't so low level, there was plenty of physical violence too. You could see it in the faces of his other siblings. It couldn't be bought off with toys.

A portrait of his mother at that time showed her looking much older than her years. In those days the whole family was subjected to her nightly rages: a terrifying, door-slamming, screaming, hysterical shit-fit almost every night when his alcoholic father would return late. She was haggard from lack of sleep and her body had an almost flabby quality, though she was still slender, but weak, defenseless.

Memories came crowding up. More pictures. Cub scouts, Boy scouts tied to church and religion. Catholic school. Khaki military uniforms.

"In Catholic school, their idea of physical education was to march you around on a hot pavement, to turn you out onto a big asphalt parking lot, and march you around in the hot Texas sun for hours," Walker related.

"By then I had become the boy with the pinwheel eyes." He gave an embarrassed laugh and thought privately: One who looks inward. Who is locked into his own mental processes.

Then there is a huge jump, no pictures from that time.

One of him with some girls in junior college. Some with a favorite uncle on an Ontario farm. One of some very hard times growing marijuana on a farm in Texas.

Finally he had those 3 in a row pictures taken at a coin-op recently, during the time Dahlia was away. She held up one of these that he found particularly ugly. "That is the most anger I have ever seen you show," she said. "You ought to hang it up on your wall. Ought to hang that one up, and this one of you as an infant, and maybe this one of you and your father and your little brother."

The group ended, and people began to get ready for bed. "Guess I'll take a shower," she said.

Walker wonder what it would be like to be able to walk around casually in the nude. He'd have to change the strong associations between nudity and sexuality. That is that when you got in the nude with somebody, it was to have sex.

"Can I join you in the shower?" he asked.

Walker slipped into the shower using the velcro snapes

to secure the curtain to ensure water did not spill out onto the floor. Dahlia had a fine, slightly rough cloth which she soaped up and proceeded to gently rub over her slick, soapy body. Immediately he became turned on by this and got an erection. This made her kind of stand away a bit so as not to encourage it. The commune men were pretty much desensitized by nudity.

Back in bed they got into a snuggle and a hug. She just put his hard cock away somewhere, between her legs, like it was some obstacle in the way of the feelings that might come up. They got really close, belly to belly in the full on hug with much loud auming and snuggling sending signals through an imaginary umbilicus of deep vibrations connecting them.

After a while she became distracted and pensive. She said, "Those pictures really shook me up," she said.

"Yea, me too. A lot comes up for me."

"Yea, a lot comes up for me when I look at my own pictures," she said.

By and by, her auming started to turn into sobs, great long aums, broken up by little shuddering sobs.

After that they got into especially deep hugs. She pulled a pillow over her mouth and was wracked with sobs for a while.

"I'm crying because of the terror that you grew up with," she said. "I can really identify with it." Soooooooobb.

And it was like she was some kind of child, back there in those times, inhabiting those feelings. She let it flow through. It is not a regression but a kind of transference of memory. And empathy.

"It was such a waste to be back in those times," she said. "Where you just had no way to be. That is how you got to be so lanky and gawky and awkward. There was just no way to be."

"Yeah."

Walker felt very caring for Dahlia like she was some young child there in his care. But then all of a sudden *she* would be the big sister. Walker looked into here eyes—tried to read her eyes. Have you ever looked into your lover's eyes? You see your own eyes reflected (try to read your eyes). You see the eyes, try to read her eyes—you see your own eyes reflected (try to read your own eyes).

He sees her lips as though huge on a movie screen. Opening to his kiss. And she was so warm and soft and loose and open, that he fell in. They merged. She cuddled up. And he hugged her, as she let out more sobs.

"It was so hard growing up," she sobbed. "There was just no way to be."

In between talking, she began to sob again and went on and continued on so. So now the sobs were made out of her aums.

Walker was really feeling it too. They got into making louder and louder sounds. She put a pillow over his face and told him, "Make louder sounds."

And he began making some of the loudest sounds he had ever made. It wasn't that loud. But they really shook him up as he really felt all that pain and terror.

Feedback loops, going back and forth, between the parents, the male and the female, getting down to the hard wiring of the brain.

Regression, going back along those early engramatic pathways in the brain, in which you felt the overt and covert terror in the house you were brought up in.

The terror of the male infant, over the circumcision.

He began to sob himself, the AUM breaking up. He held her closer to him. He just couldn't keep from crying. Big wet humbling tears. He couldn't believe it, here he was a grown man crying.

Her feelings were like his feelings, the fear of being back under the power of the Father and the Mother. Walker felt the tears rolling down her cheeks onto his cheeks. His tears mingled with hers.

She is a most lovely woman and he could tell that she really loved him. She is the quivering whore of compassion. When she cries she is like a baby, who expects the world to be changed. By her crying, that somehow the tears will foster, like the rain, the seeds of change.

Pictures came to him, of being little, like back in a dream, looking at his mother washing dishes, in the sunlight of a kitchen window. He must have been very little. He remembered never feeling like he could get their attention.

He felt the terror and powerlessness of being in that confining environment.

"Oh, Walker, I'm crying because I can really identify with what you were feeling. It is a lot like mine."

"You really do love me," he said. "I can feel it."

He started giving her kisses, one on each cheek, and some on the third eye, and some on the lips. She slipped into that special grin she gets when she is horny and Walker felt most happy. Sex. Muscles most pliable. Her flows were flows of gladness. (Watch what happens when I touch her gently here). See how she makes herself quiver. Her face goes into that pleasing grin he liked to see so much. The moons of her round bum were squeezable to the strong gentle hands of Walker. (Watch what happens when I do her like this). Her tears melted down his cool world. Her nipples were like little eyes.

He licked her pussy. It was exquisite, intimate love making, with crying and intertwining. And after he ate her pussy for a long time, licking the beautiful soft moist folds, so that they were dripping wet, he came back up and rubbed it, the pussy juice all over her mouth, around and around in circles, like feeding a young bird.

And it was like she had two heads, one with a mouth with brains and the other with the mouth of sex with no brains.

Dahlia went down on him. Giving him her special divine hum job: Auming, vibrating her lips while she felt his erect penis with her mouth.

ummmmmm mmm she goes ummmm mmmm buszzzzzzzzummm lick lick manfruit with rich creamy white center ummmmmmbzzzzzzuuuumm /
mmmmmmmmmmmmmmm
mmmmmmmmmmmomommmmmmmmmmm /
mmmmmmmauuummmmmmm lick! lick! lick! lick! lick! auuummmmmmmm the cock is in her mouth the cock, the blow job is wild is wild o auoooo auooooo the head is licked by her tongue the blow job the head is licked by her tongue the head is in a hummm job the blow job is wild is wild is wild is wild

hummmmm mmmmm
hummmmmmmmmmmmmmmmmmthe head is in the

hummmmmmmm of her mouth the head is in the
hummmmmmmmmm of her mouth o the blow job the blow
job the head is in the hum of her mouth, oooo she grabs the
cock and squeezes the head is in the hummmmmmmm of her
mouth the lovely blow job, the lovely blowjob
hummmummmmms and squeezes cups the balls in her hot
hand stretches the scrotum up the ultimate aummmmm the
blowjob hummmmmm the blowjoy
hummmmmmmmmmmm the blowjob hummmmmmm the
blow joy humm
mmmHHHUUUUUMMMMMMMMMthe pressure is
building up behind the pleasure, the pressure, the pleasure,
the pressure the blowjob, the blowjob suck the incredible
manfruit expanding and contracting organ all rigid and red
with it's creamy white center her saliva drools over him, the
little six inch man begins to shout, shocking her mouth — he
explodes in her mouth wet lips hold the magic fluid in, O
swallow it all, Gulp, holding onto the slackening manfruit
the humble man, bending over, not this time, not this time.

As usual he couldn't stand the intensity of feelings, and
had come in a huge upsurge of passion.

She admonished him for coming too quickly.

"It's the way you hummm when you do it," he said. "It's
just too much."

"I'd like to give you a blow job all night," she said.

Morning. "You stay down here and sleep," she said
when they woke up. "And I'll be back. Don't go running out
of here." She got up, and went to her young wards room to
wake him and get him off to school.

Walker was in a state of bliss feeling the imprint of her
in his body. He kept playing back the movie of the horny
moves from the night before.

She awoke him and they got into a hug.

Then amid all the hustle and bustle they went upstairs.

The people in the loft were shocked, and gave them
strange looks. They were hustling off to work and here were
these two, he not even a man of the house, hanging back.
They got under the covers, and were seen by most of the
house "writhing for hours like two snakes."

He was duly overwhelmed remembering the way he slid

his skin smoothly over her body in awe. He circumnavigated her terrain, looking through the skin. Her slender haunches rose and fell to his touch. She opened and flowered. He submerged into the vegetarian perfume of her garden, his up-periscope being touched by the eyes in her agile foot. She wrapped her sylphen sinuous thighs around him, as she shifted to his touch in shuddering lurching lunges. As desire overcame him he licked her honey flue, then getting her dew all over his face, came back up and rubbing mouths got it all over her lips and face.

Her spit curls turned into guishes as the perspiration oozes out of every pore, as they liquefy under the covers.

She puts the squeeze on him with her warm crevice. She was so warm and soft and loose and open. He fell in. He merged.

He came quickly, some fear of being seen by the house.

Mario came up to them, and Dahlia looked up into his face and Mario said, "Have you got the keys to the blue truck."

And he got scared and wanted to get up, but she was trying out her nice new body, and grabbed him in a hug and pulled him back down. Walker could just feel the eyes of the people of the house wanting them to get out of bed, almost everyone had left by then.

Someone else interrupted them. "Hey Dahlia, I can't find the gas requisition forms."

Wow, he thought, and wam, wam, wam, pow, she's going to make me confront some of the transparent forces that are pushing me around. And he was surprised and relieved to realize: I get all upset, and yet, land on my feet, and think, wow, she's a genius, she really knows what she is doing. And the intelligence acts even more like an aphrodisiac, and I am further drawn into you.

My fear is doubly confounded.

I feel all these protective vibes, so that you can open up.

I feel like it is incredibly good with you. You feel like this most pliant energy in my hands. I touch and kiss every part of you.

Squeeze your bottom, and you almost jump out of your skin with quivering and shivering delight.

Or pull on her nipples, and she rises up out of the futon shimmering, then dives back down, like a wonderful sea mammal.

Little quivering feelings swim through her, when I drag my nails slowly and gently across her back. And we were stuck so close together, she just fit into me, she wound in the horizontal position, her legs became like wonderful arms and then like vines that wound around my long snake like trunk.

He, his cock, the snake-like thing, slit, slithering he slid his not quite bonified member into her crevice not like in the old way, where he was real hard, and he was fucking her, piercing her with his rigid incredible expanding and contracting organ, driving into her, but this was her putting *him* through changes. *She* was really drawing him in.

It is such a change of head all the time with you, he thought. One minute you are perfectly cool, treating me like furniture around here, and the next you are drawing me in, like some goddess who has infinite power over me. I feel totally lost and I like it.

The penis begins to soften and *suck up* the female energy, to take it in.

But the panic of standing out in the house was really getting to him now, and he fought his way up out of her wonderful bed.

"O my god!" he says, in mock panic, "where are my clothes!"

And she looks with perverse delight on his chagrined modesty.

"Upstairs in the Loft without clothes, how terrible!" she teases.

But he doesn't find this too funny and gets his anger going, and barges on out of there, like a big kid trying to preserve his dignity.

30

Feeling 18 when you are Thirtysomething

Being part of the Loft emboldened Walker and he got into a class on monologues given by the fabulous playwright John O'Keefe. They did a lot of contact improvisation in the class and it was a total blast. Walker showed up at the Loft all bright and energized from the class.

In the kitchen little 4-year Dhyana, who was going out with his group that evening, talked excitedly about some posters of the Smurfs. Then Katie sat down beside him and started eating some lentil soup with lots of garlic in it. Dahlia sat down next to her away from him.

Katie asked Walker "Have you noticed that we smell a lot like garlic?"

"Yep. I associate it with this place. It hits you when you walk in the door, and reminds me of the good feelings I have around here."

Several people who were hanging around the kitchen were leaving to help Adrienne move into the Loft. She and Walker, being the only new people to get involved with the House at that time, were often together doing the dishes during clean up. People were encouraged that Adrienne would show such a vote of confidence during Chase's absence.

Frieda was chatting. "Tom was living with some chick named Lucille and they had a menage-a-trois going and the other guy left when she got pregnant, and he was about to marry her when he first came over to the House and we influenced him not to marry her."

Then Katie got up from between Dahlia and Walker and left the room leaving him sitting next to her. Dahlia said, "Here we have a manage-a-quarante." That cracked everybody up. He put his arms around her middle and gave her a big squeeze.

"Is it OK.? Can you take a big squeeze around your middle?"

"Yeah, it's fine."

"You're back to normal? Can handle just about any kind of handling?"

"Yep," she said with a lascivious grin.

Since the others had left, he looked her in the eye and started talking to her. She looked him in the eyes and they allowed themselves to hook up, to regard each other deeply in a feeling contemplation of the other's essential divinity in a gaze of mutual confirmation and recognition.

"It just breaks my heart to have you cry. We got into a big cry, and I had your tears dropping down on my cheek."

She said, "I think you identify with me a lot. Sometimes when I talk to you it is exactly like seeing me talking to myself."

Then feeling herself fall into a void of introspection, she caught herself and asked in a chatty way: "So how's it been going. What have you been doing?"

"Working on a monologue."

"How's it going?"

"Turning into a long piece."

"What's it about?"

"Well, It starts off..."

Walker gets up, sweeps his hands back and forth in front of himself, creating his spot, indicating this is on stage, that he is giving a monologue. "This guy is talking about this suit he got at St. Vincent de Paul, the suit makes him take on the personality of the previous owner and he goes into a rap about how, when he puts the suit on, it makes him feel like being straight.

```
Actor: I got this suit, see . . .
```

Walker points fingers in, sweeps hands down dragging his fingers over his chest indicating the suit.

```
at the St. Vincent de Paul. . .
for $12.50.
It was marked DOWN from 15 dollars.

It's a gray shark-skin suit.
I can't tell if it used to belong to a dork or
a slick.
Or maybe a slick dork, a dork that thought he
was slick?
```

Walker steps out of character addresses Dahlia. "Have you heard those terms: slick and dork a lot?"

She looks pensive, amused: "No I haven't heard those terms all that much."

Walker goes back in character of the monologist raises his arms in explanation,

```
A slick is a kind of person, a kind of person-
ality.
```

Walker smooths back his hair with both hands.

```
He's got slick hair, smooth, in place. He's an
extrovert, kind of a controller, he looks at other
people as a way . . .
```

Walker makes eyebrows go up and down, looks imperious, haughty

```
of furthering his own ends. He's more concerned
with appearances . . .
```

Walker waves hands as if touching a smooth table surface

```
and the surface of things.
```

```
A dork on the other hand,
```

Walker ruffles his hair, shows teeth in an overbite

```
is an introvert,
```

Walker brings shoulders up to ears, looks diminutive

```
he is usually the one being controlled. He may
be more sincere but spends too much time beneath
the surface of things and can't relate, or is so
afraid, he can't share.
```

Walker steps out of character addresses Dahlia. "He starts talking about what he said to his love that morning. He tells her this stuff about love being the balance between total obsession and freedom, only in a very embellished and flowery manner."

Dahlia and Walker have a long look at each other.
"He tells her:"

```
You are the self . . . same . . .
                 as I am.
We were always on the . . . lamb
via the image - in - nation.
```

Dahlia smiles and wiggles her shoulders. "I have done
that a lot, gotten totally obsessed by people."

"Then he tells her:" (getting more dramatic.)

```
I am not so much a personality or an indi-
vidual. . .
```

Walker looks pensive, touches finger to cheek
thoughtfully

```
Perhaps it is only a state . . .
      I am in,
perhaps people are the state or perhaps not
even people,
say individual personality is the state.
```

Walker draws this out and acts a little sinister, drawing
out the sibilants.

```
And say it is in face possible
for an individual,
    —an in-di-visual
           to possess
a variety of states,
a nation, within themselves united. . .
         states of hyssssterrria.
```

Walker looks at Dahlia and says

```
You are as free a state
           of this hysteria
      as I am free. . . free to be
      . . .possessed by each other.
```

And then he says to her...

```
and there is a balance . . .
    between
total freedom
    and total obsession.
You ask . . .
    openly, aloud:
"What is this balance of which ye babble, my
love?"
```

Walker and Dahlia smile at each other, "And he answers his own question with:"

```
It's a balance of possession
    . . . and total freedom.
And since we are so free . . .
we are free to really love each other.
This is the choice.
This is the balance of freedom.
Now the obsession . . . is a loss of equilib-
rium.
The loss of the free will.
Could it be . . . the meaning . . . of falling
. . in . . . love?
```

Walker started feeling all squirmy and embarrassed and getting red in the face like an adolescent. "*Any* way."

Dahlia was eating a slice of apple. And went all pretty.

To cover up his embarrassment he hugged her to him, she reaching way up to him. He sat back down as she moved over to the sink; she looked about 19.

It was like out in the suburbs. He is sitting around the kitchen of some family, talking to their young daughter. They walk around each other, advancing and retreating, playing and doing adolescent things trying to figure out some way to get her out of there so they can find some way to get naked in each others arms and do It.

They are both feeling about 17 or 18 at the time and it is the sweetest thing, the most precious thing in the world to be 18 when you are 30-something.

Walker looked over at her, says, "God I feel like a teenager when I am around you. It is always so awkward when we are together. It is always like the first time whenever we get together."

She says, "You know if anybody was listening to this

conversation, they would think we were back in high school. It sounds like a couple of high school people talking, being charming to each other."

Dahlia's built-in dependency alarm went off. Ever watchful and suspicious, Dahlia could tell some romantic hysteria when it was coming and said, "Hey, let's go see what's going on in the rest of the house."

Fleeing out of the room with her he said, "I've got to go down to the van and get some street clothes."

Walker went with his new group to the Golden Lotus restaurant in Chinatown. There was a funny scene with the Chinese waiter; it reminded Walker of that old Buddy Hackett routine with much confusion and face saving around substitutions. The earnestness and innocence of these people, the waiter and the women trying to get the proper dinner put Walker into a caring ebullient mood.

After leaving the restaurant the women - Jade and Rachel - split off with the beautiful child Dhyana to do some shopping in Chinatown, while the boys - Morey and Kevin and Walker - strolled around Chinatown with their hands in their pockets. They checked out Grant Park and Morey talked about improving its appearance with hardy bougainvillea plants. When they saw a bunch of Guardian Angels (a group of stalwart self-appointed neighborhood protector vigilantes) moving Indian file through the trash strewn streets it reminded Walker of the Peter Pan musical and he, like one of the Lost Boys, wanted to follow them under the moon.

Group Marriage

31

Tommy Boy, Wyoming and Scott

Wyoming could be an insensitive tease. She asked Scott with whom she had had really good sex the night before, "Has any one seen that Tommy Boy? We're supposed to have a session."

Big Tom was several years younger than Wyoming and she liked to keep the upper hand. Scott felt himself cringe with jealousy. He went outside for a walk around the dangerous and dirty neighborhood. He returned quickly.

When he got back Frieda came up to him and said, "I'm getting ready for our session. Are you ready?"

"Pretty soon," he said "Do you want to get together on my futon?"

"Why don't we sleep on mine. I could set it up downstairs."

"OK. I'll come over and help you in a bit."

He went right into the other bathroom from where she had come, washed up and met her on the floor of the loft. They were within sight of Wyoming's futon. Scott and Frieda talked and held each other and AUMed for a while then got into intercourse. His back broke out in a sweat as he stayed deep inside her, pinning her, thrusting and really moving her inner body. She howled and screamed with sensation and delight. His jealousy waned. Then they held each other and Frieda drifted off into blissful slumber.

Wyoming and Tom got started late, and after a while Scott found himself tuning in to their session. He was lying on his futon within sight of them. Scott's jealousy began to overtake him when he saw that she had her face buried in Tom's crotch. Tom was sitting up on his elbows watching her do him, and looked severely vexed and perturbed and tortured by ecstasy.

Scott got really jealous when Wyoming sucked Tom's cock. Scott was tossing and turning and pretending that he wanted to go to sleep. He couldn't help being very jealous and squirmed next to Frieda, stretching full out then curling up in a ball then lying on the left then on the right. He thought of going over to Tom's futon and fucking Wyoming from behind while she felt Tom's penis with her mouth! His jealousy was driving him nuts. He had to do something to overcome it.

He decided to wake Frieda up. He peeled back the sheets slowly so as not to wake her. He laid down beside her with his head toward her feet. His face was inches away from her backside and he began to kiss and suck the tender inner parts of her thighs. This woke her up. In a sleepy fog she thrust her butt back out toward him and he began dragging his tongue over her pussy.

Yet in spite of how pleasurable it was, she felt something was desperate in it, and she pulled herself away, turned over toward him and said to him in a low voice, "I'm feeling a little weird in this. Let's hook up." They held each other and aumed for a while then drifted off to sleep.

Next day at small group meeting with Tom and Wyoming and Scott and Frieda and Theo and Greg and Denise. Frieda asked Scott, "What was going through your mind when you woke me up and started to get into sex last night?"

"I was just really horny," he said.

"Well it felt good but you felt kind of desperate in it somehow. You seemed kind of distracted and desperate in your attentions. And I couldn't feel hooked up. Where did you go?"

And Scott had to own up that he felt very jealous about Tom and Wyoming. Then they had Scott and Wyoming hook up around it. Scott said, "I felt really jealous when I saw you feeling Tom's cock with your mouth. I felt like you loved him more than me."

"Oh, I love you both as much," she said. "We've got a session tonight. . . and we'll get close."

The group encouraged them with: "You two hook up."

Scott and Wyoming sat in erect yoga pose, let their eyes reaffirm and possess and relinquish each other. After a few moments they laughed.

These are some journal entries for that day:

—Scott: *April 23, 1983 Well, I got a shot of jealousy seeing Tom and Wyoming getting into oral sex together. Her face was buried in his crotch and I had that nasty little voice piping up "she never did that with me".*

—Wyoming: *April 23, 1983 Sunday. Beautiful morning out on the roof. Lazy morning writing journal pages, being with my friends. The breakfast crew was Theo, Loretta and Jenny. They made some nice whole grain pancakes with maple syrup.*

My big insight for the day (seems like I've been having so many lately): When I want something for myself, I often think of men as my enemy. Yesterday it played out between Scott, Tom and I. I wanted to have fun with Tom and before I even saw Scott, I was in a fighting frame of mind. That somehow this <u>man</u> was controlling me. This made me mad and I was indiscreet.

Of course Scott got jealous the way I set it up by teasing him. I know he really cares for me, but it is making us crazy the way he goes about it. Finally we got some help from group. They helped me see how things were setting up between us. Greg called me on it, said he wouldn't put up with it. That's when I flashed . . . I was treating Scott like my enemy! Wow this is big - I see this attitude being played out over and over in my life. I see it doesn't serve my goal of having more pleasure. Can I find another option?

—Tom: *April 23, 1983 Woke up early to Wyoming giving me a blow job. Great way to wake up! A man usually has an erection that time of the morning anyway and I felt monstrously big. I felt like she was really getting into to. Felt rejuvenated and sprung out of bed. Had whole grain pancakes with maple syrup for breakfast. Swept stairwell and kitchen and cleaned kitchen. Worked hard with Morey on shoring up the equipment racks. Did a Rainbow run with Scott after that. He seems to be getting closer after we had the small group about jealousy around Wyoming and me. We got some burritos in the Mission, got back, put stuff away in the kitchen. Had house meeting.*

Have a session with Frieda tonight. Looking forward to getting into sex.

—Scott: *April 24, 1983 When Wyoming said at group Sunday that she didn't want to be "a couple" with me anymore, I thought that I wouldn't be having such exciting sessions with her. But the group helped us understand how we were being with each other around dependency and control. Then last nigh we had a good session. I asked her to come to my futon. When she got together with me she was beaming. I felt like I had passed some kind of test. We talked for 45 minutes, fucked for 1/2 hour then fell asleep in each others arms. This morning she told me that is what she wants. She tells me exactly how to give it to her. When I listen to her my life gets alot better. She's brilliant. I just can't seem to get her out of my mind. And who would want to.*

32

Nimrod

They were in double group upstairs surrounded by soft futons and sleeping bags. Dahlia and some of her group (Aaron, Mario, Frieda, Lissa), against Walker and some of his group (Morey, Rachel, Jade). Walker is in a half-assed lotus position, his back arched up in hung low sad sack shape. It is the classical body language of the oral type —dependency, if one cared to look for it.

Dahlia is angry and looks down at Walker with contempt.

"I don't know how to talk about it but you always come too quick when we have sex."

"Whoah!" Walker reels back as if from a punch in the face! This was too much. He didn't like having his sexual difficulties broadcast to ten strange people.

It felt very weird, and no one came to his aid that night. It felt like they were trying to appease Dahlia, the general manager and most important person —in a supposedly democratic house. They just let her lay out the contempt. Walker wanted to just tell her to go to hell. But he tried to take the House Buddhist perspective that everything was a chimerical construct, an image floating in an internal phantasmal phenomenology space. He decided to try and sit with his own anger that she provoked in him.

He got through group and later that evening found himself at the huge dish-washing basin, where they put the new initiates, washing dishes next to Adrienne, a newcomer who was already a therapist on the outside, and Frieda, conducting the cleanup. Frieda had the most incredible sphinx eyes. Her eyes were like chrome orbs that burned with an ancient empathy and feeling belonging more to some alien's hell world. Her eyes fairly smoked with feeling.

During dish washing it was starting to get hot. Walker reached up and opened the big window above the sink. The rush of wet cool air quickly relieved him. "Fog-breath," he said.

"What?"

"Fog-breath. Is that a term that San Franciscans use? For the cool moist air that comes with an in-rolling fog."

"It sounds like a line from a poem," Adrienne said.

"O, yeah. 'The fog comes in on little cat feet.'" Walker said.

The slithering fingers of fog flowed down Noe Valley like lava from the diffuse burnished sun behind. The fog was rolling through very fast and the fog breath was blowing language rhythms across this tongue of land — the San Francisco peninsula. Papers blew across the parking lot. Leaves danced in the trees, annunciating the approaching cloud banks swirling in like a slow motion explosion. The fog comes in like Mongol hoards of ghost riders from the sky, riding down the valley, a deluge pouring in from everywhere. Ghost Riders come riding down on the scattering citizenry who are fleeing to the clang bang of objects in the wind. Outside the window, in the city, cars revved and roared and growled like wild animals in the jungle.

"It's different," Frieda said, "when the window is open. I can really feel the city. Sometimes, inside here, I feel like I'm on an alien planet."

Walker looked out the penthouse kitchen window and saw a face floating in the air above the ground looking back at him. It was his own reflection in the top pane of the glass, while the lower part of the window was open to let in the hellish fiery orange sunset blasting in on the swirling fog mixing with the steam rising from the dishwater. But it was scary. He was superimposed on the Sutro tower.

A wet light poured through the open window on the wind. The gog magog fog breath heralding the approaching cloud banks swirling like huge dust clouds kicked up around the legs of the Sutro Tower like it was some kind of Star-Wars planet-strider galumping through the fog banks like the hunter Nimrod with his dog pack traversing a hill, hot on the trail of some wild THING. What was it. The cold fresh embracing winds of change? Shifting turmoil of an ancient otherly planet chasing inside the little men who down below here are toiling for love and money? We were already inside.

"You are," Walker said. "This is paradise."

Sutro Tower bristling with antennas, the source for a consortium of media outlets broadcasting throughout the

Bay Area, looking for traps. Kind of a schematic skeleton structure man, a giant being whose body was raining down radio waves all over city, and it seemed like it was a big face in the spanning horizon, it was walking into this dimension from another dimension, and it was sowing little bits of Pentecostal fire at the speed of light on the populace which was ignoring it on a typical evening.

The tesselated structure towering over the city reminded Walker of pictures he had seen in Scientific American of the bacteriophage viruses. *Now THERE was evil incarnate —not even evil, not even incarnate but somewhere between alive and dead, a self-reproducing organic matter automaton, going back to the dawn of time when meteors were bombarding the planet, and injecting chemicals into a soup. The Sutro tower became like this huge bacteriophage virus striding down the hills, a giant insectoid, looking down on the humanity below. It was spidery. Creepy.*

A shiver ran through Walker. He knew the herpes was upon him. *It made your flesh crawl. Made you fear your own body. Made you not want to touch anybody. It made you cringe away, made your hair fly up and stand on its own. You knew that people walking by you might catch something from them, their disease might suffuse into you by a kind of oozemosis. Hard luck to get caught in an epidemic. You could have been too. Karma in the form of a big mechanical electrical thing, smoozing over the hills   The karma virus. We are all carriers.*

Walker shuddered. *Just as you're goin' along good in life karma made this happen. A little stress, and then the dome would lysogenize and the whole geodesic would explode sending shattering chards in a glassine menagerie of molecules, shaking the body's immune system into fits of terror and fever sending out infectious spikes of virus into the world. But also moving up into the mind, through a man's virility, forcing him to have a spoiled identity. Nimrod. Diminutive rod.*

What he feared most was getting it into the eyes. *It had gone on for two years. It changed him. His eyes went more and more into cold outrage. Makes you moody, scares the shit out of you. Got to get out of this frame of mind. Got to get into one that will not be so scary.* He began whistling while he did the dishes.

He was glad he had told Dahlia about the herpes, that is good; but he hasn't told anyone else yet and that is bad. I haven't needed to, he tells himself. He shook his head in chagrin and tried to see the humor of being in a sex commune and having to avoid sex. He recognized the mechanism, good old Catholic guilt. *I'm being punished for what? For being trusting and loving. Not fair. And in a way I am in turn punishing them, by not allowing them to make their own decisions. When was it never not so. Can you imagine the irony of that!*

He shook his head in disbelief.

Here I am in tantric heaven. Where the women are beautiful, loving, equal and easy and I've got post coital distress syndrome.

How did I get here? This is a house full of people in a real deep high. I just met this woman who really turned me on. I fell in love with her. I followed her here. I had to. Got a place in the house, joined the group, just to be near Dahlia. I put as much of myself as I could on the hot seat. As much as I could, I opened up. But knew I would get burned by this light if I approached it too straight.

Whoa! The flash of instant enlightenment! I think you're onto something here! Slow down and look at the image being propagated. Nimrod Numb-rod. A broken tower. A tower broken open. Peeking into my brain. My brain is as sensitive to the head of my dick. I'm David and the great Goliath coming over the hill is my Karma.

See? Guilt is a primitive karma recognition system. Shame is what Karma propagates, like radio waves which are picked up by guilt.

See! I'm sending and receiving guilty vibes for not informing these girls and empowering them to make their own decision.

I must be an evil person. I am the only one who has gotten this disease, because I loved somebody. I am being punished. Does Karma work like ordinary cause and effect, crime and punishment or is there some way out? I am struck by how pre-Newtonian Buddhism is, — the playing out of cause and effect, things seem to have motors, wheels, hubs, spokes and things that don't have motors are moved by external motors imparting motion to them, like a newspaper being pushed along the sidewalk by the wind; whereas animate beings have motors in them, they move by their own cause and effect. Hmmm. Maybe it's like this: If rebirth happens in this lifetime, like when your ego dies and you are reborn in another life, a life that is governed by a different metaphor or situation, then the rebirths coming in from this other dimension should provide the individual with the new life in which he can deal with this karma.

Walker was suddenly shocked out of this funk-fugue by little Dhyana who was hanging around the kitchen, balancing on a bucket. She had fallen off and got into some real loud screaming and crying.

After the screaming child had quieted and been taken up to stories and beddy-bye in her room, Frieda wondered aloud if she didn't react too strongly to pain.

"I sometimes wonder," she said, "if I've become so inured to pain that I just don't feel it anymore. Dhyana has been brought up really sensitive and she really feels it all that bad."

The House then convened in Big Group. Some very scary things were going on about Chase. They were very focused. A couple of the men from one of the research groups displayed a chart on an easel showing the various kinds of cancer therapies. It helped mitigate everyone's anxieties about doing enough for their leader, and satisfied their thirst for knowledge.

They mentioned the A.M.A. which reported about a 6% cure rate for lung cancer. It went into the Gurnsey treatment with its heavy emphasis on metabolic stimulation of the immune system. It mentioned Nipper in Germany, with his physics background, his well equipped hospital, and his avant garde European technology. They also discussed Halstead in New Jersey and Contrearas in Mexico with the Laetrile treatment, and Kelly who had cured himself of cancer.

33

Wolf Eyes

Walker had started a construction job. He started a day's work over in the city by gassing up his van. He was disheartened by how Dahlia was being so distant. Noticing a nice bunch of roses for sale at the cashier's booth, he decided to try and get something going with Anita the *au pair* girl who worked for the family of the house where there were doing the renovation. He had spoken to her. He liked her Asian beauty and he wanted to take her out to the I-Beam, a loud and ecstatic disco on Haight Street. She was Vietnamese French, extremely intelligent, teaching herself Chinese so that she would be able to command a lot more money when she went to China at the end of the summer. Walker was getting tired of the Group Mind front the House presented and wanted to check out this Asian woman. He had never gone out with an Asian woman. He wondered if they were all peaceful and sweet from being Buddhist and maybe would recognize him as one? Was there a secret Buddhist sign? Walker felt awkward and afraid. He imagined she would be afraid of him; it did look incongruous — a big construction worker and the *au pair*. He was 34 and she 23.

He felt a little ridiculous pulling up to a construction job site with a bunch of roses in his hand, so he left them in the van to see if the coast was clear. Lots of workmen were hammering and pounding on a fine labyrinthine house on Potrero Hill overlooking China Basin, not far from the bay. After a while, when the contractor was not looking, he went outside to the van and slipped the roses into the kitchen where he quickly snatchaed a vase from the cabinet and put them into water. They were a beautiful spray of red on the green tile windowsill over the kitchen sink.

After lunch Anita showed up but was too busy to really talk. Walker couldn't bring himself to tell her about the roses, and left these passion imbued flowers as a mystery standing in front of a window garden above the sink at the end of the day.

After work he went home with one of the men on the crew and drank a couple of beers. The man was married to a lovely woman, who was a scent artist —around the house she had placed various sachets from the wildcraft garden she maintained in their back yard. Imagine that, Walker thought, having a home with a wife like that.

Walker arrived at the Loft at 7:00 a little tipsy from drinking on an empty stomach while fatigued from a hard day's construction work. Then Dahlia walked in. She managed a weak not-quite-smile. Walker didn't know why she was treating him like furniture. She got into some discussion with other house members about Luke, one of the kids. Walker purposely reached across her to hand a book to someone; still not the slightest sign of acknowledgment.

Walker went upstairs to get Kevin and Morey, and get to hell out of there! Next to the futon upon which Kevin was sleeping, the beautiful Rachel was naked and on all fours like a dog with her butt in the air having her asshole closely examined by Bridget.

As Walker nudged Kevin awake, Bridget was lovingly and humorously peeking between the cheeks of Rachel's ass, and relating what she saw there. Walker was trying to be nonchalant, but couldn't help smiling as Bridget was too.

Parting the cheeks gently Bridget, a strapping dark German frau of Olympian beauty said, "All I see are what looks like little bumps where hair is starting to grow, and perhaps one bump is a little larger. I don't know. But it looks a little red."

Walker looked away from this lovely domestic scene, to the pile of futons and there sleeping among them after a few quick scans, there emerged from the gestalt of soft shapes and bright colors, the figure of Morey asleep too. Walker woke him up with two tugs on the big toe.

After a while Kevin got up to take a shower. Walker felt really hungry from working on a roof all day, and really grungy in blue jeans. He hungrily watched Rachel getting dressed, pulling on a Danskin.

Then Morey came over and they talked, Walker occasionally urging departure, for he feared that Dahlia would come and sit down and force him to say something nasty and sure enough it happened.

"Hi," Walker said.

Dahlia just gave her open-eyed sagacious look and sat down. The hackles on his neck stood up, because again he felt snubbed.

"I'd like to talk to you," he began. "I want us to meet in some neutral cafe. You come alone, unarmed to some neutral cafe, I want to talk to you."

No one laughed. He sure did find it hard to get these people to lighten up a little bit.

It is hard getting over you, he thought but was too proud to say. He was suffering sorely from a whole lot of self-loathing which started coming up from rejection. It's my fault, I'm not likable, I'm not a nice guy, who would like me, etc. I realize that I am just some love starved idiot that has followed this woman home, and now here I am at her house, and she hasn't any room to move etc.

"Well you can come and talk to me in my group," she said.

Arrrrggh. This really pissed him off. Yet he dared not show it because he was so afraid of his anger. Now he couldn't see her alone anymore, for Christ's sake. Now he had to work his way through this bureaucracy to see her!

And they were perfectly right! For I am guilty, and really didn't have her best interests in mind.

Then she said terse, angry, almost spitefully confrontational: "You only are with your group on the weekends. And it feels VERY manipulative the way you are around here."

This got Walker really pissed off. He was turning white in the face. Yet at the same time he had to admire her truthfulness. God how he loathed the healthy young people of the world who could just fuck their hearts out for the fun of it.

My days are done, my time is run, he thinks. Now I am an asexual brute who frightened women. My god that was in my dream last night. Somehow I was a hippie or wild man living in a cave, and there was a princess in the dream, and in fact she kept me in the cave. Wow. I remember there was even some stuff about me trying to see her in her castle it was a big castle with many rooms that went on and on. There was even a dungeon down in the basement. And she had all these viziers and people in her retinue that she had to keep council with and they didn't like me. But she liked me. I was like some kind of wild thing she kept. Walker was amazed at the insight available from the dream, but jumped up to run out of there anyway. He couldn't stand it.

He was afraid he would say something that would 'ruin his Karma' around the loft. He decided as usual to Run! Flee! Why talk to her anyway. She couldn't hear him. He was invisible. As he heading down the stairs toward the door he turned and said, nasty and teasing, "God damn it! I'm going to get you a sash that says, 'Winner of the Little Miss Immature Bitch of the Year Award for 1983." He smiled at the image. Then he laughed. No one else laughed, though.

Morey tried to grab him by the arm and hold him down, but he pulled away and stomped across the room and down stairs saying, "Look, I am tired, been working all day, kind of drunk, and hungry, I'll go eat, and come by and check you guys out later on."

"Wait a minute, we'll go with you."

Kevin emerged from the shower as the two men stood hot eyed on the stairs, Morey trying to cool Walker out.

"I don't want to say something that will totally ruin it for me around here," Walker said.

"A lot of people freak out around here. You often say the worst things to people you love the most."

Then Miss Immature Bitch sashayed down the stairs as though floating on clouds. Walker thought about going for her.

Finally, the men got over to Amazing Grace and had some of their vegetarian curry. At table Morey talked about one time defending his father from some thugs at the store with a lead pipe. Walker was bringing out a macho side of the housemen that he hadn't seen before.

Walker thought to test them further with: "I kind of thought I'd like to go to this art opening in Oakland. I like art openings, because you can meet lots of nice sensitive people, they all stand around with their backs to the paintings drinking, and I don't know, for some reason, it is in the stars and the moon, I feel lucky, feel like I could get lucky tonight, feel like I could get laid."

Morey visibly blanched at this statement.

"I'm having a hard time with talk like that."

Walker said: "I don't know, you guys are like married guys, you always have lots of women around to talk to, and come from an abundance of sex. It would be O.K. for me to say something like that to my unmarried buddies. You guys feel like married guys."

Then Kevin said, "Lets go down to Telegraph Hill and walk around and see what we see."

Walker had a feeling that they were going to stay together that night, and that he would see what kind of thing happened with men in groups.

As they walked to the car, Morey was cringing from the foggy cold said, "Well, it's summer in S.F."

Walker started singing, "In the good ole summer time, it stays light 'till nine."

They parked in a No Parking zone near the base of Coit tower. The top of Telegraph Hill is the best place to send and receive messages. There is a truncated tower of concrete. Walker said, "Doesn't it seem to you, and everyone who looks at it, that Mrs. Coit has erected a foreskinned phallic symbol in memory of her husband. I bet they were an interesting couple."

You could see the city only in the midst of wraithlike shreds of fog. Occasionally there was the great mating call of fog horns to the tug boats. The bay was like a big frog pond.

Then they wandered in North Beach. As they were walking across Broadway, a group of young men and women, all dressed up in formal attire (it was prom night), in a little red two door Capri started nudging into the street crossing forcing some of the pedestrians to hang back. Walker got incensed at this. He got right in front of the car, and stared at the young punk driving the car and then at his girlfriend beside him. It was the most cold-blooded stare ever. Somewhere from way inside an atavistic strata of his mind Walker was shocked to "know" it was the stare of the veteran, who had seen brains splatter against walls, who had strangled opponents with his bare hands in combat. It was livid with hatred and animal cunning. It was devoid of feeling.

Walker felt that at the slightest provocation, like honk of horn, or the slightest advance of an inch, he would go off.

Walker stared in horror and watched as some kind of monstrous alter-ego emerged from him, like an insect crawling out from under its shed skin, walked around and opened the door on the driver's side, pulled the young man out, picked him up and impaled him on the sharp steel corner of the door. Then with superhuman strength the fiend dragged the young prom-goer's body down, using the sharp edge of the door like it was a can opener to split the young man's white sport coat with the pink carnation up the back and open the lad up. Then the all-powerful monster of the Id ripped out the man's spine, and held it up for all the shocked people in stopped cars and passersby under the lights of Broadway to admire. Finally Walker's evil Mr. Hyde dopelganger grabbed hold of the young man's feet and bashed his head against the asphalt road way and the curb until his brain cavity split open and his brain flew across the sidewalk and landed in some lady's Caeser salad at Enrico's sidewalk cafe.

He was really pissed off at Dahlia. He had the look of outrage of someone that has been socially mistreated. He also envied these beautiful young people with their healthy skin and quick reflexes—their beauty, off to a prom somewhere in the city of dreams.

He looked really mean in his blue jeans.

When they got to the sidewalk Morey said, "Hey, were you trying to get those guys into some kind of staring match."

"I stared them down, man," Walker replied, his cool turning cold.

"Anger at your mother, that is what that's about."

Kevin and Morey talked to him and Walker got apologetic, for these were very kind and sensitive men and sheepishly he said, "Well, it was a cheap shot on both of our parts. He was acting like a punk trying to impress his girlfriend and I was getting off some anger. Men are like that. They like to fluff up their ruff at each other."

"What a strange thing to do," Kevin said. "You are acting out your anger. Have you been in a lot of fights?"

Walker could tell that his British reserve was quite affronted by this and felt ashamed. "I had this fantasy of pulling the door open and pounding him into the asphalt."

"I get those fantasies too, but don't act on them."

"There are a lot of guys in jail because they are angry at their mothers," Morey said as they walked up Grant, into the Cafe Trieste. In the sad cafe much talk ensued. Walker was kind of shook up by what he had done.

"It is just Texas macho bullshit," Walker said.

"You start to get loose, then freeze up, and you're back in Texas like an armadillo," Morey teased.

"I was just trying to protect my civil rights," Walker tested. "The right to walk across a street unmolested!"

"You have right on your side," said Kevin, "but you are also acting out your anger."

"I might have taught the punk a lesson. He would become a more courteous driver. He would remember to be a little more courteous to pedestrians in the future if one of them pulled him out of the car and pummeled him into the road surface."

Walker was getting into a kind of panic, and remorse over what he had done.

"In Syracuse, man, I could have seen the back door opening and a bunch of guys getting out of the car, and getting into it right there in the street."

"Yeah, in Texas too. You can get shot there for honking at somebody."

"All the more reason not to do that kind of shit."

"Ah, I can handle myself. I'm tall, fast, evasive and kick like a horse."

Walker got up and got another cup of mud. He felt actually kind of good. He had a big grin on his face, and came back and stared down at his coffee, burning a hole in his cup with his eyes.

Kevin said: "I've been kind of out of it. But I'd like to say that you both were acting like a couple of. . ." He notices Walker staring into the black void of his coffee. "What is going on with you?"

"I don't know, man, I have the wolf-eyes tonight."

"You look like you are trying to stare a hole through that coffee, I can see it reflected in your glasses."

"Both you and the guy behind the wheel were both acting like pricks out there. It puts me in mind of that kid who blew his father away with a gun. Did you read that story? He felt this incredible anger, but he ruined his whole life over it."

Walker felt like some kind of sub-human looking through the window glass at people, the couples, uncomplicated, I have never been like them and never will be.

Then Walker started talking.

"I never told anyone this before. You remember Morey, when we were in the last group, and I started to recall about how my father slapped my brother and left a bruise on his face. Well there was another part to that memory that I didn't tell you and that was I had actually put a bullet in the chamber of my gun and walked down the hall to kill my father."

This shocked them. They were kind of taken aback.

"But something came upon me, some kind of instinct, that I should not do it, that I would ruin my life, and I went back into the room and unloaded the gun."

"Where did you get the gun?" Morey asked.

"My father gave it to me, it was given to him by his father, my grandfather. I have it now."

"Wow, that's weird, this gun passed down from one generation to the next. Some kind of violent trip."

"How old were you?"

"13 or 14."

Walker could see that they were getting real edgy. He tried to put them at ease.

"But I'm on top of my anger. I studied with the NRA and ROTC in high school. Shot a lot of guns in gunsmithing school.

"Have you ever done any hunting?"

"Yeah, I hunted rabbits and deer."

"You hunted deer?"

"With my father and by myself. He was never very good in the woods."

"Did you ever kill anything?"

"Yeah. But I don't do that any more. It was a horrendous image of death the last time. It was the dirt on the eyeball that did it. The dead deer could no longer make tears and the eyeball got little bits of dirt on it."

"I've got these wolf eyes tonight." Walker said as they went outside. "Women can see it in me."

"No you don't. You have never looked like that before."

They went into the Saloon and dug on the Michael deJong blues band.

Walker was still sweating out the internal turmoil about what had happened. He drank a couple of glasses of wine and felt better.

Morey was in really good form. He loved blues music. He walked right up to the prettiest, most natural girl in the place and asked her to dance and they got out on the floor and had a really good boogie goin' on.

Walker went out. The jazz, the be-bop and the blues woke up his hearing.

"I'm kind of at the intersection of two world lines," he mused allowed.

"What is this the intersection of?" asked the ever-faithful Kevin.

"A Riemannian geometry of curved spaces," smiled Walker.

As they left North Beach, Walker hooked his two arms into the elbow crooks of Kevin and Morey, and pulled them close to him.

"Kevin, you're too literal, you've got to raise the gaze."

"Raise the gaze!" They all chuckled in unison.

Back at the loft, Walker dropped them off, he put his arm around Morey and said, "I wouldn't have done that if I hadn't known you'd back me up back there."

"No way, you're on your own, buddy."

Walker laughed, giving Morey a hug, "Naa, you would have put this broad back right into the middle of the fray."

34

A Tibetan Funeral in America

Chase died in hospital that spring in Mexico. There was a crematorium in the hospital. Harve and Carlos returned from down south with the ashes. It was a touching reunion when Dahlia tearfully embraced her brother Carlos upon his return from down south where he had spent the last 6 months with their beloved dying friend. Carlos was her real brother, they had grown up together and there was such a familiarity and love in the way the man and the woman approached each other.

The Lama had started visiting the House two days ago because he was a good friend of Chase's and the House had begun incorporating a reading of the Tibetan Book of the Dead in the meditation. Feeling was running extremely high.

Walker hadn't known Chase, had only said "Hi" to the man once. Walker thought Chase eyed him suspiciously and had right away gotten into a projection on him as the guru and chief older stud. But Walker could feel the loss of these people who were coming to be his people, the tribe he had always wanted to be part of since the hippie days.

They embarked on a Tibetan funeral, where passages of the Tibetan Book of the Dead are read over a 49 day mourning period. There are various addresses one makes to the recently deceased, some of them calming him, as his physiology recedes laying bare subtle bodies to the withering transformational lights of reality without the filter of the body. It is a supreme contemplation for the living. The Pho-wa ritual is done soon after the shock of death is expanding out into the minds of the survivors reminding them of our own mortality. It is in this frame of mind that one can conduct religion.

Maybe it was a way of trying to be there even though he was not mourning, or maybe it was his standard intellectual defense against feelings but Walker was amazed at this piece of literature   the Bardo Thodol. The way it asked you to visualize. The way it used language to construct a devotional image, that was to be held in the mind as a kind of meditation. Was that a prayer or a poem, or was it a kind of personal theatre piece. Walker liked thinking about it as a verbal equivalent of a wild tankha paintings of wrathful deities dancing in flames over the vanquished enemies of the dharma in our lives as the souls of the dead leave the body, but not before the receding body experiences the terrors and joys inherent in all things.

The Lama Dordj-em Yamdrok, an old friend of Chase had started to help the Sangha through this difficult time. The House had begun incorporating this prayer in the meditations as well.

***

(Devotion to Chenrezig)
Taking Refuge
Myself and all sentient beings
as limitless as the sky.
From this time forward.
Until the heart of enlightenment
is reached.....

I take refuge in all the Holy Lamas
I take refuge in all the Assemblage of Yiddams
I take refuge in all the Teachings of the Dharma
I take refuge in all the Members of the Sangha
I take refuge in all the Herukas, Dakinis, Dharmapalas
and Guardians possessing the wisdom eye of
Knowledge.
(Repeat 3, 7, or 21 times)

Taking refuge and generating Bodhicitta
to all Buddhas, Dharma, and Sangha
until Enlightenment I go for refuge
through the merit of my practice of
generosity, etc
for the sake of all beings may I
attain Buddhahood.
(Repeat 3, 7 or 21 times)

VISUALIZATION
I and all sentient being spread out
through the expanse of space
on the crown of the head, a white
lotus and moon

above from Hri the sacred body of Chenrezig
white and clear with five lights radiating
Beautiful, smiling, gazing with eyes
of compassion
of four hands, the first pair are
joined together.
The lower pair hold a crystal rosary
and white lotus.
Silk and precious ornaments adorn him
an antelope's skin clothes his shoulders
Amitabha crowns his head.
Two feet are placed in Vajra position,
a stainless moon supports his back.
He emerges as the unity of all refuges
in essence.

DEVOTION TO CHENREZIG
O Lord unstained by faults
with body white
with head crowned by a perfect Buddha
with compassionate eyes gazing on beings
to Chenrezig I pay homage.
(Repeat 3,7, or 21 times)

Thus having prayed one-pointedly
from the sacred body light radiates
purifying deluded awareness,
the manifestation of impure karma
the outer realm becomes Dewachen
the inner contents, the body, speech
mind of sentient beings
become the body, speech, mind
of mighty Chenrezig.
Form, sound, awareness become
inseparable from emptiness.
_____*

OM MANI PADME HUM
_____*(Repeat 108 times)
* A few minutes of silence*

I and others appear as the sacred body.
Sound, speech are all the melody
of the syllables.
Thought and memory are the vast
expanse of awareness.

DEDICATING THE MERIT
With this virtue may I quickly attain the
enlightenment of Chenrezig.
May beings, not even one excluded,
be placed in this state.
Thus with the merit of practicing
this meditation and Mantra
may I and those known to me, all beings
as soon as this impure body is cast aside
be miraculously born in Dewachen
and right after birth there, when the
ten levels are crossed.
May emanations work in the ten
directions for the benefit of others.

**

That weekend the House amassed caravan of some 7 or
8 rental sedans got transport everyoneto their land up in the
Siskyou Mountains for the Tibetan funeral, the Pho-Wa.

"Good guys in the back!" Walker taunted as they got into
the large four door rented sedan. He was in the back seat
with the divine Ms. Jade and his great new friend Kevin.
Walker had purchased a whistle and a snake bite kit for the
wild country, and one of those fine therma-rest air pads.
Rachel was in the front with Morey driving. Walker
somehow felt it was incumbent upon him to play his role as
the joker, the clown, the grasshopper—he was not insensitive
just had not experienced death in his life up until that point,
certainly not the death of someone close. He had no way of
knowing what they were going through.

There was the usual confusion of coordinating the
departure of 40-odd people at once from the House. Leslie
walked across Army Street to the corner store wearing one of
those white dust masks because she had a cold and didn't
want to spread germs.

"We certainly are an odd bunch," she remarked to
Walker through her mask.

To beguile the hours of the long drive up to their land
near the Oregon border, to try and keep things from being
maudlin, to cover up his own fear, Walker began to question
Rachel in the front seat about some of the terms and
concepts in the meditation.

"What are yidams?"

"Female deities."

"What is the sangha?"

"That is the group of people who are committed to a common path. A group of people who are committed to mutual supportive confrontation. We are the sangha."

"Let's see, I think I know what herukas and dakinis are but what is a dharmapala?"

"Don't know," a couple of people said.

"What is hri?"

"I think it is some kind of sound," one said.

Rachel said: "No it's that part of the head where like, have you seen in those pictures where there is this smoky visualization of some deity that comes up out of the top of the head. Supposedly it is easy enough to visualize deities of the lineage in front of you, but it is much more difficult to maintain an unattached space of nothingness in front of you, and still visualize the deity behind or above you."

"And who is Chenrezig?"

"Well he is a deity, but not like the lower deities, like men who have lived." Morey said.

"You mean, not like Marpa, or Milrepa, or Naropa, but a higher deity, like a psychological principle?"

"Yes."

"Kind of like god the father in the west, some kind of creative spirit that permeates all things?"

Rachel started to interpret the visualization. "Chenrizig is like a buddha that comes out of the top of the head. Like some kind of principle of compassion, or way of looking at the world."

" 'White and clear with five lights radiating'. . . That would be like the lights you see inside your head when you meditate. Like this kind of electric feeling you get," she said.

"Or just the five senses," someone added.

Walker conjured up an image of coronal discharge as he had seen it in Kirliean photography all vortexing up in a puff of smoke, as a kind of being emerged or arose out of the head of a person, and somehow this was identified as the 'unity of all refuges in essence'. This is an incredible kind of poetry and writing, he thought.

"Subcortical linguistics, a kind of hypnotic text," he blurted out to the others.

They drove on each car making its own way. Their care made a stop, way up north in the cold starry night at Weed, California. Walker enjoyed the fresh air. It had been a long time since he had spent some time in the country, and he was very grateful for the opportunity.

Just across the border into Oregon they tried to drive up to Pilot Rock. They were repulsed by the horrendous mud-slick, gullied road. They all got out. Kevin, Walker and Jade pushed from the front of the car as Rachel, in her little shirt sleeves, guided them — backing up in the dark, and Morey drove about 1/4 mile down the swervy road.

It was 4:30 AM by the time they repaired to the Klamath rest area beside the Shasta River. They flopped anywhere - Walker got to use his new therma-rest on a concrete picnic table - and were awakened when the sprinkler system kicked on shortly after sun-up, drenching them.

That morning Rachel took the wheel of the sedan and in a *tour de force* of back country driving, —she was from Yreka and could really wheel it over mud-slick roads — powered that big car way up beyond where any of the others dared to go. The group was shaking in their boots in the back seat, knuckles white from bracing and digging in — two women in front and the three men in the back for the weight.

"We can't go any further. . . Watch out for that rock!" Morey cried.

Kevin said, "Whoa . . . Look out, Rachel!"

"Wow, don't go over the edge! Not over the edge!" Walker said.

The big brown sedan went squishing and sliding through the wet red clay landscape, like one of those toy cars being run through its paces by the giant hand of a child, amusing himself going across a mini-landscape of mountains and rivers past vast flooded fields and tiny little Zuni villages with dried temples, and hanging wall gardens with ponds and bridges, and cemeteries with huge stone monuments.

"You can't go any farther, pull over here, Rachel."

"Don't stop me now, I've got to keep going!"

And the boys in the back got into it. "Keep going! Keep moving! Watch out for that stone! Oh the stone!"

Klunk!!

Tail pipe Klang! Rooster tail of mud spew from back tire and finally, she pulls into a high dry spot, hops out of the car, cool as could be and leaning against the fender folds her arms in front of her.

They met the rest of the House up toward Pilot Rock. There, the House had waiting their huge amazing jeep, an all terrain vehicle, W.W.II surplus army drab vehicle, called Kong. In two trips it would carry in all the food, packs and bedding for the 40 people. Wyoming got really excited when Ursu arrived, ran across the ground, leaped up in the air and clasped her legs around him, nearly knocking him over. People were feeling a lot, very sensitive over the loss of their beloved guru and very excited to throw off the tyranny of the city and be with nature on the long hike in.

Aaron read from the Bardo Thodol for the sixth day.

> O nobly-born, listen undistractedly. On the Seventh Day the vari-coloured radiance of the purified propensities will come to shine. Simultaneously, the knowledge-Holding Deities from the holy paradise realms will come to receive one.
>
> From the center of the Circe [or *Mandala*], *enhaloed* in radiance of rainbow light, the supreme Knowledge-Holding [Deity], the Lotus Lord of Dance, the Supreme Knowledge-Holder Who Ripen Karmic Fruits, radiant with all the five colours, embraced by the [Divine] Mother, the Red Dakini, [he] holding a crescent knife and a skull [filled] with blood dancing and making the mudra of fascination, [with his right hand] aloft, will come to shine.
>
> Be not attracted toward the dull blue light of the brute-world; be not weak.

And they set off into the cloud forest with their hands free and their feet footloose for a nice 8 mile walk in. Occasionally snow-covered Mount Shasta could be seen only as a brighter white against the shadowy gray white of the cloud-misted day. Walker could not get a view of the whole mountain, for it was enshrouded in mists all day.

In a beautiful spot overlooking a valley they sat down and had a meditation.

"That's what it must be like to die, to have no body to

hide behind against the earth and sky, but to be in a place where you feel everything," Rachel said.

Sauntering along, like cows kicking up their heels after a long winter's confinement in the barn, Walker remarked, "Wow, look at the dew crystals on the grass. Breaking up light into its colors like a prism."

The dew drew him in. How do you do, dew? What is dew due to?

Air warms up before earth does. Change of state, condensation to become more dense, to precipitate out (or in?) Dew drops created and annihilated. Microscopic spherical harmonics, caught in the webs and branching of grasses. Fracturing light into spectra. What we must do is bid adieux to a dew drop.

Some kind of phanopoeia occurred for him of mist and rays into mist-rays and missed rays into mysteries.

Coming and going from existence was. . . could be thought of as a change of state, couldn't it? The dew evaporates into the air, its molecules combining with others, becoming food for some other beings. What must it be like to die, to go out of existence and become a ghost with no body to buffer yourself against the earth and the sky, and your own nervous system, as it slowly evaporates out of activity. To be pierced by the colors as though they were rays, mysterious wave fronts crashing through in the great ocean of existence. He thought about Leoweuken's first microscope used a drop of water as a lens to amplify. Walker did a selective look at just the water elements in the purview of the scene. Starting with the saturation of the atmosphere and its effect on light, and the plumbing of the tree machines conducting water, down below the ground to the aquifers and tunnels. Not to mention the beings which were all about 70% water. He thought: Perhaps like the water, *we* are taken up again and again and dropped back into the recirculation that is the world.

The troop of hikers got more and more together as they approached the entrance into their land. Groups of hikers had been stretched out over miles. As they entered through the gate, Walker got in stride with Theo, a tall lanky guy, older than the rest, whom he liked a lot. At one point in the hike, Theo had sat down in a gnarly-to-the-max root system of an old tree trunk that had fallen over. The roots and fibers radiated out of the fallen tree trunk like a halo up to 12 feet into the air. It made a neat picture that someone snapped, like Theo had emerged through some kind of blasted nebular gestalt.

With everyone standing around him —the oldest man in the House — taking a break Rachel said, "Wow, you must feel really weird."

Walker couldn't grasp the extent of their land, but it encompassed several large hills, hills around a winding valley, at least a mile long. The tallest, maybe 4,000 feet, would take several hours to climb. At the bottom of the valley, was a flat grassy spot, where the huge army tents were permanently encamped. The great green-brown tents reminded him of an old English jousting field. Below that was a large pond and a big garden area.

Walker got in step with Jade then as they cam in, showing more solidarity with a group member. Suddenly he saw a snake move in the grass on the side of the road. He got really afraid. "Looks like a coral snake to me," he said. "They are really deadly, their venom attacks the nervous system, like the cobra, really deadly."

"It's just a non-poisonous grass snake," someone snorted at the city slicker.

Jade and Walker were pretty tired when they reached camp and they immediately curled up together in a spoon and took a little nap. As they were getting bedded down, Jade, the gardener, picked up a big black bug and said, "It's a beetle, you can tell by the number of legs. The beetles have six legs not eight, therefore not a spider."

When they awoke, Walker was still spooked about snakes. Tom, a strapping, tanned, good-looking young man, who never seemed to wear a shirt, took him over to a large oil drum where the advance team had captured a couple of rattlesnakes. He said, "It is part of our trip, that we harmed no living beings. We capture rattlers with a long pole that has a wire loop on the end. And take them out and dump them way off somewhere else.

"No one has been bitten since all these people have been coming up here," he added.

Later as they were sitting around the fire, having dinner, Tom got a tick on him. Walker saw him go over into the woods then, and when he returned Walker asked him, "You didn't take that tick back into the woods and let it go, did you?"

"Yep," he said, grinning benignly.

"I thought it was the sentient beings you didn't molest."

"We protect ALL living beings," Katie chimed in.

Walker was flabbergasted.

That evening, as the sun was setting, they all crowded into one of the big tents. It was cozy with all the colorful sleeping bags and gear. One panel of the tent was rolled up to catch the sunset. The Strawboss had the four people who had been down south, Serena, Elissa, Harve and Carlos get into the center of the big circle and they started talking about Chase's last days and hours.

Basically, the last time that he had gotten into a bad spot was two weeks before, when fluid from his lungs began to put pressure on the pericardium sac, so that the heart couldn't pump and it was difficult to breathe. They had done a minor operation and drained off the fluid, but found that it had cancer cells in it, indicating that metastasis had occurred, and that the cancer cells were getting into the immune system. Still the operation seemed to give him some relief.

The four took shifts with Chase around the clock. He was getting four or five hours of sleep in twenty-four. Chase never wanted to sleep, and he wanted to be with them. The doctors were amazed at the devotion. He was too weak to turn himself over, and had them turn him all the time. His heart was beating twice as fast as normal, like after a long jog, and had been, almost since they'd gone down to the hospital in Tiajuana.

Carlos: "The last thing he said to me was that he wanted me to turn him. I had just turned him, and we wanted him to get some sleep, and I said, 'I don't think I would be your friend if I did.' And he said, "Friend, schmen, turn me!"

"Chase seemed to sleep after that. Harve and I went out into the hall, and after a while, an orderly came in to make the bed, and found that Chase was dead.

"We ran and got a CPR resuscitation device, and later a doctor came in and touched some nerves in his feet, and said that if he did not respond to the nerves, then he was dead."

Harve: "Chase was sure he was going to die the day before."

Much talk ensued about the last words to everybody and what it meant.

Gradually, the fact that he was dead began to sink more and more into the people of the tribe. They were saddened by the pain Chase had felt. And repulsed. He had been in almost constant pain for six months! Harve shook his head and said, "The doctors said he was lucky to go, that sometimes it lingers on in that coma state for months."

Serena: "He was still able to talk to me about my stuff. He was still trying to be the analyst up to the last. He spent a lot of time talking to some of the most famous doctors in the world that we flew down to see him, about their egos. That was one of his problems, that he could be there for everybody else, but he didn't know how to ask the others to be there for him."

Harve: "A couple of times there in the last week he suggested that we just get a gun and shoot him. He was out of his mind some of the time. He couldn't get enough oxygen to his brain."

After this saddest of all Big Groups it was time for sessions.

"Let's sleep outside," Rachel said.

"It's pretty cold," Walker said.

"I've got an old futon around here, and we can get a big blanket." She looked enthusiastic, like she really wanted to sleep outside.

"Yes, it would be nice to sleep beneath the stars."

They got outside just beyond the big tent where the others were talking and laughing and moaning and carrying on like some kind of circus show in a big warm kitchen where everything was warm and intimate.

Walker got under his bag with his clothes on. Oh! It was so cold. Rachel had gone off somewhere and didn't get back for quite a long time, making the kids lunches. She stood over him when she got back. Walker thought she looked pleasant enough. Neither of them got undressed but snuggled up anyway and he kissed her beautiful classical face.

They were close, in a hug, when the teenagers Luke and Mark came up and pounced on them in the night. Then they ran off, giving the horse laugh.

Walker thought it was OK. I mean, they were just showing that they liked us, he thought.

He started carrying on a bit, saying he was afraid of the attack of the teenagers, and would have to keep a sharp look out, but he knew he was afraid of why he and Rachel don't seem to be turned on to each other, not turned on psycho-sexually at all. He thought maybe he was projecting his mother on her. She *was* a country girl with lots of brains who had lots of ambition in the city. He didn't know.

It was a fitful session with Rachel that night. The vast cross section of the Milky Way could be seen. They slept with their clothes on, and Walker was very antsy.

Walker got up real early as was his camping style and made his delicious Celebes Kalossi coffee over the fire he rekindled and broke wood for. He went for a long walk up the road and saw wild deer. He came down and had a bath out of a pickle bucket in the bathing tent. Pia was there too and Walker felt OK, about nakedness in front of others.

When Dahlia saw him that morning, she looked him in the eye and said, "I'm glad you came on the trip."

That afternoon at big group it was decided that Dahlia would take Mario to a hospital in Medford as he was sick, and pick up the Lama at the airport and drive him in in Kong.

A special tent for the Lama had been set up away from the others, so he could meditate and pray, in a little high spot, where the dry creek forked around. The lama wore red robes over yellow robes, comfortable sandals and a pair of slick-looking Air Force shades. He was informed that the preparations were not yet complete. They had to finish marking a trail up the mountain, and plant the prayer poles.

Walker volunteered to be in the path crew so he could go up on the first trip. He stood in the back of the truck as they slowly wound their way up the steep road in Kong, with Dahlia driving, about 15 of them, the bunged-up who needed help climbing, the children, and the men of the path crew. He was a little afraid he might fall off due to the swaying and jostling of this great lumbering giant assault vehicle.

It was then that he got his first view of Mount Shasta in the distance, dominating the terrain for a hundred miles all around, awesome, majestic, huge, way off a bekin in space. No wonder it was a popular UFO landing spot. He kept twisting around trying not to loose sight of it whenever a turn in the road hid it from view.

It was a long trek up one of the high hills on their property over a winding tricky path that had been set up by an advance crew with loppers. Walker was carrying a 12 foot 2x4 to be used as a prayer pole at the top. After wandering around carrying this for a while he began to feel like Jesus Christ. He had waited until the end of the line, while the others disappeared on the true path to the top. He came across Malcolm, who was sick and looking queasy, sitting by the side of the road, looking like some traffic angel, waiting to point the way to the others. Walker got into a chat with him for indeed Malcolm had been formally designated in group to be Walker's Guardian Angel and arbitrator, as there was no Chase any more, in case anything was wrong or uneven.

"Well, how's it been going?" he said.

"Really good. We have started doing a few things together. The group is feeling more and more like friends."

"That's good!"

"I've been having a hard time with Dahlia. We had one large group a while back and it felt very hard."

"Why is that?"

"She told me that I always come too quick."

"Well, you should give that up. It's unmanly. You come, have orgasm, then you roll off and go to sleep."

"Yeah, but coming feels wonderful. You get all soft and relaxed, and merge. That is what people have sex for."

"No, it is just another way of avoiding feelings. You have a lot more feelings if you stay hooked up."

"Well, anyway I'm having a hard time discussing my sex life in front of 10 people. Sleeping with men has made me feel a lot warmer to men in general. But it bugs me the way Dahlia just turns off."

"Dahlia is like that," Malcolm said. "She is like that with me."

"You mean that she treats you like furniture?"

"Yeah. If you want to have a relationship with Dahlia, you have to work through that. That's her stuff."

"Well I guess I better get up top, exercise my Jesus Christ complex. I've got this prayer pole to drag up there."

Walker finally got to the top of the mountain with his 2x4 and found a multitude of people already there assembled, around the raising of the first pole. It was a clear day in early June — not a cloud in the sky. The peak was very high, you could see all around. And there — off in the distance, floating like a giant island in the ocean of atmosphere was the massive Mount Shasta. There was a nice warm gentle breeze, slowly filtering through the few trees crouched here and there in patches of this barren craggy peak.

The prayer flags were multicolored wind socks. They were tied onto the notched 2x4s and hoisted up into holes surrounded and burmed by piles or rocks, or tied into low trees. Dahlia climbed on the back of tall muscular Tom to tie one up. David, one of the teenagers, climbed a tree and helped put one up.

The prayer flags were like fishes whose mouths gulped quantities of the breeze and fluttered out. Prayers in Tibetan and Sanskrit were written on them, and the meaning of these prayers was carried off with each flutter as though spoken by the wind.

Rachel unfurled a small white prayer flag, with Tibetan verses on it. She tied it to a branch of a moss-covered tree.

When the flags were in place, they got down in a circle and started the circle-chakra meditation.

Walker watched the lama wend his way slowly up the steep mountainside switchbacks. Jesse helped him. Both wore red hats. The lama wore an amazing one which looked like a hyperbolic paraboloid.

Everyone gathered around him at the highest point. The place was transformed with colors. Flowers were strewn everywhere, around the prayer poles, in the branches of the trees. Jesse offered the lama his prayer beads. The lama smiled indulgently, "I've got my own."

Then Jesse produced the burnished copper box. Inside

were his friend's ashes.

The lama asked, "What do we do? Do we bury it, or what did he say we should do with the ashes?"

Carlos answered him: "He said they should be scattered. That is the word he used. Scattered."

The lama handed the burnished copper box to Malcolm who said, "It seems to be welded shut."

Someone else examined it and said, "Yeah, it's soldered in the corners!"

Malcolm rose to the situation and with Swiss army knife, some pounding and judicious use of the can opener, got the box open. Inside there was a large plastic bag with a name tag and Chase's ashes. Chase's sons, Luke and Mark were close by, and they picked up the first handful of ashes. Mark walked over to the edge of the cliff and opening his hand let the ashes flow out and drift off into the abyss. The others in the sangha began to take handfuls of ashes and scatter them about, or throw them off the cliff, into the wind.

All we are is dust in the wind thought Walker as he threw the ashes, and shards of bone! (Yes! He hadn't expected that but there were shards of bone).

The wind-lofted ashes so they spangled in the sun. The wind equalizing temperatures. No body to feel it. No body to hide behind. Feel everything.

The ashes drifted out scattering in the sunlight falling scattered in the wind. One could see white bone shards, mingling with the rocks on the stone piles holding up the prayer poles.

All was hushed, there was only the sound of people solemnly walking and wending their way among the rocks, keeping their balance in the rough terrain.

The people looked sad. Serena's face was red from crying. Woman held each other and sobbed. Dahlia walked out to the furthermost point with tears streaming down her cheeks.

Walker felt an urge to hold and comfort her. He imagined what it would be like to experience through no body —the warmth that penetrated the rocks, the peak they were on, the wind kindly bending the trees, the awkward stumbling around, the great blue expanse above. What would it look like, what would it feel like. He knew we would all be annihilated by death. And felt the urgency, how very little time there was, how we had to have courage.

Ashes and bone shards. Ashes and bone shards. A state of low order, maximum entropy. Being dissolved to become part of the organic cycle again for the next recombination and reincarnation. This cycle is the ultimate expression of life. It is the buzz saw that cuts across entropy's fate.

That is what the Bardo is about. Being taken in a boat across a river from old being to new Being. The ashes scattered now go into the wind, go into everything. They become the giving of the body back to the bountiful recirculation.

And now the spirit of Chase is free, free to circulate in the minds of his friends. For that is all the dead ask, is that they be remembered by the living. They circulate in our minds ordering the way our programs allow us to see the world.

When his bag of instruments was brought up the mountain, the lama wanted to get into the grove of trees out of the relentless wind. After some preliminary arrangements the ceremony proper began with the lama delivering an incredible driving chant out of a book with a brocade cover and tied with ribon , The chant sound ran like a freight train.

He accompanied himself with a drum which he played with one hand by twirling and making little balls on strings strike the drum surface alternately. Sometimes he struck a fine long-ringing bronze bell in syncopation. Occasionally, he would lay these down and chant, then blow a long mournful note through a horn made from a hollowed out human thigh bone which had a brass fitting on the mouth end. The two large nodules that had been a human hip joint were hollowed out, with holes, from which the most mournful sound in the world emerged.

Walker was very impressed with such powerful poetry, with the lama's control of breathing, and with what he surmized from the lama's occasional starting was being in a deep visualization feeback loop. You could see it in the lama's face as he went along: his mind and forehead would be in concentration then his eyes would open wide in surprise, and he would be 'seeing' the deceased there in front of him as he was addressing him. Those ancients knew what they were doing.

It was very strange, the Tibetan language. Walker recalled when reading the horrendous Evans-Wentz translation of the Bardo every few words there would be ungodly bone crunching sounds like rDzogs-chen and Klog-chen rab-'byams-pa. The only thing in his experience he could relate it to was mathematics, where each letter stands for some concept thing, and they are yoked together in equation words.

It got chilly in the glade.

On the way down he hung back with Pia, who was favoring a leg injury, staying with her all the way down the mountain. They were the last ones off; Kong awaited them.

That evening Big Group talked to Chase's sons. That night the whole camp was awakened by an eerie glow of what could only be Northern Lights. But this far south? And in June? At the same, time Pioneer10 was the first man-made object to pass out of the solar system to wander for an eternity among the stars of the Milky Way. It informed Earth scientists about a dramatic change in the sun's heat from 9000 to 27000 degrees and of the consequent burst of solar wind activity. Changes in the solar wind effect the Earth's electrically charged ionosphere which acts like a shell above the earth's atmosphere. It is the earth's aura if seen from space. The solar flares produced the Northern Lights. Chase had given them a feeling for the halo that surrounded the earth and all living things.

The next morning Walker awoke, by himself, in the sunshine, feeling very high. He sat up and could see really well, without his glasses! It was if a miracle had occured!

He got up and made his coffee, putting on a large pot for some of the other folks. Bridget came down and was making tea for the lama. She had her chuckling grin.

"I asked the lama if he wants me to fly with him down to San Francisco," she said. "But he doesn't want me to. "

"Why?" Scott asked.

"Well, I shouldn't say. It's a private reason."

"Aw, go on," Scott said in a conspiratorial tone for he liked a bit of gossip. "What is it?"

"Well, I shouldn't say this, but he told me he has a

girlfriend and that she is extremely jealous. He said that if she ever heard about it, she would cut him off. He is completely dependent on her," she chuckled.

Scott said: "Yeah you can tell that they don't hook up at the lamasery all that well." He looked at Bridget, arched his eyebrows and smiled at her. "Did you sleep with the lama?"

Bridget raised her eyes heavenward and blushed ever so slightly and said matter of factly, "Yes."

Smiles all around. She had boffed a lama, a venerable lama. There was merit in seducing a lama.

"How was it?" Scott asked, pointedly.

"Well, it was very spiritual," Bridget said in a tone of voice indicating the topic should close, now.

Walker went down for a swim in the pond while the camp was buzzing with activity. He missed most of the morning meditation. Later, after cleanup and some hot frisbee, and getting their packs all ready to carry on the long trek out, they all went down to swim in the pond.

As Walker went by a little sylvan grotto, Dahlia emerged from it carrying a little baby fawn in her arms. For him it was like looking at a female forest deity protecting wildlife. The teenagers had found it abandoned by its mother. The lama came up and told her that she should just leave it there, and its mother would return and take care of it. Its mother was just probably off feeding or something.

At the pond Walker got Dahlia to go it by taking off his clothes first and jumping in. She did too after much teasing and coaxing from the others.

WooOOOoooaAAAAHHHHhhh!!!oooooOOOOwWHoa!! She hooted and yelled.

Tom remarked: "What incredible faces you are making! You look like those faces in the tankhas."

At the cooking tent, Walker talked to the lama about his book of rituals. The cooking tent was built underneath a tree —the tree supported a lean-to; there were animal-proof wire pantries underneath a hardwood slab counter top and it was a congregating center. The lama was standing, dranking tea, digging the camp.

Walker went up and started talking to him: "I liked the ceremony a lot. I was wondering about the book. Did you hand write it, then etch the printing yourself or what?"

"Yes we write it out by hand, then we print it."

"I think it was very powerful, the rhythms with the instruments. Is there a translation of it?"

"Well, yes." The lama mused for a while, his eyes looked thoughtful and he said, "*The Giving of the Body to Generosity* is the name of the ceremony."

"And could one get a translation?"

"Well, I have a translation for my students, who come to a retreat, in Oregon for 60 days, but most of them have studied with me for 7 or 8 years."

"Yes. I can see that it takes a lot, the way you had the lines going at full breath. You must have to practice a lot of breathing."

"Yes, our students practice a very long time."

"And there isn't anywhere I can get a translation."

"Yes it takes a certain amount of devotion. One could almost say obsession. Some of the people who seek us out have a kind of schizophrenic tendency."

Walker was kind of taken aback by this, thought maybe the lama was having a divine insight into his personality. He put the questioning on a more academic level.

"How old is this particular ceremony?"

"About a thousand years."

On the walk out when the group finally got on the road, Walker started talking about the book. He was feeling really close to these people and what they were going through, and used his intellectual verbality to defend against that closeness.

"Wow, Rachel, did you see that book? The hinge was fabric! . . . You know it kind of opened up like an accordion and he flipped the pages over one by one. . . And the wood.. And the jewels, and the little lock." He was talking to Rachel about it, because she was interested in sewing.

To Kevin he said, "The lama told me it was over 1,000 years old, that would have put it around about the time of Beowulf, around the 900s. . . It has such fabulous rhythms."

"And it was incredibly beautiful the way he started singing the OM MANI PADME HUM in all those different levels and registers, wasn't it? And all of us singing along. It was like some kind of Sweet Home Baptist church choir singing "Amazing Grace", or some other old time spiritual. It was beautiful."

"I would like to have such a book," he continued with longing, "an illuminated manuscript divulged in a dream. Wow, man. It combines breathing, and those fabulous rhythms, and dreaming, and visualization and metaphysics." Walker noticed he wasn't getting much response for his enthusiasm, and half apologized: "I don't mean to be going on. I know you all must be feeling a lot. It's just that I have this typical American mind, I have to have some product, some kind of object to carry away and for me it is in the Book.

Walker thought about the ancient tome Beowulf, with its powerful incantatory poetry. Language must have been different back then. I've always wanted to write something like that.

Then the conversation turned toward mantras. They didn't know it but Rachel was saying mantras, most of the whole time of the walk out She did that to calm herself.

"You know people who study such things, psycholinguists say. . ."

There was a rustle in the bushes not a foot away from Walker's leg. He looked over and Harve said he saw a snake slithering off into the bush.

Thump, thump went everybody's heartbeat.

"Look! It's a rattler!"

"Yeah, you can see the rattles on his tail."

This silenced even the talkative Walker. But not for long. Soon he continued his rap: " Yes, people talk about the mouth action when you make the word OM, supposedly it goes right back to the baby at his mothers breast. The action of moving from the open mouthed O to the closed lips M sound, is what the baby first does, to get a squirt of milk from the teat."

Jade sort of smiled at this.

Walker, thinking he was being entertaining continued: "Have you ever read the *Way of the Pilgrim*? It talks about this Russian Orthodox mystic, who had this mantra 'O sacred heart of Jesus have mercy on me' or some such thing and anyway he starts saying it like 50,000 times a day. He has got a sort of gimped up arm and can't work. Eventually, he gets to a place where he doesn't need to say it anymore, for he says it with every beat of his heart."

Rachel said, "Yeah. I say a mantra at work sometimes. "It helps me deal with people that I get pissed off at."

Kevin and Walker sort of hooked up for the walk out most of the rest of the way after that. He was an electrical engineer and they had much to talk about. Kevin works burning programs into PROMs all day.

Walker kidded: "You know, PROMs are like intuition, or like some basic programs that govern the behavior of insects. Did you know there was this bishop in Des Moines who programmed insects to sing an entire Bach cantata?"

This got a smile out of Kevin.

"You know, Kevin, when I read the *Tibetan Book of the Dead*, it almost feels like reading something like an information theory of the self. That is something I really want to have, an information theory of the self.

"I mean if you think about it, they are starting to get this in a kind of evolution now, like when you. . ."

"Like the way they use computers at one level to design and program computers at another level," Kevin interjected.

"Yeah, it's like evolution; you couldn't have had frogs without fish, and lizards without frogs."

"Yeah, but that is based upon reproduction, though."

"True, but if you look at it from the standpoint of information complexity, you have living things growing in increasing chemical complexity, and these silicon organizations growing in a kind of design complexity. Higher density. That is the what VLSI is about. We are in the 5th generation now."

After a while Walker, was with her Jade. He must have been too talkative because she said, "I think I'll go on No-Talk when I get back."

This made Walker self-conscious. "Did I inspire that thought in you with all my verbality?"

Finally they emerged from the country back onto the main road in. Morey was there as planned with the sedan. He had gone out earlier in Kong. "Ah, there's our man with the limo waiting," Walker said. They cruised out of there with the air conditioning on. They stopped in Yreka for a bite at Denny's. Should be denies. It's hard for vegetarians in such

places. They all ordered tall glasses of fresh lemonade.
"What could be finer than lemonade in June." Walker said.

"Do you have any sandwiches with sprouts?" Harve said
to the waitress.

"Nope. Wait, a minute. It does come on the chicken
sandwich."

"Well can I have a chicken sandwich with sprouts, cut
the chicken?"

Walker ordered a salad and got a pile of lettuce with a
couple of carrot shavings in it.

Rachel drove them around her home town of Yreka.
Mount Shasta floated heavenly in the blue skyline beyond.
She pointed out a stoplight on old highway 5. "This used to
be the only stoplight between Redding and Eugene," she
said.

By the time they had threaded their way through the
fingers of Lake Shasta, the talk turned into a hot discussion
of group dynamics.

Walker talked about that hard Friday night with the boys.

Kevin said, "You have such a cynical attitude, you say
things like 'Sperm is cheap; eggs are dear.'"

At this Jade looked at Walker with suspicion clouding
her brow.

Kevin and Rachel really got into it while Rachel was
driving. About how she was acting very distant toward him.
Walker had said as much to Jade, and a hostile look came
across Jade's face.

"I like you very much," Jade said to Walker. "Remember
that time we almost got into sex?"

Walker was begining to get the feeling that both these
women were castrating.

Walker drove for the next 100 miles. Rachel broke into
tears in the back seat. Walker was shocked to hear her talk
about how she and Chase "were into a lot of asshole stuff."

"It made me really scared and this image came up to me
when I reached inside the box to get a handful of Chase's
ashes to scatter on the mountain top, of me putting my hand
in his asshole which we used to be into alot."

Harve talked to her about how she was very
manipulative.

"You go from at one moment being angry to the next

moment crying all in a matter of seconds. It is like watching a soap opera, it makes me think that it's not quite real."

The sangha stopped at a roadside rest area for a meditation. Some of the others talked for a while about visualizations they had. It felt really good and refreshing to be in this spiritual interest while the big rigs were slamming down the highway beside them, un-noticed. Walker really felt a part of something. They could stop the world. They could turn their back on all the machinations of the world; they could focus inward on the consensus reality of the group and find peace. Walker felt a sense of belonging, of knowing another and being known by another. It started to rise up in him, a most profound experience, one of the most intimate and human he had ever experienced. He was merging, and being able to see a reality different from the one his society had constructed him in, a deeper, much more human reality.

Jade looked at Walker long and wonderful then. His eyes relaxed basking in a kind of recognition and acceptance. Morey took over driving when they got back in the car and Jade curled up in the back seat with Walker putting her head on his lap. There were many close warm feelings. He touched her beautiful face tenderly.

In the front seat Morey and Rachel talked. They talked about how she is always teasing him, and she should be more direct. He talked about what a glorious sex life they had. "It feels incredibly blissful to be in a spoon and sliding it in and out of you."

Walker felt envious of his ease with sex and impressed with the honesty of his talk. He could learn much from this man, this fellow husband in this group marriage.

As they got close to S.F. they put on rock'n'roll and cruised into the high energy on delight. The were driving down just past sunset when Jade piped up, "I gotta take a pee." They pulled across an intersection and she got out beside the car and began to struggle, and wiggle in a most delightful way, to get out of her tight blue-jean shorts.

She looked like some punk waif or some do-not-think-I'm-bad- or-bold-but-where-the-water's-deep-it's-cold pin-up writhing in sinewy S curves as she peeled them off, her haunches emerging, fairly leaping out of those ultra tight jeans looking off to the last trace of sunset, hair blowing in the breeze, then finally getting them down, squatting down to pee.

As they were coming into town with the rock and roll streaming out of the quadraphonic stereo sound system in the sedan there was a curious way that things added up. It had to do with the lights of the city being diffused by the fog; it had to do with the sky scraper buildings and strings of lights and the big steel girders and rhythms of the Golden Gate Bridge.

Walker felt a lot closer to everybody, a lot more comfortable with nudity and sexuality. Feeling somewhere between tired and psychadelicized. Somehow it was like driving into a vast mind, or circuit and the girders were long strong arms and he felt like this Shiva figure — he didn't know what it was called, but it is the being with four arms, swirling around in the dance.

It was an image of love, the way the light pulsing into the moving car flickered like soft candle glow of his friend's skin. The way we are intimate he thought, the way we are strong. We are like one large being with many arms.With all this energy going every which way. We just feel solid together. Maybe it is the city, I don't know.

The city looked like some kind of hell, from which they had escaped for a while and to which they returned. The city is this great swirling energy, in which we were dancers, and although many things would change, we would still get through. That's what it is! I and the others had become part of the sangha. We were another body besides our own, the body for each other, that allowed us to have more energy to do and to be for each other. We now had many eyes and arms to see ourselves and to see each other, and to watch and to catch and to touch each other. We could have the life outside and the life inside. Yes. There you have it. I don't know how to put it, but I now have 3 eyes, and 4 arms. I am a big good-looking sexual man, not grabby, but with plenty of strong arms to hold and enfold with.

Walker got up early for meditation the next morning at the Loft. The divine Dahlia came down in the nude, and gave him a check to pay for the car rental as he was on the car return convoy. He was now a brother of the House.

35

The Analyst at Work

It is quite a scene of activity every morning, with 40 people getting up from the penthouse floor and the loft above it, putting away their futons and bedclothes, performing the morning ablutions and getting dressed and out the door by 7:00. And now since the funeral, there is a reading from the *Tibetan Book of the Dead* each day. The sangha all knew they were in for a period of mourning. Thoughts of mortality tend to drive people close. Morey and Lucia and Rachel for example had different ways of dealing with it.

Morey had to be up and out by 5:30 so he missed the reading. I really don't have that much time for all this Buddhism, he thought, though I like some parts of it. The Lama's a good guy. He's trying to be helpful. I have to smile when I picture how the Lama's eyes got as big as saucers when it dawned on him at a meeting of the group how we all sleep together. The poor guy. This was way more of a sangha than he had in mind.

By 6:00 AM, Morey had driven the big old battered Dodge crewcab out Army past Bayshore toward Hunter's Point and was unlocking the gate to the yard of the House landscaping business — Spaceship Earth. Tom and Aaron are with him. Luna the watchdog is there wagging her tail and glad to greet him. Tom puts her in one of the bays, and puts out some chow while Morey and Aaron open up the offices, turn on the machines. Morey goes into the front office through the back door, turns on some more lights. It was very basic: desks, some carpet laid down to cover the concrete slab, wood panelling, a few plants. On the wall across from Morey's desk above his drafting table was a huge poster from the famous '70s collection of NASA artist's conceptions of the great rotating space colonies. This futuristic domed world in space is the one with the Golden Gate bridge in it and hills like in Marin.

Workers start arriving at Spaceship Earth Landscaping

and are soon loading up trucks with sand and lumber and cements and bricks and tools. Aaron has clipboard in hand doing the dispatch. About half are from the House.

By 6:15 Lucia, back at the loft, is up, bedding stowed and is getting dressed. She will be taking the 14 MISSION bus down to 16th to her morning job as janitor. She knows she will really stick out and has to dress down. Lucia is putting on a workman's checkered shirt, beat-up paint-spattered pants, hiding her hair up under a bill cap, putting on shades trying to disguise her beauty for a trip on the bus. Too many guys would be hitting on her all the time. Lucia had the most sexy smile, and relaxed way of looking at you. Her hair was brunet with highlights of sun flowing through it. She had big lovely luscious lips, curled in a lascivious smile. She had to try and hide it. Though she never wore makeup to hide her naturally radiant complexion, she could down play the radiance of her inner being. Just a cleaning woman, blue collar worker of the world on her way to a job.

Lucia earns $7/hr as a maid. Like most New Yorkers, she has no driver's license, is an intrepid user of buses and other public transportation. She has learned how to talk with the other maids she meets. They always want to know why a white girl, a good looking white girl is doing this work. I tell them I'm new to town, I have no education and this is the only job I can get right now. Besides I like doing physical work. I'm strong; she flexes her arm muscles, good at cleaning.

At 6:15 Rachel had these thoughts as she looked at the small LCD display on her wrist watch alarm: Aw hell . . . Some days it doesn't seem worth it to get out of bed. Chase is gone and never coming back and that's what we all have to look forward to. Why bother. She lay there afraid, drifting in and out of sleep.

By 6:30 a small circle of people still at the House have congregated in the main floor and Warren is reading this day's passage from the *Tibetan Book of the Dead*. Lucia is forgoing her usual jog over to the Garfield swimming pool with Pia, Beverly, Wyoming, Frieda and Loretta to get some laps in before work. They are a regular pack of wild women who have even been known to bay at the moon running around some nights on the land. But today Lucia is listening to the reading. It is the 8th day and the passage is about the fierce deities arising.

> This is the Bardo of the Wrathful Deities; and they being influenced by fear, terror, and awe, recognition becometh more difficulty. . . There are even discipline-holding abbots [or *bhikkhus*] and doctors in metaphysical discourses who err at this stage, and, not recognizing, wander into the *Sangsara*. . .
> — O nobly born. The Great Glorious Buddha Heruka . . . body emitting flames out of every pour, orange flame enhaloed head, with nine eyes widely opened, swinging a battle axe and wearing an apron of skulls, protruding teeth glistening and set over one another, singling la-la la a la
> . . . the body of the deceased is embraced by the Mother Buddha Krotishaurima, her right hand clinging to his neck and her left putting to his mouth a red shell (filled with blood) making lips smacking sounds with clashing and rumbling as loud as thunder. . .

It made Lucia shudder and wonder about how Chase's soul was fairing on its journey through the underworld. I hope he's not haunted or suffering. But how could he be suffering, he's already dead. I wish I could just hold him.

Rachel sleeps in until 7:00. By then everyone in the House is required to be up if not already out. Her love Morey, is long gone, having left her embrace at 5:00. She doesn't have to be downtown until 9:00. Her only early obligation is to help her young ward Dhyana, getting her dressed and out the door to school. Rachel is more internal, less social. Taking her time getting dressed.

At 7:00 Morey and a helper are on their way to the first client. Morey does half of the time behind the desk and half of the time out in the field, especially working with clients and estimating new landscaping jobs. He still likes to work with the plants though, when he can.

By 7:15, after chanting and meditation, Lucia is out the

door of their penthouse building and is assaulted by the swirl of sound all around. Dog whistler. Children screaming. Sound blaster. Bus going by. She is frightened by the super-aggressive urban blast.

The city is to torture the mendicants she thinks, assailed by noxious fumes of perfume, plumes — auras, sewer smells, papers flying by showing the shape of local wind devils.

Morey is driving past Candlestick park. Looking at the Bay.

At 7:20 Lucia catches the 49 MISSION to 16th Street. Where she must change to the 22 FILLMORE. Feel More. As the bus went by, it looked something like this: Asian, Asian, Mexicans, Asian, Black, Mexicans, Beautiful White Woman, Asian, Mexican . . . Lucia stuck out.

Going down Mission, Lucia looks out the bus window. Credit Facile. There is a tremendous whirring electric sound coming from the streetcar engine. The bus driver is bored and angry: alternately stabbing on the accelerator and stomping on the breaks making the bus do major jerky moves. Electric buses are hard to start. Pawn shops. Old people on the bus: like the poor (they are the poor) have time on their hands. The bus is horrendously filthy. Marks-a-lot graffiti all over. What's that. Piece of corn. Yech!! She recoiled in horror. Residual barf in the corner! Graffiti festooned buildings. She shivers as for a moment her mind presents only the scrawl of graffiti all around her, on the bus, on the buildings. She reads it as: So much anger in the graffiti; Fuck it, if I've gotta crawl, I'm gonna scrawl. Colors all over the Mission.

Morey is driving up the winding path to his clients house on a hill overlooking the bay in South San Francisco. It is an old estate. The lawn has long stretches of grass, and there are islands of flower beds in the shape of raised up circles and odd arching curved shapes; the lawn just goes on and on and is wide. There is an old apple tree with a bench in front of it. Looks like a typical back yard from the 20s or 30s. I got the design for it out of a Little Rascals movie. The old guy I built if for really likes it because it reminds him of his youth.

I first got into gardening and landscaping when we were

in Hawaii. We had a coffee plantation. There were some fine gardens there. I'm so grateful to Chase for getting me into this kind of work. Imagine a Jewish butcher's son from Syracuse now a vegetarian Buddhist gardener. I'm from the Striberg school of gardening, use the local natural environment, that has evolved to be here — whenever possible and the client willing. Some days now I get the sense of Nature herself in my garden, by copying the way nature did things in the wild.

The bench is an old church pew sanded and sealed with Varathane. It is surprisingly comfortable, because it makes you sit with your back up straight. Right behind the apple tree and its bench is a large circular bed of old roses doing very well and bathing the bench in fragrance. Makes it look almost Amish or would that be Presbyterian.

The old guy is up.

"Hi, Morey."

"Hi, Mr. Bishop. You're up early."

"I knew you guys were coming. I hope it wasn't me that broke the sprinkler system."

"We'll have a look at it; it's probably just the controller. James here is going to put down the dirt and pick up the leaves from the datura if I don't need him to dig up pipe."

They walked around the place.

Morey asked, "How do you like that swing we hung from the big live oak. Have you used it?"

"No, but my granddaughter loves it."

They walked into a more secluded part of the garden. The garden was set off from the open expanse of lawn by a large hedge; you entered the quieter more secluded space through an arched arbor. It had lilies and hollyhocks, and primadonas in beds along soft dirt paths covered with leaf. It felt enclosed, sheltered from the vast expanse of sky and hustle of the city. A quiet place inviting you to sit down and relax.

Mr. Bishop asked Morey, "What's your secret? You've got the place really fine. I could never get it to bloom like this."

"Well it might be the Miracle Grow, then again it might be love."

Rachel, still back at the Loft, having gotten Dhyana off to school is taking her time getting dressed for work. She feels like wearing a hat today, and by god she's going to. A person ought to be able to wear a hat in San Francisco. Time was when women didn't go downtown without hat and gloves.

Rachel is a very good seamstress, an occupation she picked up working in a womans' co-op boutique. She could make any article of clothing from scratch, or might pick up something at the Goodwill and modify it. For today, to pick up her spirits she decided to stand out in one of the most trendy outfits in all of women's high fashion: the three tier jacket. It opened all the way down to her knees over a long dress. It had big buttons. The dress was a knit with thin shoulder straps under the substantial jacket. They both were made of 100% Poly Crepe so the ensemble was light. The olor was a light seal brown. On both the jacket and matching dress, Rachel had hand-stitched some embroidery in an art deco motif, rich in detail.

She had to top this with a hat of her own creation, and here she had outdone herself. She modified a traditional black English riding helmet because she liked the classical shape with the elegant deep crown profile and she just thought it was a good idea to wear a helmet downtown, in case something fell out of the sky onto your head. She'd taken off the leather harness, replaced the internal headband so that it sat snugly on her head; she had widened the brim, dyed the black velvet mauve, and put lacy mesh on it, that actually could be lowered over the brim like a veil. It looked stunning and fun, and yet was exceptionally practical. It had a big bow on the front of it that shone like a coal miners's lamp. She thought of herself as Bo Derrick in a pith helmet from that Tarzan movie, wading into the corporate jungle.

Rachel is getting ready for another day, another boring and tedious day in the life of a Temp. Being a Word Processor was basically a contemptuous position, one of the human cannon fodder of the information age.

Rachel is thankful that her relationship life is so interesting because her work life consists of tedious, demeaning chores working as the slave of an evil demon "handling information" and generally being a handmaiden for and occasionally even having to kiss the ass of some male boss who ignores you. It's a life of obeying orders without questioning them, worrying about your future and lack of job security while waiting years for a promotion that never comes. It was a temp job.

She has to walk down Mission Street past the mob of laborers milling around in the big parking lot of William's Paint at the corner of Mission and Army. Hundreds of Mexican laborers' eyes, young and old, follow her as she crosses Army. (She didn't dare take any shortcuts through the neighborhood; stay to the well traveled path —Jade got mugged once a block from the loft). As she descends down the escalator into the underworld of the subway going to the life-negating "Cubicular World" of corporate culture, she thinks: We are ants crawling around a hole in the ground. To quiet her fear, she tries to relax her breathing, says the mantra, "Oh Ahh HUM" under her breath.

As Rachel is stepping onto a BART train, Lucia runs to catch the 22 FILLMORE. Morey is stepping back into the cab of his truck and on to the next client.

Lucia sees a nice woman bus driver who waits, waving the workers onto her bus. Lucia gets on for a gut-bouncing ride as the bus struggles along 16th Street. A gas bus goes by roaring its engine then slams on screaming, squeaky breaks. Gears grinding. Surely, I'm in hell, she thinks.

A huge funeral procession at Mission Dolores church stops all traffic. Everyone looks. Lots of black Cadillacs. Wonder who died. Chase died. Lucia does an involuntary shudder and shakes it off. Return to the now. The funeral holds up our progress. Must have been one of the old families. Finally, after the long procession begins to wend its way down Dolores Street, they continue.

Lucia watches a young punk woman come down the aisle of the bus toward the back. The woman has orange spikes of hair, 10 of them, carefully gelled and glued to withstand rain, wind or an unwanted touch, sticking out of her head. The effect is a punk Lady Liberty shocked. She shuffles down the bus aisle, shoulders hunched forward, head down. Her T-shirt proclaims: GO FUCK YOURSELF

WITH YOUR ATOM BOMB. A thick silver chain drapes around her neck. Like everyone else, Lucia looked at her as she walked by. Yellow-tinted glasses concealed her angry brown eyes. She had a nose ring, and a small silver ring piercing her left eyebrow, and a chrome stud protruding like the head of a nail that had been driven into her lower lip. Three chains, silver and shiny, swing from the belt loop of her baggy jeans.

Why do they do that? Identity. . . I wonder what *her* story is.

Lucia looks away out the window. People out spraying water to clean off the sidewalk in front of their business. Antique street cars going down Market. From another time. Venerable MUNI bell rings. They take off to a wild jumping start. A real gut wrencher. Lots of black people on the bus. One, a Southerner who told no-one in particular she was from Louisiana, says Thank YOU Ma'am! to the bus driver as she gets off. You don't often see that. The driver smiles a big wide satisfied smile but with the immense sagging pouch of skin under her chin it makes her look like a giant bull frog chewing gum.

We have to slip by a wide moving truck going around the blockage. Hope the electric rods don't come off. Loud disco music pouring out of every car in the Fillmore. A beautiful woman gets of at Fillmore and Sutter. Lucia thinks about all the housework she has done in these wealthy Pacific Heights / Presidio homes.

I worked cleaning the Big Apartment complex at Pacific and Fillmore. Not like jobs I've had working as a janitor in poorer housing. The poor barf in the stairwells more.

But in Pac Heights, a lot of these houses have their own maids. Some are FDWs. Foreign Domestic Workers. Imported. But sometimes they get sent back and I have to fill in. That's how I came to work at the Rheingolds. That was weird. They sure had a beautiful house. They are both lawyers. Carol and Sol. They liked me because I'm Jewish. But they kept on trying to get me to stay late and take care of the kids. I had to say no. Got commitments at the House. She sure was ambitions. And he was just out of it. She was trying to become partner in a law firm. They had a "live-in" nanny / domestic for them and their two kids.

When I worked over there Mrs. Rheingold told me they had to send their nanny back to the Philippines. Apparently she started hanging around with some guy she met. Even brought him into their house when they were away.

That Carol sure was ambitious. No "mommy track" for her. Always goin' on about the glass ceiling. " Oh sure, they let you in the door, give you an office, then shut you out of the "corridors of power." It's a Boys' Game. It's not as if you can't be a successful downtown lawyer and have a family, you just have to make sure you have a wife at home if you want to make it work."

FDWs. They have a tough life. They are like full time housewives. On temporary visas to be servants for the wealthy. Entirely dependent on the family they work for, for money, a place to live, and their very right to be here. I've tried to talk to them when we are waiting for a bus. They often don't speak English and can't even relate to us. Always an outsider on the inside.

Rachel (8:00 AM) gets on BART headed down town. Everybody seems to be looking at her. She actually gets a seat, and since there are no old ladies or old men around she takes it. She sees her reflection in the large window and is pleased. The shape of the hat is really powerful. She's going to need the edge because she's trying to get somewhere in this law firm where she is temping. She notices other people looking at her. One crazy looking guy in a suit and tie, is staring at me so hard he might be trying to bore a hole right through me with his eyes! I can't think of where to put my eyes, god damn it! Here's this asshole straight from 17 consecutive lifetimes as an axolotl looking at me in my hat. A person ought to be able to wear a hat in public! To quiet her anger, she tries to relax here breath, says her mantra, "Oh Ahh HUM" inaudibly.

Lucia, after a long ride down Fillmore has to be seen on the projects where she works, picking up trash on the grounds. She starts outside sweeping the walkways. Then inside, she mops the stairwells. The main thing is to be seen.

Rachel (9:00 AM), after getting into the lock-step flow with the great tide of well-dressed office workers fromBART thronging the downtown sidewalks and cross-walks, passes the smokers outside her building at 101 California Street. They are grabbing a last puff, taking the last drag of their fag and insouciantly making the final flick away for the day to start. "Time to go," one of them says to her. It gives them some sense of controlling time, she realizes. These outside smokers were at least more considerate than the inside smokers who actually smoked in their cubicles. Yeech. People were smoking everywhere even in the elevators up to her floor! As she rises she says a few quick mantras: "Ohm Mani Pay-me Hum" and thinks about the sound penetrating the realms and levels of existence.

Before I even got to my desk I am reeking of people's expelled death. Why do they do that? They were terrified and bored. Having to sedate themselves on their way to work. People she knew — most of the girls in the typing pool — took all kinds of drugs, little white pills for energy when on a diet. She was proud of being drug free. No weed, no coffee, just occasionally a little LSD with the group.

Rachel doesn't even have a cubicle. She has to pass through a gauntlet of people in cubicle land who were smoking, trying to get a quick glance at her as she heads on out into the open temp pool. This is a sea of desks, each desk faced opposite one other, surrounded by cubicles in the periphery. And beyond the cubicles, going around the edge of the room were the offices with walls, and doors that close, and windows. She was just another one of the corps of degraded office temps, shock troops in the advancing forefront of the information age sitting stupefied, VDT-blinded, in front of her new IBM, Intensely Boring Machine.

One big lug stood up and smoking, looked over the top of his cubicle. He watched as she took off her hat and placed it in the empty bottom drawer of her desk, then hung up her jacket on the coat rack as if he had never seen anything like that before.

She could stand it because she had an interesting relationship life. Thank Chase for that. Oh, Chase gone. Must get to work, not think about it.

She said her mantra — the mani — silently. She knows each syllable goes into one of the six realms. She had to use the mantra several times a day at work. It was the only way to get through the day without her anger boiling over. But cigarettes, that was the one thing she hated most about her job — having to work temp in offices where there was a lot of smoking.

Why do they smoke? she asks herself. And the answer comes to her: it provides the illusion of autonomy and creativity. The timing of the light up, the drag and the final flick away provide illusory moments of control.

Even though some would try to hold the cigarette away from you there was just an awful feeling of stinky smoke in the work place and in most of the department stores down town.

Rachel wondered what would people smoking mean psychologically. It was an oral fixation, wasn't it? A person has parts of his mind and behavior fixed on an earlier stage of development. In this stage there are issues around survival and control and comfort at the mothers breast. She thought of the tankhas. Pretas, hungry ghosts in the smoking hell realms.

Life in the real work world is full of stress and the worker enjoyed a smoke like it was a suck at his mama's breast and this would give him at least the sense of having some control over his environment. It is something to help pass the time as they say. Pass the Time? How can we let ourselves be this bored? It infuriated her sometimes. She started to notice the boredom. Sometimes it really got to her and all she saw in the office or on the street was the sheer boredom in people's lives.

Lucia, after making sure she was seen picking up trash and mopping stairwells for a couple of hours, retires to the janitor's closet. This is actually a small room with a window. It was the main reason why she kept this job: got my cleaning supplies and various junk. Got a hot plate and a refrigerator. Even got a large sofa. I could take a nap. Nobody comes in here to bother me. There is a large mirror she has attached to a wall opening the room.

Lucia gets in front of the mirror: I can hardly pass a mirror now without stopping and wondering. Chase got us to meditating in front of a mirror. He would put us on the yoga of sitting in front of a mirror. You had to do it for 24 hours and were supposed to do it in at least 3 hour intervals. You were supposed to do this yoga rigorously in short order, like within a week and report about it at your next weekly session. It often meant losing sleep. She smiled thinking of Kevin's remark: "Sleep deprivation is causing me to walk around in a somnambulistic infundibulum." Chase used to tease us and chastise us to see that we are not truly free if we can't find the time in our life to pursue enlightenment.

As usual now whenever she sat in the mirror to meditate it brought back her first breakthrough experience meditating in front of the mirror. It was really incredible when I did that. Of course, I had some help with LSD. It took a long time before I could meditate with my eyes open. Learning to mediate with eyes open sitting in the mirror really frightened me at what I might see. When I did it, at first I gave myself my most sexy smile. My hair was kind of wild looking, brown with reddish highlights. My big luscious lips in my big cheeky face. I liked what I saw. I tried out my come-hither smile. Gradually I let my face relax. The feigned expression slipped and some anger started to surface. I just calmly watched it. Trying not to control it. Trying not to let myself fall apart. The face I had believed to be my own looked to me with an expression so animal and uh, ... inhuman that I gasped audibly. When the fear abated I saw that the face was quite old, weathered. It looked dead. Then it became a child lookin' at me with candid curiosity.

I tried to do some Buddhist visualizations, seeing Tara above my head. I tried to visualize my face as centered in a kind of test pattern with other deities inhabiting the circles around me.

I can remember a sense of the unreality of time and space; I became acutely aware of form and colors. Mandalas like rain drops in the surface of water began to appear. A strange emergent constellation of circles drawn in black and blue and red and gold, expanding, contracting, merging, converging becoming close and infinitely large, then receding to the thin point where awareness fades and they are forgotten. The circles were like time tubes. Faces came toward me in a procession, some of them family, my mother, an uncle, my Jewish grandparents, whom I had only seen in pictures. I felt a lot of connection and longing and I had to wonder how they died. I remember thinking ghosts are un-grieved dead. This went on for a long time. It was incredible. It showed me love is stronger than death. My god you have to appreciate the generosity that built in this ability for the source to spontaneously show images to us human beings.

Chase used to tell me about how I was always holding myself too stiff all the time.

"Relax Lucia, ain't nothing in this world you would want to hang on to except your enlightenment."

We used to get into sex. It started because we used to get so close in sessions. I felt like he was the only person who really knew me. It was incredible, to let someone you had let get that close to your mind and your soul, to feel him slipping his cock into my cunt. Smiling down at me. Chase was my salvation, my mentor in this life and my lover too.

The next stop for Morey is one of his favorites. He designed and supervised the building of a beautiful sanctuary garden of an all-California woodland scene, consisting solely of rocks and native plants, lots of hydrangea and ferns. There is a circulating fountain with a good waterfall. It was quiet and dark. Contained, the waterfall masked noise from the outside world. Morey thought of it as a *sunyata*. Chase's idea. He inspired him to become a nurseryman artist.

The owner of the garden had a large greenhouse across the back of the property. It is a good size greenhouse made of green painted wood. The greenhouse is filled with orchids in bloom. The guy is an orchid expert. Morey found himself wandering in it. I like to think about the flowers colonizing the world. Colonizing the world with their beauty. Insuring they get propagated. The bountiful generosity in the brave new world.

God my knees are killing me. Hobbling around. Shouldn't have done that tile work yesterday. Got to get the younger guys to do more of that.

I get a little nervous in the presence of the orchids.

I can almost hear them talking to me. It's a kind of affinity telepathy. *Hello, big man.*

Hello ladies.

Masdevalia so beautiful, takes your breath away. I wonder if chakras are like that, can look down the flower, the cone, into some plumbing, some source that takes you back down under the ground, to the great earth mother pushing up all this.

Morey putters around amongst the plants on tables.

Gotta say good by girls. I see you're doin' good. Except for you, cymbidium. What is your problem?

I'm dying. It's just not my time, this time.

Ohhh, I know. I'm sad.

Don't be. There'll be others.

I hope you all make it.

We hope you do too, big man.

Death made him think of Chase. Morey recalled the look in his regard. He remembered his dark eyes when they could hook up. I always felt such a sense of recognition and belonging and empathy from him. Felt really seen.

Where are you now that we need you, Chase? Why have you left us? . . . How are we goin' to carry on without you?

If he could talk back to me, what would he say?

The glass is already broken; you are already dead. Step out from the small time of your control to the Big Time of freedom. This is your life; how are you going to choose to live it?

What are some of the things he taught you in life?

Chase said: Recall how you relaxed into the light. Recall the movement of internal energy as it gets aligned, facilitated, to move in channels. Project your sound, your motion, your self into a center -out there in the world. Then experience and recognize the feedback that comes back.

Seek enlightenment son, I'll be there to help you as much as I can.

What is to become of the community, Chase.

You're a good leader, got a pretty good head for business. Responsible too. . .Got to keep the business going. Try to keep people in the House working with you.

Why did you have to leave us?

I'm just going on ahead of you.

Right now I'm all split apart. My head has opened to the sky, and my body went through the flames and was turned to ashes. My soul has slipped though the ground under the turf. I get terribly afraid sometimes.

What's it like. Are you really drifting in the Bardo? How

can that be? Your body is burnt up. Is it in a parallel dimension?

I'm trying to make sense of it . . .

The great mandala of the day rising . . .

At 11:00 Morey is back in the Marina near the Palace of Fine Arts working on an private little English garden he inherited from another landscaper who begged him to take it on. He is working down the street from where Lucia is, but they do not know each other's schedules.

At 11:00 Rachel is struggling with a computer problem. She has the big three ringed binder book in her lap and is hunched over the keyboard peering from book to screen. Here I am, once again, being the first, moving from a hideous and grotesque word-processor called Lex on a UNIX mainframe to an equally hideous and grotesque word processor called WordPerfect on the PC.

She recalls with fear and loathing disgust the experience of learning Lex in that environment. The sys-admin, now there was a piece of work. She probably files her teeth. She was a fierce bug-eyed Indian woman who might have been the model for those carving-knife wielding deities in the fiercest of Indian and Tibetan Tankha paintings. She had been hell to deal with, a real Ma Sheila Ananda.

The server, . . . the Server everyone had to bow down to the server. We are all clients of the Server. It's like that in life too, it seems. We individual people are given our lives as clients of the Server. The server is like GOD, for Christ's sake and it has an operating system and a network that goes everywhere.

I'm not opposed to probing the secrets of word processing. At times it even feels creative and productive. I was the first around here to start using macros. But how long can the most advanced macro retain its freshness and meaning once it becomes just another part of the job description? The whole idea is to come up with something that added another duty to your job description to forestall your eventually having to leave. And I do often find the subject matter interesting. Last month I spent weeks typing up papers about interferon and methods for amplification of cell populations.

You have to always be on good behavior to get the full time job. At least I don't have to feel like I *wanted* this full time job. In my case going back is going back to hideous typing on a typewriter, which is even more horrendous than word processing off a UNIX server with a buggy command line word processor.

Lunchtime. Morey stops the truck for a bean and cheese burrito at a little Mexican restaurant. Rachel is sitting by herself at a tall counter table in the back corner underneath a large potted fern in a crowded yuppie juice bar next door to the Pacific Stock Exchange.

Lucia takes a cheese and avocado sandwich she has brought from home and walks a few blocks to the Marina at Fort Mason. The wind is brisk, causing the ropes on the masts of the sailboats docked there to bang against the masts. Ptink, Ptink, ptink steady rapid tapping of rope on hollow aluminum pole. The sky above the meadow is tumultuous with dark gray shapes mounting and rolling in.

She follows a white butterfly with her eyes, as it too descends going over the edge, flying down the embankment covered with a fiery tangle of orange yellow and red nasturtiums down to the water. Lucia has a bench to herself.

A group of three Filipina nannies walking a huge collections of kids goes by. Three babies in strollers; three more hanging on and walking. FDWs with a family's biggest treasure.

Listening to sound makes me feel the presence in my being more. The sea seems to be heaving too. Wheer rhaach ch ch, sound of the floating dock grinding. Against the Ptink, Ptink, steady ptink ptink of the wind slapping ropes on aluminum masts. Pay attention to the sensation. What am I feeling right now. When you listen to the sound, slow down and really listen to the sounds around you, it helps you get more into your being. Into your sensations, your internal landscape. It's all constructed by the mind. The floating boat docks are heaving, up and down, undulating hearing. Big sigh movin' undulating.

Past drifting in. Gentle as sleep rising and falling.

Wheer rhaach ch ch. Sounds of ghosts and shadows in

the underworld. Is Chase passing through? Ropes rattling, chains still attached to . . . the life he knew. Waves circling in from the North, across the bay Mount Meru — Mount Tamalpaias. Souls rising.

Shadows and sounds coming out of the creaking boats. Lines clanking on the masts. Taking a boat out. Funeral boat. Light it afire. Send it out on the tide. Burn down to ashes, dissolved into the sea.

Ghoulish big dog-face cloud with dark circles under the eyes floating over the bay. The face of Death?! Who'd have thought it. Death is a dog, a wild thing, natural thing. Maybe even a compassionate thing. Death is a god.

The book has said 'I the world departing one. . .'

Creeee-unch. Ca-blume-pha. The ghosts are restless. What a place, where time is speeded up, so fast sun races across the sky and shadows move, elongate out and back change sides. Like fun house mirrors.

Seems kind of cold, the soul on his/her journey, the pilgrim, has to tell him/herself, has to keep reminding him/herself 'I am dead.'

It is 4:00 and Rachel is still at her desk, still going strong, her posture erect, her attention full. She's been sitting all day crunching numbers and her bum is going number and number by the minute and her asshole itches. She wiggles around in her chair. She'd been trying not to think of all the physical stuff she started getting into with Chase. Sometimes in session, he'd want to get into asshole feelings. What a wild lover that guy was. He had the magic to break through my defenses. He made me feel secure. He made you feel present with yourself. Rachel saw herself in one of these, what he called "physical sessions" with her analyst. Shocked at what he had made her get into, she shook her head in dismay but had to smile too. You could say Chase took his work as an analyst literally.

He was the best man I had ever been with. He had shown me more about myself than any person ever had and I had been able to show him things about himself too. I think.

I'll never forget the first time we got into asshole feelings. We were in a session and he said, kind of scientific

like: Psychoanalysis is all about transference. It was
necessary for us to develop trust to let down the boundary of
the self, both literally and figuratively. Chase told me it was
necessary to get into asshole feelings, he said, "In an effort
to release the spasticity in the lower back, and that will
release tension in the shoulder girdle. This will relieve the
base of the neck and the jaw."

From within a desk drawer he brought out a small jar of
lubricating jelly. He popped the lid off easily with a flick of
his thumb.

Chase was the first person I ever told about my history
of troubles about my father getting into sex with me. At the
time I thought sex was disgusting, but Chase and the House
changed all that. I was very confused and afraid of men back
then. I was terrified of men. Bob had been very gentle with
me and I had this need and ability to control men. I always
had to be in control. But Chase wouldn't let me play that
game on him.

We undressed in front of each other laying our clothes
aside and sat down on a large towel, facing each other in
lotus position. We AUMed and meditated. Our knees were
touching and we intertwined our mudra fingers. We aumed
loud and long and hooked up in our eyes. Chase had a way
of holding you and containing you with his eyes. It was a
moment when you could let your defenses drop and be there
in the present.

Then Chase changed his position so that his left side was
leaning against my right side. He took a big dollop of KY
jelly out of the tube and put it on the index finger of his left
hand. He held out the jar to me and I put K.Y. jelly on my
right index finger.

"You trimmed your nails?" he said. "I don't want you to
hurt me."

I nodded my head. "Yes."

"And you gave yourself the enema?"

I felt myself blush. "Yes."

"Good," he said. "It will be a powerful experience. It
will help you open up and own your own energy-core self."

In spite of my fear I was turned on. I could feel the heat
coming off his body. I wanted to go through the experience.

He said, "I want you to pay particular attention to where

your mind goes when you start to relax the boundaries around the self and we'll explore those later."

Then he circled his left arm around me and came in behind and then slid his hand along my ass and his index finger reached between my ass cheeks. I felt him gently dabbing some K.Y. jelly on my asshole! I then reached under him and soon I felt my finger touching right on my therapists anus. He was playfully bouncing his finger at the opening of my asshole, smearing the KY jelly around the opening.

"Relax," he said. I flicked my finger around the opening of his asshole. We maintained eye contact all the time. We smiled and looked a little nervous at each other.

"Breath deep," he said.

And we had begun panting together, and then gently his finger began probing its way into my asshole! And I gingerly slid my finger into his.

We were both grunting and moaning as he reached his finger into my ass and I pushed mine into his; we breathed heavily and sighed and moaned at this intrusion across the sphincteral barrier of the self. He was being very gentle, I had never done this to a man before. He hissed between his teeth, "Slowly, work it in slowly." I shifted my hips slightly to make an easier reach and to accommodate the unaccustomed presence of the anal probe.

He asked, "Am I hurting you?"

"A little," I replied, punctuated by a gasp of breath. "Oh, it feels so weird!"

I worked my finger into his asshole.

"Let's just go slow. Relax. . . And breathe."

I gasped and felt myself opening up with surprise at the strange sensation. Rachel heaved a sigh and shifted in her chair. Felt herself getting red in the face at these memories. She realizes: It's making me horny right now just thinking about it!

We were both radiating plumes of heat. I was awestruck to be doing this. My finger penetrated his tiny hole and slid up inside. My god!

As my finger entered him more deeply, Chase was able to relax. His cock became erect.

Chase started rubbing his hand on my breasts

I remember him saying, kind of sighing, "You have such lovely breasts." He was plucking my erect nipples like a guitar player, causing me to shiver. We kissed, teasing tongues, while we were impaled and penetrated by each other.

I could tell that he had opened himself and allowed me in, but when he pressed his finger forward into me, I tightened like a vise around it with my sphincter muscle.

"How tight you are!" he said.

I gasped. "I feel like I've been split in two!"

He said, "Make more sound."

I grunted and moaned and we AUMed really loud. Really loud, it was more like Primal Scream. I'm sure we were both screaming. He eased back slightly and then I relaxed and he pushed forward entering me more deeply.

"How's that?" he whispered.

"Unbelievable! Don't move for a few seconds. I have to get used to it. I feel like I'm about to faint."

"Keep breathing," he said. "Pant. Relax."

Chase was very sensitive, I felt safe in his hands. He could tell the entry had been somewhat painful for me, but that was expected. "Feel my asshole," he said. The walls of his rectum were warm and smooth against my finger. Soon I had my finger plugged into him and he was pressing his right side to my left side so close I felt like we had melted together and become one. I could feel his breath on me and smell my perfume mixing with his sweat. He had reached all the way up inside me. And me inside him. I was starting to kind of pass out or faint or something. I could sense clouds rolling by.

When I moved my finger around inside his asshole it made his cock twitch. It was almost like it was my finger extended up through him and now was sticking up front out of him.

He had reached forward and was touching my cunt with his other hand. This got me groaning and moaning something awful. I reached over and took the tip of his cock in my hand then squeezed it. That really made him moan. Then he started really sliding his finger in and out of my asshole. And I did likewise sliding mine in and out of his. At the same time stroking his cock. Every time I shoved it up inside him, his cock would get really hard and thick and hot.

Then he reached up and touched my neck and began to pull my head down toward his cock. He said, "Oh god baby feel my cock with you mouth."

I grunted, and groaned, and impaled my ass further on his finger, and leaned over and took my therapist's cock in my mouth, while I finger-fucked his asshole. His cock was about to burst with sperm. I was snorting and gagging rather than breathing, for he had me in a tremendous energy circle and it was like lightning was going off in my mind lighting each of our integral internal perfidious abys.

He said something like "Impale your throat on my cock, and was really pushing my head down on his cock, and I was chocking and gaging and crying. He said, "Just let it all come out, all the disgust and pain and shame you felt around what was done to you." I did, I just let my mind go blank and when his cock slid down my throat and I felt him forcing my head down on his cock, I gaged and threw up a bit in his lap. He said, "That's OK baby, let it all come out." I couldn't believe it. I was crying. Outrageous. It was mind-blowing to be sharing this disgusting secret.

This same thing happened again a couple of times but then I began to enjoy it. God Damn! What a pervert that guy was. But I've got to hand it to him. I wasn't disgusted by sex after that.

He said, "Become aware of rhythmic pulsing activity within the body. Feel the core dynamo continuously throbbing and radiating energy." It was like he was trying to reach into my id!

"If done right," he had told them, "the anal probe can cause an endless flow of cellular forms and color to flow by in scintillations of point energy."

"Now I want you to contract your asshole around my finger," he said. He seemed to be testing the elasticity of my anal muscle! I was just about to pass out. Clouds of darkness were billowing up around me.

It was as if a . . . a spotlight swept through my inner being, lighting off various chakras and nexi.

He was trying to make us feel our own identity, in the

wisdom of the body, and to own your own asshole.

What a pervert. Making me horny right now thinking about it. What a bastard that guy was! Doin' that to a girl coming from my background. Incest.

Chase damn you! My guru. Gone.

Three years. Three long, terrifying and painful of years of being in therapy with you and in love with you. At times he was everything to me. He was my therapist, my lover, my friend, my father, my mother, one man — one loving, mean, compassionate, HOT, depraved, spiritual and funny guy. Three years of my life devoted to my own quest for sexual autonomy and enlightenment with this amazing man.

He became the object of my OBSESSION. Doing what he wanted was good for me and it helped the group. He was everything a woman wanted and more. I felt such love and empathy from him. I trusted him. I let my guard down for the first time in my life and let another see me. When Chase started having sex with me in sessions, I felt so special! I guess I thought we were lovers, I was pretending that I was his girlfriend! I was about to cry! But as soon as we got back, into the general population of the house he just ignored me. I loved him for three years and he helped me a lot. He wouldn't let me make him fall in love with me, and he would call me on my bullshit, he wouldn't let me live in my fantasy world. He made me feel my own emotions and it made me cry.

He forced me to confront how I think sex is dirty.

He was wrong! I suppose he would rationalized his unethical behavior by saying it was about reducing the chronic holding that most people have because of the way they have had to organize themselves for the social world by abandoning their inner child. He used to say, "Most people got up and learned to walk too soon, they have stiff knees," He'd say, "You need to hold onto your love like it was your baby, like a lost child because we are all lost children."

Then he'd ask me to own what had happened in the session, to try and talk about the place it had taken me. He'd practically grill me. "What did it feel like a few moments before orgasm?"

"I had the sensation of being high among rolling dark

blue clouds, or something similar."

"Did you see them? How did you know? "

"No I didn't *see* them. I just sensed them in the periphery of my mind. I felt like I was sinking into oblivion as if I was falling or I was being projected through something. Soaring though a portal, a cloudbank, and the sense was one of effulgence, emergence."

"You are a lovely young woman," he'd say. "And articulate." Chased really insisted we be articulate.

"What did it feel like at the moment of orgasm?"

"I had the impression of being engulfed by them as the climax grew near. And then I seemed to sink into oblivion."

"What was the oblivion like? Is it anything like the light or other things you see when you meditate?"

"I seemed to be floating in a space, standing erect, maybe riding something. And this is strange because I was so aware of being with you, I remember having to control myself from wanting to bite your cock, or push my finger way up inside you.

He looked surprised, smiled. "Well thanks for that. I wanted you to feel like you were both being inside and someone was going inside you."

"I did. I felt very close to you, and I felt you were close to me. There was a lot of trust going on."

"Yes. A lot of trust." He smiled and held me in his gaze of silent intimacy. It felt so good to make Chase smile.

Chase really was a pervert I suppose. In some ways he had girls he favored more than others. But maybe that was a projection on my part. I don't know what he was into with the other women. Or men! Rumors went around the House but people didn't talk about their most personal relationship with Chase.

Besides it wasn't supposed to be that big a deal. A lot of us went through the Orgasm training with Chase and Wyoming, but that was out in the open. Everybody was there. I know *those* two must have gotten into sex.

We were assigned to have sex for our homework! And to talk about it. What a scene. Here he would be taking me to this incredible place, this healing place and yet he really got my anger going.

I know he was getting into sex with Frieda . . . and Katie

and Lucia; and I suspect some of the other women. And I suspect even some of the teenage girls. But that can't be right. Even though I think some of the women in the house have gotten into sex with some of the teenage boys. But it's not that big a deal for boys.

Rachel did a quick inventory of current and recent relationships. It seems I always had to control the men in my relationships. The house had to separate Carlos and me because of that. Chase was just being a very good friend. He really helped me get over my dependency on Bob, and learn to have pleasure with Warren and Ursu. And then get over my dependency on Carlos.

But I wanted more from him. I had felt this way for three years. I thought I could make Chase fall in love with me, like I did with the others. But he never did anything about it. He wasn't dishonest. I have told Chase that I really cared for him. . . but he just turned me away. A therapist's reaction.

I cant tell if I'm mourning a truly loved one or mourning an introjected ego-ideal. I'll have to meditate on it.

Lucia waited for a bus at Beach & Fillmore. Tired, she finds herself enviously looking at people driving by in their Mercedes and sporty little roadsters. She thinks, "God I'd like to drive a little yellow convertible around town."

A guy pulls up and the song "Don't Get me Wrong" by the Pretenders is booming loud out of the window.

don't get me wrong / if i'm acting so distracted / i'm thinking about the fireworks / that go off when you smile / don't get me wro-o-ong

She sees Chase, how at times he appeared so poweful to her, and at time so needy. How sometimes they held each other's eyes in mutual recognition and intimacy. Seeing his eye Lucia shudders, and bending her head down she just starts to cry. There on the bus bench in the middle of the Marina in San Francisco she is sobbing. Big tears are running down her face.

After a while, she takes some deep breaths and dries here eyes with some tissues she finds in her jacket pocket. The bus is coming. She doesn't want to draw attention to herself by crying on the bus. She decides to go to the record store this weekend and treat herself to a tape of the Pretenders.

36

Deconstructing Sutra

Since the House was doing daily readings of the *Tibetan Book of the Dead* as well as saying the "Devotion to Chenrezig" (whatever that was) in the morning and evening, Walker was doing it too. He decided: I've got to do something about figuring out what was going on! It really bothers me that my own culture does not seem to have natural analogs or counterparts to what was being spoken about in Buddhism in the daily readings of the Bardo Thodol.

Since he was unemployed and free to pursue enlightenment he began to surround himself with books and started looking things up. He started to gather material for an Essay on Buddhism. He thought: I'll take the lazy man's path to enlightenment and at least look up the names of things in the "Devotion to Chenrezig" — the prayer / meditation / poem / sutra / liturgy they were all saying. He decided to deconstruct it and called his essay Deconstructing Sutra. He knew he could look to his heroes Jung and Campbell to provide the analogs. He liked the sound of that title. He didn't know at the time that the prayer was not a sutra, but the liturgy of a sadhana.

He started on Day 9; the Tibetan Book of the Dead reading was about "the blood drinking deities" and it went into detail. Days 8-14 depicts how the evaporating consciousness of the one undergoing the journey is ambushed by the wrathful deities as it wanders downwards un-liberated. The wheel of ignorance and illusion has become neither exhausted nor accelerated by the passing of the deceased. The lama addresses the recently departed:

> — O nobly born. Listen. After the dawning of the Peaceful and Knowledge-Holding Deities, who come to welcome thee . . . the 58 flame enhaloed wrathful blood drinking deities. . . Know that these yet are only the former peaceful deities in changed aspect. . . issued from the southern quarter of thy brain, and come to shine on thee. . . Fear Not. Be not terrified,

Walker was amazed that the *Tibetan Book of the Dead* (TBOD) passage seemed to pinpoint in the brain the source of archetypes. Fan out. Feed back. Push. Pull. He wondered if *these* were the objects of object relations. According to the TBOD these wrathful deities were inversions of the peaceful deities, and they emerged from directions, psychic centers inside the body. Specifically the good deities come from the heart and throat psychic centers of the Bardo-body; the wrathful deities issue from brain psychic centre —they are excited or wrathful reflex forms of the Peaceful Deities.

First thing Walker did toward his essay was pull together all that he could summarize by going through the big dictionary, about the history of Buddhism and its place in the time-line of the world's religions and philosophies. He wanted to throw a frame of time around it.

```
May 15 (Day 9) Notes Toward Deconstructing Sutra.
     The Vedas which is Sanskrit for knowledge, refers
to Hindu sacred writings from 1500 BC. The Tao is
defined as that in virtue of which all things happen
or exist; the rational basis of human activity or
conduct; a universal, regarded as an ideal attained
to a greater or lesser degree by those embodying it.
In Chinese it means simply <the way>. Taoism starts
with Lao Tsu 6th century BC and The Tao Te Ching. It
was further promulgated in China by Chuang-tzu.
     Vedanta reached its highest development in 800
A.D. some 1400 years after the start of Taoism and
some 2300 years after the original Vedas.
     Buddhism originated with an Indian prince named
Siddhartha 566-480 BC who underwent enlightenment
and changed his name to Sakyamuni when he became the
Buddha. He taught the way to ease suffering and
thereby to attain enlightenment.
     So I am wondering about how the ancient Vedas,
which I understand were based on the primacy of
sound and vibration in the world and the way the
phenomenon symbolized by the sign / sound ingresses
into the mind, are the foundation of all these
religions. In 500 BC Buddha is in India, and
Confucius in China. Confucius is interpreting the
Tao of nature into the organization of community.
Pythagoras is working in Greece. Plato 427 — 347
B.C. Later came Euclid, around 300 B.C., around the
time of Aristotle and the Buddhist missionaries
being sent out from India to other countries.
     Where do the sutras come from anyway? They go
```

back to the Vedas. Basically they are saying I have
seen THAT. That psyche at the bottom of mind. I have
seen that and it is basically the central nervous
system under the veneer of the animal, and beneath
that the creative generosity of the Universe.

Well that's fairly straightforward. But why are
we so un-peaceful? Why are we so distant from the
perennial philosophy? I mean what are we committing
to here if we were to take this up and follow it?

I liked Buddhism because we are all participants
in the body of god and don't know it, while in
Christ we have one person who is the son of god, and
we basically try to participate by recognizing and
celebrating that in the one person. Where's that at?
Come to think of it, it is like how we are with
getting excited when the home team wins in baseball
or football, or how people dote on movies stars and
rock stars. Where is that at?

Next thing Walker did was set himself up writing a book
report as though he were still in grade school on the *Tibetan
Book of the Dead*. He started to read the it. He only had the
gnarly Evans-Wentz edition. It is formidable and
intimidating. He needed some concept tenderizer. This
involved having the Trungpa version and other
commentaries open at the same time spread out on his desk,
and reading versions and ponies across the several sources
hopping from one to the other, reading the commentaries of
Trunkpa, Govinda and Jung. The humor of writing a book
report about a book in which the main character is a dead
man did not escape him.

Walker recalled having spent time with Timothy
Leary's version of the Tibetan Book of the Dead called The
Psychedelic Experience in his youth trying to understand the
the onslaught of feelings and sensations and what it meant to
how he constructed the world. He was one of the few people
he knew to take mind expansion seriously as experimental
philosophy. He found a copy of the it at Moe's.

May 19 (Day 13) Notes Toward Deconstructing Sutra.
I thought The Psychedelic Experience was
marvelous and sophisticated, making connections
between the psychedelic drug experiences and visions
of mystical ecstasy. It describes karma as a
psychological game behavior. I recalled I'm OK;
You're OK Transactional Analysis, which modeled
Superego, Ego, Id as Parent, Adult Child. That was
big stuff in its day.

The Timothy Leary version of the TBOD points out
how Evans-Wentz to a great extent, and Jung less so,
were caught up in the esoteric level of the book:
that it really was a manual for the dying. And it
is, but it is a lot more.

I was bugged by the way that the Clear Light
state was depicted as something that happened at the
moment of death, and that it was depicted as a kind
of Heaven a person could get himself permanently
installed in if only he would recognized that he
himself IS the Ultimate Reality, "the All-good
Buddha", transcending time, eternity, and all
creation and that if he can recognize this while in
this supreme state at the moment of death, he will
attain Liberation - that is, he will remain in the
Clear Light heaven called Dharmakaya forever.It
sounds like the great Catholic con to me.

Jung in his preface though, points up that the
process of descending into levels of being
culminating in rebirth depicted in the TBOD as the 3
bardos sounds like the process of analysis "if you
read it in reverse." WOW! Now this seemed like the
road in.

Lama Govinda in his preface states clearly that
"There are those who, in virtue of concentration and
other yogic practices, are able to bring the
subconscious into the realm of discriminative
consciousness and, thereby, to draw upon the
unrestricted treasury of subconscious memory,
wherein are stored the records not only of our past
lives but the records of the past of our race, the
past of humanity, and of all pre-human forms of
life, if not of the very consciousness that makes
life possible in this universe." WOW! What a
concept.

That is the Collective Unconscious. It is also
generous in its understanding of the defenses as two
faced guardians at the "gates" to the unconscious.
As seen in the next passage: "If, through some trick
of nature, the gates of an individual's subconscious
were suddenly to spring open, the unprepared mind
would be overwhelmed and crushed. Therefore, the
gates of the subconscious are guarded, by all
initiates, and hidden behind the veil of mysteries
and symbols." The defenses are beautiful things,
they protect but also isolate the ego.

Jung must have enjoyed the similarity between the
psychoanalyst and the priest. Both intoning to the
client/patient, to be brave and fully experience the
return of the repressed, as a kind of rebirth, a
kind of reversal of the death process where the
analysand is undergoing the tortures of re-
experiencing in a safe environment, the events that

got learned into the body and mind as motor and
mental defense postures — objects — to which the
client is now still relating as if real.
    So the Defenses are the Guardians!!

Walker's journal/diary reveals an exited mind trying to
make some sense out of the House and discovering
Buddhism. He began reading everything he could on
psychology, trying to become his own shrink — albeit in a
typically intellectual way. He set about teaching himself
meditation. He tried to make some sense out of the theory of
Object Relations (what an unfortunate choice of terms that
is). Reading Abnormal Psychology, he fell into the
Psychology Grad-Student Syndrome: as he learned more
about defense mechanism and energy transfers in psychical
reality, he imagined that he had the symptoms and thus the
syndromes of various degenerate mental configurations. He
spent a great deal of time imagining he had all the possible
afflictions. Was he orally compensated? Anal retentive?
Narcissistic. After much reading Walker came to the
conclusion that he was compensated oral with a Narcissistic
position. The posturing of the developing ego undergoing the
onslaught of the world trying to achieve some kind of
autonomy was touching. He was fascinated by other
accounts in which the organization of mental energy might
even map onto the structure of the Chakras.

On Day 17 Walker tried to make a table of guardians and
defense mechanisms. In one column he listed the Defense
Mechanisms: projection, de-realization, introjection,
regression, prejudice. . . and tried to find exact
correspondences to Guardians in the Buddhist cannon. But
that didn't seem to map up. Then he realized the Guardians
were two-sided figures, the defense mechanisms were one
side and good psychological attributes or skillful means like
forbearance, trust, sympathy, tolerance, were the other side
of these deities, or two-sided psychological impulses. Most
psychological impulses were like that.

At first he thought of the mind based on Freud's theory
as a three dimensional world of psychic energy economy, a
flat x-y-z space of id, ego and super-ego. With analogies
based on supply and demand and strategy. He wondered if
some economist somewhere hadn't formulated a theory

using calculus, — just as inflation is the area under the supply and demand curve, super-ego or something would be the area under the curve of impulse and restraint. Something like that. Apparently Freud's, though an older model of the psyche, was a good history of the development of psychoanalysis in this century.

Walker began to take up the philosophy of analysis. The people of the House were in constant analysis. These were sophisticated people; they were attempting to live a life that allowed them to feel more of their being. This is the state of the modern mind or at least the modern mind in California. They saw people as struggling and they tried to love them and yet develop the freedom not to be taken in by people they cared for. And they had to mourn their own wounds and the wounding they have done, take responsibility for it so that they could catch themselves in regression more often. And not be taken in by it.

Walker could see why the people of the House liked the Tibetan Book of the Dead. Most of them are therapists; the place was a graduate school of group, psychoanalytical, bioenergetic and transpersonal psychology. And the TBOD is about addressing a person —you do this and you do that. And it is like how a person might address themselves —that is the whole thrust of therapy —to get the therapist active inside yourself. In whatever way you can, come to recognize yourself and have real feelings in the body and life that you have been given. In whatever way you can do that — symbolically, energetically, you need to come to self-knowledge, painful though this "introjection of the good breast" —as the object relationists termed it, may be. On that day the reading of the TBOD was:

> — O nobly born. Listen . . . will issue from the southern quarter of thy brain, and come to shine on the, . . . Fear Not. Be not terrified, for they be thine own tutelary deity. In reality they are the Father-Mother Bhagavan Ratan-Sambhava. Recognition and obtaining liberation will be simultaneous. Merge with them.

Walker realized too that here was a terrific parallel between the color energy in the mandalas and in the devotional tankha paintings and the color symbolism in the text of the Tibetan Book of the Dead. Thought there were only a few color plates, each deity is depicted in conformity with its description in the text as to color, position, posture, mundra and symbols. He began seeing quite a lot of tankhas and mandalas in book stores around Berkeley. Berkeley is a hotbed of Buddhist activity. He got an analogy going between the energy of the colors and the various states of mind at any moment. The colors are given off by mind activity. He worked on it in his journal.

May 23 (Day 17) Notes Toward Deconstructing Sutra.
    At first I saw Freud's model of the mind as a three-dimensional space where the state at any moment was an admixture of id, ego and super-ego. Then I began to look at the mind like it was depicted in a circular mandala and made the analogy to the model of the atom. The atom — the mandala of our age — is depicted as circular with a central entity, the nucleus, surrounded by the fast moving electron smeared as probability. Like the atom, the energy of the mind is centralized around the id. And how its energy is mitigated, falling in and out of realms is modeled by the mandala. Like the atom model there is the nucleus being the id at the core, the ego being inner electrons around the core, and then the super-ego as electrons that are being exchanged with other nuclear systems in the society —the social ego, or super ego.
    Then you have another depiction of this motion in the quantum energy levels —the Bohr model which connected structure and predicted spectral lines. This model used level and talked about the radiation — color — when the configuration changed from the basic levels of the free or un-excited atom or molecule to the excited levels. The energy transitions among the levels gave off characteristic colors. Excitation causes splitting of the energy levels.
    So by analogy we would actually talk about configurations of the being as being more or less excited by radiation energy coming from without and from within. In its ground state, its un-excited state, the being is timeless. Is that the state of meditation?
    What would wisdom and compassion be?
    The energy from the id and how it is sublimated is modeled like the atom with the nucleus being the id at the core. Wisdom would be sublimated ego libido energy. The energy level diagram would show a transformation from narcissism to a deep

understanding of the nature of self. Compassion
would be sublimated object libido energy. Its energy
level diagram would show a transformation from
desire and rage through the vision of there being no
separate subject in need of a magical reunion with
either a gratifying or a frustrating other. Maybe a
change in energy levels would produce different
effect; perhaps a serotonin cascade in the frontal
lobes, a hysteresis effect due to an avalanche, a
cascade of neuronal re-alignment.

It's like Wisdom is Hydrogen and Compassion is
Helium. Whenever libido energy makes transitions it
gives off light. It's like wisdom is turned inward,
centripetal, and compassion is centrifugal. Wisdom
is a shell of energy closer around the core, and
then the super-ego is like outer electrons —
projected objects that are available for hooking-up
in exchanges with other beings out in society.

This appears to be what modern psychology has
taught us. How the splitting of desire occurs. It is
the theory underlying much clinical work. The id and
the super ego are split off parts of the self or
person. The threefold conception would then be the
extreme expression of a splitting when things have
become intolerable.

Always the text of the world and above it the
logic and themes of society through the super-ego
and below it the psychological imagery of energy.
And you want to be able to move across these levels
with awareness.

I have a bad or cruel super-ego, which I
contained or otherwise deactivated with the use of
marijuana. Where did that super-ego come from? What
did it look like?

The next day Walker even wrote up some of his own
thoughts about these two languages, the language of energy
and the language of logic. He saw group theory as the perfect
place for this, the science developed by crystallographers
intuiting the configurations of matter was like the artists
painting tankhas. The picture of the group as a closed finite
system maintaining itself seemed like the energy system of
mind. He wrote up an idealized interaction between the
Analyst and the Client. It developed into a bit of a parody of
how the House sees psychoanalysis.

May 24 (Day 18) Notes Toward Deconstructing Sutra
O nobly born Do not be afraid of your neediness
weakness and self-centeredness. Ask where does this
self-hate come from. It is not a malevolent foment

from outside, it is a looking for the weak person
you feel yourself to be.
   Guarding against the weak person you feel
yourself to be, a character type is created at a
stage in the development process.
   I am trying to see through the defenses.
   Reversal: oral person transmutes his essentially
infantile selfishly narcissistic, irresponsible and
bitter real self into a much easier to sell package
   becomes nurturing
   selfish —> nurturing
   irresponsibility —> responsibility (resented)
   so we have this group of operations depicted by
the slide arrow (-->)
   The mind is a group of operations.
   THE MIND IS A GROUP OF OPERATIONS!!
   — a central statement like "language is a virus"
   This is a major discovery. Hoorayy!!!!!
   I'm really feeling my need.
   How my needs are not being met.
   Denial   Projection   Identifying   Displacement

   Here's Dr. Benway, evil Doctor of Pho-Wha talking
to the deceased, diseased, dis-eased,
   Displace: over-consumption of food, drink drugs
   in an attempt to easily alter the internal
experience
   of loss, emptiness & despair.
   Displace the need for love of people to
   the need to be surrounded by material
   objects which are believed to offer fulfillment.
   Displace the need to a need for attention
   verbally bright
   Resistance at all levels.
   So get a map up between the colors (in TBOD) and
the resistances.
   Explain how the compensations form thought-forms
at a level.
   These thought-forms . . . are these the objects
of object relations?
   Do not abandon your child to these "Realms"
   to wander around forever in these realms.
   If the subject fails to recognize
   the machinations of the ego defenses
   for what they are, rebirth
   will not be possible.
   karma = past-game playing
   karma = the compensating for abandoning the child
   Game playing is the compensation for abandoning
the child

   Through Campbell and Jung, Walker got the concept of
Yidam. He grabbed onto it like a drowning man grasping at

straws. This was the way in. It spoke to him. Yidam, that's like your THING, man — the main passion or guiding interest of your life. What was that for him? Well, writing of course. Obviously it was writing. Writing is my Yidam. It felt good to make the connection. The line in the Devotion to Chenrezig was *I take refuge in all the Assemblage of Yidams*. Wow, there was an assemblage of Yidams. The muses? And taking *refuge* in writing? —piece of cake, done it all my life.

Finally, getting that prepatory study and intellectual defensiveness out of his system, Walker started to do an *explication du text* on the sutra.

```
May 25 Day 19 Deconstructing Sutra — Beginning
     The first part of Devotion to Chenrezig is about
Taking Refuge.
```

Taking Refuge
Myself and all sentient beings
as limitless as the sky.

```
     Now this, — limitless as the sky, — I've seen
that before. The poets who wrote the Buddhist and
Vedic sutras are often trying to get images of
clarity. Another one is the pool of ultra-clear
water, in which you can see into fathomless depths,
and your thoughts and images and ideas are like
ripples in this water.
     Another image is Diamond Mind. Another is like
the image of space curved by matter. Yes. Who
wouldn't want to, sometime in their life, hold onto
a sense of clarity. Another image of this clarity is
the mirror, looking into the Mind-as-such they say
is like looking into a sky-like mirror on a
perfectly clear day in which the endless blue goes
on and on for miles and miles. Maybe we are all tall
kites soaring up into this blue clarity —tethered by
a thin line, and looking down at the earth back out
to the blue horizon where sea and sky meet. That
would be nice. And yet, and yet, what must it be
like to actually come to know the contents of your
own mind and the contents of Mind-as-thought as
though they were some physical THING, —those great
ripples in the beyond. Wow. It boggles the mind.
     I wonder if it would be possible to have psychic
phenomena, visions, experiences of telepathy, mind
reading, clairvoyance. Synesthesia, visualization,
deep hypnotic trances. That would be cool. But you
```

can't just sit right down and . . . have these
experiences. Can you?
　　Anyway, back to the explication du text. It was a
prayer for Liberation.

(Devotion to Chenrezig)
Taking Refuge / Myself and all sentient beings / as
limitless as the sky. / From this time forward.
Until the heart of enlightenment / is reached.....
I take refuge in all the Holy Lamas
I take refuge in all the Assemblage of Yidams
I take refuge in all the Teachings of the Dharma
I take refuge in all the Members of the Sangha
I take refuge in all the Herukas, Dakinis, Dharmapalas
and Guardians possessing the wisdom eye of Knowledge.

　　The first part is about Taking Refuge. A stepping
out, a reassessment, an admission that you can't do
it alone. Where's my community? What are we
committing to here? What are the Assemblage of
Yidams, the Teachings of the Dharma, Members of the
Sangha, all the Herukas, Dakinis, Dharmapalas?
　　Well taking refuge. . . I read from Bloefeld's
The Tantric Mysticism of Tibet, that all sadhanas
start with taking refuge. To me that is a bit of a
foreign concept, but there is hope in it. And
humility.
　　Well, the Yidams I gather, are like the Muses.
That's cool. The muse of dance, movement, kinetics.
The muse of visual design, painting. The muse of
poetry, making sense. Yes, that is something I can
get into. Is there a muse of psychology? Is it
Psyche? Who was followed by Echo? No Psyche got
together with Cupid — the body - and (Psyche + Body)
produced Love. And where did the muses come from?
They were the children of Zeus and Mnemosene, a
cross between the sky and memory. Wow. What must it
have been like to experience inspiration as a union
of the sky and memory back when philosophy
celebrated the dawning of consciousness on the fresh
new world. Is it possible to do this with other
aspects of mind? With all of them? In our own time?
　　I recognized the Wisdom Eye of Knowledge. The
Dalai Lama himself had written a book of that title.
It is about consciousness opening up above the ego.
Being able to look down on the struggles of the ego
in this world from detachment. Isn't it? Above the
ego, the super-ego?
　　Heruka is the masculine energy principle in a
wrathful form. Would that be the animus? And if
there is a wrathful form is there a benevolent form?

And if there is a masculine energy principle what would be the female principle, what we might call the anima. Yep, just as I thought —the Dakini, — the feminine energy principle, associated with knowledge and intelligence which may be either destructive or creative. Is this psychic energy we are talking about— the id, the unconscious out of which the ego grows? Yes! The Sutras are a poetry of elemental psychic entities or complexes or aggregates, (or groups, called skandas) or even archetypes of mind!

I woke up with a gift from consciousness one day. It was an early morning lucid dream, and I started thinking of Herukas, Dakinis, Dharmapalas as angels that were by my side or in my mind. Helpers on the way. Archetypes or complexes being given by the emerging consciousness to help me find my way. It was up to me to make them real. To make them new. To make them exist. No wonder Jung liked this material so much.

Checking out the Evans-Wentz TBOD, what did I find? Dakini was considered like a Fairy. What?! Is this some kind of transplanted Blake here? In some footnotes I found another footnote — Evans-Wentz had footnotes in his footnotes! I had never seen that before. He footnotes a Tantric sutra which calls the Dakini the recollection of the body, — is that like somehow getting underneath the body and feeling the CNS, the first subtle body you come to on this path?

But Jung thought that the SNS, the Sympathetic Nervous System, which did not have any sense periscopes to the outside world but was yet responsible for maintaining the being of an entity. Was that the subtle body? Were these Buddhist meditators actually able to directly know these entities? Could I come to know them?

No by god the Dakini is the anima and I think Dahlia represents that on earth for me.

In another footnote of E-W TBOD, page 127 you have The Dakinis, (Tib Mkhah-hgro-ma [or Sky-goer']) fairy-like goddesses possessing peculiar powers of good or evil. Cool. Sky-goer. Luke Skywalker. There's that kenning again.

I was very excited by how kenning - the ramming together of two things, like saying whale-road for the sea - was actually a synthetic language like Sanskrit and Tibetan. Then on page 128 the TBOD finally calls the dakini the Divine Mother of different colors. Well if that's not the anima I'd like to know what is.

On that same page they describe the Knowledge Holders in the four directions of different colors. Walker began to think of emergence myths of the Navaho.

When were *they* around? Same time as Pythagoras? Or even earlier? Around the time of Buddha and Confucius? From the same dictionary, he found that the Navaho were part of the Athabascan(?) Indians. How far back does this tribe go? And their mythology? Probably back to the time of Lao Tsu too. Or even the Vedas? *Sure*. Walker wondered if it could be possible that American Indian language was from Sanskrit. Naw, that couldn't be. What a strange thought. Anyway we are reading about an emergence myth here. And I'm getting more confused than ever. But I know the mandala in the Tibetan cannon is like the mandala of the American Indian. OK keep going, what are Yidams.

The Yidam is your Thing, man. It is the central inspirational energy around which you organize your life. For me, my Yidam is writing. It was the center of my practice. Yes, dig it, I could take refuge in my writing Yidam. The thrust of the 2nd Bardo in which the "dying" person was instructed to meditate on his "tutelary deity" —Yidam — that is the particular god for whom you performed devotional practices while alive. I've never really said it before but writing is devotional practice. So who or what is the tutelary deity of which writing was the devotional act? Joyce? Borges? Casteneda?

No. These are Avatars, reflections of the writing Buddha. The real thing was the voice trying to speak experience, trying to create a feedback loop in which it could watch itself. Come to know itself through me - Walker Underwood. See so that we may see. It is the closest thing we will ever have to telepathy.

What is the Dharma, the teachings of the Dharma?
Dharma = truth, religion, law, the basic elements or realities? Related to dharmadhatu; dhatu is space, sphere or realm. Dharmadhatu expresses the idea of the all-encompassing matrix in which all phenomena arise and cease. Dharma kaya the body of truth, the absolute Buddha-nature.

Oh, oh. The bodhi bodies. The three kayas: the dharmakaya is the body of dharma or truth; there is also sambhogakaya, the body of enjoyment the aspect of Buddha nature which communicates the dharma and appears in the form of the peaceful and wrathful deities (now these would be the defenses, and the organizations —call them bodies, in the sense that they are an integrated purposive whole with their own hardware -chemical nervous system, and finally

the third is the mental objects, —phenomenal
integrities constructed by the mind to which we
relate. These are the third nirmanakaya body of
creation in which it is possible for the Buddha
nature to manifest itself on earth.
     Encompassing and transcending them is a fourth -
the svabhaavikakaya the essential body of intrinsic
nature.
     What intrinsic nature. What could that be?
Instincts? A term like Intrinsic Nature, —it's like
Transworld Business Company Incorporated Unlimited.

Walker read in Lama Govinda's introduction the story of
how Padma Sambhava, said to be the author of the Bardo
Thodol which was one of several Bardos —vehicles for
taking you across to a more real connection with how things
are — had the book hidden. Its whereabouts was transmitted
through the Dharmabody and generations later it became a
'discovered treasure,' one of many.

     What an interesting history. Govinda also
mentions how Buddhism wherever it goes treats the
local deities like guardians of the Dharma, and you
get a sense of people's defenses as being guardians
of the treasure of the unconscious. Wow is that ever
generous. We are embodiments of the dharma.
     Then the introduction by the lama mentions that
the esoteric trio is the Buddha, the Dharma (or
Scriptures) and the Sangha (or priesthood). My
community is the sangha. I know what that is. Got to
be careful here it would be a big mistake to equate
Yidam with a Buddha. That could be a primary
problem.
     Herukas, Dharmapalas. Dharmapalas,
     What are Herukas, Dharmapalas. Dharmapalas? I
know what those are. They are big, beautiful,
pronking time-animals. No, what are they?
Doorkeepers. It's a Sanskrit word — faith guarding
deities. That, and with Bodhisatvas, they symbolized
the four immeasurables —tranquil or peaceful methods
employed by Divine Beings for the salvation of
sentient creatures. (What would those be? loving-
kindness, compassion, joy, and equanimity.
Dharmapalas symbolizes a method used by divine
beings. Cool. And Herukas are a masculine energy
principle in a wrathful form so we have Heruka as
the opposite of what. Damn! the writing in these
Buddha books assumes so much! What I'm finding is
endless concatenations of interlocking nominalistic
systems. I am hungry for the experience.

Then the recitation asks us to do a
visualization.

VISUALIZATION
I and all sentient beings spread out
through the expanse of space
on the crown of the head, a white lotus and moon
above from Hri the sacred body of Chenrezig
white and clear with five lights radiating
Beautiful, smiling, gazing with eyes of compassion.
Of four hands, the first pair are joined together.
The lower pair hold a crystal rosary and white lotus.
Silk and precious ornaments adorn him.
An antelope's skin clothes his shoulders.
Amitabha crowns his head.
Two feet are placed in Vajra position,
a stainless moon supports his back.
He emerges as the unity of all refuges in essence.

What is "above from Hri the sacred body of
Chenrezig? Amitabha? Vajra position? Hmmm. I know
mudras are used to change the MAGNETIC! flow in a
person. Wow this is getting interesting. Hri. Wow,
that was a tough one. . . . "above from Hri", I
thought that might be the top knot? The cortex?
                    Chenrezig
Chenrezig or Chenrezee called great compassionate
Lord, the bodhisatva of compassion. Also called
Avalokiteshvara. Chenrezee being the patron-god or
national tutelary deity of Tibet and his mantra Om
Mani Pad-me Hum, (which apparently means Hail to the
Jewel in the Lotus) or (Hail to Him who is the Jewel
in the Lotus). Its repetition both in the human world
and on the Bardo plane is credited with bringing to
an end the cycle of rebirth and thereby giving
entrance. Entrance to what? Also, Chenrezig Che = eye
ré = corner of the eye zig = see. Was he the patron
saint of peripheral vision? Wall-eye. May as well be
praying to Wall-eye for all the relevancy this has
for me. Pity the poor westerner trying to take on
this culture. It made me wonder though. Is there a
bodhisatva of focal vision, a bodhisatva of 3D
stereoscopic audio, one of prehensile acquisition.

Then Walker remembered the Wheel of Life from the
Kalachakra initiation. It has the 6 realms, all circling around
the subhuman pig, cock and snake. Representing ignorance,
ego (narcissism) and hate. And the 6 realms each had their

own delivering Bodhisatva of Compassion. The one for the Gods Realm held up a mirror. The one for the Hungry Ghost Realm held up a bowl of symbols — spiritual sustenance. What were the other Bodhisatvas of compassion? The one for the Human Realm was the Buddha himself. What is Chenrezig? What is Amitabha?

Walker had begun to meditate and one day he got it about Chenrezig or Avalokitsvara —the being with a cape of 1000 eyes. It was mindfulness! It was basic attention, a beginning of watching yourself, of being self-aware, being aware of your sensations and thoughts, moment to moment. He had been just getting the first taste of it in meditation. He had set a little timer for 5 minutes, then 15 and gotten into a relaxed but attentive position where there weren't any kinks to bind up energy. Then he watched the flow through his mind. What a tumultuous onslaught from moment to moment! He took it to be that Chenrezig was an icon (an emblem, a symbol, a figure, an archetype, a complex) of a basic awareness that he needed to fall into more and more. It was a kind of being-in-time.

What is Amitabha? Walker played hell trying to find that one and Hri. That send him wandering around Berkeley Theological Library for days in a religious daze. Trying to figure out what was that all about. He found the Amitabha Sutra. What is Amitabha? A Western land, a Buddha land, a land where there is no longer the choice or option for Regression.

Walker read the Amitabha Sutra in a book at the UC Berkeley Graduate Theology Library. It was marvelous. It seemed to talk about a land that was generated by some ancient Buddhas, or perhaps from the officiates's own mind, that was a kind of beautiful abstract land where one need not worry any longer about falling into regression. It was in a dialog of Buddha talking to one Shariputra, and they called it the land of Utmost Happiness where there are pools of the seven jewels, filled with the waters of eight meritorious qualities; the bottom of each pool is pure, covered with golden sands. On the four sides climb stairs of gold, silver, lapus lazuli, crystal, mother-of pearl, rubies, and carnelian. In the pools bloom lotuses as large as carriage wheels with colors of green light, red light, yellow light, and white light, subtle, rare, fragrant, and pure. And in this Buddhaland heavenly music always plays, and the ground is made of gold. In the six periods of the day and night a heavenly rain of mandarava flowers falls, and throughout the clear morning, each living being of this land offers sacks filled with myriads of wonderful flowers to the hundreds of thousands of millions of Buddhas of the other directions. At mealtime they return to their own countries and after eating they walk about. Buddha tells him: Shariputra, the Land of Utmost Happiness is crowned in splendor and virtues such as these.

In that Buddhaland when the gentle winds blow, the rows of jewelled trees and jewelled nets reverberate with fine and wondrous sounds, as a symphony of one hundred thousand kinds of music played in harmony. All who hear these sounds are naturally mindful of the Buddha, mindful of the Dharma, and mindful of the Sangha.

Walker thought, Wow I'm all for it. A land of no regression. Yes that would be nice. A laudable goal, to be sure.

May 27 Day 21 Deconstructing Sutra.
What is Amitabha? I got to read the Amitabha Sutra, with those luscious descriptions of a Buddha land, Dewachen.
I found bodhicitta = unconditional love; am looking for more map-ups. I thought about how being a parent is one of the rare instances in life where you get to experience unconditional love. That must be why they do it. It struck me that this Buddha land Amitabha (Dewachen?) was kind of a picture of this perfect Platonic world of forms, where things were attracted to other things by magnetism, and one could move across the floors by magnetic repulsion - they were frictionless floors.
Ah, so this is the meaning of the cloudless sky. It is a picture of non-dual experience. And yes, Bloefeld continues, "deities are stages of progress and retrogression along the path."
A Western land, a Buddha land, a land where there is no longer the choice or option for Regression, Amitabha is "the essence of the speech of all the Buddhas". It is found if you can generate this bodhicitta, then you can get into an experience of Supreme Joy called Sambhogakaya, where angers have been extinguished.
But really, how realistic is this for a humble

layman like myself? Perhaps it might be possible for adepts who really work on it to seriously stop, in some way — in the sense of uproot it - the choice or the option of regression in the use of energy. As the saying goes, First you've got to root it up, then Push it over. I am trying to take it to heart.

I wonder what the English psychological equivalent would be for dharmapala.

I think Dakini is female archetype and Heruka is male archetype. Yidam is muse. Also from Bloefeld I realized that the "Devotion to Chenrezig" has most of the elements of a sadhana. These are: Calling upon the Guru; taking refuge; invocation of the Yidam; the generation of Bodhicitta; a brief Vajrasattva meditation for purification; - so far, we've had these. Then the sadhana should also go on to have these elements: entering the Four Immeasurables (which are the 4 noble Truths - 1) We are born to experience the humiliation of suffering and death, 2) It is thirst for this suffering which binds us to it, 3) There is a release from this suffering, and 4) letting go and becoming mindful is the way. These are depicted in the Wheel of Life, with the Realms of suffering, and the Bodhisatvas of compassion to lead beings out of that suffering. What an awesome psychology!) Bloefeld continues to say a sadhana also has meditation upon the Ten evils and Ten virtues accompanied by confession, meditation upon the voidness of the ego and non-duality and entering samadhi.

So is this next part "entering"?

DEVOTION TO CHENREZIG
O Lord unstained by faults / with body white / with head crowned by a perfect Buddha / with compassionate eyes gazing on beings / to Chenrezig I pay homage. (Repeat 3,7, or 21 times)
Thus having prayed one-pointedly / from the sacred body light radiates/ /purifying deluded awareness, / the manifestation of impure karma / the outer realm becomes Dewachen / the inner contents, the body, speech / mind of sentient beings / become the body, speech, mind / of mighty Chenrezig. /
Form, sound, awareness become / inseparable from emptiness.
I and others appear as the sacred body. / Sound, speech are all the melody / of the syllables. / Thought and memory are the vast / expanse of awareness.

Dewachen. Sounds like Wa Ching — that gang in
Chinatown. I'll be Wa Ching you. No. Dewachen. I
played hell trying to find that one and Hri.

With more reading Walker saw that the structure of this
little prayer was really fairly typical for a sadhana.

May 29 1983 Day 23 Sutra Structure
Reading The Cult of Tara: Magic and Ritual in
Tibet by Stephen Beyer. Wow. It was like reading
Casteneda. Finger mudras. Functor diagrams of states
and processes. I was delighted to see some poetry
from Adrien Rich and Artaud and Pound and TS ELiot
in that book as examples of mental states. I am
getting really excited about the possibilities of
poetry in the sutras, sadhanas and prayers. Got to
make it new for myself.
     The sutras are a web of colored thread which is a
gateway to enlightenment.
     The real intention of the prayer is to act with
the deity. The source of power is the deity. Yes
that's a good idea for prayer. Beyer talks about the
adept using a vivid imagination as a simulacrum for
events. . . a simulacrum built through constant
contemplative feedback growing in each contemplative
period.
     The person saying the prayer / and doing the
sadhana visualization wants to "construct" the
entities that they are praying to in the sutra.
     Chenrezig. What would that be. A kind of model?
Hmmm. . . A model. Chenrezig is a model, the most
important aspect of Chenrezig is compassion, so as
such he is a model of sympathetic understanding.
     Let us look at what we are asked to visualize. We
are asked to visualize Chenrezig above the crown of
your head and above the crowns of the heads of all
beings who are spread out in a tessellation
extending to infinity in all directions of space.
Chenrezig is visualized higher than yourself as
befits the quality of the enlightened mind. Which is
no longer capable of selfishness and attachment,
aversion toward and rejection of others, or
indifference and lack of concern.

     There is a white lotus and a stainless moon
supports his back. No doubt these are symbolic, I
get the image of a crescent moon with the lotus in
the center of it, this concave image is about being
penetrated. Being imbued. Being taken over.
Channeling, incarnating a superior consciousness.
The phrase — "above from Hri the sacred body of
Chenrezig" was tough. What was Hri?

Finally I found a book by Very Ven. Kalu Rinpoche on the Practice of the Chenrezig Sadhana. This is The Four-Armed Chenrezig Meditation. And I saw that the Devotion to Chenrezig that the House was saying was a variation on the prayer of the Chenrezig Sadhana. These sadhanas of visualizing the yidam are important because they work with our attachment to the idea of "I" or "I am." Kalu Rinpoche says, "As long as we have the idea 'I am my body,' we cannot obtain Buddhahood." So the sadhana gives the faithful an opportunity for visualization of oneself as another. One visualizes oneself as Chenrezig. For example, one thinks, "I am Chenrezig, my form is that of Chenrezig."

Beyer with his functor diagrams, which are a wonderful right brain layout of the processes going on in the ritual — of which the liturgy is just a part — shows how the sequence of actions in a Buddhist ritual has the same sequence of actions used in black magic. This sequence of actions has to do with the binding of power. He shows a parallel between the structural anthropology of magic and the structural anthropology of Buddhist ritual. The important insight was the sequence of actions in the Sadhana could be seen working across all rituals and poems. Perhaps across all creation? This sequence of actions is summon, absorb, bind and dissolve the entity therein.

Beyer starts to show the parallel between black magic and the rituals of Buddhism with the story of how a black magician who wishes to perform a magical operation in public, to subjugate an evil king or a fierce and troublesome demon goes about it. The magician makes an effigy of wax and generates it as the person to be subjugated. That is he dissolves the object contemplatively in Emptiness and contemplatively recreates it as a visualized image.

The black magician then summons the awareness of the victim, he draws forward the person to be subjugated, sowing the sound seed syllable into the womb of the effigy; and he binds him within.

Similarly the sequence of actions in the sadhana are:

1. Summon. Create a symbolic being, and project it upon the ultimate fabric of reality — the practitioners own visualization. That is, "the body of the deity adorned with faces and hands whose real nature is as an 'appearance' of one's own mind, a making vivid of one's ordinary ego."

2. Absorb. The ritual empowers the sense of the visualized deity radiating forth upon the perceptual organizing mechanism of the one performing the

ritual as the power of body, speech and mind, of the deity being crystallized in the syllables OM Ah Hum on head, throat and heart.

3. Bind. Into the receptacle thus prepared for it, the divine power descends in actuality from its natural abode of the Dharma realm — Dewachen. It is compelled to do this by the visualization of its appearance and often greeted with offerings and praise. This is the "real" deity, the knowledge being who is dissolved into the symbolic being with the four hand gestures.

4. Dissolve. The power is finally "sealed" into a unitary simulacrum through the deity's own ritual initiation by the five families of Buddhas.

To summon, absorb, bind, and dissolve the deity therein means "at this very moment the yogin casts off his ordinary ego and grasps the ego of the god." The deity dissolve into the yogin.

"If one makes the knowledge being enter in, his eyes and so on are mixed inseparably with the eyes and so on of the symbolic being, down to their very atoms ....visualize their total equality."

Beyer then goes on to align these steps with the liturgy of a sadhana. I was so inspired by how Beyer enumerates the steps of the procedure for a kind of incarnation that I quickly tried to do the same thing with "Devotion to Chenrezig." I found that the prayer performs several of these steps at once and on several occasions throughout the text. I tried to break it down to a minimum of detail to lay bare the structure.

So looking over the ritual sequence in the Devotion to Chenrezig, we have the Approach of taking Refuge. Even the approach of taking refuge suggests we are going to hide out or get into some space that is protected or maybe even the body of Chenrezig. After that we:

1. Create a symbolic being in the VISUALIZATION section, . . . summon

> on the crown of the head, . . the sacred body of Chenrezig . . . with five lights radiating . . . eyes of compassion. . . .four hands, . . . precious ornaments adorn him . . . Two feet are placed in Vajra position, ...

In the VISUALIZATION section of the Devotion to Chenrezig one projects the complex of <wisdom leading to compassion> as an entity called Chenrezig upon the ultimate fabric of reality —the practitioners own visualization. That is the body of the deity Chenrezig adorned: "Silk and precious ornaments adorn him."

Faces and hands whose real nature is as an
'appearance of one's own mind, a making vivid of
one's ordinary ego.' Then in the DEVOTION the
phrase, "He emerges as the unity of all refuges in
essence." suggests absorption and binding. Which
brings us to:

Sequence steps 2 and 3. The prayer combines steps
2 — absorption and 3 —binding of the ritual
sequence. A kind of iterative crystallizing, with
the repetitive chanting of the visualization 3, 7,
or 21 times and the OM Mani Padme Hum mantra (108
times). The repetitive sound work goes on while the
enticements Binding to the deity continue:

> the manifestation of impure karma / the outer realm becomes
> Dewachen / the inner contents, the body, speech / mind of
> sentient beings / become the body, speech, mind / of mighty
> Chenrezig. /
> Form, sound, awareness become / inseparable from
> emptiness.

4. The power is finally "sealed" into the space
and dissolved with:

> I and others appear as the sacred body. / Sound, speech
> are all the melody / of the syllables. / Thought and
> memory are the vast / expanse of awareness.

Then finally the prayer sums up in its DEDICATING
THE MERIT and invokes the families of Buddhas.

So the Devotion to Chenrezig is a variation of an
old sadhana and as such it follows a sequence of
actions designed to bind the visualization of a
deity in the yogins life. The prayer is also a
statement about the whole Buddhist enterprize of
emptiness.

To Walker this was a staggering discovery. It had much
to say about his efforts in art. To be sure, hadn't his creative
efforts always been about attempting to call down god into
his art? Here was depicted the a process of generation and
incarnation. And he saw the structure of ritual sequencing is
used over and over in Buddhist rituals. Sometimes in a much
more elaborate way and at other times compressed, down
into a single sound seed syllable or sigil. This is what is used
to break through the duality. Bind and sealing the deity into
the yogin's own body.

Walker had to go outside and wander around wondering about images and the forces trapped in them, wondering what was beneath them. Later he continued in the notes:

```
Money works by a kind of black magic.
We have imbued this paper with a kind of power
to transform the world.
     It even has the mystic symbols of the eye in the
pyramid. We worship it. When we have it we feel
good, even spiritual -have the time to become
Buddhist. And when we don't have it we are in abject
despair. Currency represents a conductor of a kind
of current of power from the divine. Look! It even
says in God We Trust.
```

In early June, Walker wrote a letter to his friend and teacher John O'Keefe.

```
    6.5.83
    Dear John,
        Wow, this essay I'm working on, Deconstructing
Sutra is really taking me for a wild ride.
        When I started I only thought of deconstruction
as the first step in a reverse-engineering process
(an explication du texte) — I had hopes of
reconstructing my own sutra. I am trying to learn
how to pray here. Then Beyer in his Cult of Tara,
showed how the structure of all the liturgies and
rituals in Buddhism are isomorphic to the
anthropology of black magic —imbuing an effigy with
attributes in order to get some kind of control. In
the case of black magic — control over the victim;
in the case of Buddhism — control over a deity. I
realize that this mechanism is at work in money and
art: —we imbue money with the power to conduct our
lives, and I see art as a kind of artificial
intelligence in which it is possible to contain a
bit of the transcendent.
        Then, thinking about Jung's Answer to Job, I
realized that these rituals were a re-enactment of
the Incarnation! As is the Catholic Mass an
incarnation ritual. The visualization ritual of the
sadhana is a kind of incarnation of Buddha which is
to say consciousness or some of the aspects of
intervening consciousness. Jung's book, Answer to
Job, is a classical Deconstruction of the biblical
story. A deconstruction is what therapists and
analysts do, that is, take the manifest (conscious)
content of a communication and look for how the
unconscious (masqued or reversed) is also in it.
```

Jung, in the Answer to Job, deconstructs the biblical story which on the surface is about how god became incarnated to redeem man — but underlying that, is the story of god trying to redeem himself. Are you familiar with it? Jung gives a history of the old testament god, Yahweh the Omniscient, and how many times he became enraged with anger and wiped out just about everybody on the earth, or other-wise was cruel. (I wonder if these aren't some kind of phylogenetic memories of the dinos through metieor impact.) Then Jung looks at how, in the new testament, God is incarnated in the form of Christ, who is presented as being put on this earth for Man's salvation. Jung reverses this and points out how god is trying to redeem himself for His unkindly nature. Even Christ remarks how the problem of evil seems to have taken the numinosity off God. Job is lamenting that God is blind, else why would he fuck over a good, hard-working father like himself. Jung says that God is not blind it's just that god has a personality with an unconscious which sometimes causes him to behave in an ungodly way to man. Incarnation is where the unconscious of man meets the unconscious of god. The unconscious of a man opens to admit the transcendent hand of god reaching out but also reaches back and pulls god out of nature. This intervening consciousness goes both ways. Nature, the unconscious of god, spends billions of years doing experiments with life, exercising a prodigious and tumultuous creativity groping toward an upright vertebrate with a differentiating mind so that mind which also must individuate itself can see the conscious of god.

The coming of God is the coming of consciousness — an intervening consciousness. Intervening consciousness is man's salvation from his animal nature of devouring and being devoured. Religion is the celebration of this intervening reflective consciousness for which we have great hope. The Tibetan Book of the Dead is about incarnation of consciousness. The compassion of the Buddhas is seen as the expression of a cosmic and eternal Dharma Body reaching out the hand of salvation from the transcendent. But that is something that is a gloss from successive generations of practitioners, the mistake or the thing that needs to be deconstructed in Buddhism. Buddha teaches that there is no fundamental mind at the base of the universe. And that is the bitter truth to take.

The clue that led Jung to do his deconstruction of Job and finding the personality of god was the way the problem of evil is dealt with differently in the Old and the New Testament. In the Old Testament God is seen as this malevolent, paterfamilias blind force of nature. In the New Testament, God is seen as incarnate in man and tempered by compassion for man. Buddhism also seems to have a schism like this that suggests the personality of god — around whether there is a Mind under all this nature or not. The Buddha himself originally taught there was NOT but later developers (except for Zen) keep finding one —the Dharma Body. This is reflected in the two different ways the Bible and the Sutras deal with the problem of evil. Buddhists do not think of their god as responsible for the nature of the world and its evils as their Creator while Christians do. (In Buddhism evil is explained as an illusion created by ignorance.)

Jung points out that an incarnation must be about the emergence of archetypes. Man through his individuation process, learning to let the archetypes express themselves through his individuality also has an effect on the archetypes. Reflecting consciousness intervenes.

So what is there about the sutras to deconstruct? I am staying with my first interpretation and trying to reconstruct. But I am starting to look at the method of paradox in the Heart Sutra. This has always bugged me about the Tao Te Ching. I've never been able to sit well with a method of paradox to get at the emptiness, but maybe I'll make some sense out of it yet.

Strictly speaking I should narrow my scope and call it Deconstructing Sadhana which is a Buddhist ritual with liturgy. Sutra,. . . cain't touch dat.

I want to do the Buddhist exploration of psychic energies, know the Diamond Sutra and the Heart Sutra. In the Diamond Sutra Buddha equates sangsara with nirvana. Beyer explains it. In Buddhism the phenomenal universe of physical matter is known as sangsara. Its antithesis is nirvana or that which is beyond phenomena. Also within sangsara exist Maya, Sanskrit for a magical or illusory show with direct reference to the phenomena of nature. An epiphany. Thus in the Diamond Sutra Buddha equates sangsara with nirvana since both contain "magical elements" and asserts that both are illusory.

Well anyway, I'm thinking about a lot of stuff here. I hope this finds you well.
    fortune,
    Walker Underwood

37

Wooing the Wild Tantrika Feminine

Thinking well of himself, thinking what a fine companion he would be to go to the theatre with and thinking it would be good for Dahlia to get out of the house during this time of mourning, Walker called her up for a date to go to the theatre.

"How are you feeling?" he asked

"I'm kind of having a hard time. What about you?"

"I've had a cold, that's why I haven't been over. I was wondering if you might want to go to the theatre with me?"

"Whaaaahker...."

Dahlia found herself cringing silently. Because now they were in separate groups, they'd have to get permission to go together. She saw it as, once again, a person about whom she's begun to care for setting himself up for another fall. He was avoiding the difficulty they were having in their relationship and he wasn't even aware of it. He was going to push right on through.

He pushed past her insistent whiny exasperated enunciation of his name, not wanting to get into a bunch of relationship talk.

"There's this play on, *The Joy and Terror of Being a Dog*."

"Hold on, Walker. You are leap-froging back to where you were before."

He didn't want to get into endless discussions about his psychological makeup or their unstable relationship so he said, "Say, don't you have a birthday coming up soon? Maybe we could go on your birthday."

"Walker, we need to talk. I feel all this fear and anger coming up from you. And from me. I keep going through this." Once again she felt herself being sucked into some kind of collusion. That she would be kept from having her feelings and that she would stop someone else from having his. "And I want us to get some help. It seems like a good time rather than avoid it, to go through it."

"Well I just thought it would be OK that we could go out, just one friend asking another to go to the theatre."

"Are you coming over tonight?"

"Yea, OK."

"Maybe we could talk about it tonight, in group."

After hanging up the phone, he sees a huge sign: RELATIONSHIP FEAR flashing like a Las Vegas marquee in his mind.

Walker thinks, She feels a lot of fear and anger coming from me? Towards her? What is going to happen tonight? She is going to definitely have it out with me. I can't talk in front of a large group. Why does it always feel so awkward like the first time when we are together? Disrobing, nudity, sexuality in front of the others. I. . . I find it difficult.

That day Kevin came over to Walker's place in Berkeley. A communications engineer, he was being sent by his company to take a class in C programming at UC.

Walker liked talking geek to him and could well draw him out and follow tech talk. Kevin was very impressed with Walker's education; he liked being able to talk about his technical work stuff without having the person go catatonic with boredom. They went and had coffee at Moishe's, a Jewish delicatessen on Shattuck owned by Koreans and staffed by Mexicans. They had an animated and humorous conversation about mathematics and signal theory. Walker spoke enthusiastically about his predisposition to like groups. "You know man, I really like groups. Have you ever studied group theory in mathematics?"

"No . . . I saw a little of it in linear algebra once."

"Well, when I was in school at the University of Texas Austin in the early 1970s I took a class called the vector space theory of matter and it quite blew my mind as much as any peyote or poetry trip ever did. We had this marvelous teacher who wrote the book. Matsen was his name. I still have his book." Walker got up and pulled a green hardback book off the shelves. "Truly this is one of the most amazing books to ever fall into the hands of an undergraduate." He held it in one hand and gently stroked the cover. Vector Space and Algebras for Chemistry and Physics.

"People were still in this huge argument, about particles and waves, between the time-based probability density Schrodinger wave mechanics, and the followers of Heizenburg for whom the matrix mechanics was where it was at. It was really the arguments between the analog and the digital people. And even though there was a lot of calculation, the matrix of operators really made a lot of sense to me, especially when we got the group people to relate it to the geometrical patterns of the crystallographers. It made quantum mechanics a lot more understandable. And the whole thing was projected into an abstract space, a Hilbert space of harmonics."

"It was abstract, but our teacher was very pragmatic, and said we didn't need to concern ourselves with what *picture* we had about the underlying behavior of the universe, because we had the *numbers* and we needed a theory that predicted the *numbers*. It was just an amazing trust of abstraction, because it took us beyond the world that our senses constructs."

Walker handed it Kevin who flipped through it. Walker said, " Man this was an amazing book. This idea of operators in an abstract space was so general, and it made so many other things clear. Relativity as a vector space under operation of the Minkowski space time transformation. Anyway, it was a heady time and I read Eugene Wigner, who was like the Stravinsky of quantum mechanics, and the people around called him *die grupenpest* —the group pest, because he kept writing papers where he showed that the matrix and the wave were the same and since these older physicists were trained in traditional continuous, (analog) methods they were really bugged by this guy and called him the group pest. But this abstract space of operators made it possible to relate the concrete way the *symmetry* of the atoms held themselves in crystals, to the abstract way the laws of physics were invariants, that is symmetries which were *apriori* to even space. And it was such a revolutionary take on things to just sit down and think about an abstract manifold as a thing that had nice vectors in it and operators on the vectors."

"And also there was the whole romantic revolutionary Galois. . . Have you heard of him?"

"No I haven't."

"He was this great mathematician who worked out a way of solving algebra equations by doing group combinations on the space — he died in the French revolution at the age of 21, and yet his papers are considered among the most profound thing ever done in a single sitting. Anyway, what a story. Ever since then I wanted to call myself a grupenpest.

Walker thought: and I fancied myself a grupenpest. And here I sit before you, this tall thin man collecting measurements in a space, any kind of linear programmable space, and I get this vision of myself this collegiate guy in jeans and a long sleeve white shirt, and he had this language that lets him know about the emergence of symmetry in the universe, going back to the elements emerging out of the big bang, and it is a collections of things —a space spanned by a necessary set of basis vectors, and like they are all these abstract spaces wild and tame and we are moving around in them. And yet they would still be amenable to the same techniques and rules of symmetry adaptation.

It's like the way a kid starts out with a measuring tape wanting to measure around a room, then he gets the idea of the perimeter is twice the length plus twice the width, and that it is good for any room or any rectangle. He has the formula. This is going from the intra-room to the inter-rooms — to the relationships among all rooms, with the formula for ALL rectangles. Then to take it one step further in the formula you imagine if you don't know what the operator plus is. That is trans, a further higher level of abstraction that speaks about the formula. Does that make any sense?"

"Well you're getting a little ahead of me there. But I can tell it was a deep experience for you somehow."

Walker could tell that he'd gone off the deep end a little on this stuff, by the way Kevin was staring blankly. "Anyway, it's wonderful stuff."

Kevin said, "Groups in the sense of really being with people was for me one of the most profound experiences in my life too. When I finally got over my defenses and could merge. One of the most profound experiences of groups is the experiences of merging, of feeling yourself being a part of something. Being a part of some kind of energy and belonging. Durkheim talks about it. It is very important that you be able to merge and be part of the group but at the same time that it doesn't take you over. That you are strong enough to experience this kind of love from the group, this kind of binding, but at the same time that it does not take you over".

"Wow that's really true. I was off on this abstract group thing." Walker wondered though if at the bottom they were related.

Kevin said, "Try to be in the love. There is a lot of love around the House, you have to try and let yourself be in the love."

A little later back at Walker's pad, Kevin began talking about having a difficult session with Rachel.

"She said that I always jump into sex too quick. Then Jade jumped in. And it was quite a go around. The two bitches trying to castrate me. Or that is what it felt like."

"Yea, I feel that a lot from Rachel." Walker said. Walker was afraid of Rachel. She was stunningly beautiful in a haughty, troubled bitch sort of way, and Walker didn't think there would be any way he could handle her. Besides she was Morey's favorite. He told Kevin about his earlier conversation with Dahlia. He said, "I'm really scared about what is going to go on in group tonight."

"You think Dahlia is going to cut your balls off?"

"Yea!"

"Well, that's your idea, not what is going to happen at all. We just sit down in a big circle, and you say what you saw, and she says what she saw, and the others who know you say what they see. It is just you getting some objective help."

"Yea, I guess it is me that castrates myself."

"It's your own nasty little personality and you're stuck with it. Like Bobby Burns says, 'Would that we could see us as others see us.' It is hard to be objective and see your own self."

Kevin said, "I really want to work through this. . . stuff, this feeling of being always castrated by women, this ongoing war I have about women trying to castrate me, going back to my domineering mother. I want to work through it."

"I just want to run from it." Walker said.

"To avoid it? Well in a few years you will either end up with a domineering wife in some house, thus fulfilling the prophesy, or you will end up a fucked-up lonely old man."

"No man! I certainly don't want that."

Later that afternoon Walker fell asleep. Depression and anxiety conspire to let the unemployed have naps. Upon waking he decided not to go. But then a great change of heart enveloped him. He began to see that there was something like a sacred heart of divine love burning at the center of this group of people. That it did not concern itself specifically with individuals, but that individuals did work together to create this love. It was trans-personal. That was the equation, between transpersonal and Buddhist psychology. Heart.

Walker saw himself at what appeared to be the parting of the two different life pathways he could take: "One path leads to what might be called the 'real world' as our parents understood it and how it was inculcated into us. Or I could follow the path of feelings, into the House quietly rejecting 'normal' society by declaring we want to be with the flow and be able to feel as much as possible all our lives. And not get stuck behind huge defense systems designed to cage anger and other reactions and defenses to being hurt. We want to own that we hurt and realize that to hurt and make mistakes is human and not get blocked up in it.

He got this vision, of seeing the group, as petals on a rose and in the center of that rose was a heart. We are a group, we are part of these many parallel spaces, sheathes or petals on the rose. But the same laws, the same patterns govern all these levels. These are the laws of group theory. Microworlds embedded within microworlds within microworlds. It was perhaps a gift of his unconscious in meditation. A dhyana, a profound visualized understanding. It made him feel really good.

He leapt up out of his lethargic slumber and started pacing back and forth. He wanted to reach through to something more than this beautiful woman, to this community, he felt his love for this woman expanding to a love or agape for the whole group, living for himself in this group was even more important now than living for her.

And surprisingly enough it went well in the group.

Dahlia started talking in some abstract way about how and why he didn't come around there very much. This was suspicious.

Walker thought, I better get cagey. Psychologically sophisticated. Like they are. I'll have to use some strategy; honesty won't help my cause here. For sure I can't pursue her into her group. In order to still be able to hang out with her I have to prove to her that I am not 'dependent.' Sheesh!

He blurted it out: "I started coming here because of you, and now I am starting to feel this love for my group and for the whole House. . .I have gone through the most things with you and sometimes I was rebellious against it, but it was only my ego that made me do it and it was not how I really wanted to be. . .I find it really difficult making love out in the open. My catholic guilt trip is coming up strong."

She looked at him sadly. "Me too. I have that problem too. We all do. That's the great challenge about living here. You can't hide out. You have to live a more truthful life. . . . I was raised Catholic too.

"Yea, but you guys seem so relaxed!" he countered.

The focus shifted when Dahlia started talking about Walker's pictures.

"They were so much like my own," she said. They smiled and recognized each other, moving through a childhood in mid-20th century American suburbia, coming from a lonely negativity land where the world was black and white when they were children to getting on the yellow brick road of color. The discussion of pictures caused a contagion of focus. The group asked Walker what he saw or remembered. He tried to speak in the language of the group, the language of psychology, in order to be able to be heard by them.

"I didn't see them too well," he said. "But when Dahlia covered the nose and mouth with her hand I could see the terror in the eyes. I said I thought it might be related to circumcision."

This started Dahlia crying again. She shook her head and looked down, "I'm feeling pain from a very old place." She started sobbing. "I was always in some kind of fight with my brother, Carlos, so that it would provoke my mother to come and break it up."

She got quiet as a conclusion, an insight, and understanding settled across her mind. "I guess the house is the mother," she said.

Rachel jumped in and said, "You're on such a *good-girl* trip!"

Then Rachel had her feelings about what she saw in his relationship with Dahlia even though she didn't know anything much about it. "You do the same thing to me, Walker. You put me on a pedestal and keep saying you are so lowly. It is a way of shutting me up."

Walker thought about his southern subservient smile and how he's always saying 'I'm sorry'. God how I hate that submissive crap, he said to himself. I need to knock off the subservient crap, but he did not say anything.

Then Dahlia started crying again.

Morey said to her in an almost sneering teasing way, "You told me once that you wanted to be a nun!"

"I did not!" Dahlia sobbed like a three-year old.

Morey quipped: "Nuns are like what they sound like - None! You are just this woman who doesn't get into any feelings and is married to the guy on the cross."

The whole catholic trip with it's celibate priests came back to Walker. He had wanted to be a priest. Had admired them a lot. Why had I wanted to think that women were not people too. The catholic trip, that you get to god by going through a woman, the virgin trip. Tend to hold women up so high.

Things started going his way in the court of love. The rest of the group pronounced that Dahlia had been very provocative the night that Walker had gotten so mad.

It was decided that there should be more double groups and that Dahlia and Walker could have regular sessions, on Fridays.

HOOOOOORAAAAAY!!

38

Night Movie in the Long Body of a Dream

It is late spring, on a full moon night in the Loft on top of the city. The House is all asleep floating in a flotilla of futons on a sea of acceptance. The women in the loft lie naked, bedded down with the men or the other women. Some men sleep with other men tonight.

The people are no longer interested in marriage, though some of them were/are married. They have gone beyond marriage — they are a tribe. The women dream of dominating their days, with swimming before dawn, running their own business by eight, aerobics class at noon, jogging, food with good friends, intimate conversation, and loving sex in the evening. The men are dreaming of chain saws and light assault vehicles.

Walker is stirring. And in that state between waking and dream, that hypnagogic state, a Watcher of Consciousness emerges and gives you the gift of lucidity in the dream, where you can see yourself from within and without your own stream of consciousness. He could for example pull the camera back to the ceiling and watch himself from above.

EXTERIOR Loft Floor: Walker and Dahlia's futon — Slow pan up the covers. They are in a spoon, she's got her butt cocked up into his stomach and he is snuggling into her back. He kisses the soft curve of her neck tasting the sweetness there.

Dahlia: (She *stirs and moans quietly, gently.*) mmMMm.

Walker: *(Inhaling her, nuzzling into her hair, thinking — in Voice Over)* When I woke up having slept next to Dahlia, I looked at her still sleeping. I drew a deep long breath. How beautiful she is. Inhaling, her fragrance floods my thoughts.

Here on the floor of futons it was warm next to her body. Just lying there with all this community of people pursuing enlightenment and acceptance you couldn't feel more secure. There was Dahlia in his arms and nearby was Morey and

Rachel, as was Malcolm and Frieda, and a little further away was Aaron and Katie and near the door was Ursu and Wyoming, Jesse and Lucia. As well as many other couples he loved and who loved him. You could let yourself go on into a dream.

EXTERIOR Loft Floor: Camera pans over field of futons on floor to futons suspended in black interstellar space like an armada of stuffed UFOs in black star field. Dahlia is the pilot/captain and Walker is the co-pilot. They are sitting upright flying in their little futon, just the two of them. It was quiet, — a convertible that floated through a cloudy atmosphere high over ocean and islands peeking through below. The tiny islands far below have a checkerboard of fields. Pilot and co-pilot are wearing old World War II leather aviator's hats. There is a mouthpiece on a swing-arm placing the mike in front of the mouth, like the kind that people who work at a Burger King drive-through have. They are able to communicate with other futon UFOs by subspace radio comlink.

Captain: Well, looks like our altimeters are within reason.
Co-Pilot: Yeah.
Captain: Yeah, I like that altimeter.
Co-Pilot: Boy, you know it - reads right about the middle marker there.
Captain: Yeah

EXTERIOR Plane: Pan out side flying vehicle, there is a sense of coming from space into atmosphere, floating in the wind of space. A flash of white off a sparkling plane, flying over ocean, coming to coast. The sky is blue and with big fluffy clouds.

Captain: Check out those pods of whales down the coast. *(pause)* Yeah, man. Sitting comfortable in one of our aircraft watching the dolphins and whales, getting ready to come in for a landing at Utopia feels good. *(pause)* Yeah.

Co-Pilot: Yeah. *(pause)* I always watch that radio altimeter. We should be getting something from the Tower any minute.

Captain: There are the islands!

EXTERIOR Coming in from high in the sky. Soaring into a green sun-dappled glade.

Co-Pilot: Aren't they beautiful!

Captain: *(excited)* There's so many valleys here. And look at all those stupas and ziggurats and pyramids.

Co-Pilot: *(awed)* And the gardens and fields.

Their craft soars through canyons of clouds picking channels among the updrafts. The land is very geometrical with symmetric fountains. Off in the distance are little waterfalls flowing down the mountains into pools.

Captain: Ask him - Walker, ask him if he's ready for us to land.

Co-Pilot: Tower, Flight 1-9er 6-8 requests permission to land.

EXTERIOR: *(Sound of power increase)*

Outside of the dream, in the Loft kitchen, someone has opened the door of the big refrigerator and its compressor has kicked on. Camera races across the floor and zooms into dark space between fridge and wall. Zoom into compressor.

CUT TO:

EXTERIOR *(back in the dream)*:

TOWER: *(Voice Over)* Sure am. Uh, there's a little fog, right off the end there and it's wide open after you get by that. You're about 5 miles to the runway.

INTERIOR of plane: Walker, the co-Pilot has a map unfolded on his lap and is pointing the way for pilot Dahlia to land.

They zoom fast down vast twisting turning canyons, fiords, that seem like folds and creases of soft curving enfolding flesh of a body draped in the landscape. Birds could be seen soaring alongside the craft.

Their futon banked as it rounded a corner and THERE ahead, towering up like a skyscraper, was a huge statue of a Buddha. It looked like the same material as the canyons; this shape of the Buddha had been carved out of the landscape by eons of river flow. It was ancient. They landed the craft in the shadow of the canyon wall. They got their gear and headed in.

CUT TO:

EXTERIOR: Walker looks up at futons hovering in the sky as if they are parked there. He is standing at a corner not far from where they arrived. Strangely it seems to be out near . . . their land. Mount Shasta is in the background, they are on their land, but it is also by the sea and there are airports and lots of smooth elegant pyramids and amazing geometrical buildings, spheres and ziggurats. Dahlia and Walker are on the corner, strangers in a strange land. He is looking over the map in his hands. It was a map of the Buddhist heaven Darmakaya complete with mountains from ancient cosmography. Walker sees himself in the dream and is shocked because he usually looks out at the world from behind his own face. To the south the sky had an red-orange horizon; to the east, green; to the west, yellow and to the north, blue.

Walker: *(to himself — Voice Over)* Somehow I'm lost. The map I have is a sort of haphazard creation that was some kind of half translation of Buddhism translated into Jungian psychological terminology with a filter that had taken it through American Indian cosmology. On the map all Buddhist mystical street names were being changed from language particular to an agrarian pastoral medieval society to a modern urban one. Tough break for a traveler like me.

CUT TO:

EXTERIOR: View of Dahlia looking inquisitively.

Dahlia: *(as seen by Walker)* "Hotel Clear Light?"

Walker blinked up into Dahlia's deep, dark brown eyes framed by her lively Latin face. He smiled, not at all understanding what she'd said to him.

Walker: *(trying to sound as polite as possible)* I don't speak Buddhist?

Dahlia: *(Shaking her head, creasing her brow, gestures with a smile to the mandala map in Walker's hands.)* So you like the map more than the territory, huh?

She indicated the map and he handed it to her. She took it, turning it to face her.

EXTERIOR: Walker looked around at the environment. The buildings have long sweeping horizontal symmetries punctuated by amazing rising vertical towers — stupas. These reliquaries were like stacked disks of decreasing circumference up to the sky. You could see a little of the waterway meandering behind a temple or geometrical figure.

Everything was glassine and gold. Huge faces of Buddhas were carved in the towers at every corner. A strange light was emanating from some of the stupas and geometrical buildings receding into the horizon —making the streets of this land glisten.

Objects seem deeper and there was something about the behavior of shadows here. Although some of the buildings have a shadow to the right, some have a shadow to the left; some buildings don't seem to have any shadow at all. The light's rays struck the glassine surfaces of the buildings and geometrical shapes and the surfaces refracted the light rays as if they were passing through a prism, causing the edges of stupas, steps and shrines to shimmer the vibgyor of the solar spectrum. Then these reflections criss-crossed one another in shape-shifting arabesques of unduly undulating color-shapes. The objects in this world take on their own internal glow. A different colored light emanated from each of the four horizons. Red, green,yellow,blue. The scene was a play of diffusion, ambiance and specularity. Also transparency and reflectance. There was something about the refractive index of the air here in this land. You have control over the way light moved in and around in the scene and could do to objects what light does to them.

Dahlia: *(pointing at the map and then down at their feet.)* Here is where we are.

Walker nods in understanding.

Dahlia: *(gesturing around them)* Rig-pa.

Walker: *(nodding, trying to explain)* I don't speak Buddhist. Do you speak psychology?

Dahlia: Rigpa is the word for the realization of universal mind.

Walker: *(to himself privately —V. O.)* Rigpa is epistemology, the knowledge of knowledge itself. All those old Indian philosophers were each of them as sharp as a Kant.

She smiled and nodded. Pleasantly. He got a chill and suddenly realized she could read his mind. . .

Walker: *(fearfully)* Clear Light Hotel?

Dahlia opened her mouth in a smile of understanding, and pointed to another street on the map, quite a ways away from where the two were standing.

Walker: *(INTERNALLY in Voice Over)* Before this trip I had managed to crib together some notes even though I didn't know the language. I'd crammed a few useful phrases into my head and now I was on the plane, that became the mountain. I was discovering that the terminology wouldn't get me everywhere.

The two looked at each other and Walker realized that he has telepathy too. Either that or there were special earphones for the subspace radio in his flying helmet.

Dahlia: *(INTERNAL V.O. —subspace communicator)* It's all about freedom and space. Internal space. There is a tremendous amount of freedom in there.

Walker humbly took the prayerful pose, hands clasped together and bowed to her. She nods and smiles at him.

Walker: *(tentative, as he takes back the map, as thanks)* "Space ! We are as limitless as the sky?!"

Dahlia: *(smiling)* Exactly. . . Follow me.

Walker grinned and nodded back, and they began walking.

Dahlia: Be careful. In-the-Between the souls are moving. They are looking to get between copulating couples. Come with me. The Tibetan Book of the Dead warns again and again, about being watchful not to be reborn in a lower realm.

Walker: *(looks at her,shaking his head, V.O.)* It was something I didn't understand. I wanted to follow her. She, her, unconscious. Hypnagogic State. Talk to Her. Be present in Her. Court Her. I followed her.

Dahlia: *(pointing at herself, V.O.)*Dahlia

She points to him.

Walker: *(offering)* Walker Underwood.

Dahlia: Ah, Underwood. Do you like walking in the woods under leafy boughs?

Dahlia pauses for a moment, pinches her chin.

Dahlia: I wonder what would be a good Buddhist name for you. *(She pauses for a moment, thinking.)* I will give you a Buddhist name.

Walker: *(laughs.)* What will it be.

Dahlia: Ee-oh —awe qua outremonter ring rchS/Z bwa.

Walker: Wow. That's quite a name. I wonder how you spell it. What does it mean?

Dahlia: (Getting *a teasing look on her face)* Ee-oh —awe — literally translated, (for it is only a sound movement) means, "he who has come to the isles from the other side with ideas."

Walker: *(smiling in delight)* Wow. Ee-oh —awe qua outremonter. I like it because and it sounds so exotic to my American ears.

CUT TO:
EXTERIOR Loft Floor: Someone has opened and closed a bathroom door leaving the light to splash for a moment over the inhabitants sleeping on futons on the floor. Walker startled up from his dream momentarily and sees a shocking black and white landscape of rumpled angels or heavenly host, like a Dore print but then snuggles closer to Dahlia relaxing in the scent of her closeness. He settles in and follows the light.

The light swirled and tangled in Dahlia's long hair as they walked. She was close, on his left.

Walker: *(thinking to himself, Voice Over)* Communists have such a different sense of personal space.

He breathed in the smells of Rigpa —Window to the East, and reveled in their exotic flavor.

EXTERIOR: Walker notices the light feels different, it is almost like they are underwater, in a large motel swimming pool, or looking through glass at a world underwater on the other side of the glass. Like an aquarium. And he thinks not water exactly but we are immersed in some kind of fluid, —Time, perhaps, what has sustained me this long. You get a sense that it is a very ancient atmosphere, one that has seen a long evolution from heavy duty monsters and dragons and mahakalas and entities who had evolved over eons of time into these much more benevolent sea horses. It's like sea monsters from long ago turned into these sweet, lovely life-forms.

Then in the dream for a moment he recognized it. It was the light that he saw inside of himself when he meditated — looked down inside. It was actually starting to break up that night. That light was starting to move out into other things. He thought that he could see that same light was, was in everything, and at first he just thought it was the way that the light played on things because they reflect onto water, but this was the real true way light played.

Dahlia: *(indicating the canals flowing by)* Elio quay symslio clion noats. *(She looks at Walker.)* Translated — "We like the way the water flows in our canals."

They walked through the streets, actually they glided evenly, effortlessly. The curbstones seemed to be open raceways whose bottoms were paved with integrated cirucit chips whose gold traces glistened carrying current along. Here and there wading pools could be glimpsed, their waters gently undulating, carrying giant lotus pads as big as wagon wheels. Somehow the ground of this world was frictionless. They "loomed" along.

Sphinx-like temple dogs guarded entrances. Railings and banisters always ended with marvelous upswept curves. The whole place looked like it was set up to attract energy. As they turned a corner, Walker gasped in amazement. In front of them was the giant carving of the Buddha atop the temple. It towered up some 20 stories, shaped out of stone. The gigantic Buddha was sitting in Vajra pose. Of his four hands, the first pair are joined together. The lower pair hold a crystal rosary and white lotus.

EXTERIOR of TEMPLE: They went up the wide steps made of lapis lazuli, trimmed in silver and gold. The stairs were flanked on each side by fearful Chinese Temple Dogs straight out of cross-breeding hell from the steppes of Tibet. The building was like some kind of library. They walked up the steps and entered a temple so wide and vast that Walker "understood" it could only have been a government monument.

INTERIOR of TEMPLE: Inside the temple it got dark. It was vast and windswept. They wandered into a central hall, and could not figure out which way to go from there.

Walker had a machine he had designed. He took an orange shockproof case out of his back pack and set it on the floor. He knelt in front of it. He opened up the double clasps, lifted the top of the case off, leaving the unit exposed. He pulled up two large antennas telescoped inside it then turned it on. It looked like an old World War II radio. The twin tuning antennas were about 3 feet long coming out the top. Two green dials glowed and a potential energy was induced across the two antennas.

Walker: *(explaining)* It is an In-between detector. The Shrodinger Gap Resonator is based on the radio tuning coil. But instead of a mechanism that created a resonance frequency by varying the length of the coil, this one generates a magnetic field that induces magnetic flux. This magnetic field detects openings in the material where the polarities are quiescent — holes.

Walker picked it up and began sweeping it back an forth in front of all the tankha paintings that were gracing the walls in that room. It found an opening behind a great gigantic Wheel of Life painting. Walker stood before the horrendous black mahakala with long teeth and skulls coming out of the top of its head, holding the Wheel. Each of the realms were well represented, especially the human realm: there were many scenes of tiny figures in caves, and in grottos and in large tree trunks, as if they were smoky clouds and they existed in the spaces between the shreds of moving clouds. Some seemed to be living in tents nearby one starting a fire. Here one is giving another a drink; there two traders are arguing and gesticulating. A number of priests are standing before a very much larger yogi with an emaciated body. It had the "stations of the cross" Blind man, potter . . . But the Great Black one, holding the Wheel, — it was as if his body had been ripped open and this Wheel of Life is what we saw inside it — it was really the center and subject of the painting.

Walker: *(explaining)* The Shrodinger Gap Resonator generates a strong magnetic field and then tunes into the eigenvalues in gaps for magnetic probability density. When the spectral gap is perturbed by a strong magnetic field this machine is tuned to eigenvalues above the fixed energy level E inside the gap. Then, by vibrating at that resonance frequency, it can decompose "natural" boundaries along their edge and recombine the boundary around a bigger hole.

Walker was sweating profusely, his forehead glowed as the Wheel in the center of the square began turning slowly and the scenes around it began to twist into a vortex chiaroscuro, pulling the pictures into the wall like fluid down a drain, swirling and turning, sucking inward. Walker felt himself being drawn into it. Dahlia had come over to stand beside him. Just then a sound like a seal being broken preceeded a circular door opening. Going through brought them inside another room. It was not dark; it had its own illumination with which it just seemed to be imbued. Across on the opposite side was a huge double door. Beside each door sat huge monstrous guardian dogs in bronze, their manes flaming death's heads.

The two onernaughts pushed this door open and they entered a vast long hall, like one of the burying chambers of a great Lama —Milarepa or Padma Sambavda. It was long and lined on each side with large glass museum cases with statues of Buddhas and Bodhisatvas from past eons. They looked like they had been carved in stone by natural elements over eons .

Dahlia is looking around, but Walker is struck by what appears to be a glass museum case at the far end of the hall. As he walks up to it he sees a stele stone inside it. This headstone shaped way-marker had universal colored carvings on it. They appeared to Walker to be kind of symbols of group symmetry, icosahedra intersected with the triangular planes. Walker looked puzzled. He wondered what it was.

Walker: *(V.O.)* It is somehow like a picture of dimension or like something out of Kandinsky or . . . Yesss! That's what it is. It is the top view of the chakras seen on end from above! Yes, and somehow I KNOW this, down deep in every part of my being, know it with my i and my I and my "I/alter-ego".

Walker is staring at it with awe. He begins trying to identify it. Dahlia is busy doing something, taking inventory and Walker is standing transfixed terrorized and very afraid in front of the symbol.

Walker: *(V.O.)* It is not just some arbitrary model nor is it some simple Kandinsky abstraction. It is a Hri! Hri --> H_{iel}

Whatever it is, it suddenly begins growing and MOVING in a glowing roseate field! The elements of the chakras break out and separate. Some go in front and some go in back .

$$(( )) \cup \nabla \, \lozenge \oplus .)(.$$

Their parts and the hooks and half moons and spheres of their sigils and symbols mix, as do their individual mantra sounds. The resulting sound is very strange and is becoming modulated and the Hri is generating into strange concatenations of sounds. It is like some low subsonic throb, as if spoken really low and gutturally by monks somewhere in the temple.

CUT TO:

EXTERIOR Loft Floor: OUTSIDE THE DREAM (At that very moment outside of the Loft building in the Mission, huge garbage trucks were at the building docks downstairs revving electric motors, straining as they lifted and banged huge hollow dumpster bins over their tops and the sound was being integrated by Walker into the dream.)

CUT TO:

INTERIOR INSIDE THE DREAM The monks are chanting low and their wall of sound is flowing like lava from a volcano.

Monks: *(low, guttural changing)*
Dwo two chye dwo ye . . . / . . . Dwo de ye two
E mi li du pwo —pi
E mi li dwo syi dan pwo —ki
E mi li dwo pi jya lan —di

Dahlia: *(who has come over is standing at his side)* Would you like me to translate?

She listens intently. She begins speaking out the words as she catches bits of meaning here and there translating phrases as she goes along.

Dahlia: It's a chant about the elements of the world and how they are coming into the body. . . Flesh, bones: earth — smelling . . . Blood, liquids: water —taste . . . Warmth: fire — sight . . . Breath, sensations: wind —touch. And it's a chant about the elements of the world and how they are coming into the mind! . . . ground, water — induces: continuity and adaptability! . . . fire —clarity and perceiving . . . movement space —emptiness. Wow, they speak of time as if it was a fluid in which they are buoyed up.

CUT TO:

CLOSE-UP OF WALKER: His eyes open in surprise as the carvings on the stone signposts in the glass case begin to peel off and and start moving, start to loft, begin expanding out into the room. Dahlia turned to see Walker standing transfixed looking at the swirling sigils. He looked straight at it with a frightened intensity.

Walker: *(softly, entranced, with awe)* Synchronica.

Walker's hand went to his forehead which was beaming. His deep blue eyes held the casement in an intense stare. He let the motion of the symbols take him in as he is pulled head first soaring along with his arms at his side, into the landscape. The light was not so sharp as the atmosphere was becoming more viscous and he more buoyant. And he was flying pretty fast, across an abstract landscape. There is a round white moon way above somewhere and he is in a dead man's head first dive off the side of a long fall, Walker is flying head first with his arms by his side.

He is soaring out over the landscape, like it was a foggy San Francisco shoreline with yellow sky filling the horizon, a very thin band of yellow. Walker sees another traveler flying beside him through this landscape, he is not sure if it is male or female, and it looks over at him and points, but it has only white in its eye sockets and Walker is afraid.

Walker: *(wondering, perplexed)* Is it the Father? It is some guide, the Guide that he had once sensed in meditation when he fell down inside himself and relaxed in the light.
Yes there is a built-in Guide and you can give it a lot of other names, worship it in a lot of different ways but it is just kind of a guide, a shadow or an anima or an animus.

Walker: *(wondering, perplexed V.O.)* There was one ancient symbol of a planet seen from within the meniscus of a crescent moon (like a concavity receiving and being pushed into. And there were other symbols emerging.

$$(\,(\;)\,)\quad .)(.\quad \nabla \cup \lozenge \pm \times \oplus$$

Walker follows her pointing fingers. Falling forward endlessly into the fall, and controlling yourself so you loft, it reminded him of the Milikin oil drop experiment where they looked at tiny oil droplets, —bubbles through a microscope moving in a viscous fluid under the influence of gravity and an opposing electrostatic force field, which he could control.

And the two figures are seen making a long swimming fall along down canyons, back to their pond on the land in Mount Shasta. The other flyer lands butt first with hands in the air shouting a gleeful WHEEE! splashing lake water, and the lake water immediately turns into the soft foaming top of the wave, as Walker butt-lands too in this Buddha land, and the two of them are swimming under water . . . but it is not water but something like slow air or viscous external memory. The bottom of the lake is covered with golden sands and strange looking tubular weeds and cilia are growing out of it. This underworld was rapidly being populated by a sprouting kelp forest, and the city metamorphosing into ancient rocky reefs. Yet on the surface, there was a most beautiful lotus floating in the placid lake.

They swam down into it. The moon was a small white pearl almost directly overhead, and its light shimmered and re-focused and undulated its way down slowly into the depth of the "water." Shadows shifted sometimes moving away from where they were as if they were being struck by light rays from different source directions. Things were tinted with delicate shades of ultramarine and further out in the distance at the edge of his vision the colors turned to a purer darker blue before becoming a vague shadowing.

And he touches down into a soft sandy bottom which is becoming all frothy and labyrinthine and mitochondrial with grooves and striations conductin' fluid. In the distance he sees the other traveler.

Walker: *(wondering, perplexed)* is it his yidham? his muse? his alter-ego? his ulterior motive? his major imago figure? sitting on top of a conic frustrum pedestal. Looking at me?

He is walking through what appears to be a quickly sprouting garden of succulents and tubers emerging and encroaching from a rich swarming life-broth that has become a soupy gel.

And dropping through this viscous fluid a small white bubble drifted down. And the Guide figure catches the tiny pearl and holds it with loving intention and swirling his hands around and around he makes it grow bigger into a golf ball and a softball and soon his is holding a small white sphere of light that he shapes like snowball until it is perfectly round. Then with a quick gesture of his hands tearing it apart, he throws it into the exponential air and the white sphere has become again the elements of the chakras.

The Guide, who is above him by a distance, has begun

juggling and shaping and moving the parts of the chakra abstraction system in the air, the parts of the Kandinsky symbols on the air, and they grow larger and larger, and begin spinning and moving, in and out like mathematics, dishes turn into radio telescopes, sine waves turn into bits of DNA, triangles fill out and become big solid yet droopy soft pneumatic shapes.

Walker: *(astounded, in amazed V.O.)* This is the stuff life is made up of!

And arising out of the background there starts to appear in the air, . . . the air starts to be filled with these little butterfly men.

Walker: *(astounded, triumphant V.O.)* —El hombre mariposa!

And the alter-ego or is it the animus? —the Guide, is swirling and agitating, and molding that shape into a huge fluid that begins twisting and turning and sloshing in its own momentum and in the kneading of the malleable elemental images, their arose larger images in Northwestern American Indian paintings. And more than that —energy shapes.

CUT TO:

EXTERIOR Loft floor. At that moment someone slid open the sliding glass door that leads out to the roof. Walker opens his eyes a slit. He listens to the other people asleep or stirring, spread out around him on the floor. He opens his eyes wider. He looks over Dahlia's lovely rump through the sliding glass door onto the roof into the opaque sky. He gets a sense of belonging, as he senses the room and the people in it as all around him worshipping something just by their being. Peering beyond that opaque sky, he somehow knows there is a gestalt light where the ocean and the sky meet out at sea. He thinks: "There, lightning bolts are stored behind screens, charging up the outlines of things." But the dream is calling him and he dives back down into it.

CUT TO:

INTERIOR OF VAST OPERATING AMPHITHEATRE. Large multitude of people sitting tier upon tier, each seat an individual glass container holding a being. The butterfly people have turned into church-goers each in their own cocoon or capsule. Walker is in some kind of theatre, a laboratory, a theatre as in an operating room theatre but he is also right back in the Loft.

Suddenly the alter ego does a diving flipping somersault in the air, and with long reaching gestures starts passing out bits of the colored energy shapes with his hands like he's sowing seeds or dealing cards. With great aplomb he is making the streaming colored energy shapes fly through the air and they go directly into the open mouths, or hearts or butts or sex organs or third eye of the theatre goers.

He is penetrating and they are receiving in a re-enactment of that great Eucharist, that is the generosity that supports us all, and he is doing the dealing out with very skillful means, and snaky moves like a dandy crack dealer doing fancy back-handed moves slipping nickel bags into the internal cavities of his constituents.

And some of it starts to circulate and congeal and vortex around Walker, abstract shapes of color, bits of chakras and semantic symbols, and his Guide has sped up now and flies around Walker, around and around him in the vertical plane, and soon begins to stretch and elongate like those great elastic beings in the American Indian sand paintings arching across the sky and sinking beneath the earth, flying faster and faster becoming an almost continuous circle spread out thin as light around him.

Then as if struck by lightning Walker is one moment there then the next he is dissolving in the air and falling like sand, into a shape, — "Walker" has turned into an avatar, a statue sitting cross legged in a glass museum case on the trapezoidal pedestal in the vast operating amphitheatre. Meanwhile all around him, the glassine cocoon enclosures of the people are starting to wear thinner and thinner and are starting to become porous and the fluid people inside the cocoons are leaking out all over the place and mixing and flowing into the "water" all around it. And these separate entities are starting to grow together.

Then just as quickly we are back in the in the big room, where he has left his pilot Dahlia. And Walker is looking at, now, a stature of *himself* solidified in solid sandstone in the museum case.

But there is no time to ponder, because the walls are coming down or wearing thin and clumps of people growing together are sprouting out of the floor and waving and dancing like undersea plants flowing into the "water" all around. Becoming one within it and indistinguishable.

The people of the Loft are starting to emerge as Walkers' consciousness surfaces back in the Loft. Everyone is starting to merge and float off into the waters of Time that they have been part of for all this time, for they realize it is a kind of time fluid, one that supports them and carries them along, and are coming up through the floor, cracking the floor and getting large and green very fast like the stalks of onions.

CUT TO:

EXTERIOR Loft floor. Walker wakes up again shivers at what is a rather frightening dream. What does it mean he wonders. He thinks about getting up quickly, not wanting to disturb Dahlia with a cuddle, and sees himself out the door before he has to talk to the others around the breakfast table.

There are laborers waiting outside the doors of the Labor Exchange on Mission and Army. He sees himself walking up Mission past the Safeway where they will be hosing down the parking lot and unloading trucks. He sees himself following the light and warmth into The Mighty Nice bakery, which is just now putting the finishing glaze on their delicious fruit rolls. Or his consciousness can float out the door and down Mission Street and hover over the city, he thinks, and moor my floating body at the old odalisque in Dolores Park beside the giant old pine tree over three hundred years old there acting like a laser antenna to the past as it remembers in its peripherals and R.O.M. stored in the core of its bark sights from the past it has seen.

But he decides to hang in. Snuggling close to the warm body of his love. Thinking about all the other people snuggling around him on the loft floor. They were all one mystical body now. The whole room was one big blanket that he could pull up over his shoulders and feel secure. The mystical body that he put on was the community — he had seen pictures of it in holy cards. It was like a cool Lord's Robe with an ermine collar. The lord is this regal bearded young man, wearing a prelates crown. It is a long blue robe with millions of tiny people woven into the fabric like what the Hawaiian priests wore, made out of millions of soft downy feathers from birds' breasts. And Walker drifted down into that Mystical Body. And in that dreaming, in the night, they encountered other people from the Sangha, and they put them on in sex and wore them on their bodies. Pulling the covers up he started descending into the others' dreams.

CUT TO:

EXTERIOR: Pan over field of futons on floor to view of Morey and Rachel on her fluffy celestial futon: He is turned toward

her nuzzling her in a spoon. ZOOM in onto Morey's head.
INTERIOR: Morey's dream —his futon has lofted down among
the canyon skyscrapers of his old stomping grounds — New
York City. He steps off it. He is wearing a suit and tie. He is
walking down a New York street which opens up to the United
Nations plaza. He crosses the space and is reaching to open
the door to the UN with his right hand. He is carrying an
oversized flat leatherette artist's portfolio satchel by its grip in
his left hand and has a collapsible easel under his left arm. He
makes his way down the wide corridor and enters the great
open meeting hall of the General Council. He takes up
position under a panel of judges on a high bier. He looks
around and sees spreading out as far as the eye can see to the
horizon a vast expanse of potentates behind long desks, and in
the audience.

Morey: *(thoughts heard as Voice Over)* I'm pleading my case
before the United Nations!

Morey: *(addressing the august body there assembled)*
Gentlemen, I represent the sovereign state of Buddhist Utopia.
I am here today to apply not just for non-profit status but for a
new statehood.

Morey: *(indicating the large map on his easel)* The Buddhist
Utopia is comprised of three submerged islands in the Pacific
Ocean halfway between Hawaii and Palmyra. These newly
forming islands we call Dhyana, Sattva and Sunyata. They
form a base upon which will be constructed huge tesselated
space structures, platforms adapted from oil drilling
technology to house the newest of the new world orders.

Morey: *(looks for a reaction from the judges, sees mild interest,
continues)* Our new country is not within 100 miles of any
other nation's boundaries, therefore we beg the United Nations
for their support and protection, while we are in the crucial
development and construction phase of our new country.

Officiate: *(looking down from judges bench)* When are you to
begin construction of this new country?

Morey: We've already begun it. We've been established since,
(pauses, thinks for a minute) since 1968. Yeah, 1968. That was
the year.

Morey: *(continuing)* We are a consensus democracy, that has existed since 1968, and has 41 citizens at this time, but we look forward to having many more join us in the very near future. The New Utopia started by the Sangha of Dorje Chang is a Buddhist Utopian community currently centered in San Francisco.

Morey: *(addressing the august body grandly)* The Principality of New Utopia has established a beachhead in our hearts, but at this point it exists only in our hearts since the three submerged islands of the Mahayana Buddhism don't have anything built on them by us as yet.

Morey sighs. He indicates the second page of a map he has set up on his easel a large picture of Chase.

Morey: *(continues)* Our founder and head abbot, Chase Lang has seeded us with Buddhism and now it's up to us to help it grow. The organization of the Buddha state begins with accepting a little seed and watching it grow.

Morey: *(spreading out a large mandala, which is also a painting and also a psychic map before the august governing body)* How do you get there? You just have to be seeking refuge . . . And then turn left at the moon and continue straight on 'til morning.

CUT TO:

EXTERIOR Loft floor. Walker, struggling, pulls back into his own dream, he wants to know how it will come out.

CUT TO:

INTERIOR: Walker's dream. The pilot and co-pilot Dahlia and Walker look at each other in fear. They realize they have to run and are soon running out of the temple out of the ziggurat out of the mandala city, and the life forms are multiplying in quick profusion and seeking to entangle their legs, not maliciously but curiously and glassine cocoons are dissolving and their innards are flowing out into the medium. Walker and his pilot drop their instruments and continue running, and the whole ground outside has grown thick with plants standing up like tender shoots, like vines, like sprouts, like tube worms and they wade through the stuff. The sky overhead is filled with fractal butterfly men.

Walker: *(in V.O.)* It's as if I know what they are dreaming! *(alarmed)* Oh my god, they want to get me in between them!

CUT TO:

EXTERIOR Loft floor. Pan over field of futons on floor to view
of Malcolm and Frieda's futon: He is turned toward the middle
hugging his pillow; she is away from the middle at the edge.
ZOOM in onto Malcolm's's head. There appears to be a door in
his head and we enter in:
INTERIOR: Malcolm's dream — he is wearing a lab coat and
working in a psychology lab. There is a huge soft plastic
Magnetic Resonance Imaging machine and a patient lying on a
moving table which is being slowly slid into the opening of
the machine. Malcolm is speaking to his lab assistant.

Malcolm: *(indicating a computer monitor)* In the mind there are
thoughts constantly percolating through the brain. If we
approach from a black box standpoint and name objects in the
box by their functions and signals that we see outside the box,
these "objects" would be constellations of brain wave activity
which we are just now starting to measure and observe with
MRI.

Malcolm and the lab assistant are looking at colors coming up
on his computer screen.

Lab Assistant: *(looking with admiration at his professor)* SO
professor Phelan, what do you see?

Malcolm: These are thought-forms, neural nets of ebb and flow
of brain activity in parts of the brain. *(Pause. Looks over at
Lab Assistant, taps the monitor.)* Well here, looking at these
purple hues, we are entering the realms of dependency where
alcoholism and romantic love and drug addiction occur.

CUT TO:

INTERIOR: Therapist's office. Malcolm in priestly robes having
a clinical session with a client who is stretched out on a
Freudian couch. In a room very dense with symbolic paintings
and tapestries. Malcolm is talking to the patient on the couch
like he was administering to the dead.

Malcolm: O, orally fixated one.
Now that you have passed out of the realm of collapse you
will feel a sense of extension and want to extend yourself into
life and aggrandized and apotheosize yourself to the level of
exalted grandiosity,
Do not go there for that one.
You will feel an attraction to overwork and plow yourself

under so you can feel the need to try to attain that which you know somewhere in your heart is unattainable.
This push into grandiosity leads to poor self care, overwork excessive drug use, excessive nurturing and responsibility.

CUT TO:

EXTERIOR view of Malcolm and Frieda's futon. Camera moves slow pan over field of futons on floor to Walker's futon. ZOOM in onto Walker's head.

INTERIOR: Walker's dream — And the butterfly men are flying about the verdant habitat and all around everywhere. This world has grown into a giant garden, where the flowers are much bigger than houses. The pilot and co-pilot find their ship all encroached upon by cilia and vines about to overrun it. When it starts and they break free of the vines that would entrap them and lift off, they fly up among the undulating flows of flowers which are now as big as skyscraper buildings. They are for a moment flying along on the Embarcadero freeway going among the big buildings in downtown San Francisco which has become a profusion of giant flowers they are buzzing. Lifting higher and higher they soar above the top of the giant Buddha head which is now all but submerged in a most precious garden of riotous profusion and verdant fecundancy. And they are soaring through the air and Walker sees in the distance a dense vast number of naked human beings flying after him and together they are all soaring and hovering over this landscape of huge flowers in which either they have become small or it has become very big, and at last they are back in their own Loft in the general ensemble amongst the flying naked people of the Loft and the swarming flock ensemble of flying naked people smile at them as they leave and they soar away from the planet.

CUT TO:

EXTERIOR view of Dahlia and Walker's futon. Walker awakens. Eyes open.

Walker: (*blinking the sleep out of his eyes. Voice Over, thinking*) What a strange dream!

Dahlia wakes up and he tells her, "What an incredible dream I had. It was like we were in the same dream together! I was dreaming about flying through a Buddha land and there were strange temples, and everything, with all these plants growing really fast, like fast forward time-elapsed photography!"

"Wow. Really!" she said. "I was dreaming about flying too. It was back in Hawaii, I think, we were flying over the islands."

"Really! Wow! That was in my dream too. . . Man. That's weird." Walker shivered. "You were in my dream last night."

"Yeah, we might have been in the same dream."

"Yeah, or our dreamtimes might have intersected."

"Wow. That would be wonderful."

"There were some weird symbols in it. I'll have to get a piece of paper and write them down before I forget them."

39

A Recidivist at the Court of Love

Walker felt a delighted affinity for the innocent children at the house. He was a single guy, no recent experience with kids, since being the older brother in his family, but he was good with kids. I'm just a big kid myself he often told himself. He was there on a night that kid's committees met. Dhyana had been sent home from pre-school for hitting one of the other kids.

She had to undergo a group process. It was hilarious, to see this cute little girl going through all kinds of defenses.

She took the long way around the room dawdling along, coming toward the group. She sits on the floor, shows off her legs straight out in front of her. She smiles up at the adults and looks cute. Assumes a casual pose. Hummms softly to herself.

"What happened at school today?"

"Nothin'."

"Why were you sent home? Your teacher said you hit someone."

"I didn't."

Dhyana heaves up and down. Looks around suspiciously to see who's on her side. Feels embarrassed. Feels conspicuous. She squirms like a 4-year old. She is.

More things are said to her. She does not respond. Acts like she didn't hear. Tries to look invisible.

She denies that she hit anyone at all.

"You mean that your teacher lied?"

"Yes."

"Your teacher is not like the other kids. She doesn't need to lie."

She tilts back. Jiggles her legs. Dhyana chews on her bottom lip. Gets uncomfortable, squirms some more. She extends her lower jaw and exhales hard over her upper lip to see if she can make the hair on her bangs rise up.

Dhyana dawdles, looks all around, appears to think seriously, then sticks her tongue out, waves it all around in the air before pulling it back into her mouth.

People talk to her about doing that, being distracting and not paying attention to what is going on.

She heaves upward, holds herself erect. Hunches over, looks bummed out, looks both ways, wiggles eyebrows.

Walker was fascinated watching all this delightful behavior in its pure state. He thought about how his own defense mechanisms are so well formed, their formation going way back into time to early childhood.

He went out and got a glass of white wine at La Boheme. It felt good to be walking around in the Mission fog thinking about stuff.

40

Thought Forms

Since there was no longer a head charismatic figure, there were more double groups. One group to referee the processes and interactions of another. The House was relying fully on the group process now. There was a great excitement too. Though they were scared to be on their own, they were going into second order group theory now, an unchartered land. Malcolm, Wyoming, Rob, and Denise, among the several people who were PhD. graduate students in Clinical Psychology, thought there might be a tremendous opportunity for them here. For example, the group with Wyoming, Lucia, and Bridget was monitoring and participating in Walker's group with Jade, Rachel, Morey, and Kevin. In that group Wyoming was especially good as was Lucia, Bridget, and Morey.

The main issue was between Jade and Rachel: who was the Beautiful Woman. Rachel gets dressed up, and wears make up and goes downtown to work in a big corporation. Jade wears blue jeans and is a gardener. They are both beautiful women. The have a lot in common.

Malcolm had written this about the two women in his session notes: *Though they have seemingly different defense styles it results in the same distancing. Jade launches into these long monologues, which are interesting but space everybody out; Rachel gets really dramatical and emotional —she is bound and determined to get to the feelings. She gets really angry, and hysterically pissed and gets this soap opera thing going, so that you want to change the channel. So either woman makes you spaced and wanting to not pay attention with their defenses.*

But Walker was not that sophisticated yet to see through these defenses. Walker was quick as usual to blame himself, Maybe it is just my defenses against feeling another person.

In the dual group session, Jade began: "I think of myself as ugly. . . I walk in front of the mirror, and see my pot. And fast for a day. And feel better. I look at the pictures of me on the trip, and I am my mother looking at me, feeling like being really critical and picky toward myself."

"I had this dream the other night," she continued, "I was in somebody's bed and I was masturbating, then I started to shit all over everything, and I was trying to clean it up with my hand, and this zombie came in and told me in this weird, eerie zombie voice, that it was OK."

Rachel was glaring at Jade with a very unsupportive, condescending look. She rolled her eyes to the ceiling at Jade and let out a sigh of condescension.

Wyoming observes that Rachel who certainly looks "angelic" has gone into a "Queen" mode.

Malcolm thought to go into interpretation of the dream. "Hmm," he said interrupting her. "Hmm." He rubbed his chin thoughtfully. "The zombie is obviously the shadow. . ."

But Morey interrupted him with a look of exasperation on his face, thinking the focus was being lead away. He said, "Hold on a minute. Slow Down."

"Yea," others said.

There was much discussion back and forth to unfold this competition between the two women.

Bridget looked at the Morey, Kevin and Walker. "Do you feel the competition between these two women?"

The men were silent, not wanting to get into this fray.

After a while Morey wanted to hook up with Rachel and publicly own the feelings he had had with her the night before.

He looks at her. Holds her gaze and their eyes lock for a moment and the others let them have this moment. Morey started: "I had a lot of deep feelings when I was with you last night. . . It felt so incredible movin' in and out of you. I really like it the way you held me into you. . . And then waking and getting close to you in the morning, I really liked it when you let me enter you from behind. . . But the night before, I had these images coming up of being a baby. I felt so safe in the way you held me. I cried."

Rachel looked please at this honor. She said, "I wanted to get into more feelings. But you had fallen asleep."

From this response, though it was an attempt to get into more feelings, the others felt Rachel was in a Haughty Bitch mode.

Morey came back with: "This is your stuff. You are getting into a dependency thing."

Wyoming said: "This is your style because it was expedient to have a man fall in love with you. You have a man fall in LOVE with you so you can CONTROL him. You couldn't do that with Chase, so that you were able to really feel a lot of things with him. You can't do that with Morey either. But with Carlos, he was in love with you, you could CONTROL him."

"This is the same kind of BEHAVIOR you were doing in the last group, and now this is a chance for you to get out of it," Wyoming said.

At one point, Rachel ruffled her skirts, moving them around haughtily.

"Quit acting like a QUEEN!" Wyoming said. "The Queen. You ought to be over on Castro Street — swishing your skirts *around*!"

" You use tears if you can squeeze them out; they make the lies and the faux-pain behind them look MUCH more authentic to make it LOOK like you are actually working on your own behavior, and accepting responsibility for your actions, when, in fact, the real motive is to arm yourself with distortions of the therapist's words and tools, in an effort to heighten and increase the psychological warfare. . . Come on, this is someone with whom you have stayed up and screamed throughout the night!"

Walker began to see something in all this. A projection is a thought form. Something like a program that routes the bits of information from memory and senses and presents it to the brain for handling with actions and feelings. It has to do with the way that we even perceive reality. Competition is a thought form. Isolation, a defense beginning in childhood, is a kind of thought form.

Guilt is a thought form. It keeps one anxious and scattered, unable to lead a free and productive life. Leads to all that weed and eating and consumption to deaden the body so that it doesn't feel. Must look for the opportunities to really feel something. We spend our whole lives trying to avoid feelings. The thought forms are what project you into realms from which it is sometimes very hard to get out.

41

In a San Francisco Bath-House, 1983

"Ha-low?" Walker heard her English accent through the door.

"It's Walker, we met one night at the I-BEAM".

Her name was Jennifer. She let him in. She looked different, her hair was a lot blonder, she was more tanned, wearing hot red jogging pants and a striped pullover, pulled over her lithe, well-developed torso.

He had met her a month ago —rather she had met him, at the I-Beam disco on Haight St. This was a vast, cavernous, totally SLAMMIN! and FUN dance hall that Walker loved to go to because one, the women of the house showed up and he was able to lose himself in dance ecstasy with them without having to be some sort of suitor, and two, a cadre of gay boys led by a wild Rastafarian man, all wearing cute little gym shorts and without shirts set the energy of the place so high by the way they danced their hearts out with the wild rastaman flinging sweat over the crowd when he swung his coils of dreadlocks that being present on the same floor with them meant you never had to worry about anything you did ever being considered outrageous or untoward. The I-Beam was about a totally whacked-out and eclectically manic experience engaging in wild and crazy dancing, moving to floor-shaking Western pop, blues, English and Euro-trash while being among the crowd of ecstatic celebrants engaging in tricky fascinating tribal body communion in 'dancing with myself'.

He was standing in this great unholy din of laser, smoke and mirrors by the stage, and someone came up and just yanked the shirt out of the back of his pants! Talk about the direct approach! He spun around quick and there stood a good-looking blonde woman with long hair down past her shoulders. They drank and danced and he drove her back to her profusely carpeted efficiency in the Gaylord Hotel on Jones street. They toked and talked. He had enjoyed the conversation with her, she knew something about Tibetan

Buddhism. She had lived all over the world, and studied some Buddhism in India. He thought to get her in a hug and when he tried, she froze up. He left, chalking it up to her being a lesbian. But now it was past Solstice, there was a lot of beginning-of-summer madness about, it was a full moon in June. Walker was disheartened by how things were going with Dahlia, he wasn't having any sex with the women in his group and he thought he would check this Jennifer out, see if she was still in town.

They circled around each other, and Jennifer Smythe jumped back onto her bed and Walker sat down a good distance away. She got out her bong, and loaded it up. The apartment was extremely clean and elegant.

"Haven't seen you in a while," he said.

"Yeah, I tried to call that number you gave me but nobody was home," she said.

After an awkward silence she asked, "Are you still neurotic?"

"Yeah, but starting to understand it better. I went up to a Tibetan funeral up in the mountains, and the lama came and gave this beautiful ceremony. Since then I've been reading the Tibetan Book of the Dead. Have you ever read it?"

"Yes I have."

"And I was picking up the idea of Thought-Forms. You know, like how thoughts go through your head?" Walker started, listened to how incredibly condescending and nebulous that sounded and said, "Well now, my that sounded innocuous enough. I meant sometimes you can just be detached and watch the thoughts go by."

She nodded yes.

"Well Thought-forms are like pathways that guide thoughts. They are the big program that channels around thoughts in your mind. Like guilt. Or isolation, a defense technique started in early childhood. Mine is guilt. Have you studied much Buddhism?"

"I lived in Asia for four years," she said. A slow lascivious yet whimsical smile spread across her face. "See I'm a professional call girl. I make a lot of money. I lived in Japan for 9 months working. Had a good time. Went to lots of ma´ssage parlors, lived in India for a while.

She handed him the bong.

"That's what I do. I have worked in South Africa, and made a lot of money in Australia, invested it and live off the interest at 30%. I keep a level of money at $10,000, then I have a vacation for a while. That's what I'm doing now."

Walker just took this all in trying not to appear uncool.

"I am my own person, and I have learned how to be with people." She finished packing the weed tightly into the bowl of the bong.

"I met this coke dealer a couple of days ago, and started hanging around with him. I cleaned up his room, did his laundry for him, and gave him a ma´ssage and he kept shoving this free- base cocaine in my face all the time. Then he had to fly away somewhere on a business trip and there I was out on the sidewalk, and I could barely make it home. I have been recuperating for a few days.

"I don't know what it is but I have not been able to get out of this bed all day."

"Me neither," Walker agreed. "Must be the full moon."

"It's like some big hand comes down" — she put her hand on her forehead, pushing herself down into the bed, elbow poking straight up, "and is keeping me here."

"I got this nice radio," she said, pointing to a good quality boom box on the dresser. She had a good view out her 10th story window; the Cancer moon seemed lonely and mysterious as it majestically filled the clear starry cityscape sky.

"Isn't it a beautiful night?" he said.

There was a long pause. Then she asked, apropos to nothing, "Have you ever heard of Psychic Death?"

Walker was a little startled at this — here he was in an old creepy Gothic hotel downtown, with dark Bavarian woodwork and exposed beams everywhere almost like a mead hall in Beowolf, and a certain kind of 'a person could go mad in a place like this' or 'watch out for Vampires hanging in the elevator shafts' *je ne sais qua* about the place.

She continued: "It first occurs in children around the age of five, when they find out that their parents aren't the persons they really thought they were. The children kill a part of their own minds."

He looked at here with admiration.

"It occurs later in adolescence too," she continued.

"Then, the *world* doesn't live up to their expectation. And plus they are having a lot of guilt around their sexuality, and they turn a portion of their mind off."

Walker was impressed. "It's like Psychic Numbing." He explained it to her. They talked for a while, she had other insights. It was a good conversation. She was a well-traveled fast-talking quick-thinking woman.

"You live over in Berkeley," she said. "You hang around the college towns. I mean, you don't hang around the college, but you hang around the young people. . . You ought to be over in the city more, maybe make a life for yourself over here."

Walker moved a little closer. "Yea, I've been thinking about that."

"Sit down— here! This is the guest's chair," she said indicating a chair closer by the bed. "Would you like a nice hit off this bong. It is some good grass I get for $145 an ounce. I can get you some if you like."

After a couple of hits Walker began to feel stoned. But when he got stoned he got either amorous or intellectual, sometimes both. It made him agitated to get out of there. "I was going to go for a drink," he said. "I was wondering if you might like to go. I had come over to check out that statue by Ruth Selwa at the Hyatt House."

"Is that so," she said. "I was thinking about going for a drink over there."

"Maybe we could go for a hot tub, or go dancing at Bajones," he added. One of the first things his new group had done with Walker was introduce him to the California hot tub experience. His entire group, Morey, Rachel, Jade and Kevin had all gone over to a very lovely open-air hot tub with oak trees climbing through the redwood deck in a secluded patio in Oakland. It felt incredible and clean for all of them to be in their birthday suites together especially with these two beautiful women Rachel and Jade. Things were really looking up in this honeymoon period of the new group marriage. Walker thought he might be able to create an equally good experience for Jennifer who was obviously messed up around sex and intimacy. And who wouldn't be in her situation.

Jennifer got dressed in a hurry, and looked really fine,

bordering on outrageous. She had on an elegant jumpsuit, with a plunging neckline. The pants were flared like jodhpurs, like what Hammer wears in his high energy routine "Cain't touch 'dis". The disco outfit had lots of gold thread running through it. She slipped into some black pumps and wore a sequined head band like a diadem. Then with a swirl she swept a long stylish jaguar-skin ski jacket around her shoulders. The spots in the pattern looked like eyes. The pants suit was a light, subdued green. It went well with the gold earrings, gold bracelets, and it had an elastic band around the waist. You could see the VPL underneath the thin material.

She had a lot of makeup on and he asked her, "Why do you go out like that?"

"Because it makes a lot of things happen," she said with a sly grin. "When I go out like this I get treated a lot better. Doors open for me. There is a lot of power in it."

Down in the lobby, she hung back talking to her friend at the desk. Walker played the tourist looking at the elegant tile and woodwork from 1929. It was too late to go to the Keystone, so the night person turned them on to the Van Ness Baths to which they proceeded.

As Walker maneuvered the van into a parking space, he started getting the FEAR —the AIDS hysteria. What had started out being a kind of gay cancer, had become something that infected gays and hemophiliacs and intravenous drug users. People were just starting to become aware of the AIDS epidemic and didn't have good information. It wasn't something that could affect heterosexuals, was it. And if it was, how was it passed. No one knew.

Here I am, he thought, going to a San Francisco — and therefore gay — bathhouse with a professional hooker, where anonymous sex might occur!

"I don't want to stay, if there is a heavy gay scene around there," she said.

"That's cool," he said, relieved. "We'll go in and check it out, and if you don't want to stay, we won't. We're just two people, out doing what we want."

They decided to get a sauna / bath.

At the desk as he was about to pay she asked, "Do you

want some money?"

"O.K."

"Separate?"

"Yes."

She seemed miffed by this. As they walked by the counter where the man handed out the towels she pointed back over her shoulder and said, "He can pay the key deposit."

The room was down a carpeted hall, lighted by red neon lights running horizontal. Inside it was steaming. There was a nice tiled jacuzzi, a sauna, and a queen sized bed at the right level for giving massages.

She was undressed in a jiffy, long before he was.

"It looks like a bordello, doesn't it?" She winked.

Walker's heart sank.

"Yeah, it's not like the ones over in Oakland, where you have the redwood hot tubs, where it's outside, and there is no bed, just wooden benches. I guess this is what you might call your x-rated sauna." He was really starting to get the fear.

Jennifer walked over to the tiled tub, and laid her towel down on the edge of the water. "I guess I'll use my towel to sit on," she said. "You never can tell who was sitting there before you."

She got in the water, and Walker sat on the edge.

"When I was "working" in Japan at the massage parlors, we would massage the men, then, touch them down here," and she reached out and slowly her fingers just lightly brushed his thighs and hips, "and if they got turned on, we would ask them— tell them, 'for a little extra money we could satisfy them some way'."

She had the gift, alright, for the slight touch got him immediately aroused, his cock swung out huge and hard, balls dangling down. He got into the water and tried to avoid her. She started grinning, as he gave a little embarrassed pre-oratory cough.

Action at a distance with only words, suggestion and looking at her beautiful tanned trim body in the gently glowing lime lights of the steamy little room. It was really sensuous, and apparently she was flattered and turned on as well. "The old field effect working again," he said. "Aren't women amazing."

She kept rubbing up against him, touching him with her leg. He got into the hot water, thinking the shock would change his attitude, but it only got hotter and harder if that was possible.

He was really enjoying the sensuality of her kittenish turn-on. She was obviously enjoying the effect she had on him too. At one point she pushed him against the side of the sauna and took his cock and balls in her hand and examined him closely all over, while blowing on him, a cool jet of air from her mouth. It was quite delightful.

He reached up and hugged her. Started gently touching her body.

"You don't have to touch me," she said. "I don't like to be touched. I've been touched by so many men, that I don't feel it any more." This really shocked Walker out of any fantasy he might be getting into. God, she must be angry, he thought.

Walker had her sit down in the warm water anyway and gave her a gentle massage on her shoulders. She seemed to enjoy it.

They got into the super hot sauna, and she got into a perfect lotus pose. Terrific alignment and elasticity of leg. Then she went over and lay down on the bed. He went into the lime lit pool.

She was lying on the mattress luxuriously stretching like a cat. "Do you come quick?" she asked.

"When I'm afraid I do. But I usually like to hang in there and prolong the feelings, when I'm relaxed and into the woman."

"Come over here," she said.

"Well I don't know."

"Come over here and lie down beside me, just for a minute. This place is really erotic, it has me really turned on."

"Well I don't want to get into anything," he said. And he really didn't. He was into the prolonged tease. She was just acting out of nervousness, not knowing how to be, she didn't really feel. But when a beautiful lady calls, you come.

He went over and lay down beside her and immediately started to get the Fear again.

She put her hands on his chest, and got between his legs

and went down, rubbing his hard cock on her cheeks and forehead, her long hair teasing the big brute thing.

Then she quickly came back up and tried to put him inside her! She was on top! It scared Walker anyway when women were on top! And with no condom! With a hooker in a bath house! Who knows who was there fucking on the mattress before us. We might exchange bodily fluids! AIDS!

And he started writhing away from this beautiful tawny strong lithe bitch. He had the fear, and also he was determined not to be just another trick in her life. He wanted them to be really there with their feelings. He had just wanted the sensual tease.

She kept on trying to put him in her, and he kept slithering away. O ever-wretched man-thing.

"You are going to miss a wonderful opportunity," she said. "Look I'll just put you right here," and she pressed his member up against the hard bone of her pelvis, and held him there hard.

Gently moving back and forth she said, "I've never had anyone behave like this before."

He managed a limp smile.

"Look I'm very good at this," she said with pride. "It will just take a second. A lot of men would pay a lot of money to be where you are now."

She made one last attempt, and she was strong, but he was impelled by fear and would not let her impale herself on him, and gently wrestled her and kept her off.

"O.K. I know what it is like, a lot of people have made me have sex with them and held me down when I didn't like it."

"I like to make love with a condom the first time with a new lover," he said, "because it is so traumatic and awe inspiring. Plus there is different acidity, and different microflora in there."

"I never let the men wear a condom, I can't make sex juice when one of those is up in me."

She got up, kind of disappointed and went over to the bath. She lit a cigarette in the closed room. He got his glasses on and looked at the clock. "I got pregnant on the pill once, and once with my tubes tied. Now they have been cut and singed. I'm still afraid I might get pregnant. Very fertile stock." She laughed.

"We can leave if you want to," she said.

"It's only 12:30, we still have another half hour. Let's stay."

Things simmered down between them, and she got kittenish again, and played with him some more. "You know, you're pretty good looking in a rugged sort of way," she said. "You need a haircut. You should see my hairdresser. . . I picked you up in the I-BEAM because you looked decent. Everyone else there looked grotty."

"Grotty?"

"You know, heavy, tight-assed, violent, cheap, grubby, dirty."

Then they had a shower together. Under the shower she kept moving away from him, when he got near her. "It's O.K.", he said, "you can get under here too." She liked the shock of the cold shower.

Her hair was curly from the steam, and the make up had all been washed off. She looked really good now, more wholesome. He watched her put on her little pink panties and bra. The cold excited them when they got out on the sidewalk.

She created quite a commotion as they walked through North Beach, people were coming out of bars imploring them, (her) to enter.

They went to Enricos, a sidewalk cafe on Broadway in North Beach. She attracted all kinds of leers. Men were actually tripping over themselves looking at her.

Sitting at a table near the street, he asked, "Have you ever been to Paris?"

"Lots of times. . . I started going there when I was in the escort service. I would fly over and stay with this boyfriend I had. It turned out that he was a famous cat burglar."

She looked like one of the wild creatures in her Jaguar coat.

They drank Orange juices.

"You know, a lot of people in this town would like to take me out and pay."

"I know."

He just wanted to be real with her. Maybe it would help her if there was somebody real in her life he thought. When they went back to her place he wanted to try and get her into a real hug.

They got into bed, drinking tea. It was beautiful looking out the window. She kept on shying away, when he tried to touch her. She really didn't like being touched. What a terrible thing to do to your own sexuality he thought.

She kept eating and drinking and smoking bong after bong of the potent weed, all the while talking.

Her brother was cruel, her father and he were always putting their hands on her. She had escaped from home when young, and taken up with an older man, who exploited her eagerness to please. Eventually while working as a secretary in London, she applied to an ad for escorts.

She was a straight escort.

"You see," she said, "they have about 70% of what they call `bent' and the rest straight. I was a straight escort — went around with clients who just wanted somebody for political functions, or business men, who weren't into sex."

They talked and smoked on, and he got drowsy. But then after a while, due to all the tea flushing his kidneys, he got mincturation. He had to get out of bed every couple of minutes to pee. He didn't know now if it was his fear of pussy or of the VD or both, but every time he came back to bed he would put on another article of clothing, and lay there in pain having to take a pee until it was time to go again.

"Lucky you, we didn't have sex," she said, "or you would have accused me of giving you something."

By then his penis was dripping like a lonely lost little boy crying for his beautiful young mama. La mamma et la puta. Why is it always one or the other?

"What are you doing on Monday?" he said getting dressed to leave.

"That's the day I'm going to Lake Tahoe. You want to go with me?" she asked.

He could tell that she was starting to like him, that there hadn't been that many real men in her life. That she was starting to have some feelings.

He wanted to go to Lake Tahoe, he had never been there. But he had an obligation to his group marriage now. He wanted to be with some good women who knew him.

"Naw, but thanks. I'm into too many things here."

42

Ring Around the Rosy

Walker was at the Loft leaning against the red brick wall reading, trying to be inconspicuous, when Frieda — the slender willowy Frieda — dragged him by the feet out into the middle of the room and started tickling him.

"Ah, so you ARE ticklish," she said, "and I've found the spot!"

"O nooooo. Yes!"

As they rolled around on the floor her red dress rose up to her waist. She had nothing on underneath. Walker liked Frieda, gave her a big smooch on the cheek. The first. She seemed surprised and delighted. He was pleased with himself. They both wondered if it was manipulated. They both concluded it was spontaneous.

After meditation, they got into small groups. Walker was by himself, a lone representative of his group visiting Dahlia's group.

Dahlia said, "I can't accept that I am loved. Somehow my mother gets in the way. It is like in my house: whenever me and my brother were going to get close I would somehow end up doing something to provoke her into a rage and she would make it hell for everybody." People in the group thought about this then turned the focus on Walker.

In keeping with his strategy of non-pursuit and not showing his dependency Walker made a statement to Dahlia: "You really have helped with a lot of stuff and we seem to have gone our separate ways, and have been through a lot of changes in the past month, and I want to get current with you. I want to be committed to your growth, just as you are committed to mine. I really trust you a lot."

He was mustering his courage to call back his projections, trying to be free in the now moment, be in that moment between needing and letting go. He was trying to be objective about her, because if he was going to open up with her, he had to take a chance of losing her.

"You have such verbal ability," she said. "I wouldn't be

able to say that so easily."

Walker made a statement to Jade: "I'm getting closer to you and my group, and the more I can trust you, the more of myself I can divulge. I realize that the group is like myself, the group of myself."

Things seemed to be going all right. It was a summer Friday night, summer had just begun. It was decided to go to a place called Prince Neptunes on Haight Street. When the girls came down Dahlia was wearing a dress! A flowery summer print! It had an open neck and looked almost disco! What kind of place is this? Walker wondered.

In Prince Neptunes, there was a young foreign crowd,. African couples in dashikis and wild colorful clothes sitting at tables drinking fancy drinks with little umbrellas in them. Nancy wanted to check out the Prince whom she had met once in New York but she was afraid to approach him. Dahlia and Walker slipped into the couples role. Like experienced lovers they advised the timid Nancy and encouraged her to pursue the object of her affection. He was a beautiful black man, with rich deep black skin, a mouth full of gold, gold pendant on a chain hanging around his neck and a gold earring. He brought aperitifs to their table. They ordered drinks,

There was some kind of a performance art thing going on. It started with some beautiful soulful reggae harmonica playing, and a man dressed in women's clothing waltzed and sashayed through the restaurant throwing nasturtiums and roses around out of a wicker basket. It was a poignant frieze against the long preternatural fauvist mural which graced a wall. Nancy went off to talk to the Prince.

Dahlia asked Walker, "What kinds of changes have you been going through since we were last together?"

He had a hard time getting started, then finally started telling her about it.

"I am feeling a lot more for myself now. I can be in a situation and be more real, feel more comfortable." He told her about the scene in the baths with Jennifer. "She wanted me to go to Lake Tahoe with her. "

Dahlia said, "You were probably the most real person she had met in a long time." Then she looked thoughtful, "But it is covering something up. Chase told me, that every time somebody tries to feel something, the seed is sown for the forces of the ego to rise up and suppress the feeling. So look at what is in it for yourself."

Then groping even further she said: "Why did you have to prove that you are not a jerk to this woman?"

Walker got defensive, but smiled — up to her tricks: "That sounds like one of those double bind things. Like, 'When did you stop beating your wife?' — Have you stopped proving that you are not a jerk yet?" Walker found himself laughing at the abilities of this woman. Sometimes he had to wonder if she wasn't always just playing with him.

"OOOOOOOFFFF, the stairway up to the Loft," she said as they trudged along.

They went up onto the upper loft. She got out her futon and told him where to drag it and lay it down. Right next to her brother! Her real brother Carlos of the stocky and powerfully rugged build!

Walker began getting paranoid that her kid brother might be a parent by proxy. But Wow, he began telling himself, if I could just get through this paranoia, and see it as just the conjuring of my own mind, then I bet I could come to know something about what we are trying to do here: culture - independent awareness. What a sense of acceptance it would be. I would be definitely in her tribe. He decided to hang in with his fear and go for the feelings.

With the brother there in the next futon on the floor you had to watch while you fuck, be aware, no time for closed-eye fantasies. Damn right. Or you'll roll onto somebody else's futon and that might turn into a whole different situation!

At one point they both started laughing a lot at his fear. He got in her and rubbed her real hard and she came. It was beautiful to watch her face.

And that night Walker and Dahlia did make moan and a lot of good fun for themselves right there in the middle of God and everybody, her neighbors, friends, husbands, brothers, sisters, lovers —both male and female. He most truly did feel love for her.

It's true! In tantra the women are aggressive and the men don't come. So after she had already come a couple of times he was still after her. He would catch his breathing and just relax and OM with her for a while. In the OM sound they brush lips in a kiss, and it sounds like the chants of 25 horny monks on speed reverbing up from deep down in the bottom of a cave.

The next morning many of the people in the House went to the Hands Around Livermore protest. As they arrived they saw thousands of people milling around huge parachute tents. They were part of some 6,000 demonstrators there to descend on Livermore and hold hands around the facility.

For the House, the protest is a kind of American folk ritual. They tried to support as many as they could. If for no other reason than to walk in the sunshine down the middle of a city street. They parked and hiked a long way into the UC Berkeley facility at Livermore against the burnished yellow hills of a late summer California.

A flyer explained that 90% of all atomic weapons were designed at Livermore. NUCLEAR WAR BROUGHT TO YOU BY LIVERMORE.

Walker liked this kind of folk festival around the Bay Area. People go out to passively glare and witness about some outrage or another. A kind of birthday, or carnival atmosphere abounds. Nice women, active, tanned, politically correct, concerned. Stand around in the heat, mill around.

Zen monk pounds drums and looks at guard shack. Chanting occurred for the 1000 arrested the previous week for civil disobedience.

Afterwards the group drove back to Walker's place in Berkeley. He was delighted to have some people inside his small apartment. Rarely had anyone visited him. He served them refreshments, and the transplanted New Yorkers took the opportunity to sit outside on a real stoop.

Aside he said to Dahlia: "Say, why don't you come back later. I'll leave a key under the mat. You could stay here."

"No," she said.

As she was leaving, she leaped on him and in front of everybody held him in a ferocious bear hug.

43

Stonewalling the Brute

The House was making another trip to the land taking a long weekend. Walker was going up to the land because Dahlia had sort of promised to sleep with him on this trip.

Being an interloper into a group marriage will really get you in touch with your craziness. Walker began spending more and more time at the House. He felt like the poor brute crashing around in the fine china shop of these people of highly developed spiritual and aesthetic sensibilities. He was some wild man living in a cave out in the hinterlands of Berkeley tied by obsession to a Princess living in a strict Buddhist land. The Princess had all these commitments and responsibilities and expectations to live up to and yet he felt that she did truly love her brute. In order to be near her, and also to explore the possibilities of poly-fidelity, Walker wanted to be an active husband in the group marriage with Rachel, Jade, Kevin, and Morey but right away he got Dahlia and Rachel into the projection of the Good Mother and the Bad Mother. He was not aware of this. In the few sessions with Rachel he was uncomfortable. She seemed so controlling and programmed. Was he projecting his mother on her as people said, or feeling her the way she really is. There were hard times going on in his group. Walker had, so far, managed to keep himself out of them.

As soon as he arrived at the Loft for the trip Walker picked up on the tension in his group. Rachel and Morey weren't speaking to each other. It was so tense that they decided to have a group on it in the car on the way up. (If Chase had still been around they would not have allowed this level of insatiability behind the wheel. But they were on their own.) For Walker, always afraid of confrontation, it felt really hard. Though he didn't recognize it, in the unconscious layer of his mind he was present at the archetypal scene of his parents fighting. He had slipped back into that timeless circle of family where nothing ever changes. He didn't know where to turn. He left himself kind of out of it, just kinda' going along with the flow. Kinda feeling it out. It was an old feeling to be disconnected. He reminded himself that you can't have these peak experiences unless you take risks.

Morey was on the run, Rachel was pushing him away. It was interesting to observe, this pushing away behavior between these two because everybody knew they had such a hot passionate love for each other. He 'knew' he was in some kind of space, archetypal or Freudian or Buddhist and he would try not to become caught up in all the fear and anger and agitation it was generating but to use the time well and learn perhaps how to reconstruct the psycho-archeology of a person's behavior — say, maybe his own?

In a roadside attraction called Poltroon Flatonia in a small town off I-5, the intense animosity between these two lovers started to really boil over and have a cowering effect on the rest of the group (Kevin, Jade, Aaron, Freida). The group pulled into the parking lot and looked at what had obviously been a large country bordello here in the north woods. Now it was a weather-beaten run-down but very busy restaurant, country store and truck stop.

"Looks like a warm and cheery place," Walker said viciously.

Aaron says: "Wait till you see the bathroom in this place. It's really something."

The got out of the van, the car door slammed and there they were in the cool moonlit parking lot. Frieda and Walker stepped in out of the dark starry night. Inside Walker took the opportunity to flirt with Frieda. While the others were still groggily staggering into the place it was him and Frieda sitting cozy together trying to decide on whether to split a cup of that unwholesome American addiction —coffee, or go for each one having his own.

"Cup of coffee to go," Walker said at the counter.

Frieda chimed in: "Two coffees for here." She smiled and said, "Lets each get a cup." The waiter brought them two mugs.

And there was Frieda, a very intense looking woman in her late thirties. Long hair and eyes that glowed like bright ball bearings. She was a calm woman. Walker liked calm women.

Aaron came in smiling, happy, high.

Walker noticed there was a pool table in the back, and thought it would be good to move around and bend over and do some standing and moving around to shake off the cramps of the road.

While the others were going off to this bathroom in the place and coming out with strange grins on their faces, Walker put a quarter in the slot, and heard the avalanche of pool balls crash into the trough. He racked them up and went in to get his order of french fries and coffee. Walker thought to get Morey into a pool game. He knew Morey was good at pool, having a hard time, feeling a bit down, and maybe it would make him feel better to win a game.

After a couple of shots, Morey said, "Let's hit the road, nobody is going to win this pool game."

"Why. . . man, let's finish the *game*."

Morey gave Walker a condescending and painful, harassed, baleful look which he just managed to temper into thoughtfulness. Nothing escaped Morey's attention and at this moment he was seeing the unfolding of a primal oedipal scene clear as a Christmas creche: Rachel was the Mother, Morey was the Father and the infantile baby Walker was wandering around being out of it and helpless.

Shaking his head in resignation Morey said: "I thought, man. . . I don't want to get into this pool game because it will end up me proving to you that I'm your father. You know you would be hard put to walk around in any pool hall and find someone who would beat me."

They got out of there pretty quick after that. Walker wondered if there might not be another interpretation of this event. The "lesson" was lost on Walker's conscious mind. But underneath he saw it as being the Bitch humiliating the Man, and the Man being angry about it and taking it out on the Child. Trying not to see it this way Walker felt angry at Morey's arrogance. It seemed like ▢Morey had laid out a bunch of anger and asserted his dominant position over Walker as low-man interloper on the totem pole. To Walker it seemed to be rubbing it in a bit but he had to admit, yes his father did that. Yet, Walker rationalized, that he was really beginning to trust Morey. They were all 'brothers of the flesh.' They had all made love to Dahlia and all felt the affinity. The males are not going to attack me or be jealous of me. Can't be when making love right on the next futon.

On the way out Walker took a quick look at the bathroom to see what they were all smiling about. The bathroom had some kind of denuded and debauched mannequin in the bathroom tub. What was so funny about that?

Back in the car Rachel started throwing a fit. She kept on asking why Morey kept avoiding her. She really got herself going.

She demanded of Morey: "What were you doing in there so long?" like a mother scolding a dawdling child, who was trapped in guilt.

Walker explained like a scolded child: "We were just in there being silly, and Morey and me shot a pool game."

Rachel started to get wilder and wilder as they drove the main drag of Yreka. It was her home town and she didn't want to spend the night there. She had made a vow to herself to never go home EVER again. Flashbacks of being in motel rooms with her father were edging their way into the periphery of her thought as she struggled to keep them out. But the group, exhausted and not willing to give in to Rachel's hissy fit, decided to rent a room there anyway.

"Don't plunk me down in Yreka!" she whined. She was in quite a panic. As they drove around town, haunting memories of being taken to motels by her father for the purposes of sex tried to edge their way into her consciousness and she was doing all she could to repress them.

All seven of them rented a motel room for 45 dollars. They crowed into one room with green shag carpeting that looked like a bed of writhing snakes and frightful orange flowery bedspreads on its three dark wood double beds. Frieda and Aaron got one for their session. Rachel jumped into one of them, but by this time Morey was too burned up to want to have a session with her.

Rachel started crying and screaming hysterically. She started stuffing her sleeping bag into its stuff sack saying, "I'm leaving. I'm going to the Yreka bus station and going to take a bus back." She screamed, "You go fuck yourself Morey!" And later again, "Oh go fuck yourself!"

Morey and Walker slept on the floor and gave the girls the bed. The men got into a hug, made a few sounds, conked out from the shrillness of the day's events, like two cowed kids. Kevin had a bed by himself.

Walker's final thoughts before merciful sleep were about how this touching primal scene brought up a lot of memories of his parents fighting all the time. He started becoming really suspicious of Rachel. This one bears watching he told himself. Meanwhile, for Rachel the repressed images were trying to leak past the doors of her consciousness and she was saying her mantra and trying to be there while the monstrous images she had repressed sought to get at her psyche and she tried to be a good Buddhist and be there with her pain. Some of the memories were very old from when she was very young of her father taking her into Yreka and undressing her in hotel rooms and how awful that felt. It made her shudder all over like some kind of terrible bad trip. Jade's compassion rose to the occasion and she held on to her friend in their session. Walker was having his own hard time remembering his parents fighting at home over his father's drinking. It brought to mind the screaming shit-fits his mother would throw every night when his father came home drunk. She would go around slamming doors making the children jump and start nearly out of their beds.

The traveling group all seemed a little better after a night's sleep. Morning found them all sitting swaddled in a ponderous pea-green naugahyde booth around a table at the local IHOP, looking furtive in the redneck enclave, feeling like fish in a tank behind the vast expanse of window pane in the restaurant facade. Except for Walker, he had long ago learned to navigate the middle-American redneck strain in Texas. Rachel started making snide remarks about there being so much southern drawl in the cowboy accents.

Walker observed in the slowest, most obnoxious of southern drawls, "Whaah they don't sound too Cow-buoy tuh mey." This cracked everybody up.

The long walk into their land helped relieve the bad feelings. Nothing like having to watch your step, one foot in front of the other, in snake country to take your mind off your troubles. Large groups of people hung-in and stayed together. Walker felt out of it most of the time. He helped carry a huge brain mushroom they found, a giant puffball. It was as big as a pumpkin weighing at least 15 lbs. People would slice huge slabs off of it and toast it on the open fire like bread. Flesh of the gods. *Teonanacatl*.

That evening Walker's group got in a double group with Malcolm's who had been in on the scene on the way up. This marathon group went on and on, the rest of the House dragging their sleeping bags and reaching for their stuff over their heads. Walker had to get up and leave, he was just totally overdosed on the data flow.

He lay down with Jade. They held each other close. She was a beautiful young woman. She took all her clothes off. "Aren't you going to take yours off too?" she asked.

Not wanting to disappoint her or make her look bad in front of the others Walker obliged. He screwed up his courage, and said, "Listen. There's something I have to tell you." He hesitated, he really wanted to make it with this fresh-faced young lovely. But she had the right to know. Since he didn't have so much wrapped up in Jade he blurted it out: "I've got herpes. I was going to tell you if it looked like were going to get into sex. And I'm not symptomatic at this point."

She stared at him blankly.

"It's like a cold sore I get on my penis sometimes."

"I know what it is. We know a lot about that."

"Well you know you can't catch it from door knobs, or towels, or toilet seats. Can't catch it from touching it, unless you get it into an open sore. It is passed by vigorous intercourse, and even then, the mucus lining of the vagina is made to flush out foreign bodies."

Walker could see that this was not the most inspiring of pillow talk. So he finished up quickly: "The main rule is, if it is not uncomfortable when having sex, then don't worry about it. If it is, then use a condom."

She seemed all right with that. They hugged and aimed for a while longer. She reached over and played with his cock gently for a long time. It felt great. He rubbed it between her tight twat lips and legs.

Then she fell asleep on him. No wonder he thought, not

much sleep the night before, long walk in, much hassles in big group.

He got up early the next day to put in a hard day's work. He asked the strawboss, "What's my job?"

He shouldn't have asked. "Oh," said Denise, "I forgot about you. Would you like to do compost?"

The crew of Theo, Katie, and Loretta and Walker limbered up by turning some of the other older thirty foot long piles. Walker was glad Theo was there. It was good clean compost, no longer hot. It was beautiful stuff. Theo said, "They always like to put the new guy on the compost job. It brings up a lot of disgust."

It was truly an amazingly big mountain of compost. Theo said: "When these piles are really hot they catch on fire. I've seen blue flames coming out of them at night. We've even had to station personnel down here with a hose."

Then they began builing a new pile. First they laid down about a thirty feet long and four feet wide pile of sawdust and wood pulp. Then they poured the shit in. The shit came in sealed pickle buckets from the two-seater outhouse up by the tents and stunk terribly. Drizzly slush for the shit shleppers. Walker began singing an old Fugs tune: 'It's a big wide river of shit that we live in' to the tune of 'It's a big wide wonderful world we live in' — a Lawrence Welk tune. Everybody laughed.

Theo talked the whole time about "pathogens". Theo said, "The mind is like a compost heap, out of a lot of waste and shit, good things grow." It made Walker think of what people of the House were into — as they say, digging into someone else's shit. Turning it over, providing stresses, so that it forced them to look at themselves. Hoping good stuff would grow out of it.

They covered the top of the pile with horse manure. Loretta worked real hard. It was the most disgusting experience Walker had ever stood still for, especially cleaning the buckets out afterward. Loretta showed most exemplary mindfulness and service.

As Walker's group was having such hard times; they were again brought before Big Group that evening .

Dahlia looked at Walker and said: "I was really floored when you told me the other day that you are not having sex with the women in your group."

"OHHHHH," and "oooohh" it went around. People wondered why Walker was being so passive. He wanted to tell them about the herpes but was terrified. But he knew he had to do it.

It was expected that Jade and Walker talk about last night's session. Walker smiled when Jade started with, "I've been having a hard time with penises lately." It felt pretty ludicrous. (Jade was so serious she didn't *even* get the pun.) She just continued right on, "I don't like men to touch my body with them." This got everybody in an uproar.

Scott engaged Walker in mock sympathy with: "I can just see you — here's poor Walker going around in the cold and dark during the night, none of the women in his group will keep him warm."

Walker laughed.

Then everybody jumped on his case, told him to take it more seriously. Then he just decided to blurt it out. "Well I've got herpes and I'm really cautious and afraid about getting into sex."

People just looked at him matter-of-factly.

"And I've been careful," he continued, "I wasn't going to get into anything with the women until I had told them."

Walker shook his head waiting for a horrified reaction. Christ now everybody knows.

So what? was the attitude of the group.

It didn't seem to bother them. The Time cover story about herpes as the scarlet letter had come out. The House people seemed totally accepting of it. Walker felt he had to explain. "It's not casually contagious and not contagious at all when you don't have symptoms. It's like a cold sore. And you can use a condom." But everybody seemed to know all this and were blasé. They didn't seem that interested. It was no big deal. The ensemble broke up and individuals headed for their sessions. They were all pretty sophisticated about it, and compared to the AIDs epidemic which was just starting to surface as a gay and intravenous drug user's disease it wasn't that bad.

But unburdening himself to Big Group was a truly

liberating experience for Walker. He sat there astounded. He was not run out of town or tarred and feathered. He had taken hold of the demon that had been bothering him for so long by the shoulders, and putting his knee into its back had broken its spine. He could feel it giving way. Walker floated out of this session with light glowing around his head.

Later when they were alone, Jade said, "I'm sorry. I completely stonewalled you last night."

Walker was supposed to have a session with Rachel. She looked at him with hard eyes and said, "I want to take some space. You can put your sleeping bag down beside mine if you want." Walker thought this might be a good opportunity to slip over and sleep with Dahlia.

At first Dahlia was amenable but Morey came over and had to interfere. He told her that Walker was running away from the hard times in his own group. Walker wanted to say, What an asshole you are, Morey! but held his tongue. After much hassling with Dahlia, Denise (Denise from Dahlia's group had come over and joined the fray) and Morey, Walker was pissed and went up the hill to sleep on the barn site by himself.

It felt good to take some space, to lay back and watch the shooting stars. Morey came up after a while and sat down on his mattress and shared a dube with him and talked to him about anger for the mother and that what Walker was seeing was how it worked at the House. He said "We are here to pick up on each other's anger, to make each other feel their own craziness. It is a way of fighting fire with fire. And here the fire is in sex and trying to get close. You can't really participate in the house unless you take some chances and go for the feelings."

The next day, Walker got kind of spaced-out up at the Christmas camp on top of the hill. He recognized his isolation and distancing were part of his severely handicapped avoidance personality as a defense and wandered back to the group. He felt scared of snakes walking down the hill.

Morey said "Snakes are representatives of the Mother. You could never know when she was going to strike."

Walker got into the pond after everyone else was getting

ready to leave, or standing around and walking around nude. He was the only one swimming in it for a while.

Rachel came out and jumped into the water and got hold of his inner tube and was pushing it around. He decided to just react as to what was going down, and not to try and control everything. But this felt weird. He had become an object of her affection. God help me he thought. He felt like a shy kid trying to escape from the mother's gooey embrace.

It was decided that the men and women of Walker's group should ride back in different cars. Walker wore one of Rachel's famous bill caps all the way back. They were made out of wildly colorful paisley prints and held on the head partly by the long hair of the wearer. They were the envy of all the Deadheads. They had little dope pouches in side of them closed with velcro. He appreciated the excellent design and craftsmanship that went into them.

On the ride back Malcolm sounded like a horny old Scotsman, "I don't get enough sex," he said. "The only person I get into sex with is Frieda."

Frieda talked about how this created a dependency on her. Walker could see many similarities between her situation in the house and Dahlia's.

In trying to understand the mechanism of projection Walker thought of other similarities between Rachel and his mother. Both had been raised in the country, moved to the city, hated the country ways; yet Rachel had the good sense to pick the useful natural knowledge out of it. Knowledge of the woods. Both were very manipulative. The attention of the group is always on Rachel. She is the one going for the feelings.

I can just be there for myself he thought. My body is something to feel with. We are both laying out a lot of anger on each other, maybe I am laying it back out.

44

The Unconscious Group

from Walker's Journal July /12 / 83

The unconscious group, that is a group which we should define and study. . . by the use of sets, subsets and symmetry . . .

The unconscious is a more primary, general, mind-manifold of pattern and interlocking implication that is not logical and is not touched so much by time. In mathematical groups one uses sets, subsets and symmetry to explore reciprocal closed relationships of similarity and sameness by means of seriality and classification.

You can feel the unconscious at times moving and organizing beneath the consternation of your brow. Example: I was feeling guilty over a phone call with my mother and I asked Dahlia to spend some time and she said she was too busy, and I was having trouble struggling to get my flying machine up into the air and start writing, and I was trying to be part of Dhyana's kid committee - I asked if she wanted to see some of the cube but Dhyana said she didn't want to and she just wanted to keep playing. I was also going to ask if Dahlia would help me with my posture in mediation. I cringe now at my pulling for always engaging her female nurturing (motherly) capacity. Anyway, we all inhabit two worlds — the inner and the outer - and they are very different. Where these worlds overlap we have a set of elements common to both to provide a transition between worlds and/or across time. The overlapping worlds are sets: a collection of things that have a common element. The set of all doors, for example: {a sliding glass door, the black door at number 10 Downing Street, the green door to the ultra-room, the open door and the closed door . . .}. The set of doors has subsets {doors that are all black, (doors that are all black with brass furnishings)}.

So I was feeling the movement of my unconscious when I was carrying the un-manageability of my relationship with my mother and transferring it (the un-manageability) into my relationship with my love Dahlia and the kid Dhyana.

I am angry at my mother and since there is much of my mother in Dahlia, they are similar - in some sense belonging to the set of people I am feeling divorced from.

It is a very uncomfortable feeling.

Sets, transference and counter transference.

Dahlia and I are locked in this relationship of anger; it is also my assumption that the feelings are reciprocal.

My mother and I are joined by the relationship mother and son. And these get interchanged sometimes. Parent, adult, child. Super-ego, ego, id. When you get into a sense of similarity between the past and the present or a similarity of relationship then you know the unconsciousness has been activated.

At any given movement going across time the present is populated by a large web of relationships, which have permutations and combinations among themselves. It is the synchronic aspect of our world - outside of time.

Sets, subsets and symmetry.

When you start to look for symmetry, for pattern, you get into the concept of the sign.

The symmetry group is what brings continuity to the past and the present. The symmetry group maps continuity across from the past to present. The symmetry group operates across and outside of time. Charles Sanders Peirce and the sign.

$(( ))$ interlocking circles

In the world of the overlap you have these entities that belong equally to the past and the present, in time just as in space, the inner and outer sense of the person's self. Or the sense of self and other.

You sense this relationship of dependence. It is binary. Binary logic and set theory. The formation of signs. They are special entities that inhabit two worlds. Symbols.

$(( ))$ interlocking circles

This special sense of similarity between the past and the present, like a ghost, gives you a sense of this world of the logic of the unconscious, this non-stop wild land that we constantly inhabit. And which we are constantly feeling from and seeking out, either through projection, wanting to separate out what comes from whom in any two person relationship.

Un-manageability and rejection is what gets projected across time. Group is a collection of objects, the relations among which we are constantly trying to determine. Groups are wild and primitive structures before algebra, logic, syntax, grammar, and even before time.

The sub-personalities of Walker Underwood
   1. The observer
   2. The hungry ghost
   3. The great hideous black one (Fear of Death)

   Alignment: There is a symmetry on each side of
these symbols or complexes, the dual seen in a
mirror. The flip side of 2 - the hungry ghost - is
the hunger for the divine, for real spiritual
nourishment and to not be accepting substitutes and
artificial imitations. There is Left & Right-handed
symmetry. Uncertainty. Chirality. The flip side of
death is not so much the tempus fugit, hurry up and
achieve but more the recognition of a death wish
inside. Is depression due to knowing about this
necessary shutting down of the life force? This
knowing also leads to a letting go.

   To visualize these complex basic organizations of
the psyche, you have to let these parts come into
you. And to feel them adjusting around within
yourself. And to feel them percolating up images and
symbols. There are many others present there.

The unconscious group and the tankha.
   We see these ugly, frightening sub-entities or
organizations and we want to get them aligned in
their dual aspects.
   Let alignment occur naturally as a result of
Entrainment.
   I was trying to take care of my inner child,
another element of the group of the unconscious, by
writing, patiently waiting for it to divulge its
insights and it wasn't doing that, being too
preoccupied with some external lack or perceived
slight. I know by now creativity has a time frame of
its own with which I must allow synching to occur as
it unfolds through its own nature.

Notes on a space of magnetic tensions.
   We are talking about three dimensions: id, ego,
superego, and how I am under constraints of these
three dimensions. Look at how this space is
organized by the diachronic and the synchronic.
   On the axis, on the cross.
   Synchronic vertical; diachronic horizontal.
   Synchronic, outside of time, the structure (group
structure) of symmetry, pristine form.
   Diachronic, across time, with time, beginning and
ending, moving through distinctions.
   Synchronic: grammar, grid, syntax, logic
   Diachronic: sentence, plot, theme, proposition,
phoneme.

45

Trust and the Trans-parent Self

The House had a well-established sense of ritual and habit but without their spiritual leader Chase, they were on their own and these rituals and methods would all have to be tested one by one to see that they still worked and were relevant. Though the people of the House were used to long Big Group sessions which were something like *punjas*, — Buddhist initiations that might go on for a day and a night or a night and a day and sometimes for an entire weekend — they occasionally were called upon to perform a hands-on ritual related to Primal Scream therapy that released a lot of mental and psychological energy for the initiate. It was able to release "knots," jammed-up places relating to chakras that had damned up the flow of vital energy so bad that they had to be released. Walker took part in one action on an evening when it happened to Theo. It was on the 30th day of Bardo Time (they were re-reading the Tibetan Book of the Dead) and the evening's reading had been on defeating rebirth in lower realms by closing the door to the vagina.

Theo started talking at Big Group. "I know it's not the women in my group, it's me. I've had trouble with women all my life."

The skinny tall older white-haired man looked sad and almost in a panic. "It's anger at my mother," he said. He started to show a lot of pain.

Malcolm nonchalantly handed him a pillow. Theo started to cry and make primal screams into it. Soon some of his group members were around him, touching his chakras. They laid him out flat on the ground, some were holding hands over his ears to protect him from the loud sound, while he screamed as loud as he possibly could into the pillow.

He sat up and said, "I remember having to be grateful to my mother for stopping my father from murdering me!" He sobbed. "I remember her out there with the rest of the family after my father died, and me in there, in incredible pain and her out there singing."

Once again the House drew up around an initiate experiencing an ungodly release of great psychological and physiological power. The whole House began OMing and touching the people of his group who were around Theo touching him. Walker allowed himself to pull in to the edge of the outer circle and complete the circuit by touching people close to him.

Theo was laid out there on the ground, screaming with all his might. This galvanized the whole House. Walker was shocked by this and imagined Theo traveling down neural pathways with tremendous energy release. Theo's arm became rigid holding his hand up in the air hooked like a primordial claw as he screamed with all his energy. The rictus of the arm and the hand being supported by something other than self-control bespoke tapping into energies supporting the self from beyond the individual. They were seeing the Self.

Several people were pushing with all their weight into his stomach. Some later said that they could feel the knot there. "The knot, what knot?" Walker asked Morey, later when things had settled down.

"The place where the tension of holding yourself together lies," Morey had said. "The knot of not being able to feel your own body, or to feel the self in the body. Or to feel the body as a device for feeling. Chase used to say, 'The body has its propensities for making all these potential connections and they get twisted into knots'."

Later that evening Dahlia came up behind Walker as he was bending over and grabbed his buns. He jumped up, shocked —whirled around ready to register umbrage only to find her smiling at him. She sauntered off on her way to sleep with somebody else. Walker had a session with the lovely Jade that night. They got onto her futon and under some sleeping bags and hugged and OMed for a while. Walker was not feeling all that connected.

Jade got a lascivious look on her lovely boyish face and asked, "Would you like to get into some asshole feelings?"

Walker's eyes got as big as saucers even though he didn't know what she meant by asshole feelings, he didn't think he wanted to find out. "Uh, no thanks," he said.

The next day, still shaken, back in Berkeley he wrote:

July 29/83 These gentle people. I need to let
them touch me more. What goes on at the neural
level, the level of breakdown, the disintegration of
personality so that another personality can come to
the fore.
Primal Scream sounds and what is inside them.
Energy spectrum of psyche, the most esoteric black
box in the world. It made me have a tremendous vote
of confidence in the whole group process.

Trying to let the boundaries reside, Walker wrote of
himself in the third person as though he were a character in a
book.

"He was trying to penetrate a dimension to which
the eyes could no longer be closed and whose being
he forever more would be not dead to. It was the
obscurity beyond sex. He becomes like a wind across
the planet on which we find ourselves meeting
ourselves."

A few days later Kevin wrecked his car. Numerous small
groups and numerous big groups were convened about why
he had done it. There are no accidents in the Freudian
universe. Everybody thought it was some terrible haunting
energy attempting to incapacitate the body so it would be
held in a state of dependency — an attempt by the ego to
maim the feeling experience. Kevin's brother Malcolm told
him: "It is the movement of the self against itself —the ego
against the self. You might be experiencing the Thantos
impulse, experiencing a depth of his self-hatred, causing you
to go into the car accident." It was even brought into doubt
whether Kevin should go to the land at all.

Kevin enjoyed hanging out with Walker more because
Walker didn't subscribe to this world of Freudian
determinants. Accidents were just accidents. Walker was
feeling closer to Kevin than anyone in his group, and was
afraid of what would happen if Kevin were to be away from
the fray and he had to face the women in his group on his
own. Walker and Kevin started hanging out together more,
started going for long walks. They were quite enjoying each
other's company and could speak of most anything. Kevin
had that elegant obdurate horniness Scots are famous for.

"Let us look at the molecular structure of women, first"
Walker might say.

"Yes let us see what gets into her!" Kevin would reply,
fervently.

Kevin became Walker's confidant in Walker's pursuit of Dahlia. Walker confessed to him, "I hate to go from week to week without talking to Dahlia. One of us could get run over by a car, and then where would we be. That would really fix it, wouldn't it? I have so much I want to talk to her about!"

Walker felt inferior because the people of the House were way more sophisticated than him at analysis. He did suspect that his coming and going and not being on a regular schedule seemed to really bother Rachel. Because it bespoke a lack of commitment. She used it as an excuse to not have sessions with him.

He had never been involved with groups before. He started to get the picture of what the house was into and some of the experiments of the past. But there was nothing written down, there were just so many implicit agreements and assumptions that were tacitly assumed. He felt that he had to drag information out of the people. They kept on telling him that he used intellectuality as a defense not to feel. He felt that they were being evasive to his questioning.

What bothered him most was that they hardly ever did the meditations anymore. And there was so much hypocrisy in it! They have orgasms left and right around here. It was comical. They try not too. You see the men in their groups, shaking their head in disbelief and the self doubt of their recalcitrant obdurate incorrigibility. Hand hits forehead, "And then I ejaculated." They seem to miss the joy of what is happening.

Walker tried out his fledgling analyst chops by trying to own the projection he thought he might have on Rachel. He didn't feel or understand it but thought if he said how he was projecting his mother on her, it might clear the air. But she slipped away, saying the subject was too hot to be handled. "Men and women have so much trouble with each other," she said to Jade as the two of them sashayed off to their session with each other. Walker thought: The girls just want to be with the girls. But I'm hangin' in, just waiting for my session with Dahlia.

Finally Walker's session with Dahlia came around. And he went to spend the night with her even though he was terrified at the large herpes outbreak he was having.

He had to tell her. "I've got the finishing end of a herpes outbreak. It's not contagious. I could just wear a condom."

She is one hell of a woman he thought. She was right there for him. Her fingers flitted over his cock under the sheets. One minute squeezing the shaft, then the next rubbing her palm over the knob. Amidst the struggle of the autoimmune system with the virus, pleasure *could* be found!!

And he kindled a fire in her with all that. She got on top of him and they both came. She enjoyed it.

She started playing with his asshole! She started patting his butt letting her fingers linger and dance lightly on his asshole.

Yikes! Walker thought. I'm just an ordinary off-the-shelf dude got picked up and thrown in here. What's going on here? Many nights I don't even know with whom I'm going to sleep.

"Ahhyyaahh," he said. He could not let her take control. Just could not let go and try to be in the experience. Frightened he made a joke of it: "Do you know how you can tell if you been abducted by aliens?"

She stopped. Looked at him quizzically.

He smiled and said, "If you've had the *anal probe*."

They both laughed at this and just lay side by side.

"Have you ever wondered why those aliens would come 25 million miles across space to abduct some poor joker from New Mexico and stick an instrument up his butt? I mean what *are* the looking for up there?"

She started laughing at this.

Encouraged Walker continued: "You know what they've found? They've found one in ten actually enjoys it.

"Hmmmm"

"What do you make of that?"

"Well, I actually enjoy it."

"You do! Hmmm. Well, we'll have to investigate that some day."

The next morning he got into oral sex with her. She just rubbed his cock on her.

Although Walker wouldn't have believed it, he had a lot of feelings. In fact he started crying with her for a while. He felt himself in the presence of this most beautiful woman.

They were both in the same situation, that would not be forever and he was crying out of relief, that he had found a woman in this world who was like him and who he could trust to be there, and to be sensitive, and to play with him. Boo, hoo. Sniff, sniff.

Walker's Journal 8/1/83

It was a kind of vulnerable bliss trust.
Vulnerable bliss trust. Note the naming of emotions
in 3-noun chains. Kind of like an ideogramatic
language, or like Tibetan a synthetic language.
Might mean there were some kind of interlocking sets
up there, like the grids of emotion that can be
superimposed on top of each other. This would be a
subspace that spanned emotions. An emotion was a
vector with components from 3 or more sections of
the brain. Has anyone applied vector analysis to
neural functioning?

This is an opportunity to get into the synthetic
language of the sutras in Sanskrit and Tibetan. In
English we have kenning.

Along about that time Walker told Rachel in small group: "You seem really bitter." He said that maybe he was really projecting his mother on her, that it was a new thing for him to see that and that maybe by talking about it, he could somehow transcend it because he knew it was not her, was it?

Walker's Journal 8/3/83

We are learning to take people's anger and how
not to get caught up in it. Things become so loaded
that we can't talk about it unless surrounded by our
group.

I am reading Jourard, The Transparent Self and he
writes about speaking with the first voice, the
voice of free association, before the second voice
censors. He talks about listening with the third
ear, that as you begin to trust yourself the trust
comes out of a response to a person.

This is the generation of good karma in
conversation. Feeling your own authentic voice. But
first you have to go through a lot of bullshit. You
have to be able to feel inside yourself and see
beyond your own projections. It really makes you see
your own insanity, and that is hard to live with.
Makes you feel a lot of pain. But this is how you
really get to know real people. When you can laugh
and joke with them, that is when the other person
becomes human, otherwise you are just a robot to be
turned on and turned off. I want to learn how to

speak to people in this feeling way.

The body itself is a sender and receiver of signals in the group. It is an instrument to study the world with.

It is natural for a group of committed people to want to go to bed together, and get closer, more intimate.

But I feel the disclosures that Rachel has made to me have been contrived. Either that or I am so insensitive that I can't feel for her. Where's my empathy? Is it that my own stuff, my feelings and emotions that make me the way I am keep me blind?

What is all this worrying about schedules that she does?

She speaks to me in two languages. The intellectual language of the mind, and the language of the body. You have me in a double bind. A cunt is a mouth with no brains. It just feels. It speaks the mute language of the body, it comes out in the smile, or a softness around the eyes.

Does she smile pleasantly when you mount her I ask myself.

No.

I don't know. Maybe they equate this with fantasy but I guess that is where I come from still hung up in the romantic paradigm. For me these are signs that my lover wants to be with me, for you they are signs of some kind of submission to an irrational, reactive world view.

That is what they mean by speaking in the first voice. It means spontaneously having feelings about other people.

Projection, that's an old dope term. Like when you walk into the group, a room full of people and you're stoned and they are not and you know that they are going to know. And you look at them and one of them makes this movement of his eyebrow, and you see it and react to it, and he sees you react to it, and others see your reaction too and they react to it, and you react to their reaction, and you know they know that you're not STRAIGHT, and they sense your fear and they get afraid of you being afraid. THAT is projection, where your mind works to produce all kinds of evidence from the world to substantiate its own way of thinking.

A man has to learn how to look into his own physiology to know what he is feeling, to know what is going on with his mind. You have to use it to program your own evolution in this lifetime, to take control of your own immune system.

And that is by feeling the world of unconscious realities, the learning that has been going on since childhood in every encounter.

46

Mr. Nice Guy

Walker went to the Loft, where he saw Dahlia with some old friend of hers, a guy with whom she appeared to have a romantic connection. She seemed a little sheepish as she introduce him.

Walker said, "Hi."

He looked at the guy, saw he was a nice respectable looking guy, probably was into shiatsu macrobiotics and tai chi and loose cotton clothing. Walker felt a lot of jealousy and had to act like he didn't.

He hung out with Pia a bit. She said, "You look kind of nervous and anxious."

"So what else is new?"

They ate in silence. Pia meditated.

Walker went to small group. They got on his case about the image he projected in pursuit of a job. They talked to him about being inauthentic in his resumé and job search.

Then as he was laying down on the floor, kind of stretched out, not paying much attention to Big Group, he heard his name called: "Walker, would you come to the center of Big Group."

Yikes! Oh, oh. It really made one feel like you were being called out on the carpet. But it went well, at least no big confrontation ensued. Many people expressed feelings for him around the room. Betty said: "You have a lot of words in your head, but they start to have a lot more feeling, when you start to feel more."

Walker wanted to talk to Dahlia about his relationship with her, but she had this *outsider* with her, and Mr. Nice Guy took over. Walker couldn't bring himself to broach the subject. He had to swallow his feelings. Inside he was relieved. Looking around Walker sensed that others in Big Group realized this bind he found himself in too. Leslie took the heat off by talking about her own self.

Walker had a session with Jade later that evening, but she had put the futon smack in the middle of the floor again, and so there was no room. And he let this get to him and his anger controlled him and kept him from the feelings. They did get into a hug, made OMing sounds but he did not feel connected up. Jade talked about her anger. He would not have been able to admit his fear and anger kept him distant though in the frustration of not being able to feel he was starting to understand something about where he came from and this so disturbed him that he classically projected his bad feelings upon the group and decided to try and get into another group. This is how he put it in his journal:

Aug. 6/83 Part of the process of making it more equal between the sexes, seems at first to be reducing the figures of the girls to that of boys, the desexualization of women. So that they are just like one of the boys. We did not get into sex, I just wasn't that interested. Jade is a very good looking woman, but she doesn't feel there for me.

This spurned me to make an important decision. That is to join into this new group. Consider a new partner in my romantic plans. What would this mean? The group. Sleeping with women in the group. Can I do that in front of Dahlia? A whole lot of shame comes up. I want to have sexual feelings with more than one person.

I can feel a lot of my father in me, and a lot of his father, my grandfather. I can see it in various ways I hold my hands, in certain looks my father has in pictures, in his ways of reacting to new situations. Almost like I was looking at the world from behind his face.

These are a kind of learned reflex, this is like the unconscious mind. They are ways that the unconscious feels like it is protecting the conscious, but really, they are ways that stand in the way of conscious feeling, being mindful. I need to overthrow, the you in me.

Walker had sessions two nights in a row with Dahlia. He had to stop and recall that it had been eight years since he last spent two nights in a row with the same woman. That was back in Montreal with Suzie. Come to think of it she had been one of the most evil, vile women on the face of the earth. Yet even after he left her, he had gone back to her. Hitchhiked all the way back across the country to spend the night in her dog house. God how humiliating. When was it ever not so.

That second night Walker had a session with Dahlia, that

sweet dark transcendental heart-mate of his dreams, it became a darker fantasy sexual-trip with him having to abstain from normal intercourse —herpes outbreak, a casualty of the sex the night before. The anger at the dependency played itself out in him over-acting out the overcompensating Mr. Nice Guy sex slave role in bed. Walker was afraid he was going to loose Dahlia to this new infatuation and he was jealous of this individual's apparent normalcy. In Walker's mind there was a lot at stake. The gods had been known to give up even immortality for an opportunity to experience love the way humans do.

He spread her legs and began sucking on Dahlia's pussy. Slowly he started from the top and worked his way down her lips. As he reached the opening vagina, he inserted a finger and began pumping it in and out of her wet cunt; then he inserted a second finger and with his two fingers spread her vagina open. Dahlia was delighted at him taking his time and rummaging around inside.

Dahlia felt her asshole becoming sopping wet with his saliva and her pussy juice dribbling down over the perineum into her crack. "Feel my asshole with your finger," she whispered. She pulled her legs back higher up to her shoulders, presenting her beautiful ass to him.

Walker is desperate. He can't take his mind off the competition he is feeling with this interloper guy. I was born to be Dahlia's love slave. He thinks to follow directions.

With his big finger he spread the drool and pussy juice around her little nether hole and gently started drubbing his finger on it as she relaxed. Even so it seemed kind of dry. Then he thought, what the hell, she had just come out of the shower and was clean and fresh as a flower down there, and he was just a love slave anyway, and he starts to tenderly kiss and lick her cheeks that he is holding in his hot hands and while this is spreading wave of warmth through her he spread her wide with his thumbs and he flicked his hot wet tongue in and out of her tight little anus. He licked up and down and all around her hot crack with his even hotter tongue.

Oo, Yes! She shouted.

He looked up at her. He saw that she was on the horns of a dilemma, whether to let herself continue to be defiled by what was called at the house, 'dirty sex.' Then she thought, what the hell and moaned, "Oh, Yes! YES!"

Oh, yes. She moaned aloud and he continue doing it, up and down, up and down and then, he poked his hard little pink wet tongue in and out of her tight little butthole again and again.

Walker looked up at her, tried to make eye-contact, but she had this kind of imperious, haughty, wretched, perfidious look on her face — lost in space that she might burst into tears or explode at any minute. Walker shrugged his shoulders and smiled for his function on this earth was but to serve his Princess and he put his finger where his tongue just was and it slides right inside of her hot tight little asshole and her eyes got wide in surprise and her mouth fell open in shock. And she moaned a loud Ohhhh!

Dahlia inhaled sharply with a slight shock of pain as Walker's finger penetrated her ass. Then as he slowly inserted his finger into her well-lubricated asshole Dahlia moaned and OMed very loud. Slowly he started sliding his finger it in and out of her rear.

Then with the two fingers still spreading her cunt, he moved his mouth back up to the top of her cunt where he began playfully sucking her erect clit. Dahlia moaned and started to rotate her hips in time with Walker's fingers. Rolling his tongue around her clit and then licking up and down on her cunt as his finger is sliding in and out of her tight little anus made her thrust forward each time causing his finger to go in deep.

She grabbed his hair and pulled his head as hard as she could into her cunt. Walker forced his tongue directly onto Dahlia's clit and she began to buck her cunt on his face.

The different sensations are becoming too much for her and she had the sense that she was being flushed through clouds, or was skimming along like a slide board beside the ocean spinning and turning with her legs high up around her ears. And she starts to buck faster and faster, making him suck and finger fuck her faster and faster.

Bucking and thrusting harder now as she slide her swee ass up and down his finger, she is starting to twitch and she tells him, "Ooh, Walker. I'm going to come." She *knew* she was going over the edge, no holding back this time.

"Ahhhhhh YES!, yesssssss," she hisses as she is kissing him with her pussy lips, pushing her cunt/mouth into his face while her ass is clenching his finger.

Walker began to get angry and really started forcing his finger up inside her ass trying to turn her pussy inside out. Dahlia screamed and moaned. She started thrashing and yelled Oo - ooohoooo! sliding her asshole up and down impaling herself on his finger faster and faster as she feels her orgasm starting.

Dahlia started yelling loudly. She howled. AAArrroughhhh. She cums over and over and over again soaking his mouth and face with her juices as he continues to suck and finger fuck her relentlessly. She thrashed on the floor, bucking her hips into him, enjoying her climax.

She collapsed back panting hard and slides her asshole off his finger. Her body is trembling as he gently kisses his way up her body and gives her a kiss on her sweet lips. Dahlia reached for him and pulled him close. She began to lick her own cum from his face.

Dahlia went completely limp after her orgasm. Walker snuggled up close and kissed her cheek as she passed out.

In the morning she said, "I wish we had been more connected in our breathing."

47

Book of Matches

A small close-cover-before-striking matchbook became the repository of a whole weeks worth of anxiety, when Walker's group finally got the sleeping schedule down.

It was done quickly, easily, and democratically when Small Group convened after a hot game of frisbee up in the park off Clipper, way up in the Diamond Heights hills overlooking San Francisco. Jade, Morey, Rachel and Walker.

Kevin had gone up to live on the land. And Walker was on his own. He missed him.

They made a grid on the back of the matchbook. Across the top were the days of the week. Sun Mon Wed Th. Fri. Beneath each day was the name of someone in the group. Walker, Morey, Rachel and Jade. Down the vertical was also the list of people in the group. If you intersect the vertical and horizontal there was a couple in each one of the intersection of days and people. Sun Mon Wed Th. Fri. Rachel and Morey, Rachel and Jade; Walker and Jade, Morey and Jade, Walker and Morey. Rachel and Greg were having session on Fridays. As were Walker and Dahlia and this made it all worthwhile.

So now they would know beforehand who would be having session with whom.

A strange sadness started to overcome Walker as he became more liberated. He took a break from writing in his journal because he began to become suspicious of it. At the house this was technically understood to be getting more in touch with the core or autonomic self. One feels less the desire to engage in symbol formation.

48

Feeling / Defending

Walker was having a lot of trouble giving up the romantic paradigm. He was feeling very angry. One night in session with Dahlia, she was kind of spaced out, and Walker felt how desperate that made him feel. The passions did not meet and feed each other. That morning Walker was replaying the sex: I came in her mouth last night and was kind of half soft when we made it again in the morning. Then he admonished himself, to not be counting orgasms. What was important was to really be there in feelings.

"Do you get sleepy when you ejaculate?" Dahlia asked. "I heard that there was some kind of chemical released . . . in a man's body, when he ejaculates that makes him tired and want to go to sleep."

"It makes you very relaxed," Walker said dreamily.

He thought: Not as young as I used to be? Feeling the fall of the rigid male armor?

When they got up that morning, Dahlia seemed kind of disappointed. She said, "I don't know where our relationship is going."

Walker thought, I'm just trying to hang in! It almost always feels like the first time and last time every time we get together! I can't handle all this poignancy. His diary:

8/11/83 I feel a lot of love for the group, for the women, all the women in the House, feel for myself, feel for them. It felt good what we were into, you were kind of relaxed and cool, and a little bit spaced out and I was kind of desperate, trying to act cool.

I feel my male armor dissolving, feel I have to let you in.

I feel a real meltdown of the male armor, of the genital character.

Walker had had it with his own small group marriage. Trying to hang in with evil bitch-woman Rachel was driving him nuts. At the next small group meeting they told him: "You need a couple of days in between coming to the Loft to marshal the forces of your ego."

"I'm getting lonely and kind of restless. Yes and bored,"

Walker complained.

"Well it's not up to us to keep you interested," Rachel snapped back.

"I just don't feel connected."

The upshot of all this was they put Walker on the yoga of no-sex.

"It will help you examine the image of you being the stud," Rachel said.

"Mm muh me? A stud?"

—

```
8/13/83
     In the last session with Dahlia, I saw the light
flower. That is a flower whose edges were light and
who's surface petals were a sort of softer light, or
darkness fading into really more darkness.
     My 3rd eye opens. Intuition. The instruction that
comes from within. Part of learning to speak with
the first voice and listen with the third ear, to
see with the third eye.
     I use the virus to see. The virus gives me
feedback about the kind of stress in my life. It
makes me get to where I can feel like I can trust
women, were I can talk to them about myself.
     It serves to remind me that I am meat, tissue,
matter.
     Constantly live with it. Lot of responsibility
not to pass it.
     Responsibility to myself, not to let it destroy
my sexuality which is getting heavily overthrown a
lot around here. The genital character having to
reform.
     My ego uses it to translate me into isolation and
into making all kinds of defense mechanisms. I'm not
going to let that happen any more. I feel my
character changing, feel the male armor eroding.
```

—

The Loft people took pride in their powers of observation. They relaxed and trusted their intuition. They studied and watched the energy motion in blushes and body language to penetrate silences. They were very keen on hearing and seeing and feeling each other more deeply.

They tried to be sensitive to the anxiety that surrounds psychic birth and were very aware of the anti-change forces, the way anxiety is defended against and how this blocks change. Dahlia often repeated what Chase said: "The way Chase put it: 'Every time you feel something you are sowing the seeds for the ego to come up and strangle the feeling'."

Seemed a little radical to Walker until he slowed down and watched the ego at work sometimes.

8/15/83

From the seed of feeling the psychological
defenses spring forth with issue to strangle it.
Like a tree the ego, with bitter fruit of
psychological defenses. Every emotion has its
opposite side and one's self oscillates between the
two extremes like: generous / selfish, loving /
hateful, envious / knowledgeable, treacherous /
nurturing, frightened / acting into, phony / real
and these could be seen as shades of gray on a line
going from one extreme to the other. Like the Signal
to Noise ratio S/N.

I wondered if it could be the basis vectors that
spanned a semantic space. Now let's see. All people
could be described or rather the emotions and
feelings people put out could be described, in a
kind of 3-cluster, ideogram - a phanopoeia. Like one
might say, Jade was [intelligent, very good looking,
OK. company] or [untrustworthy, isolated and angry].
Or Rachel. He took delight in netting her in his
semantic space. She was [OK company, very good
looking, had to be the center of attention] ,
[flighty, standoffish, morbidly introspective].

Walker was delighted by this, felt he was in blue-sky phenomena creating new images of psychology for himself by translating the ancient terms from Tibetan Buddhist psychology into modern English.

For Walker, being in feelings felt like being in Physics. He had time, and he had freedom, and he could feel his motion, because there was a basic awareness. Being in feelings meant opening up to more and more of what was going on around you. He realized this must be what the Buddhist meant by mindfulness. It was so strange and wonderful and the thinking part of his being immediately stepped up and began sketching out notes for writing. He could watch and feel this happen. And even though he knew his way of avoiding the feelings was to get intellectual about it, he could not stop himself. Being in Physics for him meant he was able to drop or let go of the bad things, the neg-ativities, the things that people told him were wrong about him or that he had come to believe were wrong about himself. It was very liberating. He was just this beautiful machine held in god's love. Really. What if there was nothing wrong? What if you were OK and everyone else was OK? Imagine. You didn't want anything from them, you were just going to be present. You are just going to show up and be yourself for yourself. With your pain. With your negativity. With the whole in your personality. With your shadow side. This was so empowering, to be able to walk around in the world without a bunch of negative energy dragging him down that he got frightened of this power and could not maintain it, and yet in an attempt to maintain it went home and began working on a paper about the analogies between mindfulness and permeability. He began to wonder about the fundamental invisible force of attraction at the bottom of all phenomena relating and moving together in time. He wrote:

8/18/83 Hermetic Magnetism: Poetry and the Permeability of Mind
Reluctance / permeability is a model.
Coercivity / Retentivity. It is an analogy to flow of current, but here it is a reverse flow together with an attraction. Current is inversely proportional to the resistance. We make the analogy
Reluctance = Permeability
Resistance   Conductivity
Conjecture: The basic Buddhist concept of mindfulness can be understood by analogy to the concept of permeability in electromagnetism.
We are electromagnetic beings!
We have auras around us like luminous eggs!
The duality E/M   Electricity / Magnetism
We have our feet in two worlds: the timeless spirit world and the here and now.
Like right now I am conflicted between thinking and feeling. It is like the hysteresis curve, an S curve chasing its tale coming back upon itself. An image, an attractive magnetic flux sets up a polarizing movement say in the direction of feelings, and depending on the permeability of the subject he is able to be present with more and more phenomena coming into his storage capacity. It is like he can store more of the moment up to a saturation point. Then he must start generating a reverse field to stave off this influx. For fear that he will be overwhelmed or become too saturated and unable to move.
Are there other homeostatic processes around the polar pairs of sensing / judging, intuiting/ perceiving, extroversion / introversion as well as thinking / feeling? Wow. We might be on the threshold of a theory of personality here.

Permeability and mindfulness. We are all like antennas, like a surface of RLC traps (Resistance Inductance Capacitance), and with education or with relaxation of rigid defenses of narcissism, we are able to be more mindful. Able to allow more phenomena to penetrate us, and to let our boundaries down and let ourselves dissolve and flow in and flow out of ourselves. Why RLC and not RIC. Convention.

Got to FIND WAYS to communicate this. This is like the Q of the coil, there is a Q of the personality. It measures personal magnetism! Everybody is RLC

Resistance Inductance Capacitance
R   sensing / judging
L Intuiting / perceiving
C thinking / feeling

More of the incoming is stored in one side and used in the other. Stored in the electric field, stored in the magnetic field. Stored in the capacitor. Stored in the inductor. RLC sequencing.

Coercivity: how hard it is to de-magnetize
a soft —temporary magnet
—Knee curve, saturation magnetization—
permeability: is amplification factor
    magnifies the induced magnetic field
    Permeability is the inverse of coercivity;
    core is self.

Is mindfulness and permeability the reverse process of the Image. Just as the image is acquired through filters, the effect of the image on organizing the mind/body mitigates those filters.

Electric AND Magnetic. You're a girl and I'm a boy. You're a south and I'm a north. We each have two poles. Sometimes when we are turned around we repel each other, and sometimes we attract.

You might think about the mind that you have and what a wonderful thing it is, and then you might think about the place that mind came from: it would be nature, evolution, a great Mind at the back of things and you might feel it is very far away, but yet it is right here as close as your breath.

To feel your anger yet not act out on it is a wonderful thing. It is trying to be present in the moment. To feel the presence of the mind of nature as close as your breath. To really come to know it. Would that actually be possible?

It is the Magician that makes love happen. Who is that. An Archetype. It is simply about coming to feel the presence of these archetypes in your life.

You cannot figure it out!
You cannot transcend it!

It is here for you. It is always here for you
and yet you say you must find your way back to it,
or find your way into it.

What keeps you out of being in this core self,
keeps you drawn out on the eddy currents of flux is
the fear of feelings. Feelings become so foreign, I
mean like anger, and love, and yet you have to
martial the energy of anger and hate in order to be
able to love. And we are completely robbed of that
in our society. Completely blind to that.

One is constantly being attracted away from
this . . . this mind that is taking care of you at
every breath, and you have got to be able to be in
it with other people more. There are a lot of
things that will throw you off. Take them as yoga,
this is a message from the divine. Don't kill the
messenger but be with your anger, it will enhance
your awareness.

About this time Walker caught the flu and was laid up
for over a week. It was hideous and grotesque. The virus
made him cough constantly like the incessant barking of a
dog left out for days and days and days, and days and days.
What other kind of sadhana would make you do that? Get
in touch with that aspect of yourself?

He had no T.V. Just had to stay up all night looking at
the walls. After a few days of no sleep he decided to try
and get Buddhist on it. He tries to look at all the fevered
dreams coming up in his mind and project them on the
wall. In his fevered dreams he kept thinking of pussy and
cunt and more cunt, and eating pussy because he wanted to
feel horny.

It usually involved him rolling over on his stomach and
he'd be looking at a pussy again, he wasn't even sure
whose. She is sitting at the head of his bed, her back to the
wall, with her legs spread open wide and her pussy right
where he can turn on his pillow and rub his face in it. She
opens her legs as wide as she can and her cunt opens a
little wider too as she ooches herself forward to offer her
cunt to his tongue which he taps on the tip of her little
clitoris. He was the cunning linguist. He had no choice in
the matter; it was a manifestation of his longing getting out
of hand. He mushes his lips back and forth on her slit.

At times he wondered if he was going crazy. His being
was just unbelievably noisy, constantly shaking and

agitating, feverish tremors running through his body, extremities being extremely cold while his face was flushed hot. A running battle —a war, inside the body — was raging out of control. A matter of life and death. Foreign invaders had set up a beach head and were colonizing his nasal passages trying to cut off his air! Unseen terrorists armed with hooks and knives were coursing down other tunnels into his stomach, up into his ears, his brain, infiltrating all through his being, taking control! Protecting deities were all running around trying to fight, to defend, to do something! Who WAS in control here? The dispatcher? Surely he was the hero, the savior, conducting the fighting force of the immune system, dispatching killer T-cell warriors through the blood into the interstices of the body, a battle space of lines and points, a space of nomographs, logarithms, titrations and concentrations. In the real world it involved sending Walker to the drugstore for lozenges, Sudafed, expectorants, decongestants, pain killers and all manner of cough syrups and nostrums. He starved himself, couldn't stand to eat anything, just listened to the great growls of his stomach.

He realized he was constantly in longing, his whole being was about longing.

Or was the bug attacking the unconscious? Yes that's it, or his unconscious was attacking him. Because the most terrible thing of all was that he didn't have any sex interest whatsoever. Just, . . . oh my god he didn't know what to think of himself down there. It was gone! As if he were completely smooth like an anatomically incorrect doll. At times he would rub himself against the bed and think about pussy, cunt and his mind would move a lot faster, the images would start to come into a play of their own playing in the field of sex, giving him some relief. The woman of his dreams is serving him with her cunt and he is the master of making her come, and he lets this anima sit on his face by turning over on his back: he sees she is nude straddling his waist. He has her move up and with each of her knees beside his ears, she hoists her hips up and gently kisses him on his lips with the lips of her pussy. They kiss like that long and passionately, she can barely stand it as he French kisses her cunt, sticking his tongue as far up into her as it will reach and she moans and slowly moves her hips back and forth, rubbing her clitoris on his tongue, her wet lips sliding over his wet lips and in a few instants she becomes possessed by a force that is endless and eternal, and cums shooting a jet of her hot eggy sauce onto his lips and dribbling down his chin and she slides off him and lies on top of him, and kisses him on the lips, dipping her tongue into her own pussy juice on his lips, and licking it off his cheeks and chin. Then he realizes the pussies need to be banged! They are like flowers in a psychological garden, they need to opened and absolutely paid attention to. It is the desire to enter and re-enter life and if his cock could project out in front of its insatiability, as if he had the power to touch what goes on in the images and if the one he liked could be here to touch his standing cock, if she would wrap her hand around his pole, it would give him a boner and make him want to stuff it up inside her. And she reaches down and impales her cunt on his erect cock, and slowly lowers herself down on the stiff cylindrical shaft taking it up her as far as it will go until she feels his penis touching her cervix.

He was totally invisible in all this, he was nothing but hunger and longing, covered by skin. And yet in his thrashing she kept bringing him back to that one part of ourselves, of our exterior image which is the only part of ourselves that can satisfy the insatiable hunger and yet that untouchable part had been made into a sin.

He saw the anger, fear in his body and the chaos and the tumultuous flow by applying the basic Buddhist methods of bare attention, and concentration in hopes that he would maybe finally get down into analytic meditation.

One day he thought he could speak Chinese. He saw the ideograms in the air as one might see cartoon bubbles floating over people, people doing detailed moves of chi gung, and the ideograms were an expression of this movement. He was coming to understand that these ideograms, the way they were built, related to how *people* were built, in hierarchical levels. Levels is what the ideograms are about. They are actional, adverbial. And from these vertical organizations there were embellishments and expansion out into the horizontals. He thinks: I can kind of read *Chinese* in the dream.

At other times in the flu he starts seeing the fearful wrathful deities of the stomach, rising and taking shape in the gas. He starts being frightened by the fearful wrathful deities of the lungs rasping, gasping, grasping instead of being enlivened and carried along by the spirit and energy in the oxygen of the air. Wrathful deities, fever, the fearful wrathful deities of fever. He imagines he has cancer. He manages to really terrify himself. He became afraid of going to sleep, he was afraid he wouldn't wake up, he realized: my, my, my personage is held in the hands of so many deities, and systems and they were all held together and here they are all playing their evil side, instead of the benevolent side.

He tried concentration meditation — intensely looking at a deck outside. It made him think about a caravan of airstream trailers going underwater on barges in France. It came to him that Death is an owl. He was taking dictation from the owl. The owl was telling him he must go into these huge cranking generators of the alternating current dynamo of our time and they want him to keep on the job and that is what will keep him working on the magnetic field.

When he got better Walker wrote this whole paper on analogies between the principles of Buddhism, Taoism, Magic, the esoteric and perennial philosophy and magnetism. He wanted to go through some of the basic principles of Buddhism and overlay them with Physics right quick. Some of these esoteric principles (for Walker these insights were like deep, swaying, swooning feelings) were coming up again in his studies and practice of Buddhism in the Sangha of Dorje Chang and from what he recalled studying Physics in school. They called it Natural Philosophy back then. Walker smiled recalling: I actually hold a BA in Natural Philosophy, though I feel far from being natural.

Buddhism, Taoism, and the Perennial Philosophy as a Sensual Intuition into Electro-Magnetism

The three basic principles of the Perennial Philosophy (and by that is meant Buddhism, Taoism, Magic, Hermetic and Esoteric philosophy, old world, ancient philosophy, philosophies that contain mythological elements and procedures for conducting yourself in the world, — philosophies that hold a belief about and stand with awe and respect before a

supremely creative and generous manifold source
energizing the world) can be collected into three
groups: {Polarity, Duality}, {Rhythm, Vibration,
Frequency} and {Correspondence, Mind-Mentalism}. I
would like to examine these basic principles using
parallels with magnetism for an esthetic intuition
into that source.

First, is the principle of {Polarity, Duality}.

The Principal of Polarity: Opposing polarities
are contained within everything in the universe and
everything in the universe is continually in motion
between the poles contained within. There is a
fundamental dualism is all things. Everything is
dual in that it contains its opposite. Opposites are
identical — either reflections, or displacements
differing in degrees along a continuum connecting
them. The most basic principle of esoteric
philosophy is Polarity containing the unification of
opposites.

A simple bar magnet is a good illustration of
this belief. Polarity is the most obvious fact about
magnetism. Opposites attract and likes repel. This
is the first fact people think about when they think
of magnetism. Magnetism seems to contain the dual
nature of the world. The perennial philosophy sees
the events unfolding in the world as an expression
of split potentialities existing in and unfolding
from an equilibrium.

The principal of polarity and dualism is
reflected in Gender which nature uses to express
Herself. Both masculine and feminine properties are
contained within everything, yin-yang, sangsara-
nirvana, passive-aggressive. Polarity, dualism is
true of all planes, including physical, mental and
spiritual. The substance of the world of Taoism,
Buddhism and other esoteric philosophies is a
unification of opposites, glimpsed through the
method of negation — it is not this and not that. In
this unitary transcendental substance, all things -
though in constant motion - are seen for a moment to
be held in a static potential, each holding the
other off in a state of détente, a state of
potential energy brought about by being in quiescent
equilibrium with its opposite.

Sounds like Dirac's ocean, the vacuum. Dualism
in physics? Position and momentum. Energy and time.
By knowing one thing you can figure out another. The
dual plays a big part in Quantum Mechanics,
conjugation of operations in a vector space, allows
one to find the unknown by looking at different
representation of the known.

Dualism in Psyche? The dual nature of the
guardians of the unconsciousness is well known:

while they serve to protect the individual from bearing the full brunt of psychological insight, they also deprive of that insight.

Second, is the principal of {Rhythm, Vibration, Frequency}

The Principal of Rhythm: Everything in the universe has its own particular rhythm as it moves between its internal poles — that of a rock is much slower than that of a person. At the same time, everything interacts with everything else in a rhythmic manner, although it might take centuries for the rhythmic pattern to repeat. The rhythm of our heart pulses life constantly all the days of our lives into our bodies. The rhythm of our heart evolved in the circadian rhythm of the planet's rotation. Rhythm brings time into the static picture of polarity and its potential. Vibration and Frequency are variations on rhythm in other domains.

In Buddhism and perennial philosophy, seeing rhythm in the unfolding of time is coming to know the sense of being in time, as opposed to seeing yourself as a being in space with a fixed core of longing. To be in rhythm means to be in synch, to be following destiny, accepting and being in vibrational affinity atunement, being attracted to rather than grasping for.

In the vibrational and frequency aspects of rhythm we see parallels in magnetics with the concept of resonance and induction in electromagnetic waves, light, heat, color, sound. We are all antennas and tuning receivers of vibrations. The principle of vibration sees everything in the universe as having its own unique vibratory rate — its characteristic frequency, its fundamental harmonic, its eigenvalue. All manifestations and interactions of matter, energy, mind and spirit result from varying rates of vibration slipping into harmonic synch. Quantum numbers are the integer multiples of the harmonics of the fundamental. This principle finds its most elegant expression in Maxwell's Rainbow, the electromagnetic wave frequency spectrum of how all things interact with each other in vibrational fields. Esoteric philosophy structures itself upon the spirit vibrating beneath it all at the fastest frequency. The shimmering behavior of light is used over and over again to speak of the Buddhist mental sense.

Third, is the principal of {Correspondence, Mind-Mentalism}

The Principle of Correspondence: There are many levels/layers of existence, all happening simultaneously and what happens on one level affects what happens on others. The Principle of Mind-Mentalism: Everything in the universe is conscious and is all of one mind. What would be the analogy between {Correspondence, Mind-Mentalism} and magnetism? It is the sense of influences penetrating all things, actions at a distance: the field. Magnetism gives us the first experience of the field.

Buddhism sees this correspondence between the same pattern being repeated over and over on different levels in different domains and niches in analogies across domains as the principle of Mind Mentalism. You can feel the nervous system beneath your self, and beneath that sometimes a Mind. Jung speaks at the same time about the Brain and the Transcendent. Teihard de Chardin called this layer of mind in the evolution of geogenesis to biogenesis to psychogenesis — the noosphere.

Bohr's Principle of Correspondence set the tone for the whole oeuvre of making the transition from what was experienced in the macroscopic world to a world of abstraction beyond experience in the quantum world. The early workers in quantum mechanics relied on the correspondences between the microcosm and the macrocosm. Just as we explain the magnetic field of the planet aligning compasses by the swirling current set up by motion of the earth's liquid core, so too we explain by analogy the magnetism in matter by the spin of electrons and other charged bodies in matter. The explanation of the invisible subatomic world is arrived at through reasoning by analogy because of a heuristic correspondence between the macrocosm and the microcosm.

When these correspondences have a clear connection in the unfolding of time, they can become strongly correlated to the point of being cause and effect. It is this aspect of mindfulness that has found itself to be the most useful in the material world. When they are not so clearly correlated they might be occurrences of synchronicity. Opening up to feelings opens one up to the synchronic. With practice this aspect of the perennial philosophy becomes a way of life, and is called by Jung and Buddhism analytic philosophy.

Perhaps the man most compelled by magnetism was Tesla. He gave the world the marvelous AC grid we have today, based upon electricity generated by water motion, a renewable source. He wanted to take this further, by developing a free energy that could be broadcast to everyone on earth. He thought of what was called at that time the luminiferous ether as of two aspects: electricity is the static or potential aspect of this ether and magnetism is the dynamic or kinetic aspect. He thought that the energy of space was kinetic and that everyone should be able to attach their machinery to this wheelwork of nature.

It wasn't until he was influenced by Swami Vivekananda who was the first to bring Vedic Science to the west that Tesla began to have language and framework with which to understand and describe the source, existence, construction and equation of matter and energy. Unfortunately J.P. Morgan, because of the potential for commercial interests in a fossil-fuel driven economy, pulled the plug on Tesla's development of free energy.

It wasn't until a few years later when Einstein published his paper on relativity that matter and energy were equated and what had been known in the East for the last 5,000 years was then known to the West. Then with terror driving the accelerated development of the nuclear bomb, and all that infrastructure having to be supported after the war, the world turned again away from free energy to nuclear energy.

We ought to, by now — as a race, be able know what is good for this planet, our home, and thus for us. We are struck by how this planet is a living entity and archetypes are about and moving through our world and we are influenced by them and influence them, if we let ourselves. One gets a sense of our world as this evolving generous entity trying to communicate with those who are willing to listen and be enlightened. We actually know the method for this and it is Perennial Philosophy, but it is very hard to practice it.

Is the meditator in a state of sensible intuition?

In Buddhism there are no substances and all things are created by mind. In Pure Land Buddhism, an important meditative practice is the visualization of the Pure Land of the Buddha Amitabha. It is a practice of using the entrainment of images to see beneath them to the attraction of the images. The Transcendental substance of the Pure Land is like magnetism. This land is a picture of perfect non-attachment reached by a method of visualization. The metaphysics implies the Pure Land is actually created by the act of visualization, since all things are mind dependent. In a Kantian sense the sensual intuition —the sensual feedback-enhanced visualization — rises to the status of an intellectual intuition. Buddhism is a form of mysticism in which the transcendence of this world is brought about by the meditator realizing the one substance of the Pure Land is a vacuum of potential energies in which the meditator identifies with that mystical object. The question of existence is facilitated by the absence of any substantiation or incarnation and one can interpret the sensual intuition as independent of any real existence of the Pure Land. Similarly, the Tibetan Book of the Dead urges the deceased to realize that the vision of the hereafter are not independent but created by their own mind. Just as a child constructs the a priori elements he needs to create and organize his world out of experience and the connection of neuronal masses, it is the action of the Transcendent or Intervening Consciousness which constructs those neuronal masses. The Transcendent or Intervening Consciousness is creating the neuron mass so that it can be known. The substance of the Transcendent or Intervening Consciousness is pure mind. This transcendental substance is like magnetism. It is a field creating potential by containing opposites. When put into motion it radiates and shimmers differently in different time frames and niches and levels. The Transcendent or Intervening Consciousness is a field imbuing all things, sometimes realized by induction which in the mind appears as intuition.

In the practice of Buddhism and other perennial philosophies one constructs his personal path to enlightenment and salvation in hopes of meeting this Transcendent or Intervening Consciousness. In this world of one substance, — things held in détente of mutual potential — the hand of the Transcendent is a fluctuation, a swerve, an instability which off-sets the equilibrium causing energy to occur. At this point it is possible for the Transcendent's existence to be presented to the meditator passively.

The pull, the attraction beneath the image is the Transcendent or Intervening Consciousness trying to have knowledge of itself. The mediator is at that moment given a sensible intuition thus relating him/her to the independent transcendent object which cannot be created by one's knowing it. Thus the Transcendent or Intervening Consciousness creates its own existence, and if the mystic is identical to the Transcendent or Intervening Consciousness s/he will see that everything else is also created through intellectual intuition.

49

Like Two Carnivorous Waterbeds

Walker's journal Fri. Sept. 12

> Starting to blur the boundaries between group and mind. For the mind is a group. And the group is the extension of the mind. We are held together by relationships.

Walker went to the loft and started with the new amalgamated affiliated group. I feel a little scared about trying to avoid stuff with my old group, but things with Rachel feel so uneven.

I just can't deal with her.

Various combinations of sessions were written up. People had some feelings as to what their preference would be. We had various options called arrangements: from 1 to 4.

"I'd like to go with #3," I said, "then me and Beverly could have a session."

They talked for a while. Morey came in, kind of tipsy.

Walker had seen him earlier come up to the Loft as far as the landing, then turn around and split. It turned out he was all worried about a bid he had made at a job. He had made a mistake and underbid by some $30,000. He talked a lot about losing his contractor's license and was pretty scared and out of it.

So Beverly and Walker have a session. They went out to the Cliff House, had a drink and a talk. They walked along the sea wall feeling the fog, and the cool air. Felt close, arms around each other.

"Lets go back and go to bed," she said. She seemed really enthusiastic.

At the loft she set up her futon and comforter. Morey was lying beside them. "It's so much easier to hook up with new people," Beverly said.

Morey answered: "That's because you don't have any projections on them."

Beverly and Walker got into a hug and made some sounds. It felt really good. She is a soft Italian woman. "We could get into sex," she said, bright and enthusiastic. "It would be just like holding hands. But don't you come inside me."

Walker started to laugh and said, "Yes."

They went in and out of wanting to hook up and Walker kept pulling away, and she did too. Finally they got into sex.

After, she said some good things to him. "You use my fear to stop feelings. It is some kind of male control trip."

Walker said: "The society castrates the males and the males then in turn castrate the females. I wish society did not get into the bedroom. Or in this case the floor."

Later, in the morning, he got a lot of insight. "We were wanting to get our stomachs more together and talked about feeling more in the stomach."

"The numbness starts there," she said.

And they did get more hooked up in their breathing. We were like "two carnivorous water beds," Walker said.

He could feel the male genital character armor falling away, feel himself opening up, the armor, the rigidity easing down.

50

Reconstructing Sutra

By now Walker had looked up the words and names in the Devotion to Chenrezig, had understood the ritual sequence of the sadhana and had said it so many times that he practically knew it by heart. He made a premature attempt to start a re-constructive translation of the Devotion to Chenrezig. He walked around in his small apartment in Berkeley, saying it and translating it on the fly:

```
Taking Refuge
Realizing that the mind is like a clear pool into
which impulses are constantly being introduced and
fanning out, feeding back and cross aiding and
canceling each other, between the resolve to escape
and the desire to cling,
    I take refuge in my self. For I am suspicious of
authority other than my own.
    I seek to merge with the flow in the source of
inspiration.
    I seek to merge with the flow of muses, with
humor and with love.
    I take seriously art and science and the
perennial philosophy.
    I take refuge in all the community of feeling
people who are aware and sensitive.
    I take refuge in my animus, my anima and the two-
sided mitigators of psychic energy, which seek to
protect and inspire me.
```

Looking over his first attempt Walker thought: My, my. That's dreadful! But it was all he could come up with.

Were these just the foolish stutterings of a writer and physicist caught up in an attempt to have a metaphysical experience? (He could call himself a physicist, couldn't he? After all he had been awarded a Bachelors Degree in Natural Philosophy, what they used to call Physics back then.) He realized that a modern reconstruction of the Devotion to Chenrezig was not going to cut it. For one thing he was really having a hard time with the term God, as well as the idea of calling the deities Lord. And it all seemed to be such a masculine pantheon.

Walker was conflicted because he came from science. He thought of science as the religion and mythology and mystery of our time. He thought in order for a person to understand modern spirituality he should know a little radio astronomy as well as some evolution and ecology. He made another start.

```
    Sept. 14  Reconstructing Sutra
    The ocean, — I have trouble with the term God,
that term got abused when I was a Catholic, I like to
think of the term Ocean — that is a great image of
deity: leveling, all pervading, dissolving,
transporting, alive with exchange, rain, steam,
exotranspiration in plants.
    I was walking in Golden Gate Park - ground all
mushy after a rain, so much life coming up in all
directions, so green in the glades. I was walking
through the gentle grasses seeing the dead dying down
into mulch and the green life coming up out of it and
I suddenly got it about the Deity — THAT's what
Darwin called the Deity with a capital D. How the
Deity recycles everything, how life comes forth from
death. And I was awestruck by the generosity all
around me.
    The intricate beauty
    of the Earthy bountiful generosity
    comes up and kisses us on our eyes, and we fall
    in love with her tremendous generosity
    that is everywhere.
    Let us just call Her the source immediate of me.
Mother and Father. This goes back to the ultimate
Mother and Father, back into evolution.
    Blessed be Then.
    That certainly is a deity,
    the long chemical interaction,
    the curl of the wave
    of which I am currently riding in time.

    So we take Ocean as the image of deity; that is
we take the entity who generates the image. Ocean is
the image; may the phenomena behind this image
animate itself to inform our discussion.
```

Yes, he thought. DNA, thread, strands woven into me — a seine, a weir — against the flow, held up to capture life out of time. A Sutra is a thread in a weave, a yoking together of golden strands of logic and imagery leading us into the divine. The intellectual counterpart to physical yoga.

But we need new images; something modern like a Mind

Movie for our time. He liked the idea of trying to create a mind movie because it was both narrative, and visual, and audio, a good depiction of the simulacrum.

He sees himself as he slips into the darkened theatre of his mind. I say some control mantras to darken the theatre, to shush the crowd and hunker down into the mind movie. Alone. It is best in the middle of the day when others are working and the sun is shining beyond the walls of the darkened theatre. There is the stage. The curtains are pulled back, they are seldom used any more. We just want this all to play out and sit down and watch the mind movie. I hunker down in my chair feeling self relax spine, get into my hippie slouching curve going down notochord by notochord letting the breath brighten the dark corridors on inhale and set us into blessed dark on the exhale, in the great cavernous theatre and in between, at the still point at the bottom and at the top of breath, I pause, and let it take over, and feel it caring for me. It is into that place I want to go. Into the emptiness.

Yes, consciousness emerging from matter is sitting here in a movie theatre chair.

He could place his sensitivity, his attention, wherever he wanted. It is something we can all do with our mind. And he started to just construct the eyelashes around one of her eyes. He makes his first attempt to construct the deity.

> Avalokitsvara and Tara are in the wind caves
> And the internal eyes guided down and he looked inside at his coming and goings.
> He would know the deity in the In-Between states.
> In-Between breathing in,
> In-Between breathing out, he could sense in the centers of will that ran up and down the central axis of his spine the dimension of the possible becoming open to him. The eyes and the sex were on a channel and he could loft from out of and into these various areas and they were seen as expressions of the possibility of necessity, for the eyes are not possible without the body and the body is not possible without sex and the sex is not possible without the body, and there are so many things without which nothing would be possible and you have to be possessed of these centers of organization — ontological beauty and the force of will.

Walker knew he was going to try and apply the theory of Summon, Absorb, Bind, and Dissolve in some kind of poem-like verbal construction. He liked the idea of the point of view for this emptiness just being the idea of the eye floating over and into the ocean. Walker saw himself as inhabited by these entities, call them archetypes — animus and anima, the bohemian artist, the respectable adult. These archetypes were at war in his psyche and caused cognitive dissonance. In trying to give them an image he narrowed down to the three, at waist, heart and head. He made a first attempt at a prayer.

```
Prayer to Tara, my female archetype
The eyes are born of the two sexes and revel in
the pleasures of bilateral symmetry.
     May my eyes play and come to arrest themselves on
and in what is really there on the other side. May
they come to see the unified view which is
constructed out of the play of the two sexes —
though they seem to be separated one from the other
- really each eye is the inverse of the other,
seeing what the other lets us see. Showing to the
other what it can see.
     I bow from the waist opening up my spine and my
heart to accept and visualize the luminous egg of
compassion growing around me. From these precious
places - waist, heart and head - until I can feel
them for myself, I pray you hold me tighter with
your loving hands of compassion.
     From the three beings within me who live in those
precious places: the big relaxed affable guy down at
the waist; the shy underdeveloped sensitive guy with
glasses at the heart; the penetrating, thrill-
seeking abstract mountain-climbing esthete in the
head; we pray to you really and truly be with us
with your grace.
     The intellectual one in the head tends to guide
the others around. Top-heavy and awkwardly looming,
looking for the next aesthetic kick, he spends way
too much of his time in the false gods realm. Bring
him back to be with the others.
     The pushed aside guy lingering quietly in the
corners of the heart would roar like a lion, but
needs to get a start.
     The big guy at the waist, has spent all of his
life trying to look smaller to fit in, to be more
aware of others. He is unable to be generous with
himself.
     We turn to you who are our inner source of
compassion and grace. If I could start to see with
your eyes, if I could take refuge behind your
```

protection, your generosity, it might empower me
enough to let that compassion begin at home, let
that be happening for myself.

Something of a transsexual nature, a being of a
transsexual nature begins to emerge it is a dual
being, a being on the other side of every breath.
And s/he has got an individual eye and an individual
sex made into two eyes and two sexes. And we have
two eyes because there are two sexes one in each
eye. The orb of one carries the form of the male sex
and the other that of the female sex but in each one
of the two there is the other and we carry one as
normal, but in play inside our private selves, there
is always the two sexes engendering what the eyes
see and each is sometimes a separate world and
sometime together.

Walker wanted to construct some kind of Buddhist
mind-movie meditation. He found that the easiest way into
that was Images. The body expresses itself in a language of
images. The personal mind likes to communicate with
images but the deeper mind communicates with light energy.
To get his start into the altered state of meditation he used a
little battery-operated egg-timer he got at the Ashby flea
market. He got going with an image. For some reason he
started by remembering a little piece of land in Canada, near
the Lower South River bridge crossing where there was a
mill, an old stone whitewashed mill down at the water's
edge.

He got this image of *himself* as the stone mill, with the
sun on it on an October day when most of the leaves were
gone and things were down to simplicity. And he could see
this mill house was divided right down the center. The left
side was strong and erect, and the right side was sagging
with structural damage, parts of a roof were caving in. It was
leaning onto the left side which had to hold up the right side.
He intuited it was his own body image.

He imagined he had gotten stuck into his bent shape
from a couple of sources. One while hitchhiking around the
US in the 60s with a suitcase (and in a sport coat! replete
with skinny tie, clean cut collegiate looks, before long hair
and backpacks) had made his posture lopsided because it
was a suitcase full of manuscripts. Another, he realized — it
goes a ways back to much earlier — it is a fighting stance,
very tense, frozen. There it is again in a later picture of him

in his marijuana patch.

He attempted to write his first sutra. He was trying to construct a deity by imaging a simulacrum. He was trying to reconstruct himself.

Ocean Sutra

When I meditate I get the feeling of being a drop in a great Ocean.

And the eyes open and close keeping the great orb bathed in a saline solution, with little cilia lashes waving like underwater plants anchored to the rock of the lid in a great ocean of light.

The eyes open and close like a pussy opens and closes —the eyes look out and bring in and the pussy looks in and brings out. And the Sea like an orgasm is a harmonic of the great rhythm coming in and going out - the great Mother rhythm. The rhythmic movement in sex permeates the body with joy. The rhythmic movement of the eye permeates the sight with de-light. A pussy is an eye that sees ontology and phylogeny and the pussy opens and a new body is cruising down the highway of evolution. And the eyes close and all those instants of spacetime are lost as if the body had never found its way. And who are we that accompany ourselves, we open the eyes and let the light slide down into the sight where it is partitioned off into action items.

Or not.

There are the pleasures of the un-grasping gaze.

Which leads to a deeper being. We open the eyes and enter into the skies. We close the eyes and look within and enter the entity. And just as light enters the eyes and slides down into the sight, we enter the world of our body because the world is like our body - our body is made of the world, and at the end of the world when we open our eyes for the last time, for one last look at the sky and cross over through that door the threshold into death and a world we do not know where. . .

Oh don't go there.

Take another notion. Think about your Yidam. I think about Joyce. In Heaven. Yes. Even there he has to steal pencils, so he can continue his novel about the Sea.

And the sex opens us like the ocean it approaches and touches us and invites us into it, though we are scared and have to let down our defenses, let ourselves be penetrated and let it penetrate us, and though we might feel like the most insignificant drop next to that ocean, we are part of that ocean and it is part of us. It is only our shadow side that keeps us from opening to it. Devotion to the Involution Ocean!

Close the eyes and open up to the involution ocean. Inside is a light as big as the sky. See what a marvelous symphony you are and fall down into that night.

But after writing this Ocean Sutra he felt creepy. Like he had defiled the pristine beautiful mindfulness spoken of, that he had somehow defaced the idol. This was not his intention at all. He recognized his Shadow had got into the works.

He had tried to avoid going into the shadow of death by invoking his Yidam, Joyce. Alas he was once again lost in the realm of the false gods; and yet he had recovered with an insight into his shadow who is also there and must be accepted.

Sept. 16   Reconstructing Sutra
I am learning to be an analyst, to look at the reverse, look at the opposite, look at the blocks of what is getting in the way of being in this primary relationship with the Deity.

When one sits down to meditate, he becomes like a drop moving toward the ocean, showing himself to the ocean. How does he do that? How is the human mind-brain system allowed to be a part of that? How can it allow itself to not be part of that?

What has to be overcome or better accepted or just dropped? What are the obstacles of alienation and avoidance, and slithering away.

Dahlia is Buddhist and she wants to be able to feel in the moment — the great oceanic moment, to whenever possible, realize you are present in that.

When we are confronted with that Ocean and feel ourselves to be a drop of that ocean, it so confronts our Narcissism, that we get closed off and we run away from it feeling inadequate, like Adam from paradise. Adam stopped the Dialog, he stopped the relationship because he felt like he a had broken with some code, some contract written down somewhere. I am trying to find the words for that dialog but I suspect as the Buddhist say, there is no code.

There is no somewhere.

What if everything was all right? Look at the flowers nodding to each other in the breeze.

The involution ocean is always there wondering where we are, what happened to us, when we hide ourselves in the obscurity of our shadow.

```
The Shadow
Insight into manifold. A Sutra is a thread in a
weaving together in space and time. Were the writers
of Sutra coming to know the spacetime manifold?
    Now, the way the resistance comes up, the
opposite comes up — you even get this picture of a
shape that is reversing its curvature, where the
derivative is the inverse, something digging in its
heels and working on a second order, the
acceleration of the rate of change in a
relationship. The Shadow is a derivative! It
operates as the "rate" of change to stop or reverse
the change. The reverse magnetically induces force
proportional to how fast the change occurs.
Reluctance times rate of change. It is always there.
Everyone has it. It operates like this: you have the
linear going toward, being attracted in, or at least
getting to a stasis of standing before, and knowing
and being known; then something operates in reverse:
look at what a terrible sinner you are — black with
sins. Or, look at how you have built up all this
world order and it is not good enough.
    And you stop the dialog, stop the relationship —
money, relationship, creativity — these are the
realms you operate in whether you avoid it or not.
    The Image is on the surface of this manifold.
What is beneath it? The Image is just a surface, and
look at how we imbue the image with a power, almost
like a kind of black magic at work.
    But by what authority? Where do you come to have
your authority to be standing-with the Ocean?
```

He began to wonder what words he could come up with
that would perform the Absorb, Bind and Dissolve actions
with this Deity he was trying to call down into his art. He
started to cluster. For Absorb, he thought of the commercial,
'absorbs 47 times its own weight in excess stomach acid.'
Wonder where they came up with 47, such a gnarly prime.
All primes are gnarly. What kind of writing would get
Absorbed across. Little fish words swimming together in
schools all moving in unison? Or maybe something like
Allen Ginsberg in Wichita Vortex Sutra or was it in
Plutonium Ode, coming to absorb the evil of plutonium in
his plump cherubic bardic body.

And Dissolve, what would that be? He got onto the
diffusion equation, what was the difference between diffuse
and dissolve and absorb for that matter. The diffusion

equation showed how the movement of something through a surface in space was related to the using up of its density in time. Here he had equated the HRI of Buddhism, with the H_{iel} of psychology, with the H, the Hamiltonian of the energy of a mind system. Now that was abstract. Yes, a wave/diffusion equation. Too abstract. He would absorb the deity with:

```
    the energy H_ieI
    where i is impulsive id
    e is negotiating ego
    I is social super-ego
    H_ieI = ∂(i)/∂t + ∂(e)/∂t + ∂(I)/∂t = ∇²(Ψ)
    a shape undulating in spacetime.
    a combination wave / diffusion equation
    (this must have blown Shrodinger's mind forever)
    and feel it separating and splitting
    out into time and other realms,
    meeting other entities like itself.
    Curving the spacetime around itself
    at great moments
    of birth and death
    when it comes in and goes out.
    For example where it creates the wind.

    In the process of therapy you might get pushed
into a paralysis, etc., have to feel these painful
things about yourself and be kind of stuck in that
for a while.
    And when you are doing constant therapy
everyday...
    You don't have the luxury of letting yourself
    deny and repress from one session to the next.
    Calm  — H_ieI = C, constant
    derivative = 0
```

And binding, fixing, gluing down. He would bind the deity with:

```
Tractor beams
    the light rays are really tractor beams,
    they attract you to certain realms.
    light path — optics they are creating an internal
physiognomy of clusters of control

    a kind of synesthesia must be going on down there
    you are following a script.
    light for clusters, organizations
    acting as tractor beams
```

```
Do not yield to attraction
toward the illusory lights of the 6 Lokas
Lust , hatred, stupidity, pride or egoism
jealousy
coercivity, susceptibility, permeability,
retentivity
induction, deduction, abduction, reduction
get picked up by the tractor beam of the light
rays of compassion
internal cinema - mind movie?
the subliminal opera, synesthesia
... dazzling and clear, adorned with glistening
drops and droplets.

I am falling headlong am zooming
    down an entrance ramp
    to a free way of light packets
    like a dew drop on a spider web
    we are all streaming into a great city,
        a light at the center.
        Signal on, I must merge with the flow,
            merge with the light
            merge with me.
```

And he wondered what would work to dissolve the deity into emptiness? What would that mean actually.

```
We want to sense this mind movie. We want to know
the entity behind my eyes. And this is where we
enter into a kind of emptiness where there is not
necessarily me watching? What would that be like?
    We can, it is difficult, but we can detach
ourselves from our regard and get back to the person
who is looking through our eyes, but then we can
only see ourselves from outside and we can't see
ourselves from inside.
    And the sky that we are looking at
carries the eyes along.
    The eyes are the sky's eyes.
    And we get these flashes of light first,
    and try to sink down into that
    and extend our awareness into further and further
    by trying to imagine these deities, doing
acquisition
    or approach to me deity.
    And the other way we get to approach it is
through sex...
```

During this time Walker spent yearning for and in one way or another attempting to generate something like the kind of metaphysical self-experiences spoken about in the Bardo Thodol and other works of Buddhism through writing and science, he began to get the feeling that he was getting in his own way. Theoretically it seemed straightforward enough: shape a work formed to call down the deity from nothing, then try and describe it by getting as close as you can with intricate rhythmic artwork until it lets us relax into the freedom of emptiness beneath it. But it just was not happening. Walker felt very grateful for the gift of these images from the Great Beyond that was trying to communicate with him. But he couldn't follow them; he couldn't have any control over them. He became afraid of not being able to go further, he became afraid that he was not worthy, that somehow it was something *he* was doing. Or maybe he just became afraid of following the unfolding of a deep sense of source connected to the Self. He couldn't follow them.

The writer in him was getting his ass kicked by the Deity for his attempts to observe and comment on his experiences. It is the hardest thing in the world to run with the Deity. And yet it should be just as natural as conversing. He concluded to drop that writer identity and put on his scientist identity.

Sept 25 Reconstructing Sutra
When you relax in meditation you feel a warm
brightness within. Sometimes there are flashes of
white light. It is the body expressing its joy that
you have come here to be with it and it is beckoning
you to approach. It is always sending out these
signals. In the books these are pictured as
elaborated Sanskrit letters for sounds and sound
particles called bindu, a seed syllable. Each sound
in a mantra is a seed syllable. Often depicting the
coming of a Bodhisatva to deliver you from out of
one of the six Realms. But they also have symbolic
design shapes, having to do with inviting
penetration of some kind, being open to receiving
the kind of energy, partly psychic, partly physical
that there is from this moment of your practice.
Meditation wants to entice you in just as the
dream does. You must get into the appropriate state.
You must tune the instruments to the phenomena that
you are trying to measure and explore. This is the
experimental method. Especially in the modern age of
uncertainty.

Mind Movie

EXTERNAL VIEW: We are looking at bubbles rising in a liquid. It is the Milican experiment. Slowly the white bubble sinks, and a red bubble rises. We get a feeling of being supported in a fluid.

SOUND TRACK: Breathing, rhythmically.

Voice Over: The flux lattice in the Buddhist H_{ieI} is rather loosely defined. It does not have the normal Narcissistic core seen in a standard population. The sublimation potentials in the Buddhist H_{ieI} are stronger than those in normal personalities which allow an unacceptable amount of flux creep due to magnetic field gradients. (Flux creep also occurs in the Buddhist H_{ieI} but at a much slower and tolerable rate.)

For the Buddhist who has learned meditation and mindfulness — that is has lowered his threshold of sublimation — he finds himself less and less trapped in the flux vortices and he finds more and more external magnetic behavior is reversible. (Yes yes yes yes yes, let us name these entities with these physical variables, — may as well, they are about as real for me here now, a guy trying to study the east - here in the west.) Look at how they describe Dewachen; it is the physicality of consciousness!

Dewachen

In the Tibetan Book of the Dead (by now my copy had pages flying out of it and was held together with a rubber band) it says:

If the consciousness escapes through the crown of the head (the opening of Brahma) the being will be reborn in Dewachen, the western paradise of Amitabha.

They want to block all the other portals for consciousness to escape and allow it only to come out the crown. All these different Buddhas, the Sambhogakaya Buddha, and the Amitabha Buddha.

Wow these guys are thinking of consciousness escaping and going to different places. Each place probably has a good side. The route through which consciousness passes. . .

Focus your mind on a HRI in the heart of the deity. Different lights radiate out to all the Buddhas and Bodhisatvas, and to the peaceful and wrathful deities.

They in turn send forth light which is the essence of all the Buddhas.

This is absorbed through the top of the head.

To bestow benefit by compassion the consciousness becomes a white HRI "standing on a sun-moon seat."

465

Light radiates from the HRI to the Buddhas and Bodhisatvas of the ten directions who descend to bestow their body, speech and mind empowerment and to offer a way out of the wheel of becoming onto the human path. The HRI is transformed into the Yidam with whom the being wishes to merge.

Wow the HRI is a sigil that is used to seed exchanges with the Buddhas. What an amazing map and technology this is of consciousness.

With his compassionate eyes Chenrezig sees the needs of all beings. Make your gaze into the gaze of compassion itself. The Bardo Thodol was Padma Sambavda's HRI. Complete Joy. Beyond the divine body of incarnation representing complete joy beyond dualistic grasping.

Yes, Yes! YES!! I'm on the right track! The physicality of consciousness. What on earth would that mean?!

This is describing light channels and their subtle shifting due to magnetic alignments, which can be changed by something as simple as a mudra hand position.

You are going back to the "real" world but now know you are carrying a special kind of understanding of how the mind constructs phenomena, that you have more control over things and a better understanding than you did before.

To visualize the chakras it was easy enough to imagine a chord stretched up straight with colored beads on it. It made sense, the talk about the internal lights, and being asked to visualize these centers which represent evolutionary organizations.

Then upon zooming in and closer examination one could see that they ARE perhaps little worlds, these centers of organization that had evolved their own spaces perhaps, and that a human being was held up and healed up in a great part by these centers of organization — called chakras.

Struggling even harder against the terror of identity loss, Walker went into a manic phase. He decided to treat the work of generating interior lights, bindu as they are called, with the seriousness of science that it deserved. After all this was Vedic Science. He began to conceive of an experiment that would involve psychology and mysticism. He would sit himself down and using Auming, Chanting, and perhaps Primal Scream Sound (if necessary) see if he could generate and move intereoceptive lights.

He started to write up the experiment in a traditional experimental write-up just as he had been taught in school. He'd have to have the Purpose, a Description of the Apparatus, the Observations, and the Conclusion. The Conclusion should, if possible, agree with the purpose which was to examine and verify some theoretical position.

Walker got the key to the Sound Proof Room in the warehouse theatre from the owner. The sound proof room had been built by Doug in the 1970s for what Doug called "scream travel" — uninhibited, long-duration Primal Screaming. Walker was terrified of this idea. And hoped he wouldn't have to use it to get results. But he decided to go ahead and try to experience it if necessary. The intense sound would be provided by Auming and at times primal scream.

O'Keefe showed him the Thai Buddhist position, kneeling with a cushion between the legs. Walker found he could go the longest in this position. And it started becoming wonderful. He dissolved into lights, which came and went, and could be bent according to how well his spine was balanced. Balancing well for a very short time might occur, and this symmetry reduced the noise in the system allowing atunement.

He thought of this as building the apparatus.

The bubbles or bindu — in sound they are seed syllables; in visuals they are small spheres — bubbles, of light. He would be moving a bubble of white light down from the brain to meet a bubble of red light moving up from the waist, and these two would collide and in some way ignite at the heart. He would also attempt to monitor the bubble size and have it grow from something internal to expand outside the body into a kind of aura and perhaps even further. He would also investigate possible resonating with the earth's magnetic field.

Walker thought about how thrilled and astounded Tesla had been by the possibilities of using the (7.8 Hz) resonance frequency of the earth for the transmission of electrical energy without wires. Tesla wanted to tickle the capacitance between the earth and the sky with radio frequencies to deliver free energy to everyone. This was for him a means of furthering world peace. He said it seemed as though the Creator himself had electrically designed this planet for this bountiful expression of its generosity. Reich with his orgone would have understood this too.

Moving Seed Syllable experiment
Definition.

Somatoluminescence is the experience of interior lights in that hypnagogic or hypnotic, somnambulate state between waking and sleeping, assisted by the use of sound and resonance. Interior lights were first documented over 5000 years ago in the Vedas.

Purpose.

The aim of this work was to construct apparatus to enable the excitation and observation of Somatoluminescence, and to investigate its basic properties. Somatoluminescence is a little-understood phenomenon whereby intereoceptive lights are observed and manipulated. Ancient Vedic Science literature and basic meditation visualization asks the student to visualize small pinpoint scintillations of lights, a white one in the brain and a red one in the genitals, and to move these lights toward each other until they merge in the heart.

Apparatus

Preparation of the body to be used for the somatoluminescence vessel.

I started meditating using lotus position because it provides the greatest stability and straightest, least-fatigued spinal column, though it can only be held for short periods of time due to pain on the knee joints. Switching to the Thai meditation posture got much better results.

A great deal of the ouvre seemed to be finding a way to rest the body on its own skeletal structure, to minimize dependence on the musculature holding the body up. In particular to get the butt to relax, let the gut hang over the hips and reach a state of easy breathing. This took a long time, to achieve balance of the spine as if you were being suspended on a string from the ceiling.

We began to think of this as the vessel or the container in which the experiment phenomena was going to take place. The whole idea is to reduce mechanical stress on the joints. To allow muscles to get to a state of quiescence and relaxation. The work of holding up the body was to be done by fascia tissue.

Conjecture:

Theoretically this alignment would allow light to be polarized by the human magnetic field which should also flow best in a state of minimum resistivity.

Theory suggests that stable trapping of a bindu at the center of the human neuro-perceptual system

localized in the torso vessel requires a shift from
a spatial to a temporal metaphor. This is because
the Sympathetic Nervous System has no direct sensory
inputs, observations must be transduced through
synesthesia. We would be setting up an acoustic -
synesthetic standing wave in the perceptual medium.
To get maximum energy the vessel must be excited at
its natural resonance frequency.

Human Resonance Frequency approximation.

For simplicity, we assumed the resonance cavity
vessel could be approximated by a round-bottomed
flask filled with water. We calculated the volume of
the column for a person with a 34 inch waist and a
trunk of 3 feet. Plugging this value into the
formula for resonance frequency of a cylinder yields
a resonance frequency of approximately 2.1kHz. for
the human body. Note that this frequency is a
harmonic of the resonance frequency of the earth's
magnetic field (7.8hz.). Note also that the 1st, 2nd
and 3rd harmonics of this frequency in the audio
range correspond to the phonemes OH Aaah Hum.

Resonator Instrumentation

Now the mechanism to tune or resonate is also the
vessel. What resonates? It would be when acoustical
cavities are filled with energy? There are three
acoustical cavities, in the nose, in the head and in
the chest; there are others. The phonemes Hum, OH
and Aaah are the respective resonance frequencies of
these cavities.

The object is to vary the volume and pitch of the
Aum mantra sounds to achieve maximum resonance. This
is tuning the sound generator to the best resonance
with the vessel (body). A weak correlation
relationship was found between bindu movement
characteristics and sound intensity. (See below.)

I found it useful to recall the Milican oil drop
experiment: one looks through a small telescope into
a small container of viscous fluid suspending tiny
and quite lovely bubbles. This fluid is between the
+ and - of a voltage potential and you can move the
bubbles because they hold a charge that is a
multiple of the number of electrons on the bubble,
up and down by changing the field. It gives the
first physical intuition into the reality of the
electron. I started with this memory and using the
imagination, visualized the medium as something like
the clear fluid of Buddhist clarity - this against
the background of a spotless phenomenological mirror
surface. Upon this visual space I was to project -
first one bindu and then the two bindus which were
easily observed to emerge. Somatoluminescence!

The observations were what kinds of condition
enabled the bubbles to glow more and to remain

stable, rather than dissolving into distraction. The idea is to vary the sound input into the human perceptual mechanism and to look at the output on the screen of the imagination.

It was found that the sound was not necessary to produce bindu but once produced did enhance stability and intensity. The ancient Buddhist mantra Oh, Ahh, Hum! which resonates in the head, the waist and the heart produced the best results. These do indeed seem to be the resonance frequencies of the body acoustical cavity.

Viewing the glowing bindu

Sound was not necessary; breathing and focus enable one to trap a small stable bindu, both in the mind and in the lower chakra area. The bindus could only be held in place for a short while before the mind was pulled into other considerations. A faint bluey-white glow, like starlight, was seen from the bindu in the center of the human neuro-perceptual system localized in the torso vessel - Somatoluminescence! If the drive level was cautiously increased, the glow from the bindu could be made brighter, and more all-pervading but too great an increase caused saturation to occur and the bindu to redissolve and be lost in self-consciousness and spiritual materialism. When lost, the drive could be backed off a fraction, and relaxation usually precipitated a new bindu. After stabilizing for a second or so, the new bubble glowed as before.

Conclusions:

Under all circumstances, best Somatoluminescence was observed when the vessel was held in a stable, symmetric, well-balanced meditation configuration. The use of sound furthered relaxation, but did not influence the onset of bindu production directly. Sound did increase the intensity of produced bindus but was not pivotal in their production.

The bindus excited a somatoluminescence, a fluorescence, a harmonic resonance in the body which could be sustained for varying lengths of time, at certain times. They could be expanded outward to surround the body like a luminous egg. It was felt they are synonymous with Sympathetic Nervous System resonance to the expression of simply being.

But that wasn't getting him any closer to what he desired. One day he got mad. Started crying. Started raving. I'm tired of always having to be someone else, some other identity than who I really am, tired of not feeling like myself of having to be another. Tired of being a slave to my Yidams, even though I love and admired them. What if I just dropped all this striving? What if everything was OK just the way it is and I could be just the drop in the ocean that I am.

He was finally starting to ask the question. The question who am I. That would be his mantra. Who am I.

The Freedom of Emptiness

I have to let go of that science guy, as an image, as the mythology I am trying to live up to, that I am using to defend myself against the emergence of my real identity. Identity is being trapped in a defensive posture. And I have to get rid of the lone writer myth guy identity. That is also an individual I am organized around and an identity I have to drop. Drop these identities and slip into the ocean of being. How do I do that? I am trying to get to a place of emptiness where I can truly say I am no one.

Who are you?

I am no one.

Oh, it was so terrifying to say that, to do that. But I know I must drop this identity and that identity and all the various identities that I present, and just say I am nothing. I am emptiness.

And for a moment he saw his own face from outside of himself. Looking at himself sitting in a chair he saw, instead of his face, there was a black void, filled with stars and planets. It was the face of the universe itself.

Who are you?

I am no one.

The universe is always out there always providing sustenance and energy, it cares for us in myriad ways because it wants to be known by each of us, and through each of us. That is why we are different! Through each one of us the universe has expressed itself in different ways. So that we may know this universe in different ways.

All these differences are ways that we get to know the one. It is like the separation out of the many from the one, the primordial separation of the waters. This is the way that makes each of us an individual knower of the one.

How would I know? What evidence would there be? Evidence of emptiness? It is a dialog? Yes. And the way you start it is with Who are you. I am no one.

And in that emptiness there is a great freedom, freedom to move around, freedom to be who we really are. Back to the person we were before he was bent. Back to when we were whole. And lived in relation to that wholeness.

We know. We've recognized our wholeness, at

moments, in jazz music sometimes, in poems
sometimes, in creative works —paintings, science, in
business, in family.

The Freedom of Emptiness

This is what if feels like to be in this place of
wholeness said John Coltrane.

This is what it feels like to be in the center
said Thelonious Monk.

This is what it is like to be touched by mastery,
and to get out of the way and let it talk through
you says Borges.

Art is made for the viewer to recognize the
wholeness in himself.

That is the welcoming.

From this time forward may I do everything from a
place of wholeness and a place that recognizes the
wholeness in others. May I tie my shoe from
wholeness. May I sweep the floor from wholeness. May
I cook from wholeness, do everything from wholeness.
Love with wholeness. Create my art from wholeness.
Then the world's just a kind of play. When you drop
the tension of maintaining a false identity, you can
feel the Movement of the universe within and without
you.

When you move you are reaching out for the
generosity of the universe and pulling yourself back
to your center. Back to the center. . .

So your practice is to observe both the wholeness
you are and to observe that in the context of moving
away from that and to observe that in others. Simple
isn't it.

That wholeness is expressing itself through you.

Don't get in the way.

Maintain the dialog. Ask:

Who are you.

I am no one.

People will knock you off your wholeness and you
can bless them for that.

Just remember over and over again you must
experience the primordial separation away from the
center. In order to know The Freedom of Emptiness
you must get into a dialog with deity. Ask yourself:

Who are you?

Let yourself answer: I am no one.

It is scary, you have to let go of the person you
think you are. To know The Freedom of Emptiness you
must ask yourself:

Who are you?

I am no one.

To let go of the person you want other people to
believe you are, and to become the person you really
are, ask:

Who are you?

I am no one.

51

A Gardener in the City

Theo gave Walker a much needed job doing labor in his
landscaping business. Walker took the opportunity to throw
himself into doing physical labor with plants because it was
a relief from his moody self-preoccupation. Theo had a very
large clientele among the sumptuous landscaped apartments
on Lombard Street, and the old money mansions on
Telegraph Hill. Theo had been a professor of Asian history at
the University of Hawaii, and had given that up to become a
gardener. He had apprenticed himself to Japanese gardeners
for many years and was very good at it. He had an old beat-
up Toyota truck with a camper shell on the back that was a
gardener's tool shed, full of mowers, shovels, picks and
rakes and saws and clippers. He and Walker trucked all
around Telegraph Hill and up and down Lombard Street. The
scenery and setting was so beautiful, moving in and out of
these sumptuous pads and palatial grounds, that it sometimes
was hard for Walker to concentrate. It was like having the
privileges of money without the burden. At each step you got
more scenery and a better view of the city. They were a
team. Theo installed microprocessor controlled irrigation
systems; Walker did the grunt work, digging ditches and
laying tubing, fitting sprinkler heads. He did the general
lawn mowing and clean up. Occasionally other members of
the House would be brought on to do the fine carpentry work
on more intensive landscaping jobs.

Theo brought an oriental look to the trimming and
pruning he did. He told Walker: "You've got to be like those
Japanese gardeners, out there with their brooms," -he
showed a relaxed sweeping motion back and forth- "they
sweep up every blade of grass. When I was apprenticed to
them they'd come along behind me and would find any
blade of grass that wasn't swept up."

Walker kept an eye out for the old guy, worried about
him climbing up and down trees, and volunteered for the
high work. Walker began to think of his work with Theo as

an opportunity to learn a new trade. Sometimes the view from a balcony or a gazebo was just stunning and the two ate their lunches in some of the most beautiful places in America. Walker took every opportunity to engage in discussions of Marx and Freud and Jung during their lunch hour.

Walker began to feel like he was in a utopian fantasy of Buddhist gardeners changing the world going in and out of these fine places and offices. Theo taught him some interesting Hawaiian like *haoli* and *pue kai ha wahine* which he understood means "ravish the young virgins." Walker bothered him a lot with questions about Buddhism in general and the practice and theory of the House. Walker tried his theories and ideas on this intelligent man to see if they might fly. He was working on what he called an Information Theory of the Self.

```
Sun.Oct.14.83
Notes Toward an Information Theory of the Self.
We write this like a program. First we define the
functions then we use them in programs which used
the hyphenated noun clusters as places in memory.
Phanopoeias.
We are designating areas of the brain as sources
of images, and as storage places of images. Storage
places of part of a much larger figure. Built with
Mantras and Visualizations. A subliminal opera.
```

Theo, though he liked the intellectual challenge, held the House position that excessive intellectualization was a defense mechanism. Sometimes, depending on the urgency of the job, Theo would take umbrage when Walker tried out ideas on him. "Subliminal Opera, what you talkin' 'bout boy?"

```
So we have clusters of sub-personalities or
collections of yidams.
We have gates that are opened and closed.
We have yidams and what guides the yidams, what
makes coalitions among the collections of yidams, or
what represents various organizations of the nervous
system. Call them psychoneural textures. These can
be like muscular knots, blocks, or they can be free
flowing sheets that go out of the body like jazz
music. Presence. The RiNpoche has a tremendous
presence.
```

The feelings that were coming up with his relationship life were so threatening to Walker's defense, that he called on his best defense against Eros, —Logos. He was aware that the House would think that by the intellectual machinations of creating theories about the mind he was masking the feelings that he doesn't want to feel. He rationalized it by recalling what Plato says: That a person touched by beauty would eventually want to study the theory by which Beauty was perceived.

Walker started asking more and more questions about Buddhism. He started making map-ups between Buddhism and computer science. He drew a picture of a being in meditation posture. All across the cortex there were wave shapes. He wrote in his diary.

```
   At the 3rd eye: Intuition (teaching from inside)
video screen of synesthetics.
   Throat: voice. How you make yourself heard in the
world.
   Thymus: seat of the Immune system, that which
differentiates between self and other.
   Heart: love
   Solar plexus: Breath, ATP distribution Wind
spurts, energy , lungs.
   Genital: the mixer, seat of attraction, a later
stage of
   Anal: The base chakra.
```

He asked Theo if the Buddhists can maybe feel the parts of their minds and chakra system. "It's like how the word Muse comes from Memory plus the Sky. Wow, can you imagine it at times when you just feel so loose and you've dropped the grubby parts of your personality for a while and you just want to be present and feel. Compassion is an attitude about time that helps in the dropping of tension so that you can sense the movement of the generosity in the world."

Theo smiled at the distraction. He said, "Buddhists start to feel their crown. The cortex. They feel the other chakras and the spaces or dimensions which these chakras center."

Walker said: " Wow. It's like these weird topologically connected spaces. . ."

But Theo interrupted him. "Well I'm not payin' you to theorize, lets get back to work."

Walker became more sensitive of Theo clamming up

after a while, thinking maybe Theo's just a quiet Buddhist and I talk too much. Maybe he just wants to do quiet meditative work.

Computers were starting to proliferate, and they were using a microprocessor in the irrigation system. Walker had studied architectures in school, and now he began trying to understand both the computer and the mind by making analogies between them.

We organize space with an array of memory. Architectures of microprocessor-like architectures of Buddhism.

You have a basic operating system. Then you have memory being used up in the same amount by a part that processes language. Then a larger section allocated to working storage, how we process the verbal flow, then an unused section in which there is much room for expansion.

We are talking about the ways that one should organize his memory allocations. And how one can exchange old outmoded paradigms and attitudes for more streamlined and useful ones.

What has happened to us by the hard behavior modification of social injustice? The cortex has come to dominate the autonomic nervous system. This is antigenetic. The autonomic nervous systems is the operating system, being influenced by the compiler.

What is a compiler? It is a negotiator and collector, a way of translating one language into another, where the new language is of a greater depth, in terms of being able to communicate more directly with the physical hardware. What gets compiled are the parts that the program needs to be present and to work, they are pulled together and linked up by the compiler. For example, the integrative facility necessary to read this text is literacy. Literacy is a compiler. Feel that under your brow. We have the cortex or superego as the compiler. And the CNS as operating system.

It is not a good idea to let the compiler have so much control over the operating system. So one should go into the mind and get the compiler out of the operating system.

A rallying cry.

GET THE COMPILER OUT OF THE OPERATING SYSTEM! Or we need to get a new compiler. This is like the negotiator who tries to keep peace among the sub-personalities.

The negotiator. He moves things around in the memory.

How wonderful it would be to be able to relax and feel yourself beneath the ego, feel the unconscious protecting the conscious, feel the self protecting the ego. Instead of the ego fighting with the self, instead of the self being thwarted from having feelings.

This is a different way around from what it usually is. Makes me feel kind of lonely, like because the women are so distant, so clinical.

Walker was always thinking about Dahlia. Right after they were together the last time, they had had breakfast and a nice talk at the Acme Cafe on 24th, she went to a ballet class, and in doing a leap, had broken her foot. Now she was hobbling around the loft with one foot in a big cast. She had gotten into some horrible fights with Malcolm and others as they explained to her how she was trying to do herself in, etc. Many eyebrows were raised when it came out that Walker was the last person she had been with before the accident, etc.

Early one morning Walker saw Dahlia, moving around the loft in the nude. There she was with crutches, foot in a cast thumping along like a damaged angel being the 6 to 8 person (a person who woke up early and, with a list, went around and gently awakened those who had requested it the night before). This angel was the first person they saw in the morning. She looked good. She is getting a little fuller in the hips. She is the spirit of mirth and wit, contained in a body that is getting stronger. Good. Need to encourage that.

At work with Theo one time, Walker was talking about what he had read in Freud. Talking about the map-up of the stages of arrested development, or the various neurotic positions and the theory of the chakras. Talking about Freud's theory of energy. Authenticity. Walker noticed when Theo was getting kind of testy around all of his questioning and went into the garden they were working on. Walker picked a beautiful rose.

Theo teased him. "Why don't you take it back to the commune and give it to Dahlia?"

"Naw, I'd be laughed out of the commune if I did."

"Yea, you sure would. People would start to say, 'What

has she done to that boy?' You know what Freud said?"

"No. What?"

Theo smiled a teasing smile and said, "Love ain't nothin' but a non-familial libidinal object cathexis." Theo laughed. He had a big grin on his face and wiggled his eyebrows up and down, as if to say: see I can talk that talk.

"What?!" Walkers eyes grew large as he tried to figure the meaning while feeling bested at the word game.

"That's what the man said."

—

One day Theo said, "You would not make a good permanent gardener, because you have studied all this physics and are going to be looking for a good job. You are going to be wanting a lot of money. And plus I hate getting involved with people from the House, because pretty soon, they are going to want to bring it up in Big Group, find out what kind of trip is going on with us."

Walker said, "What trip? What we're doing is going in and out of these fine pads in San Francisco's Russian Hill section, laying in irrigation systems with microprocessor controls. What else is there to say!"

—

The next time Walker was in front of Big Group, Theo was very helpful to his cause. He said, "I wonder if he knows what goes on around here. Maybe he just thinks it's 'Make love to a pretty girl and then she shrinks your head'."

52

Dolores Park

Walker went to the Loft for the first time in a long while. He pressed the buzzer to the Penthouse. Someone going out held the door for him. He went up through the roof garden, up to the mirrored sliding glass door. The loft lay inside. Would it be like always, like going from shadow into light? From black and white into color? From the macrocosm of Kansas into the microcosm of Oz? Where broken hearts, weak minds and slippery spines are made strong?

He knew he was in deep trouble for not going on the Labor Day work trip up to the land. He had gotten 'the fear' and called up Dahlia and not knowing how to ask for what he wanted gave her an ultimatum, either he gets to ride up to the land in her car, or he's not going.

He ended up not going.

He had projected his paranoia onto these good people. Would they have him back? He felt much fear and trepidation.

He stepped over the threshold and was in. He sat down on the stairs to take off his shoes. Tom came by, gave him a smile and rubbed his hair. Waker's hair was radically short, the shortest haircut he'd had since he was 13. He felt like about 13. He got a plate, listening to remarks about his short hair and chides as to why he hadn't been around in a long time. He joked, "Yeah, I was thinking about waiting until it grew back out before I came over."

He got into a hug with Beverly, tanned, back from the land.

The strawboss directed him outside onto the roof to get into a session with Eric. Eric starts to subtly grope into him. He fills Walker in on the seriousness of his standing and the situation.

"Tell me something about where you come from?" Eric asked in a casual, interested way. Soon they have discovered a similar background with alcoholic parents. Turns out his mother was an alcoholic.

"She would sit in the chair when she came home after drinking and nag," Eric said. "She would nag all the time. That's what she would do. Nag."

Walker said: "My father was an alcoholic too. For 20 years. Every night it was the same thing. He would come home late for supper after stopping at various ice houses in San Antone to drink a beer. He had a great attraction for these dark rundown dingy dives. Soon my parents were raising their voices in anger at each other and it would escalate into a fight. It was the same game every night. He would provoke my mother and get her so worked up about having to hold dinner, that this fight would allow him to storm out of the house and then to drink and carouse to all hours of the night. Then he would come home way past midnight and my mother would begin screeching and walking around slamming doors. Horrendous fights. I hated her for being so dependent, for having to stay with him. And for waking us up, it felt like she was punishing us to get back at him."

After a while he and Eric stopped talking and hooked up. Walker looked into Eric's kaleidoscopic green eyes. Eric has a round bright playful Cheshire cat face, with a mischievous smile. Walker took off his glasses to let him look more into his eyes.

"You've got a very Texas face," remarked Eric.

"What does that mean, I come from Canada."

"It has this set in the lower part, that is very much like what I've seen in men from the south." He grinned, "It's sort of a John Wayne face."

"O *nooo*! I've got a John Wayne face." Walker grimaced like the man on the bridge of the Edvard Munch painting.

Eric started talking about paranoia, and about when you are in paranoia, small remarks get made large. He summarized his understanding of Walker's fear: "It was probably a fear of facing something that would have come up on the trip."

Then Eric talked about his own father. "He would say things like 'I'm not good enough for you' to my mother and really put himself down. It was very sado- masochistic."

"How was it sadomasochistic?"

"It was sadistic, because it was designed to control my

mother, to keep her in a dependency. And it was masochistic because he put himself down so much in it."

"Oh, I see."

Walker began to get this image of how it was in his own family between his parents. A realization tried to struggle to the surface. He struggled to keep it down. He felt a lot closer to Eric though, for giving him a parallel form with which to probe his own memory and situation. The same. Identify with some other situation. Yes, my mother and father were in a the same sado-masochistic romance. Was all romance sadomasochistic. Was the Catholic Church sadomasochistic, with this picture of the family, the mother having to intercede with god the father who was also the son. Incredible male control trip there. Or maybe it *is* the natural way of things or was once.

"Well they are probably going to want to talk to you in group."

"O no! Are they going to have a Big Group about me?"

"I used to be scared to be in Big Group. I remember one time when I shaved my hair off, when my parents came to Hawaii I wasn't even going to see them on the second day, I was so freaked out."

They were all sitting in a circle. Dahlia on one side of Malcolm, Walker on the other. Theo was sitting in beside Walker. The rest of Dahlia's group — Nancy, Mario, Denise, Lissa, Scott. were there. Rachel, Morey and Jade from Walker's old group were there.

Eric came over and said "I hooked up a bit with Walker before in a session, and I'd like to sit in for a while."

It was like a convocation of chameleons. Everyone was looking around and away from each other. Some behind the scenes power struggle and machinations had gone on or so Walker thought. Dahlia had her hair pulled back in a severe bun.

"Why don't you start," Malcolm said, looking at her.

Dahlia cleared her throat: "I need to talk about my dependency. I'm worried about my own dependency on Walker. I use it as a way to run away from the hard times in my own group."

Walker saw little six year old Dhyana off out of the

corner of his eye. She smiled at him showing her new front teeth. She came around in a wide circle out of the edge of Walker's peripheral vision and when she got near to him, she touched his head from behind.

Jade smiled.

Walker could feel the child's good feelings coming up through most everyone. Then it all started to come out. Walker said: "I was just scared that I wouldn't be able to hook up with anyone on the trip and that everybody would be talking to me about getting a haircut and my dependency on Dahlia."

Then Theo talked to Dahlia. "It is like the Catholic trip, going to the confessional the way you listed off the things that you said."

Then Malcolm talked to her. He told Dahlia: "You use Walker to manipulate your relationship with me."

Then everybody was saying lots of stuff. Walker thought Theo, especially, was on his side. He talked slow and calm, was really sure. He and Walker had gone on jobs together and hung out together and drunk beer together. Walker could listen to what he's saying.

Then Morey said, "Sometimes double messages have occurred in the past, because of our own hard time. But now we want to get more serious. You've got to treat this like you would an appointment with the doctor. So let's say that if you miss another day, then you have to take a month off."

Walker opened his eyes wide to register shock. He thought: They are really putting the screws to me. My name is mud. I have no place to bargain from.

"Well I have no manual to read, and I just wander around and blunder into things, and then people tell me what to do," he said, feeling sorry for himself.

Dahlia looked pensive. She said, "I admit, that sometimes I have sent double messages in the past because of my own dependency."

Walker countered: "I use the good times I have with you to motivate me to come over here and work on myself."

"Run!. . . Run!" Morey shouted. "You use them to run! You use them to run away from your own group."

"No I don't."

"I think you're lying," Scott snarled.

"I think that you know more than that," Theo said. "You know more than what you are talking about. We all have a hard time getting together. It can't be that scary."

Rachel got all huffy and irate: "This is our HOUSE, and we really don't WANT to have you come over here and ARGUE." She glared at him. To Walker she looked like his enraged mother. "We don't CARE to have you come around here on your terms."

Dahlia said: "I can't believe you decided to act out that dependency, calling me on the phone like that. It felt just like boyfriend and girlfriend! . . . I feel like I'm my MOTHER and I'm hiding my father out at my house. Like I'm hiding you out here."

Rachel said: "And then you called over here yesterday with the mistaken idea that you thought you had a session with her. So we don't think it is appropriate for you to be having sessions with Dahlia for a while."

Theo and Morey were discussing the situation.

"Yes," they pronounced, "we don't think it is appropriate for you to be having sessions with Dahlia for a while."

Both Morey and Rachel emphasized the verdict in unison, "We don't think it is where IT'S AT for you two to be getting together."

Morey said: "So no sessions for two months."

Walker was severely stricken with anger upon hearing this. It was all he could do to keep himself from jumping up and shouting, Fuck you Rachel. You're just vindictive because I wouldn't get into sex with you if you were the last woman on earth!

And walking out of there.

He felt completely blown away. Unable to speak.

"*AND* we think that you should also make it part of your agreement to come on Thursdays."

Walker balked: "I've got something going on on Thursdays."

"What?"

"A dance class."

"A dance class! I'm insulted!" Scott exclaimed.

Rachel pushed forward enjoying having the upper hand. "Yes. We'll make it part of your agreement, to come over here on Mondays and Thursdays. . . And if you miss, to not come over for a MONTH."

Wow. Walker was shocked and hurting, but remained silent. Then they talked to him about his humor.

"It must be some kind of defense mechanism," Walker retorted.

"Don't be so naive!!" they exclaimed.

Walker was glad when they finally let up and he was out of the center of attention.

His feathers were certainly ruffled, but he managed to hang in for this rocky patch. Even though he was shocked he also felt like he was on the receiving end of something like tough love. His mind drifted over the events of his being in love with Dahlia. There was so much come-here and go-away ambivalence with Dahlia all through our love. This was just more of it and it too would soon blow over. Or at least I hope it will.

So he decided to stay. He got down on the carpet to listen to a tape that Denise had made of a phone conversation with her brother and her mother about going down there for a visit next weekend. At one point in the taped conversation, loud moaning and auming could be heard in the background. Mario and Walker giggled.

To Walker, Dahlia said, "You could be taking this more seriously," in an arch, disapproving tone.

Like a child being chastised by his mother, Walker retorted, "Well he was doing it too!" And then quickly thought: O, NO! What have I done.

Everybody looked at him like he had just made the most odious of *faux pas*.

"THAT was a very punky remark," said Theo.

Dahlia reached over and abruptly snapped the tape player off. People drew up into group position, sitting cross-legged, spine elongated, serious focus on, as though the group had reconvened and they were going to focus on Walker again.

Walker quickly drew himself into lotus position for the words that were about to be coming down.

"I can't believe we just spent an hour talking to you about taking all this more seriously," she said. "What's so funny?"

"Well. . . the situation. Somebody outside the house

hearing all that moaning going on in the background through the telephone!"

"It is NOT a funny situation," Denise said. "I was contemptuous of my brother, and I was subservient to my mother, and I'm getting ready to go down there this weekend."

"You're talking to Dahlia like she was your MOTHER," Theo said in an exasperated way.

And indeed I had, Walker realized. Here I am . . . being scolded by her and I'm in that old familiar kid-with-ruffled-feathers look again. O, my God, I'm acting like a 4 year old.

How obvious, how terrible, how naked, he felt.

To Dahlia, Theo said: "And you're being very scolding, and acting in it WITH him."

After this replay, they settled down and Denise spoke about her situation. Walker just wanted to keep a low profile.

Later, Walker saw Leslie through the glass doors on the staircase. She came down and said "I was looking for you. You're my session person for tonight."

Walker was standing there looking like a lout drinking a Heinekin out of a paper sack.

"Lets go for a walk," he said. "It's such a nice night."

Walker put his arm around her as they walked out onto Army Street across to the little mom and pop grocery and headed toward Dolores Park.

"Want to walk to Dolores Park?" he said.

"I wasn't in your group tonight," Leslie said, "and here we are going to have a session. What went on with you? I don't want to just be light."

They got to Dolores Street. Walker was thinking, Leslie seemed like a good ole girl. A good humorous woman, he corrected himself. It felt good to be with her. She was gentle and had a light touch.

Walker didn't know what to say.

How do I feel? I have lost Dahlia. . . Now it was formal and out front. I couldn't sleep with her, they didn't think "it was where it's at" for us to get together.

He dropped his empty beer bottle into a large unlocked bin where it clanked in the hollow eptiness and bonked in the bottom of night. The night was warm. Sultry.

"I want to walk on Dolores Street."

"What's the thing about Dolores. Did you have a girlfriend named Dolores?"

"No I just like the name. It means sad, kinda hot and sad . . . like tonight."

Or inflamed, and soulful, he thought. It *was* a soulful night to be out walking with a soulful woman. They walked along and he thought of Dahlia, and all that hot dark-eyed sad-eyed Mexican beauty and he had been her Lucky Pierre lusty French Canadian.

Getting more maudlin about it, he thought: We had walked our time together upon the stage but all paths are confluent with underground paths found when you exhume the surface of the soul. And the great heaviness of his broken heart came rising up into the body and the sad city undulated with a vague movement like a gravity wave and he missed a step and the soul moved up and down like a perfect bi-winger dragonfly on the in and out of respiration and caught him from falling.

"I think I'd like to write a piece about Dolores Park" he said. "It was incredible here last weekend. Did you see Whoopie Goldberg? She just completely dominated this whole big mob of snarling punk rockers in black leather jackets. Had complete control. It was a thing called Rock Against Reagan."

"No, I didn't."

"Well anyway, I think to write about the HHG gang, the Happy Homes Grande gang. They run this turf around here at night. About the Mission and the life here."

"Why not the Golden Gate park?" she suggested.

"Too big. We want a small microculture, so we can think about it. One that reflects the city."

It would feel better around the loft. The loft is like Dolores Park. I would just kind of be invisible. Nobody says Hi. Nobody says anything. You are just simply and existentially there. For them most of life was projection.

It's not just the sex I'll miss but the high conversation. A conversation that touched into all those individual interior complications and admired and adored them just like how I touched all her body.

What is it that gets between.

Dolorous: to feel pain, grief, mental suffering, anguish, sorrow, inflammation of the heart.

Walker had to steel his heart, could not loose it.

Maybe I wasn't Mr. Right. But I was Mr. Right Now. He tried to catch himself up into the present now moment of existence. I am out with this good woman. Maybe she could take my mind off my troubles. There was a good-spirited humorousness about Leslie. Maybe not all of it was intended.

Romance. So? So what if I can't hook up with Dahlia's good female energy any more, and feel the firmament in her body through my fingers traversing her skin.

Couples were strolling hand in hand or arm around each other across the top of Dolores Park. They appeared to be in love. Look at all the pitifully deluded romantics still believing in all that. So what if we don't hook up in sex and fall through the night like a shooting star. So what if she isn't my guiding light through the emptiness and obscurity I feel. So what if my day will be entirely bare of her girlish spirit from under the skin. So what if I won't be able to crawl into the warm bed of my protectress.

So what if we no longer make that complete combination trance to see the inner lights with. I couldn't care less. If I no longer felt the tender invisible fibers of belief. I have to find out if it is really me feeling all this and it's not the combination being that we were, the star-gate that we created together. But I can't hold onto romance because it's not Real and this door is not open to me anymore. And that like my mother pushing me out into the world I'd have to go it alone. I'd have to leave this bright orbit and cruise through hell but could stay in the influence of the House and that for a while we'd have to be like ghosts for each other, untouchable and invisible. Because we have and there are only memories.

I cast my gaze upon the larger humanity of the tribe. She was the cause of my attraction and exerted strong forces of gravity to change my ways, for my own betterment. And hope that there will be a day, for there still is hope, that we will get together again. Where we will lay side by side basking in each other's warmth and we become again one continuous being and meltdown, dissolve, fade entirely into the earth and time.

That thing that a man and a woman create from the best part of his male energy —fast aggressive — is complemented by her female energy — nurturing, caring, future-involved.

Back at the loft Walker helped Leslie set up her plush futon outside on the roof underneath the city skies. Then she came out with some dope. He could be a happy man, propped up on an extra sleeping bag, another cool Heinekin by his side, and a smoke of some fine herb and a very fine warm humorous woman being there with him.

Now these women who have been in the House for a long time always pretty well speak their mind. And Walker was finally letting some of his uptightness drop off.

"I couldn't find my cervical cap," she said.

"That's sort of like a diaphragm, right?"

"Yeah. . ."

"I couldn't find my gel either," she said.

"That's like a spermicide, right?" he said.

She looked at him quizzically. They started hugging and auming together in a most gentle way. She feels very slow, soft, light, yet there and sure of herself.

Then he felt her pull away and become pensive.

"I can't believe I can't find my contraceptive kit. Jade came and borrowed my cervical cap, and I told her to put it back in the same place." She continued: "I am part of this study going on at San Francisco State, where they fit this average sampling of women with a cervical cap and another bunch with diaphragms. I am supposed to keep a record of my periods and a diary."

"Have you been doing it."

"Not that much."

"How long ago did you start this program"

"Around 4 months."

"And you haven't kept any record of it?"

"Yeah, there is some record."

After a while she said, "I think I'll go look for it."

She was gone for a long time, because after he gazed at the stars for a while he kinda was dozing off. It was so nice and snug under the blankets out on the roof.

When she got back she announced triumphantly, "I

couldn't find the cap, but found the spermicide!"

"You don't believe in the condom?" Walker asked her again.

"Yeah, well . . . I think it is a good idea to use both."

She proceeded to fill a large hypo with the creamy stuff and insert it way up her vagina and fill herself with spermicide.

He said, "I always like to use a condom. That stuff scares me."

"Why?"

"Well, it might go after bigger stuff."

"What do you mean?"

"Well it kills sperm, it might go after bigger stuff, might go after the source."

They got back into position and as Walker was about to enter her, she pushed him off her. She gets her tube of spermicide and proceeds to fill up another hypo full and insert this large cylindrical applicator slowly up her vagina and plunging the valve shoots a huge load of the white stuff up her.

Kind of grossed out by this he said --trying to avoid any hint of sarcasm, "If you want I'll put on a second condom."

"Might be a good idea," she urged.

"So I'll put on this more deluxe lamb-skin condom over the other one."

It was that old perverse influence again. Going along with the ludicrousness of the situation. He would not be able to feel a thing. On the other hand, he could hang in and have sex for a long time. The long hard ride.

He got on top of her. He was getting limp from lack of stimulation. He had to put his hand down there to pry the rascal into her.

"You sure did use a lot of that cream," he said. While she wasn't looking he rubbed a bunch of the gunk on the pallet.

He slipped it in and began working. He hoisted her legs way up over her shoulders, and began slamming it deep into her. She seemed to enjoy it although she looked a little askance at first. At him working so hard at it. But all the friction had made him good and hard again and he liked the work.

like a mirage moving across a landscape in Spring-time

Part of *Dolores Park* first appeared in "Scanner Magazine —
Proceedings of the 8th Actualist Convention in Berkeley, 1984"
under the title: Notes for Culture-Independent Awareness.

Dolores Park

Cultivating the Texas Twister Hybrid

Michael Lyons

HiT MoteL Press

Zenobia

Michael Lyons

The Indigenous Tribesmen of Neverland

Michael Lyons

The Secret of the Cicadas' Song

Catalog of Works
Current
&
In-progress

A Blue Moon in August

knight of 1000 eyes

Michael Lyons

Other books in the "My Years of Apprenticeship at Love" series

Dolores Park is the third book in the series. Lonely Texas redneck cowboy pursues love interest into a feminist Tantric Buddhist sex commune. He falls in love with a beautiful Tantrika and through the magic of romance, psychotherapy and Buddhist trance he discovers the path to enlightenment.

It is a seeker's journal experiencing the coming to acceptance of psychic reality. (2001)

Dolores Park

a novel by
Michael Lyons

Zenobia

Michael Lyons

Zenobia is a psychotherapeutic journey exploring the Mother and the Whore syndrome, common in the American male psyche. It illustrates Freud's precept, that a man is born of two women. Walker the down-and-out Berkeley slacker creates an alternative astrology for the modern world with new signs for a blues zodiac. He learns to dance to swing music.

A Blue
Moon in
August

A Blue Moon in August is about marriage and children late in life. It follows the character Walker struggling to be a new parent and juggling creative with financial and married life. It also is about the discovery of Bodhicitta, unconditional love.

www.hitmotel.com

Also enjoy these books in the earlier "Little House on the Prairie" trilogy from Hit Motel Press

Cultivating the Texas Twister Hybrid
is the first book in this series. It is about the adventures of a city guy on a farm growing weed. It is a gardener's journal teaching the growers craft and something of the connoisseurs's educations as well as a criminal's internal monolog. (1998)

Cultivating the Texas Twister Hybrid

Michael Lyons

The Secret of the Cicadas' Song is a second book about events on the farm. The time of the book is an extended peyote trip in prose and poetry. The reader is welcomed into to the immediacy of the psychedelic experience through haiku poetry; the reader is brought to the ineffable aspect of the trip experience through object verse and semantic object modeling of the archetypes of perception. (1998)

Knight of 1000 eyes is a third book about events on the farm. The time of the book is a tai chi session. It reflects the struggle of the western mind coming to understand the spirit of the universe. It has an essay on western space time motion philosopher Laban and a modern commentary on the ancient I Ching. Gottfried Wilhelm von Leibnitz puts in a secret guest appearance as the Knight. (2001)

The Indigenous Tribesmen of Neverland, is a kind of Tortilla Flat about bohemian life in Austin slacker enclaves. It looks at the Peter Pan syndrome of males in the late 20th century. It explores living and creating in a regime of oppressive paterfamilias Texas. Main characters are Walker, an over-educated slacker, and Wild Bill the fabulous furry freak brothers' answer to Arnold Schwartzneger. Follow them on peyote hunting trips into the tribal mythology of old Mexico and encounters with Janis Joplin and Juan Mateus.

The Indigenous Tribesmen of Neverland

Michael Lyons

Check out this audio CD from HiT MoteL Press

The Background Hiss of Summer

Catman in Dogwalk House
Loafers of the Kandinsky Sound Museum
The Background Hiss of Summer
Stockhausen
Sometimes He'd Dance at Night
Caterwauling at the Speed of Light
The Mirage Symphony
Oxygen
Green Bank Parade

Set against the music of storms, winds, and the natural environment of cicadas, crickets, frogs and birds these radio plays enacted by voice-over actors speaking lines from novels by Michael Lyons present a very special 3D sound experience. In particular the Mirage Symphony shows how a symphonic structure imbues the ambient sounds of the world, indicating a dialog or a thought in the universal mind.

You can read the script and listen to samples from the radio play on the website at

www.hitmotel.com

HiT MoteL Press
www.hitmotel.com

These books can be ordered from any book seller or on-line . They are deeply discounted on Amazon, Borders, Barnes & Noble, others. Check www.hitmotel.com for selections and recordings.

Boho Novels
The "Little House on the Prairie" Trilogy:
Cultivating the Texas Twister Hybrid, a portrait of the artist as a weed gardener (1998) ISBN 0-9655842-0-8 $20.00
The Secret of the Cicadas' Song, a peyote trip in poetry and prose (1998) ISBN 0-9655842-1-6 $20.00
Knight of 1000 eyes, about Tai Chi, movement, Laban, and the I Ching (2001) ISBN 0-9655842-2-4 $20.00

The Punctual Actual Weekly, about the life and times of a small mimeograph literary rag centered around artists living in a Berkeley warehouse and the Amphictionic Theatre ISBN 0-9655842-8-3
The Church of the Coincidental Metaphor, youthful adventures in Mexican radio ISBN 0-9655842-7-5
The Indigenous Tribesmen of Neverland, bohemian life in Austin slacker enclaves (2001) ISBN 0-9655842-6-7 $20.00
Sex is the Anti-gravity of Metamorphosis, tales of romance and despair hitchhiking in US, Canada and Mexico. ISBN 0-9655842-9-1

Novels:
The "My Years of Apprenticeship at Love" Series:
Dolores Park, Texan joins a California Tantric Buddhist commune (2001) ISBN 0-9655842-3-2 520 pages. $25.00
Zenobia, a journal of psychotherapy
(2001) ISBN 0-9655842-4-0
A Blue Moon in August, about marriage and children late in life. ISBN 0-9655842-5-9

CD-ROM
Cultivating the Texas Twister Hybrid CD-ROM, radio plays of actor's voices performing bits from the novels, the Mirage Symphony

Nonfiction
The Diamond Cutter's Sutra, about semiotics, logic, semantic object modeling, mathematics --a kind of Varieties of Logical Experience

Check into HiT MoteL at www.hitmotel.com for cover art, interactive Table of Contents, e-book sample chapters, recordings and other mindware.

Dolores Park

When Walker Underwood left Texas he was escaping oppression and seeking a more loving and spiritual home where he could live closer to the heart of his own creative nature. In San Francisco he fell in love with a beautiful woman who belonged to a Tantric Buddhist commune.

Following in romantic pursuit, we are brought through shifting points of view into the lives and struggles of the people of the commune and the Group Mind at the center of Tantric Buddhist spiritual practices.

Such was the impact of this experience confronting his ego defenses and indeed his whole world view that Walker chose to say yes to the call and go into the Sangha of Dorje Chang community. Find with him a terrific sense of self-acceptance — from him and toward him — as he finally "comes home".

Dolores Park records the poignant year that began in the fall of 1982, when the nuclear freeze initiative was gaining momentum, and the AIDs epidemic was just starting to surface. A precious time of inner renewal and sexual self-discovery.

Here are recounted the philosophical assault and resulting ego death one encounters when pursuing enlightenment through group marriage. With humor, Walker describes how the experiences changed his attitudes, salvaged his sexual life and enriched his spiritual life.

Rich in psychological insight, flowing with lyrical beauty, and depicting the sadness at the heart of all attempts to live an authentic feeling life, Dolores Park invites the reader to join this hapless southern writer on his journey to a deeper understanding of the divine and the human community.

$25.00 Literature / Psychology / Art / Poetry / Buddhism / Humor

HiT MoteL Press   **www.hitmotel.com**

Printed in the United States
1258000003B/134